VIRALS

KATHY REICHS

An Imprint of Penguin Group (USA) Inc.

VIRALS

RAZORBILL

Published by the Penguin Group
Penguin Young Readers Group
345 Hudson Street, New York, New York 10014, U.S.A.
Penguin Group (USA) Inc., 375 Hudson Street, New York, New York 10014, U.S.A.
Penguin Group (Canada), 90 Eglinton Avenue East, Suite 700,
Toronto, Ontario, Canada M4P 2Y3 (a division of Pearson Penguin Canada Inc.)
Penguin Books Ltd, 80 Strand, London WC2R 0RL, England
Penguin Ireland, 25 St Stephen's Green, Dublin 2, Ireland (a division of Penguin Books Ltd)
Penguin Group (Australia), 250 Camberwell Road, Camberwell,
Victoria 3124, Australia (a division of Pearson Australia Group Pty Ltd)
Penguin Books India Pvt Ltd, 11 Community Centre, Panchsheel Park, New Delhi – 110 017, India
Penguin Group (NZ), 67 Apollo Drive, Mairangi Bay, Auckland 1311,
New Zealand (a division of Pearson New Zealand Ltd)
Penguin Books (South Africa) (Pty) Ltd, 24 Sturdee Avenue,
Rosebank, Johannesburg 2196, South Africa

Penguin Books Ltd, Registered Offices: 80 Strand, London WC2R 0RL, England

3 5 7 9 10 8 6 4 2

ISBN: 978-1-59514-342-6
Library of Congress Cataloging-in-Publication Data is available

Printed in the United States of America
Book design by Tony Sahara
Maps designed by Ray Parrish, Cuberis LLC.

This book is dedicated to the good people and dogs of Charleston.
Thanks for welcoming me to the neighborhood!

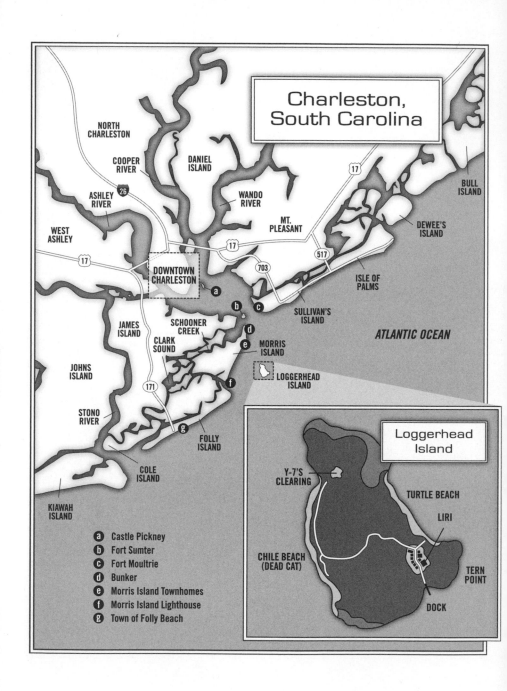

Charleston, South Carolina

NORTH CHARLESTON

COOPER RIVER

DANIEL ISLAND

WANDO RIVER

BULL ISLAND

ASHLEY RIVER

26

WEST ASHLEY

MT. PLEASANT

DEWEE'S ISLAND

17

17

DOWNTOWN CHARLESTON

703

517

ISLE OF PALMS

a

JAMES ISLAND

SCHOONER CREEK

b

c

SULLIVAN'S ISLAND

CLARK SOUND

d

e

MORRIS ISLAND

ATLANTIC OCEAN

JOHNS ISLAND

171

f

LOGGERHEAD ISLAND

STONO RIVER

g

FOLLY ISLAND

COLE ISLAND

KIAWAH ISLAND

a Castle Pickney
b Fort Sumter
c Fort Moultrie
d Bunker
e Morris Island Townhomes
f Morris Island Lighthouse
g Town of Folly Beach

Loggerhead Island

Y-7'S CLEARING

TURTLE BEACH

LIRI

CHILE BEACH (DEAD CAT)

TERN POINT

DOCK

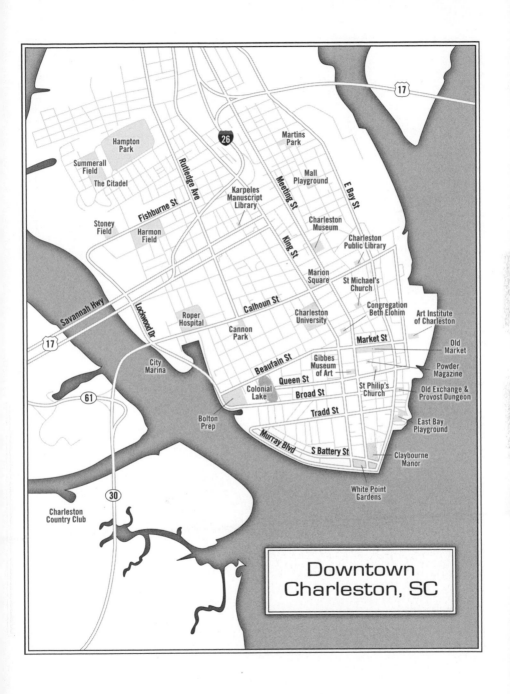

Downtown
Charleston, SC

VIRALS

PROLOGUE

A gunshot is the loudest sound in the universe.

Especially if the bullet is coming at you.

Crack! Crack!

Bullets slashed the forest canopy. Overhead, monkeys screeched and scattered.

Down below, I ran.

Heedless, legs hammering, I pounded through the undergrowth. Mind blank. Terrified.

Find the path!

Shapes zoomed by in the black. Trees. Bushes. Startled creatures. Gun-toting killers? I couldn't tell. Heart thumping, I barreled forward in a dead sprint. Blind.

A root snagged my foot and down I went. Pain detonated in my leg.

Get up! Get up! Get up!

Something large zipped past in the darkness. I froze.

"Ben?!?!"

No reply. Sudden stillness.

Waiting here means death. Move!

Scrambling to my feet, I bolted into the night.

Was Hi up ahead? Shelton had gone left, darting into the foliage.

Please be Ben that ran by me!

We hadn't had a plan. Why would we? No one knew we were here, or what we were doing.

Who the hell is trying to shoot me?

Exhausted, I gulped air.

Later, after the change, I could have run forever. Fast. Tireless. My perfect vision piercing the night's shadows. Not gasping, lost in the shapeless dark.

These thugs wouldn't have stood a chance, whoever they were. Not with our powers unleashed. My pack would have savaged them. Planned without speaking a word. Stalked them like they were kittens. Then taken out the trash.

But not that night. I was in trouble. Fading. Scared shitless.

So I ran. Hard. Branches clawed my limbs and ripped my skin. Finally, I hit open space.

The beach! I was close.

A voice hissed from the void.

"Tory! Over here!"

Shelton.

Thank God.

In the starlight, I could just make out the boat. Vaulting the railing, I dropped into the bow and turned to scan the shoreline. Clear. For the moment.

"Where's Hi? Ben?" I whispered, panting, sweat-drenched. I was definitely on tilt.

"I'm here." Ben eased from the darkness. A quick bound and he was in, sliding behind the controls. Keys in hand, he paused, afraid to turn the engine. Afraid not to.

Hi was still out there.

We sat, tensed, waiting. My courage leaked from my shoes.

Come on, Hi. Show. Please, oh please, oh please, oh please . . .

PART ONE:
ISLANDS

CHAPTER 1

The whole thing started with a dog tag. Well, a monkey with a dog tag. Take your pick. I should have known it would be trouble. Should have sensed it. But I wasn't as perceptive then. I hadn't evolved. Yet.

Wait.

I'm getting ahead of myself.

It was a typical Saturday morning at home, though my home is anything but typical. It's unique—bizarre even. Which means I fit right in.

There are lots of interesting things about where I live, if you like the outdoors as much as I do. Not a nature lover? You might find my hood a bit . . . out of touch.

Because I live on a deserted island. Well, a pretty empty one, anyway.

Morris Island. My home away from normal homes. The end of the line. Nowheresville. The back-ass of Charleston. It's not so bad, if you aren't prone to loneliness. Which I am, but whatever. I've come to appreciate the legroom.

Morris isn't imposing, as islands go, only four square miles. The northern half is an unremarkable strip of rolling, sandy hillocks. Then, in the middle, sand hills rise thirty-to-forty feet, marching south as the island widens. The western reach consists of dense marshland bordered by shallow tidal bays. To the east, the boundless Atlantic Ocean.

Dunes, swamps, beaches. And quiet. Plenty of quiet.

Only two modern structures exist on our teeny little landmass. One is the complex in which I live; the other is a road. *The* road. Our only connector to the outside world. It's a one-lane, unmarked, narrow strip of pavement that winds south through dunes and marshes before leaving Morris and crossing Lighthouse Creek to Rat Island. Eventually the blacktop meets the highway at Folly Beach, then passes Goat Island on the way into the city.

Rat. Goat. Folly. You'll have to ask the Charleston Historical Society who picked such delightful names. There are dozens more.

It was all new to me. The year before, I'd never been south of Pennsylvania. Then I crashed into my dad's life.

About my "roommate" . . .

Christopher "Kit" Howard is my father. Kit and I have known that fact for exactly six months. That's when I moved to South Carolina to live with him.

I had no choice, after what happened to Mom.

After the accident.

I'm not sure why, but Mom never told Kit about me. He had no idea he was a father. Had been one, in fact, for the last fourteen years.

Kit's still not over the shock. I see it on his face every now and then. He'll wake from a nap, or come up for air after a long stretch of work, and literally jump when he notices me. I see it register: *That's my daughter. I have a daughter who is fourteen and lives with me. I'm her father.*

Same shock for me, Pops. I'm working through it, too.

How do I describe my newfound dad? Kit is thirty-one, a marine biologist and research professor at the institute on Loggerhead. A workaholic.

He's also a clueless parent.

Maybe it's all too new—you know, the astonishment of learning you have a half-grown kid. Or maybe Kit remembers his own wild youth. In any case, he has no idea what to do with me. One day he chats me up like one of his buddies, and the next he treats me like a child.

To be honest, I own my share of the blame for things being sticky. I'm no saint. And I'm just as lost about having a father.

So here we are. Together. Smack dab in the middle of nowhere.

That day, I was classifying seashells by species. Corny? Maybe. But I'm a science nut. I live for figuring things out, finding answers. Mom always joked that it was hard raising a kid who was smarter than most college professors.

My take? I just do what I do.

Piles of shells littered the kitchen table. Sundials. Shark's Eyes.

Turkey Wings. Recently cleaned and buffed, they gleamed in the early morning sunlight.

I removed a new specimen from the bucket at my feet, making sure not to dribble bleach-water onto my clothes. It was a Scotch Bonnet, easily recognizable: white, egg-shaped, with red and brown spots circling its grooved outer surface. Pleased with the rare find, I set it aside to dry.

Reach. Pull.

My next draw was a mystery. Ark? Cockle? Both clams are abundant on the South Carolina coast.

Despite having soaked in bleach for almost two hours, the shell's exterior was covered with caked-on debris. Barnacles and encrusted silt obscured all detail.

Excellent. I'd been looking for an excuse to use my power tools. They were a gift from my great-aunt Tempe.

You may have heard of her.

I was shocked when I found out. I'm related to Dr. Temperance Brennan, the world famous forensic anthropologist. She's kind of my idol. When Kit first told me, I didn't believe him, but his story checked out. Tempe's sister, Harry, is my grandmother.

So there's a celebrity in my family. A renowned scientist. Who knew?

Okay, at that point I'd only met Aunt Tempe once. But that wasn't her fault. After all, like Kit, she'd only known of my existence for six months.

Aunt Tempe's job is pretty intense. She identifies corpses. Seriously. A dead body might be burned, or decomposed, or mummified. It could be maggot city, or just a skeleton. Doesn't matter. Aunt Tempe determines who the person is. *Was.* Then she and the cops try to figure out what happened to them.

Not bad, if you've got a steady stomach. I think I do.

Learning about my aunt helped me understand myself. Why I have to answer every question, solve every riddle. Why I'd rather read about fossilized raptors or global warming than go shopping for handbags.

I can't help it. It's in my DNA.

Aunt Tempe's specialty is teasing facts from bones. What better way to use her gift than to clean dead mollusk shells?

That's all shells are, anyway. Bones.

Digging a Dremel cordless rotary tool from my kit, I attached the bristle brush head and gently abraded the encrustations on the shell's surface. After a few moments I switched to a sanding drumhead to remove more dirt.

Once the larger barnacles were gone, I grabbed my Neytech micro sandblaster, hooked its line to a small air compressor, and delicately bathed the seashell with aluminum oxide sand. Next, I used a dental pick to scrape off the final pesky particles. After washing away the remaining grit with a Water Pik, I went back to the rotary tool, this time with the polishing head. Done.

The shell glistened on the table before me. A spotted tan oval with a purplish interior. Four inches long. Prominent radial ribs running from the hinge to the edge.

I double-checked my guide to the South Carolina coast, confirming my guess. A Giant Heart Cockle. *Dinocardium robustum.*

Mystery solved, I placed the shell in its proper pile and dipped back into the bucket. Empty.

Time for something else.

I decided to fix a snack. Slim pickings, since Kit hadn't been to the Piggly Wiggly in over a week. I suppressed a pang of irritation. The supermarket was located thirty minutes away on James Island; it's not like he passed it every day.

Island refugee living. It's a blast.

I settled for carrot sticks. Old ones. Addicted, I popped a Diet Coke. I know what you're thinking. But I do try to eat healthy. Just leave me my caffeine, thank you. The heart wants what it wants.

I checked my phone. They were late. No text, either.

I considered my options. Zilch on TV. No surprise. Nothing called out from my unread book pile. The Internet was a snooze. Zero news on Facebook.

No homework that weekend. It was late May, and most of the teachers seemed as anxious as the kids to end the year gracefully.

I was stuck. Only fourteen, I couldn't exactly hop in the car and take off. Plus, where would I go? To hang with my pals in town? Please. Everyone who likes me is an island refugee, too.

That left local options. Limited, to say the least.

Where *were* they, anyway?

Have I mentioned that my block is the most remote strip of housing in Charleston? On Earth? No one else lives anywhere near us. Most maps don't even acknowledge that Morris Island is inhabited. Our whole neighborhood consists of ten townhomes built inside a single 430-foot reinforced concrete structure. Forty souls total. That's it. Nothing else.

From our place it's a twenty-minute drive until you glimpse the first road sign. At that point you're still far from civilization, but on the right track. My friends and I usually skip the road and travel by boat.

Impressed? You should be. After all, how many people do you know who live in a converted military barracks? And I'm not talking this century. This building is super old.

During the Civil War, Morris Island guarded the southern approach to Charleston Harbor. The Confederate Army built a stronghold called Fort Wagner to block access to the island's northern tip. Good call. The rebels had big honking guns up there. Wagner straddled the only path the Yanks could use to get to them.

Fort Wagner, Fort Moultrie on Sullivan's Island, and Fort Sumter, a manmade hunk of concrete in the middle of the harbor, formed the core of Charleston's defense against attack by sea. In 1863, the Union army tried to storm Wagner. The 54th Massachusetts Infantry, one of America's first regiments of black soldiers, led the attack. It was brutal. And, unfortunately, a total bust. Even their commander was killed.

I watched a movie about it once. I think Denzel won an Oscar. He earned it, made me cry. And I don't often do that. Maybe I was supposed to root for the Charleston soldiers, but I'm a Massachusetts girl. Besides, I'm not siding with slave owners, no way. Sorry. Go Union.

Fort Wagner was abandoned after the war, but the basic structure survived. Now Morris Island is a nature preserve held in trust by Charleston University. That's my father's employer. Ditto for everyone else living out here. When the university converted the old Fort Wagner barracks, it offered free housing to faculty working on Loggerhead Island, its offshore research facility. Loggerhead is even smaller and more remote than Morris.

My dad jumped at the offer. Ever try to live on a professor's salary?

I continued to wait impatiently. I'd planned to go down to Folly Beach, but my ride was AWOL.

It felt like a no-show, so I decided to go for a run, one of the things for which Morris provides a great venue. I climbed to my room to change.

Every home in our little world is identical. Four stories tall, each goes up more than out. Any variation comes from personal taste in decorating and allocation of space.

In our case, the bottom floor is an office and single car garage. On the second floor, you've got the kitchen, dining, and sitting areas. Floor three has two bedrooms—Kit's in back, mine in front overlooking the commons.

Our top floor has a large room we use as Kit's media center. I call it the Man Cave. It opens onto an outdoor roof deck with an incredible ocean view. All in all, not too shabby, though four flights of stairs can be a killer.

While lacing my Adidas, I glanced out my bedroom window. A familiar figure was bounding up the jetty from the docks. Hiram, at top speed. Which, to be blunt, isn't impressive.

Hi was puffing hard, chugging up the incline toward the main building. His cheeks were flushed and his hair was pasted to his face.

Hi does not run for pleasure.

I grabbed my keys and bolted.

Something was up.

CHAPTER 2

Outside, I waited for Hi to appear.

I stood on the common fronting our row of townhomes. Sun pounded the grass. Half the size of a football field, our lawn is the only large green space around.

Beyond the common, palmetto palms curve up from the sand, defiant, determined to add character. The trees were the only objects breaking my view of the sea.

Hand-shading my eyes, I squinted westward. A soft morning haze shrouded the ocean, cutting visibility. *Somewhere out there is Loggerhead*, I thought. And Kit, working another weekend.

Out of sight, out of mind, I guess. Whatever. He rarely spent time with me.

Still no Hi.

Only May, but already temperatures were hitting the nineties. The air was heavy with the smell of grass, salt marsh, and sun on concrete.

I admit it. I am a sweater. I sweat. I began doing it then. How do these Southerners stand the heat?

Back in Massachusetts, the late spring days would still be pleasantly cool. Perfect for sailing on the Cape. It was Mom's favorite time of year.

Finally Hi appeared at the side of the yard, chest heaving, hair and shirt soaked. I didn't need psychic powers to know there was trouble.

Hi trudged to me, clearly out of gas. Before I could speak, his finger shot into the air, begging a moment. Hands on knees, he worked to regain his breath.

"One." Gasp. "Minute." Gasp. "Please."

I waited, thinking he might pass out.

"In retrospect, running up here was a bad plan." Quick inhales, more hiccup than gasp. "It must be a hundred degrees. My boxers are toast."

That's Hi, always the gentleman.

Hiram Stolowitski lives three units over from Kit and me. Mr. Stolowitski, Linus, is a lab technician on Loggerhead. A quiet, dignified man. Hi does not take after his dad.

"Let's get out of here." Hi was still sucking wind, but less than before. "If my mother sees me, I'll be hauled off to temple or something."

Hi's desire for cover was not total paranoia. Mrs. Stolowitski's sporadic bursts of piety often led to forty-minute drives to the Kahal Kadosh Beth Elohim synagogue in downtown Charleston. Took practice, but I can finally pronounce it.

While we may not see eye-to-eye on the whole God thing, most Morris Islanders agree: we live way too far out to be regular churchgoers. Or temple.

To be fair, the Presbyterian church I allegedly attend is miles closer than Hi's synagogue. Kit and I attended a service once. Took me ten seconds to see he'd never been there before. We made no second appearance.

I hear the Big Guy's pretty understanding. I hope so.

Ruth Stolowitski also runs the community watch program for our complex. Unnecessary? Absolutely. But don't tell Ruth that. She's convinced that the only thing preventing a Morris Island crime spree is her ceaseless vigilance. In my opinion, total isolation works pretty well. Who's going to rob us? A crackhead crab? A jellyfish junkie?

To avoid his mother's ever-watchful eye, Hi and I trooped to the side of the building. Which, mercifully, was in the shade. The temperature dropped ten degrees.

Hi's not fat, but he's not slender, either. Husky? Plump? You pick. With wavy brown hair and a penchant for floral print shirts, Hi certainly stands out in a crowd.

That morning, Hi wore a yellow-and-green vine arrangement over tan shorts with a torn left pocket. Uh-oh. Don't let Ruth see that.

"You all right now?" I asked. Hi's face had moved from plum to raspberry.

"I'm exceptional," he replied, still short of oxygen. "Wonderful. Thanks for the concern. You complete me."

Hi Stolowitski is a master at sarcasm.

"What possessed you to run all the way up from the dock?" As the words left my mouth, I realized the insanity of my own jogging plan.

"Ben crashed his boat while fishing for drum in Schooner Creek. He drove too shallow and ran aground." Hi had finally regained his breath. His distress was evident. "He went airborne and slashed his leg on something. I think it's bad."

Ben Blue lives in our complex, but sometimes stays in Mount Pleasant with his mom. I'd been waiting for Ben and Hi to take me to Folly.

"How bad? When? Where is he?" Worry made me babble.

"He got the boat to the bunker, where I was, but then the engine died." Hi smiled ruefully. "I paddled the old canoe back here to find Shelton. Thought it would be faster. Dumb move. It took forever."

Now I knew why Hi was so exhausted. Canoeing in the ocean is hard work, especially against the current. The bunker is only a mile and a half from the complex. He should have walked. I didn't rub it in.

"What now?" Hi asked. "Should we get Mr. Blue?"

Ben's father, Tom Blue, operates the boat service connecting Morris to Loggerhead Island, and the ferry running between Morris and Charleston proper.

Hi and I looked at each other. Ben had owned his runabout less than a month. Mr. Blue was a stickler for boat safety. If he found out about the accident, Ben could lose his favorite possession.

"No," I said. "If Ben wanted his father's help, he'd have come back with you."

Seconds passed. On the beach, gulls cawed the day's avian news. Overhead, a line of pelicans rode the wind, wings outstretched to catch the best breeze.

Decision. I'd try to patch Ben up myself. But if the wound was serious, we'd get medical help. Angry parent or not.

"Meet me on the path." I was already hurrying toward my house to grab a first aid kit. "We'll bike to the bunker."

Five minutes later, we were racing north on a strip of hard-packed sand slinking through massive dunes. The wind felt cool on my sweat-slicked skin. My hair streamed behind me in its usual hopeless red tangle.

Too late, I thought of sunscreen. My pale New England skin offers only two tone options: white or lobster. And sunlight really kick-starts my freckles.

Okay, full disclosure. Modeling agencies aren't trying to sign me or anything, but I'm probably not bad looking. I can admit it here. Already five-five and hoping for more, I'm graced with my mother's tall, slender physique. She left me that much.

The path we rode swept northwest from our complex to the tip of the island, Cumming's Point. On the left, high dunes. On the right, sloping beach, then the sea.

Hi pedaled behind me, panting like a steam locomotive.

"Should I slow down?" I yelled back over my shoulder.

"Try it and I'll run you over," he called. "I'm Lance Armstrong. I live strong."

Sure you are, Hi. And I'm Lara Croft. I eased off gradually so he wouldn't notice.

Since much of Morris Island is marsh or dune, only the northern half has ever been suitable for construction. Fort Wagner was built there. Same with the other old military works. Most were simple ditches, trenches, or holes.

Not our bunker, baby. It's killer. We stumbled on it while searching for a lost Frisbee. A total fluke. The thing's so hidden, you have to know where it is to find it. Long abandoned and forgotten, no one else seems to remember it exists. We intend to keep it that way.

Five minutes more pedaling, then we cut off the path, curved up and around the face of a gigantic sand hill, and plunged down into a trough. Another thirty yards and a wall of the bunker was visible, barely, among the dunes.

A dozen yards to the right of the bunker's entrance, a side trail wandered to the beach below. I could see Ben's motorboat tied up to a half-submerged post at the edge of the surf. It rose and fell with the low waves breaking the shore.

I dismounted and dropped my bike to the sand. Just then, a muffled curse broke from the bunker.

Alarmed, I ducked inside.

CHAPTER 3

Tight squeeze, then I was in, blinking to adjust my eyes. That first slap of sunlight and shadow is always a shock.

As hideouts go, ours may be the best ever.

The main chamber is probably fifteen by thirty. Wood-beamed walls rise ten feet to the ceiling. A window slit runs the length of the wall opposite the entrance, framing a kickass view of Charleston Harbor. A wooden overhang masks any hint of the opening from outside.

A second, smaller room lies to the left of the first, accessed by a low passageway. Same squeeze as the front door. From that chamber's back wall, a collapsed shaft leads deeper into the hill. Mongo creepy. No one goes in there.

Ben slouched on an old bench in a corner of the front room, injured leg propped on a chair. Blood trickled from a gash on his shin.

He regarded me a moment. Then, "I asked for Shelton." Ben never wastes words.

Nice to see you, too.

Behind me, I sensed Hi shrugging. "Tory found me first. Ever try telling her what to do?"

Ben rolled his eyes. Nice ones, dark, with lashes I'd die for.

I arched a brow, revealing what I thought of their comments. "I brought a first aid kit. Let me see your leg."

Ben scowled, kept a close watch on my movements. I saw through his macho act. He was afraid I'd hurt him, but couldn't let on.

Good. Be nervous, wuss.

Unlike the rest of us, Ben has reached the magical age of sixteen. Shelton rounds that corner next fall, and Hi just turned fifteen this spring. We are closing out a rough freshman year. Ben is finishing up as a sophomore.

Instead of buying wheels like a normal person, Ben had just put all his savings into an old, sixteen-foot Boston Whaler runabout. He calls her *Sewee.*

Don't get the name, right? Neither did I.

Ben claims to be part Sewee Indian. I'm skeptical, since the Sewee were absorbed into the Catawba tribe over a century ago. How can anyone actually claim ties? But Ben has a temper, so it's not a point we argue.

I guess a boat's better than nothing. A non-wrecked one would be, anyway.

"Is there a reason you were showboating in the tidal bay?" I was dabbing iodine on Ben's shin. The wound wasn't a stitcher, thank God, just ugly.

"I wasn't showboating." Ben sucked in his breath as I tied off the bandage. "I tried to get closer to shore, where the fish were. I misread the depth."

"Catch anything?" I asked innocently.

Ben's scowl deepened. My guess hit home.

"And how about putting on a shirt there, pal." Hi needled.

Ben's eyes rolled to him.

"Hey." Hi spread his palms. "This is a classy bunker."

Having delivered his opinion on clubhouse etiquette, Hi crossed to the room's only table and sat. The rickety wooden chair listed to port. Reconsidering, Hi moved to the bench.

Ear-tucking thick black hair, Ben leaned one muscular shoulder against the bunker wall. Of medium height, there wasn't an ounce of fat on him. Ben's eyes were brown-black, his skin copper or bronze depending on the season.

"I thought Shelton could figure out how to fix the runabout," Ben said.

Diplomatic. He was trying to apologize without actually apologizing.

Ben obsesses about his boat. Sensing he was more worried about the damage than he was letting on, I accepted the olive branch.

"If anyone can fix her, Shelton can," I said.

Ben nodded.

Ben's mother, Myra Blue, lives in a condo near the Mount

Pleasant marina. Ben and his dad share a unit on Morris Island. Though the marital status of the senior Blues is unclear, taking our cues from Ben, the rest of us honor a "don't ask, don't tell" policy.

My guess? Ben bought the runabout because it's easier to zip across the harbor to Mount Pleasant than to drive all the way around.

"I've got my phone," I said. "I'll text Shelton."

"Good luck scoring a signal," Hi offered as I headed for the door. Ben remained silent, but I felt dark eyes on my back.

Hi was right. Cell reception is sketchy on Morris, practically nonexistent at the bunker. After zigzagging the dune-top for a good ten minutes, my message to Shelton finally went through. Descending, I was pleased to hear my phone beep an incoming text. Shelton was on his way.

Worming through the entryway, I thought about Ben. He was cute enough, but Lord was he moody. I'd moved to Morris six months earlier. Since then we'd had almost daily contact, but still I couldn't say I understood him.

Did I like Ben? Did that explain all the verbal sparring? Closet flirting? Or was Ben simply the only option in a very, very small pond?

Or was I just nuts?

On that happy note, I popped back inside.

Hi had dozed off. Ben was still slumped on his bench. Crossing to the window, I hopped onto the ledge and nestled into one of the old cannon grooves.

Out in the harbor, Fort Sumter looked like a miniature Camelot. Well, a gray and crappy Camelot. My mind wandered. I thought about Arthur and his knights. About Kit. About poor Guinevere.

About my mother. The accident.

Deep breath. The memory was still a raw wound I tried not to poke.

Mom was killed last fall by a drunk driver. A mechanic named Alvie Turnbauer ran a stoplight and T-boned her Corolla. She was driving home from picking up a pizza. Turnbauer was leaving Sully's Bar and Grill where he'd been downing Coronas all afternoon.

Turnbauer went to jail. Mom went to Resthaven Memorial Garden. I went to South Carolina.

Nope. Still too soon.

I turned my thoughts to other things. Sandals I'd seen at the open market. Paint colors I might like for my bedroom. A rough spot on a molar I feared was a cavity.

Eventually, a voice boomed from outside the crawl. "Someone call for a mechanic?"

In popped Shelton, holding a manual and a paper-stuffed folder. Ben perked up immediately.

Shelton Devers is short and skinny and wears thick, round glasses. His chocolate skin favors his African-American father, but his eyelids and cheekbones hint of his Japanese mother. Shelton's parents both work on Loggerhead Island, Nelson as the IT specialist, Lorelei as a veterinary technician.

"So wise to consult an expert." Shelton raised both arms. "Be at peace, brother Ben. I can save your boat."

A beat, then Shelton's mock-solemn expression morphed into a grin. Snorting laughter, Ben shoved to his feet, anxious to get to work.

No surprise that Ben wanted Shelton's help most. He's a whiz at anything with pieces, parts, or pixels. Shelton loves puzzles, ciphers, and anything with numbers. Computers, too. I guess you could call him our techno guru. It's what he calls himself.

Shelton's weakness? A fear of all things crawly. At his insistence, bug spray is kept in the bunker at all times. He won't win any athletic awards, either.

Ben and Shelton spread the manual and papers across the table. Soon they were bickering about the nature of the malfunction and how to fix it.

Who knows? If they hadn't repaired the boat, we wouldn't have gone to Loggerhead that afternoon. Perhaps none of this would have happened.

But we did.

And it did.

CHAPTER 4

"If you can't find the problem, just admit it." Ben's voice carried a sharp edge. "I don't want more damage."

I could tell Shelton was irked by Ben's lack of confidence. His body tensed. At least, the south half of it did. His head and shoulders were hidden inside the boat.

"I'm just running the possibilities, one at a time." Shelton's head re-appeared. "Relax, man. I'll figure it out." Clutching a schematic, Shelton dove back into the wires of the boat's electrical system. Ben loomed over him, arms crossed.

"Anything I can do to help?" I asked.

"No." Two voices, one reply.

Well then.

While Hi lounged in the bunker and Ben and Shelton argued over the boat, I sat on the beach. Out of the way.

In front of the clubhouse, a stone outcrop curves into the

ocean, creating a small, hidden cove. The rocky spur protects the shoreline, conceals the boat and its tie-up from passing crafts, and, my favorite, isolates a cool little beach just five yards long.

I glanced at the narrow path ascending to our sanctuary. Even this close, the window was impossible to see. Uncanny.

Shelton says our bunker was part of a Civil War trench network known as Battery Gregg. Built to guard Charleston Harbor, much of the maze remains uncharted.

This place is ours. We must keep it secret.

Strident voices crashed my thoughts.

"Is the battery switch on?"

"Of course it's on. I smell gas—maybe the engine's flooded. Let's give it a minute to clear."

"No, no, no. Maybe the engine doesn't have *enough* gas. Pump the rubber ball."

"You can't be serious. Hey, make sure that silver toggle switch is pushed into the cowling or it'll never start."

Fed up, and feeling useless, I decided to rejoin Hi. No matter the heat outside, the bunker always stayed pleasantly cool. Halfway up the path I heard the outboard roar to life, followed by howls of delight from the amateur mechanics. I turned. Ben and Shelton were high-fiving madly, grinning like fools.

"Well done, genius squad," I said. "I'm impressed."

Parallel tough-guy nods. *Man fix boat! Man be strong!*

"What now?" I asked, hoping to divert the two from actually beating their chests.

"Let's take her out, make sure she's good," Ben offered. "Maybe run down to Clark Sound?"

Not a bad idea. Boating had been our original plan for the afternoon. Then I had a sudden thought.

"What about Loggerhead? Maybe we can locate the wolfdogs. The pack hasn't been spotted for days."

Confession. I am a canine fanatic. I love dogs, maybe more than humans. Heck, no *maybe* about it. After all, dogs don't gossip behind your back. Or try to embarrass you because you're the youngest in your grade. Or drive cars and get killed.

Dogs are honest. That's more than I can say for a lot of people.

"Why not?" Shelton replied. "I wouldn't mind seeing the monkeys."

Ben shrugged, less concerned with the destination than the journey.

"I can't believe you jokers fixed it." Hi was picking his way down to the beach.

"Believe it, clown. Too much brain power here to fail." Still pumped, Shelton threw another palm Ben's way.

"Oh, I'm sure." Hi stretched, yawned. "It was something highly technical, I suppose? Something requiring mechanical ability? Nothing as simple as tightening a wire or flipping a switch, right?"

Ben reddened. Shelton developed an interest in his sneakers.

Score one for Hi.

"You up for a run out to Loggerhead?" I asked.

"Let's do it. Monkeys are always funny. You pretty much can't go wrong with a monkey, right?" Hi paused. "Well, unless that monkey wants you dead, or does needle drugs or something. Then it's wrong, and a bad monkey."

Hi dropped into the boat, oblivious to our stares.

Minutes later we were skimming across the sea. I have to admit, it was wicked cool. Even for someone who spends as much time on boats as I do.

I bet I'm the only person you know who ferries to school. Twice a day, straight shot over the harbor. Monday through Friday. Rinse. Repeat. It's the only reasonable way to get there.

The gang and I go to Bolton Preparatory Academy in downtown Charleston. Very hoity-toity address, all antebellum homes and Spanish moss–draped trees. With ivy-covered walls and pigeon-pooped statues, Bolton Prep is as pretentious as its neighborhood.

I shouldn't complain. Bolton is one of the best private schools in the country. Kit could never afford the tuition, but the university picks up most of the check. Another perk for CU parents working on Loggerhead.

One tiny problem. No one there likes us.

The other students are all super rich. Most never let us forget that fact. They know how we got in, and why we arrive each day as a group. I've lost track of the things they call us.

Boat kids. Charity cases. Peasants.

Trust-fund babies. Elitist jerks. Snobs.

Frankly, I was happy to be going anywhere that day besides school. We Morris Islanders stick together. The guys were already tight when I arrived. Especially Shelton and Ben. Hi's a bit of an oddity. Sometimes I'm not sure any of us know what to make of him, but he definitely keeps us on our toes.

The boys accepted me right off. Not enough options to be choosy. Plus—tooting my own horn—it was clear from the get-go how bright I am. Like them.

Unlike most of our classmates, we actually like learning new things. Must come from our parents. For me, meeting other kids who are into science was like finding buried treasure.

Kit wasn't thrilled that my only three friends were boys. I pointed out that no other high school kids live on Morris. And that he knows all their parents. He had no rebuttal. Whitney, Kit's girlfriend, is the only one playing that song now.

Though we may have started as friends of convenience, the four of us have really connected. Of course, I had no idea *how* connected we'd eventually become. Or why.

Ben took the long way to Loggerhead to avoid shallow water. It adds time, but the shortcut through the sandbars is too risky at low tide. Better to play it safe.

Shelton rode in front, scanning for dolphins. I sat in back with Hi.

Bow and stern, I reminded myself. The boys spent hours learning nautical terms. Future pirates? News reports say they're back in business.

Now and then the bow rose, dropped with a smack. Spray washed over us, salty and cool. I loved every watery drop.

I could feel a smile spread over my face. The day was looking up.

After twenty minutes of open water, a blue-green blur took

form on the horizon. I watched it grow and solidify into a landmass.

Eventually we drew close, slowed, and pulled alongside a sugar-white beach.

The sand stretched ten feet back from the water. Beyond it, high-canopied trees and a dense understory shrouded any view of the island's interior. Waves lapped the shore. Frogs and insects performed an afternoon symphony of whines and hums. Now and then a branch rustled and an animal barked overhead.

There wasn't a man-made thing in sight.

Ben throttled down. The boat bobbed gently as we cruised by, observing the landscape in silence.

A sense of mystery cloaked it. Something primal. Untamed. Wild.

Loggerhead Island.

CHAPTER 5

"**W**hoa whoa whoa! Comin' in hot! Hit the brakes!"

Shelton recoiled as *Sewee* clanged into the pier. I lost my footing and smacked the deck with my butt. Hard.

The boat scraped along the wharf, screeching in protest. Tough day for the mighty vessel. Complaint box material.

Springing up, I somehow managed to snag a stray mooring line attached to the quay. We steadied, came to rest. Docking complete.

Not exactly smooth, Captain.

"No brakes on a boat." Ben grimaced, disappointed with his seamanship. "Parking's tricky. I'm working on it."

"Work harder." Hi rubbed a banged knee. "You currently suck."

"*I* couldn't do it," I said, hoping Ben wouldn't sulk.

He chuckled instead. "Not my best effort, but the ship's okay." A strong backslap. "Come on, Hiram. No harm, no foul."

Hi conspicuously pointed kneeward.

Ben shrugged. "No blood, no foul?"

"Sure. But now my back hurts, so you still lose."

Shelton popped onto the dock and secured the lines. A few loops and tugs, and we were moored. Practically valet.

"Done."

"Let's hustle, people! Go time!" Hi, looking green, climbed over the side and wobbled down the landing. "I have something 'natural' to do in those woods."

Seasickness. Look out.

I disembarked and followed with the others.

Loggerhead Island is a speck compared to Morris, only half a square mile. No residents. No roads. No Starbucks. Just a few buildings clustered together on the southern end. Don't be fooled though, it's a serious place. High tech. Top-of-the-line labs, state-of-the-art equipment, twenty-four hour security. Small, but expensive.

The Loggerhead Island Research Institute. LIRI. But Loggerhead works just fine solo.

The island got its name from the sea turtles that nest on its eastern shore. Pirates were the first European inhabitants. Seeing it as a great spot to dodge colonial authorities, Blackbeard and his pals holed up and stored "inventory" between attacks on merchant ships. Or on other pirates. Or maybe they partied with other pirates. I'm not really sure.

Anyway, that phase didn't last long. Eventually, the Brits rousted the pirates and some Lord Powderedwig built a cotton plantation. Slaves did the work, of course. Jerk. But one day they got him. Big lesson. If you're a jackass who buys other people, don't set up shop hours from help. Should your slaves object to the arrangement, you're fish bait.

The military took Loggerhead next. Bases, guns, et cetera. After that, the island lay empty for several decades. In the seventies title was given to CU, and the university filled it with primates.

No kidding. Most of Loggerhead is now a monkey colony. Free-ranging rhesus monkeys. Hundreds of them, literally running wild in the trees and on the ground. It's not like they can escape. Too far to swim elsewhere.

True, the research compound is fenced, but that's to keep primates out, not in. The chain-link is only partly effective. Smart little buggers, they sneak through constantly. Like pocket ninjas.

The island truly is an amazing place. Wander into a simian clash and the sound is unbelievably loud. I mean, who wouldn't want to hang out in a giant monkey cage once in a while?

To be clear, the institute does *not* conduct product testing or anything like that. The research is purely veterinary medicine or observational work, like behavioral studies. Otherwise, I wouldn't go there. Or let Kit work there.

Pretty awesome, huh? There are only a few other places like this on the continent. Scientists come from everywhere. You need beaucoup shots and major clearance to get access.

Well, most people do. We just crash the party.

I stepped from the dock onto a narrow beach flanked by high, rocky promontories. Seagulls fluttered from our path, squawking in annoyance. I scanned my surroundings.

Loggerhead is shaped like a penguin with the "head" facing northwest. The penguin's middle bulges slightly, making him appear well fed. The docks are located on the southern end, extending from the imaginary avian butt. From where I stood, features composing the penguin's feet limited my view.

To the right, a conical peak sprouted from the island's southeastern corner. Tern Point. To the left, a tree-choked plateau rose sharply to twenty-foot cliffs overlooking the sea. The small bay by which we'd entered lay cupped between the point and the plateau, its beach and dock completely shielded from rough seas.

No wonder pirates loved the place. Seclusion. A good place to stash a ship in a pinch. Yo ho ho!

The island's northern end is marshland that peters out into a short tidal flat. You can't walk the last hundred yards, too marshy-mushy. Not that you'd want to. Gator country. Snap, snap.

Though Loggerhead's top and bottom are inhospitable, its sides are beautiful. Nothing but white sand. The long, narrow western stretch is named Chile Beach because of its shape, but old-timers call it Dead Cat. Hear the surf whining across the sandbars, just once, you'll understand. The real prize lies on the eastern shore: Turtle Beach. Shorter and wider, it's paradise. Best in the world.

That covers the perimeter. The island's interior is all closely packed forest crisscrossed by creeks. Plus monkeys.

From the dock where we came ashore, a trail climbs northeast, up and over a steep rise that hides the LIRI buildings from sight. Hi was halfway along it.

"He's useless on boats," Ben said.

Agreed. Hi even got sick on the ferry.

"Let's give him a second to . . . unwind," I said.

"He's looking for somewhere to puke." Shelton was somewhat less delicate. "A man needs privacy in his weaker moments."

No one argued with that. We'd all seen the Heaving Hi Show. Sequels always disappoint.

"You really want to find the dogs?" Shelton tugged his earlobe, a nervous tic. "They're no joke, Tory. You got lucky last time. It was crazy."

Half right. What I'd done *was* stupid. Wild canines can be unpredictable, even deadly. Especially wolfdogs. And I certainly had put myself in danger. But I don't believe luck played a role.

Point of fact: I've never in my life felt threatened by a dog or wolf. For some reason, canines respond to me. It's like we speak the same language. I can't explain it.

The pack didn't scare me; I was looking forward to seeing it. But I knew the others were uneasy with the idea of drawing too close.

"Shelton's right," Ben said. "Dog whisperer or not, you can't take a risk like that again." He skipped a pebble over the water. "I thought you were done. I wouldn't believe it if I hadn't been there."

"The whole scene was unreal," Shelton agreed.

Here's the story.

Some years back, a graduate student departing a research station in Montana found a half-dead female wolf cub buried in a snowdrift. Having no other option, and against all rules, he smuggled the puppy with him to his next posting—Loggerhead. Somehow he lost track of his ward. Upon completion of his project, unable to find the pup, he simply left.

Over time, the wolf pup became an unofficial pet for Loggerhead's staff. Nicknamed Whisper, she moved like smoke, appearing silently for her meals, then disappearing into the woods.

Whisper grew and matured. Well-fed, she remained playful with people and unaggressive toward the monkeys. Though never officially sanctioned, Whisper was allowed to live where she chose and roam free on the island.

Roughly a year after Whisper's arrival, a male German shepherd mysteriously entered the scene. No one knows how he got to Loggerhead. No matchmaker ever claimed responsibility.

Miss Whisper must have fancied the boy. The first wolfdog puppy was born a few months later. For a year the canines rolled as a trio. Then a second cub joined the family. I was first to notice the new addition, two months after my own arrival in November. I even named him.

How did we meet?

The gang and I were lounging on Turtle Beach when a splintering sound drifted from the woods. Intrigued, I snuck through the trees, expecting monkey mischief. Instead, I found the dogs circling a hole, whining and darting. A tiny cry was rising from somewhere below.

Hearing, perhaps smelling me, the pack froze. Six eyes locked on my chest.

I stopped dead, not moving a muscle.

Whisper stared in my direction, snout up and sniffing the air. She's big, the pack leader. A full-blooded wolf. Upset. At me.

Yikes.

My sweat glands kicked into high gear.

A growl rumbled deep in Whisper's throat. She stepped toward me, ears erect, fur bristling her spine.

A rational person would have retreated. But when it comes to dogs, I'm certifiable. Something in that hole needed my help, I was certain of it.

Slowly, I inched ahead, willing Whisper to understand.

Trust me. I'm not a threat.

Whisper's eyes were so wide I could see the whites. Her lips curled, displaying gleaming incisors. The growl morphed to a snarl.

Second warning.

"Shhhh," I cooed. "I'm a friend." I inched forward. "Just one peek. I promise I mean no harm."

Movement flickered in the corner of my eye. I stole a peek.

My friends, safely distant, watched with disbelieving eyes.

Ignoring them, I took another undersized step.

Whisper lunged, stopped two feet before me.

A third growl, full throated. This time, the other dogs joined in. The sound was fierce, terrifying.

A flood of adrenaline shot through my body.

Maybe this was a bad idea.

Lowering my gaze, I slowly spread my hands. Stood rock still, urging Whisper to understand. I knew my safety balanced on a knife's edge.

No sound. No movement.

Blood pounded in my ears. Sweat trickled my back.

Keeping my chin down, I raised my eyelids. Whisper's gaze locked onto mine. She seemed to hesitate, to debate in whatever way wolves do.

Then, abruptly, she circled to stand with her mate and child. As one, the three glanced at the hole, back at me.

I had permission. I thought. Hoped.

I risked another tentative foot forward. The pack watched intently, but held position.

Quickly, Tory. Your pass will expire.

Moving forward, I looked down into the hole, an abandoned shaft, once boarded over. The brittle wood had just given way.

Ten feet down, a small furry bundle yelped pitifully. Two perfect blue eyes gazed skyward. A wolfdog puppy.

Seeing me, the pup scrambled to its feet and scratched the dirt wall with its small paws, desperate to be reunited with its mother.

Without thinking, I dropped to my stomach, grabbed a ropey vine, swung my legs over the rim of the shaft, and braced my feet against the wall. Death-gripping the vine, I began to lower myself in a modified rappel.

One hop. Two.

A shadow fell across me. I looked up. Three canine faces hung above my head, eyes following my every move. No pressure.

Oh so carefully, I descended.

Three. Four. Five.

Halfway down, my feet encountered a series of narrow shelves. Using them as stair steps, I closed the gap to where the terrified puppy crouched. It barked in excitement, eager for rescue.

When I reached the pup's level, I sat, catching my breath. My new friend crouched on a broken barrel with *Cooper River Boiled Peanuts* stamped on its side. He crawled into my lap. Face lick. Adorable.

That's when I named him. Cooper.

A sharp bark sounded from above. Whisper was growing impatient.

Carefully lifting my cargo, I stood, back to the wall, surveying my options. The shaft was uneven, with protruding rocks and roots. A relatively easy climb.

Easy, if a pack of angry canines aren't topside, waiting to eat you for lunch.

Cradling the pup in one arm, I began hoisting myself up with the other, one foot at a time. Grab. Pull. Step. Grab. Pull. Step.

Wiggling close, my passenger gave a funny little bark.

"I agree, Coop. Hang on."

My arms were burning when my face broke the plane of the ground. And came nose-to-snout with a wolf.

Whisper. Jaws inches from my throat.

Moving slowly, I placed Coop on the ground. Mama wolf clamped her teeth on his scruff, lifted, and bounded into the brush.

Two more flashes. The pack was gone.

Trembling, I pulled myself from the shaft and tried to dust off.
I grinned. Mission accomplished, and me not dead.

Still brushing dirt, I looked over at my companions. Hi was
hyperventilating. Ben and Shelton were slowly shaking their
heads. The collective relief was palpable.

All three made me swear to never act so recklessly again. I
promised, but just to placate. I knew, given the circumstances, I'd
do it again.

Returning to the beach, I sensed, more than heard, rustling off
to my right. I glanced into the woods. Two golden eyes gleamed in
the shadows. Whisper. She studied me a moment, then disappeared
into the forest.

Perhaps my proudest moment.

Months had passed since that encounter. I'd seen little of
Whisper or her pack.

If I found them, would they remember me? Would Coop?

Yes. I was sure of it.

With that happy thought, I was ready to explore.

After allowing Hi a few more seconds to regroup his gut,
we strolled over the rise and down the path to the research
compound.

And ran smack into trouble.

CHAPTER 6

Hi had been captured by the enemy.

Okay, I exaggerate. But not much.

As we crested the rise, the LIRI complex came into view downslope. A dozen structures stood tightly packed within eight-foot-high chain-link fencing. Glass and steel buildings contained research labs. Aluminum sheds provided storage for equipment, monkey chow, supplies, and vehicles. The perimeter fence had only two openings: the main gate leading to the dock behind us, and a smaller one leading to Turtle Beach.

Hi was standing by the main gate. He wasn't alone.

"Now he's done it." Shelton shielded his eyes as he peered downhill. "We're gonna catch hell."

"Crap." Ben's voice was tense. "It's Karsten."

Of course, I thought. *Who else?*

"He's waving us down," Shelton said. "Anybody else care to

run for it?" Sarcastic. There was no point in running. Professor Karsten knew who we were. Worse, who our parents were.

Ugh.

"Let's go." I spoke with more confidence than I felt. "Karsten knows we're allowed to be here if we don't break the rules. I don't get why he's always hassling us."

Loggerhead is essentially closed to outsiders. But since our parents are employees, the Board permits us to visit as long as we avoid restricted areas and don't cause problems.

"Dr. K's never liked us being on the island," Shelton said. "My dad told me he constantly brings up banning us, but can't get the votes. The jerk acts like we're terrorists or something."

"You did break that ATV." Ben, deadpan.

"Right." Shelton's eyes rolled. "Shelton broke it. Not Ben and Shelton, because Ben is better at hiding in the woods. So only Shelton." He cuffed Ben's shoulder. "By the way, you're welcome, Blue."

"I said I owe you one."

We began trekking downhill. To either side I could see nothing but trees. No surprise. No permanent structures exist outside the main facility. Some rough paths crisscross the island, but very few. From the get-go, LIRI was designed to have as invisible a human footprint as possible. The reality comes pretty close.

As we descended, I thought about all the cool research hosted at Loggerhead. The primates are my favorite, but there's also a stacked marine biology station. That's where Kit studies his beloved turtles and dolphins. The nature preserve attracts ornithologists and botanists. Butterfly guys, too. Swamptown brings the gator fans. Archaeologists have excavated a few sites on the plateau and in the interior.

An elite confederacy of nerds. My peeps.

By the time Shelton, Ben, and I got to the gate, Karsten had dragged Hi inside the enclosure. At our entry, he spun and angrily gestured us to him.

We obliged. No choice.

Dr. Marcus E. Karsten: Professor and Department Chair, Charleston University College of Veterinary Medicine; Head Administrator, LIRI.

Head Ass, if you ask me. That's where he kept *his*, most of the time.

Famous for his work on the Ebola virus, Karsten had an impeccable reputation in animal epidemiology. He supervised all research conducted on Loggerhead.

The man was also a complete tool.

Not much to look at, either. Late fifties. Skinny. Glasses. Dark, thinning hair worn in the ever-popular comb-over. Lab coat pressed so sharply the creases could probably slice cheese.

I'll give him this: he didn't treat us like kids. He treated us like criminals.

Karsten and Hi stood in front of Building One, the complex's largest structure. Inside are the most elaborately and expensively outfitted labs. Hi's dad works there. So does Kit. The security office is housed there, too. Great.

"Get over here and explain yourselves."

We obeyed the first part, but not the second.

Karsten turned on Hi. "Mr. Stolowitski. Why were you sneaking through the woods?"

"My plane crashed. I've been living out there for months."

Can it, Hi! Not smart.

"That's terrible." Karsten's tone was icy. "Your mother will be thrilled when I tell her you survived. Shall we call her now?"

Hi's eyes widened, then dropped. "I was sick," he mumbled. "Rough crossing."

I felt for him. He looked miserable.

"And the rest of you? Also unwell? Here for veterinary treatment?"

"Dr. Karsten, have we done something wrong?" Shelton asked, ultra-politely. "I thought it was okay to visit, since we're on the approved list. You could check it. We're happy to wait."

"Cute." Karsten wasn't fooled. He never was. "You're only allowed here if you don't cause trouble." His eyes crawled the group. "But you always do."

I felt my face flush with anger.

Mouth, here comes my foot. This is ridiculous.

"Professor Karsten, I'm here to see my dad. I've come straight from the dock. And last I checked, my inoculations were in order. Is there anything specific I can help you with? I need to get going."

You know that sound a needle makes when dragged across an old record? It happened.

The others inched away.

Karsten studied me. Seconds ticked by. Agony. Then he smirked. "Ah, Miss Brennan. Always a delight." He regarded me another moment. Then, under his breath, "And nothing at all like your father." A pause. "But *exactly* like Tempe."

I wasn't supposed to hear that. Secretly, I preened. Karsten knew Aunt Tempe professionally. I'd never heard the exact story. I'm not sure if the family tie was a strike for or against me.

Suddenly, Karsten was all business. "Stay off Turtle Beach; an ecological survey is in progress. I suppose Chile Beach is open. Tern Point is off limits. As always." He checked his watch. "Above all, stay out of everyone's way."

Karsten began to stomp off, stopped short.

"Miss Brennan."

Gulp.

"Yes, sir?"

"Dr. Howard is occupied with a patient. A boat propeller struck a turtle crossing the channel. Your father is not to be disturbed." A quick pivot and he was gone.

Phew.

Triple stares in my direction.

"What?"

"I can't believe you popped off at Dr. K like that." Shelton looked shocked.

Hi chortled. "You've got bigger balls than I do."

"Thanks, Hi. Noted."

"Whatever, it worked," said Ben. "Good job, Tor. Nice cover about your dad. Quick thinking." He glanced toward the rear of the compound. "But maybe we should scrap smoking out the dogs?"

"Wolfdogs," I corrected. "Well, two of them are, anyway." I peered at my reflection in the glass of Building One. Seeing Kit would've been nice, but going inside now would be tempting fate.

Sorry Kit. No can visit.

"No way," I said. "Let's find the pack."

"And some monkeys. I want to see monkeys." Hi's good spirits had returned. "*Won't-you-take-me-to, Monkey Town!*" He broke out a dance move. The shopping cart.

"Sure, Hi," I replied, eyes still on the lab. "I will take you to Monkey Town. Just never sing that again."

"Awful," Ben agreed. "Terrible, terrible joke. Shameful."

An earnest nod from Hi. "Not my best work."

"Saddle up, yo!" Shelton circled a finger in the air, ready to hike.

Like Snow White's dwarves, we marched one by one out the back gate.

Heigh-ho, heigh-ho, it's off to search we go . . .

CHAPTER 7

The man gazed down from Karsten's office window. His close-set eyes flanked a bulbous nose spidered with veins.

Watching the four teens disappear through the Turtle Beach gate, the man cracked his knuckles. Nervous and angry at the same time.

Punk kids on Loggerhead? Why? What are they doing here?

The man moved to the desk and folded his burly frame into the leather-bound chair. Leaned back. Lit a cigar.

Time to remind Karsten who's in charge.

Moments later the doctor bustled in, oblivious to the presence of another. He stopped short, startled by the smell of burning tobacco.

Seeing the man at his desk, Karsten stiffened.

"Why is a pack of kids roaming the property?" the man demanded coldly.

"I can't keep them off the grounds." Karsten swallowed. "Children of LIRI employees have the Board's permission to visit the beaches."

"Aren't you the director? Can't you control your own facility?"

Karsten bristled, but said nothing.

"I want all outsiders banned from the island," the man said. "Immediately. Keep them out of the woods."

"Why are you here? It's madness for us to be seen together."

"I took precautions. No one knows." The man's voice went even colder. "And watch your tone. I'm here because you've failed to show progress. Perhaps you've forgotten our agreement."

"I'm working on it."

"You made promises. You have obligations."

"What you seek is extremely complicated. These things can't be rushed."

The man simply stared.

"Give me more time," Karsten whined. "I'm close."

"You'd better be. I hold my partners to their bargains. Count on that."

The man rose, drew on his cigar, then dropped it, burning, into the wastebin.

"Impress me, doctor," he said. "Your time is running out."

The man left without a backward glance.

CHAPTER 8

L ight flashed.

Flit. Was gone.

What *was* that?

It was the third or fourth time my eyes picked it up. I thought the glint came from the trees but wasn't sure. I scanned the canopy, looking for a clue.

When a gumball nailed my forehead, I figured it out.

"Ow!" My hand flew up in surprise. "A monkey just pegged me!"

I was sitting in a glade with my back to a tree. We were far from LIRI, in a little-traveled quadrant of the forest. Hi was stretched out beside me, shade-happy.

Ben and Shelton were searching for the trail. Again.

We were out-of-bounds, but so what? Following the path to Dead Cat was *très* routine. When Ben spotted an older run heading north, we'd decided to go off-road.

Screw you, Karsten.

We hadn't located the pack. No surprise there. The entire island was their turf, and canines are masters at stealth. They could be anywhere.

Last year, an enterprising lab tech had installed a timed-release food dispenser in a cave below Tern Point. Whisper and her crew took to it immediately, and were rarely seen near the compound anymore.

Well, until the howling started.

Recently the pack had begun circling the LIRI fence each night, baying up a storm. No one knew why. The guards were thoroughly creeped out.

The change in behavior worried me. If the pack kept making a racket, eventually they might attract too much attention. They weren't really supposed to be there.

But my concern went deeper. Only three members of the family were appearing each night. Coop was missing.

Despite our mission failure, I was enjoying the trek. At one point we'd startled a group of monkeys clustered at a feeder. Somewhat used to people, they'd scurried into the trees to watch us from a distance.

Young males barked and bobbed, putting on a show in the branches. Babies peered from their mothers' backs or bellies. Big ears. Big eyes. Total cuties. Females groomed each other like they were prepping for a prom.

To that point, the hike was a winner.

But after the primate encounter, the track had narrowed, penciled, then disappeared altogether. Glumly, we'd conceded to being lost. Spotting a clearing, we'd cut over, hoping to find the trail on the far side.

Nope.

So there I sat, being bombed by a monkey.

Finally, I spotted my assailant. A big female with gray-brown fur and one notched ear. The tattoo on her chest said *Y-7*.

Y-7 wasn't happy. Restlessly shuffling from branch to branch, she paused now and then to lunge in our direction. Fear and anger drew her lips back in a full-toothed grin.

Y-7 let fly again. Retreated.

Good aim! I rubbed my shoulder. *Good arm, too.* I scooted behind the tree, taking cover.

"Looks like you have another fan."

"Shut up, Hi." I peered around the trunk, trying to locate my attacker. "I've never seen this behavior in a female." Air whooshed as a missile zipped past my ear. "What the hell? Is her baby nearby? I don't see one."

I peeked again. Another projectile drove me back.

"She's pretty agitated." My warning to Hi was an understatement.

"Great call, Captain Obvious." Hi hadn't moved. Not smart. *Whack!* He took a direct shot from on high.

Cursing, Hi rolled from the line of fire. "Agitated? That monkey's rabid. Out for blood. She went for my bad knee." He snatched a spiked gumball fruit that had fallen from the tree. "This means war."

Hi stood, took aim. "Payback! Don't start what you can't finish."

Y-7 easily dodged Hi's weak throw. Returned fire.

Hi ducked back, panting. "I'm overmatched. Call for backup."

Flit.

There it was again! A quick burst of light.

"Did you see that?" I asked.

"Yeah." Hi crouched beside me, gazing upward. "I think Donkey Kong has something on her wrist."

Overhead, Y-7 sprang with outstretched arms, went airborne, landed. A threatening branch-shake completed the display.

I saw another flash.

It clicked. "She's got something in her paw. Something reflective."

"Yep," Hi agreed. "It's metal. Maybe glass."

We were pressed shoulder-to-shoulder behind the trunk of a live oak. It wasn't big enough to shield us both. Sardines in hiding. Sitting ducks.

Suddenly, our adversary leaped into the branches directly above our heads. Hanging low, she drew her lips back and screeched.

Alarmed, I fell backward and curled into a ball. Monkey bites are not pretty.

Y-7 hurled what was in her hand.

Branches swished.

Quiet.

I sat up and unwrapped my arms from my head. Dirt coated my shirt. Twigs adorned my hair. Nice.

"Hi, next time you want to throw something at a monkey, don't."

"It was only a gumball."

Hi had rolled to the bottom of a slight incline. He righted

himself and glanced at an elbow scrape. "Man, this is not my day."

Curious, I scooped up Y-7's projectile.

"What are you fools doing?" Shelton called. The trailbreakers were back, having missed our brief firefight.

"Monkey attack." Hi slogged back up the grade. "The enemy had air superiority, but we survived." He swatted Ben on the shoulder. "Don't worry, I sent a message. They won't dare return."

"Guys, check this out." I rubbed Y-7's missile with my finger, trying to clear gunk from the surface. Thin and flat, the thing weighed maybe an ounce. A tiny hole punctured one end.

Shelton joined me. Hi was busy explaining to Ben how many punches he'd absorbed before body-slamming the primate gang leader. His audience looked dubious.

Y-7's weapon of choice was about two inches long and one inch wide. Though a hardened crust covered 90 percent of its surface, one outside edge glinted in the afternoon sunlight.

"Definitely metal," I pronounced.

Shelton nodded. "It's practically fossilized. I'll bet it was buried at some point."

Nose close, I gave the thing a careful inspection. It smelled of rust and embedded dirt.

"It's pretty banged up, but I can make out indentations," I said. "Lettering, maybe?"

Shelton smiled. "Come on, girl. Think! A metal rectangle with symbols punched in?" Smug. He knew what it was.

"A strike pad?" I hate guessing. It's so inexact. "Like for a stamp or something? Or a stapler?"

Shelton's grin widened. "Use your brain. Who prints things on small pieces of steel?"

Of course! And the hole. Duh.

I met his eye. My grin mirrored his.

"You got it!" Fist bump. He turned to the others. "Guess what we found, ya'll."

"It's a dog tag," I blurted, stealing his thunder. "A military ID."

Shelton nodded. "No doubt about it."

"What's it doing out here?" Ben asked. "More Civil War stuff?"

"Crazy talk," Shelton scoffed. "Metal dog tags first came out in World War I. Standard issue ones, anyway. It's at least from this century."

I handed Shelton the tag. His show now.

"If we knew what was printed on it, we could date it," he said. "The type of info that was stamped changed over time." Another thought. "The material used to make them changed too."

I frowned. "But Loggerhead was empty for decades before the university bought it. It's been vacant most of this century."

"Sure," Hi said. "Officially. You think people didn't cruise out here looking for some action?"

Good point.

"Waste of time," Ben said. "You'll never be able to read it. The lettering's too far gone." He checked his watch. "We should head out. I found the way back."

"*We* found it." Shelton shrugged and tossed the tag.

The boys moved off.

I stared at Y-7's prize resting in the leaves.

Why not try to clean it? It's not that different from a seashell.

The tag held someone's name. Not trying to decipher it? Crazy. I scooped it up and hurried after the others.

Man.

If I hadn't done that, everything would have been different. *Everything.*

That whim changed my life.

Opened the door for what came.

Paved my path to monsterhood.

CHAPTER 9

A t home, disaster lurked.

Terror. Horror.

Her.

The conversation was always the same. Bombast. Then reproach. Followed by thoughtlessness. Always draped in tones as syrupy as molasses.

And she was off and running.

"Why, Tory, look at you! You're gettin' to be so lovely! Angel eyes!"

Oh God.

"But, dear thing, why not a sundress? Girl as pretty as you shouldn't slum around in T-shirts and shorts."

Stop.

"I cannot wait to take you for a proper haircut. My girl Da'Nae will know exactly what to do with that tangle."

Kill me. Kill me now.

Dinner plans had taken a dreadful turn. Kit's "lady friend" had been added to the guest list. I was not consulted, perhaps because my feelings on the issue of Whitney are clear.

I stared full bore at Kit. He kept his eyes on his plate.

Thanks for the heads-up, jerk.

Ladies and gentlemen, meet Whitney Rose Dubois.

"Have you thought about what I said last time, sugar?" Whitney feigned nonchalance. Failed.

"Yes, Whitney, I did." I tried to be diplomatic. "I don't think it's me."

"Not you?" Mascara-laden lashes fluttered. Bleached hair swished. "Not you!" A manicured hand fluttered to rest on jacked-up boobs. "But of course it's you!" Saucer eyes conveyed total lack of understanding.

Swing and a miss. How to put this delicately?

"The whole idea is ridiculous. Stupid."

There. Oprah would be proud.

"Tory!" Kit said. "That's enough."

I resisted an impulse to sigh theatrically. "Thank you for the offer, but I'm just not into the whole 'deb' thing."

For a month, Whitney had worked to convince me to make my debut as a lady. I had zero interest. White dresses. Satin gloves. Being displayed like cattle. No thanks. I'm just not that into you.

My mind raced to find a new topic. Blanked.

"But sweet pea, you'll soon turn sixteen. You simply *must* be introduced to society." Whitney trained her baby blues on Kit.

This was clearly the most obvious thing in the world.

"I'll meet society later."

"Nonsense! And Tory, darlin', I'm your lucky day!" Looking pleased with herself, Whitney placed her hand on Kit's. Gross. "Now, we only have six months left in this season, but I happen to have *considerable* influence on the committee. You're a shoo-in to be selected." The woman positively beamed.

"Tory, Whitney's offering you a special opportunity." Kit, trying to smooth the waters. "You could use a little branching out. These are the nicest families in Charleston."

I felt a twinge of sympathy for the old man. This wasn't his idea, and he worried about my level of "girl time."

Nevertheless, I crushed the feeling like a bug. Eating with Whitney only reminded me that Mom was gone forever. She had no right to play at being my mother. Out of bounds.

"I go to school with those girls, Kit. They aren't that nice."

"But I can help with that!" Whitney looked so eager it was painful. "I know all the etiquette. I can teach you the dances. I'll find lovely dresses for you to wear." She leaned close. "I'll coach you the whole way."

Scramble. Change subject.

"Kit, uh . . . how's the turtle?"

He blinked. "The what? Oh! The turtle that took on a propeller. It's fine, just a scrape. Those shells are tough."

Kit downed a forkful of Whitney's lasagna. Which, admittedly, was excellent.

Grrr.

"Sea turtles are such beautiful creatures." I encouraged the current line of conversation. Kit took the bait.

"Yes. Boaters really must be more careful. But the pilot thought enough to bring the animal to us, so he's not a bad sort. Surgery took about an hour, and . . . " He stopped. Pointed with his fork. "Wait. Who told you about the turtle?"

Shoot.

"Who told me?" I stammered.

"How did you find out about the injured sea turtle?" Kit spoke slowly, as though addressing a toddler.

"We sort of motored out to Loggerhead this afternoon. Coop has been missing, and I wanted to figure out what's upsetting the pack, so—"

"Stop. Who is 'we'?"

"Just me and the usual guys. Hi, Ben, and Shelton."

A sharp tsk from Whitney. She had strong feelings about my being with boys unescorted. Puh-leeze.

"I didn't see you," Kit said.

"We went straight to Dead Cat. No big deal." Here goes. "We did chat with Dr. Karsten for a few minutes."

"And?" Wary.

"And what? You know how he is. We didn't do anything. He's all, 'you kids always cause trouble,' and 'you're going to burn down the island because you're such idiots.' We just left base and went out to Dead Cat for a while. That's it."

Close enough.

"Am I going to get an earful from Karsten?"

"No, Kit." Heavy mocking. "You're not 'going to get an earful from Karsten.'"

I hoped.

"Why would you want to play on that stinky old island?" Whitney's perfect little nose crinkled in disgust. Stopped. I actually saw the thought cross her mind. "Unless you're doing work like your daddy does." Again, she turned the big blues on Kit. "Important work."

"Like I said, I wanted to check on the wolfdogs. Coop's been missing lately, and the other three are agitated about something."

Whitney donned her long-suffering face. A parent confronted by childish obstinacy. "I thought we were finished with the dog debate." Prim. "Your father has spoken."

Okay. I may stab her. I would probably get a medal.

"I wasn't asking to get a dog, Whitney." Kit had refused my repeated requests. I suspected Whitney was behind his opposition. She detests pets. "I was referring to the wolfdogs out on Loggerhead. The puppy is missing."

"I'm sure he'll turn up." Softer. Kit knew I wanted a dog more than anything on earth. "It's a big island. He's probably just nosing around by himself."

"But it doesn't make sense. Wolves develop close relationships and maintain lifelong social bonds. They have a deep affection for kin, will even sacrifice themselves for the pack." I grew more distressed just talking about it. "The others would never let Coop go off alone. He's not fully grown."

"Wolves?" Whitney's eyes were saucers. "You're cavorting

with wolves?" Her head whipped to Kit. "That's ghastly! She'll be mauled. Or eaten!"

Kit looked trapped. Two angry women. Tough spot.

"Only one is actually a wolf," he said to Whitney. "She's harmless."

"A harmless wolf?"

"She's been on the island for years. Her mate is just a normal German shepherd."

"Their pups are called wolfdogs," I explained. "Half-dog, half-wolf. Coop is the youngest." I appealed to Whitney's warm fuzzy center. "He's a puppy, only a few months old."

"You mean a diseased, wild mongrel! Someone should call animal control. Aren't those dogs illegal?"

That's it. I'm done.

"Thanks for dinner." I shot to my feet. "I've got homework."

A drive-by wave.

I hit the stairs before either could utter a word.

Two steps at a time.

CHAPTER 10

Safely locked in my room, I seethed.

Downstairs, Kit and Whitney were undoubtedly discussing *The Problem of Tory*. Every time, like clockwork. I didn't eavesdrop. I was sure my head would explode.

Diseased mongrels? What the hell did she know?

Wolves are noble, caring animals. Though I hadn't told a soul, I'd thought about studying those "diseased mongrels" for a living, thank you very much. They ranked well above Whitney Dubois on my list.

"I'm not prancing like her show pony," I vowed to the dog figurines lining my bookshelf.

Not going to happen. No ridiculous fluff for me. *Nyet.*

I punched a bed pillow.

Easy. Don't make it about Whitney.

Okay. I had to admit that dressing up a few times wouldn't be the *worst* thing to ever happen to me. I like wearing white. And pearls *are* nice. At school, I'd seen girls looking at dress designs. I thought I could pull off the look. Might even turn a few heads.

Also, shocker, my social calendar still had a few openings.

"Who knows?" I asked the empty room. "On that special night of nights a handsome young bachelor of the aristocracy might choose *me* off the menu of virgin chattel!"

Getting snarky again. How bad could a debutante ball be? And frankly, you need help on the girlfriend front. Point of fact, you have none.

I knew Kit blamed himself for my lack of gal pals, but it wasn't his fault. I just hadn't clicked with any of the resident Mean Girls.

Full disclosure: my isolation was a teensy bit my fault. Sure, the girls at Bolton Prep were terrible, horrible, despicable fembots. Yes, they teased me relentlessly. But I found most of them shallow and vapid, and never showed the slightest interest in their superficial world. So the disdain had been mutual. Plus, I'm smart, care about schoolwork, and wreck every curve on which I am graded. That hadn't won me any popularity contests.

It didn't help that I was the youngest in my grade. I'd just turned fourteen. Skipping ahead had seemed awesome when I was twelve. I never considered what the impact would be once I reached high school. Now I was feeling the downside. I wouldn't score a driver's license until the very end of my junior year.

I knew the formula. To get girlfriends I had to fake interest in the silly things the fluffbrains found important. Boys. Shopping. Reality shows starring rich dimwits devoid of talent.

On second thought, being friendless gave me ample opportunity to read.

So I ranked low on the social totem pole? So what?

On third thought, cotillion offered monthly events leading up to the November ball. Hanging with the debs might score me some friends with double X chromosomes.

But then Whitney would win. I couldn't allow *that*. Could I?

I leaned back on my pillows, worries elbowing for center stage in my mind. Coop. Whisper. Kit. Whitney.

Thoughts about Whitney were always painful. They led to thoughts about Mom.

My mother, Colleen Brennan, grew up in a tiny New England town called Westborough. She and Kit met at a sailing camp on Cape Cod. They were both sixteen. Maybe he noticed Mom because her last name was the same as his mother's family. Maybe not. Brennan is common enough. It may have been because Mom was gorgeous. That works for most guys.

Kit and Colleen must have determined they were not related, because they hooked up. Big time. I came along nine months later.

I don't know why Mom kept my existence secret from Kit. She never saw him again. Probably didn't consider him prize parenting material. Who knows? She may have been right.

For a while Mom and I lived with her parents, but they passed away when I was a toddler. All I remember is gray hair and cookies, and the smell of cigarettes. Both had lungs like Swiss cheese but still smoked. Don't get me started.

Raising a kid solo must have been tough on Mom. She never finished high school, I suppose because of me. She waited tables, worked at a Walmart, a movie theater briefly, but then that closed. Meanwhile, I was taking advanced classes because my teachers thought I was a genius. Mom never let on that it bothered her.

Lost in memories, I missed the first half of my ringtone. Startled, I dug through the bedding, finally found the phone. Clicked on.

Too late. The call had rolled to voicemail.

I checked the screen: *Missed call—Jason Taylor.*

My heart pumped faster.

Other than my island pals, Jason was the closest thing to a friend I had at Bolton Prep. We shared two classes, which likely explained the call. Always fleeing at the bell, Jason usually forgot details of homework assignments.

I was surprised Jason was thinking about school at eight thirty on a Saturday night. He was an A-lister. Why wasn't he at some party way too cool for me?

With his blond hair and blue eyes, Jason could have been cast as a Norse God. The Mighty Thor. He was also a lacrosse star, a starting attacker. Not bad for a sophomore.

In other words, Jason was out of my league. No biggie. He wasn't really my type. Don't know why. Just no spark.

Jason was a genuinely nice guy, though. In class, he listened when I spoke. And not the spiteful, mocking attention of the other popular kids. He seemed to actually value my input.

My cell phone beeped an incoming text.

Tory. Party @ Charleston Harbor Marina. Chance boat. Interested? J

Jason again. Whoa.

I re-read the words. Yep, still there. The message was real.

I'd just been invited to a party. A popular person party. Unexpected, to say the least. Astounding.

I flew to my Mac, searched the location. Patriot's Point, Mount Pleasant. *Damn, damn, damn!* I had no way to get there.

Kit would drive me if I asked, but getting dropped off by my father wasn't an acceptable option. Plus, the trip would take forty-five minutes by car. No good.

Could I get Ben to run me over there in the boat?

And what, leave him standing on the dock?

Cold. Out of the question.

I was so busy crunching the numbers on transport that it took a second for the rest of the message to sink in.

I read the text again. *Chance boat?* What, like gambling? One of those casino ferries that drives out to international waters so yuppies can play craps?

Then it hit me. Of course!

Chance Claybourne's boat. The party must be on his father's yacht, docked at the marina.

So, this wasn't just *a* party, it was *the* party.

And I couldn't get there. Crushing.

And, honestly, a huge relief.

It took me thirty minutes to compose my reply. I read the final

copy out loud. "Sorry, can't make it tonight. Don't have too much
fun, smiley face, exclamation point."

After final consideration, I hit send. Ten seconds later, I really,
really regretted the smiley face. Ten more seconds, and I hated the
whole damn message.

I was busy searching for a recall feature when a new message
beeped in. Rattled, I dropped the device. Then I dove on it, fearing
the worst.

Boo! Next time then ;).

Winky face?

"What the flip?" I smiled, feeling better. "Dork!" I meant both
of us.

Then I frowned. Wait. Was Jason hitting on me?

Get a grip! Stop over-analyzing a one-line text.

I looked for the TV remote, anxious for distraction. Like the
phone, it eluded me, hiding somewhere in my covers. As I rolled
to check between the bed and the wall, something sharp jabbed
my butt.

I checked my pocket, pulled out the crusty dog tag.

"We meet again."

Crossing to my bathroom, I filled the sink with warm water,
deposited the tag, and added a half bottle of Body Shop papaya-
scented hand soap. Classy.

Back in my bedroom, I turned on the Discovery Channel.
Shark Week. Nice!

An hour of sea carnage later, I remembered the dog tag. The
sink now contained a chocolate-colored puddle. Ew.

I pulled the plug and sludge swirled down the drain. The tag lay on the porcelain, still coated dark brown, indecipherable.

I ran the water as hot as I could stand, and gently scraped the metal under the flow. No go. Even under my desk lamp, the letters were unreadable.

Hmmm.

I could've used my rotary tool, but I didn't want to scratch the metal. And the sandblaster might damage the lettering. This task required something more delicate.

I could have let it go right there. Thrown the thing away. But I didn't. I wanted to know what the tag said, pure and simple. Had to know.

I get like that.

I kicked into research mode, and, a few minutes later, confirmed my hunch. A LIRI lab had everything I needed. The process would take twenty minutes, tops.

I posted a tweet on the gang's private page. Minutes later I had three replies, all affirmatives. We would go early the next morning.

Time for a stealth mission.

PART TWO:
INFECTION

CHAPTER 11

Damp gusts tugged at my flimsy Gap poncho. A steady drizzle tapped techno beats on the hood drawn over my head. Once more, I wished I'd worn my North Face jacket. Too late. I was soaked.

Sodden hair clung to my face and shoulders, wilted by the rain, humidity, and stifling heat. My sweat faucets were working overtime.

Ignoring my discomfort, I tried to concentrate on the task at hand. Surveillance.

Crouched behind a boulder on Turtle Beach, Kit's binoculars in hand, I studied the back entrance to the Loggerhead compound. Inside the fence, forty yards distant, the grounds appeared abandoned.

"All clear," I called.

The boys emerged from the rocks, one by one.

The early morning sky and roiling Atlantic were both the color of pewter. The sun had yet to penetrate the low-hanging fog.

Lousy weather, but excellent cover. Perfect for espionage.

Choppy surf had nearly scrubbed the mission. But the weather channel had predicted only passing squalls and ruled out the possibility of a major storm. If we hadn't gone that day, it meant a week until our next opportunity.

My curiosity was far too pumped for that.

Shelton had agreed, which swayed Ben. Hi, outnumbered, had relented. The barf bag he brought had been put to use. Twice. Rough ride.

We bypassed the main dock, churning instead to a little-used equipment platform off Tern Point. At times, turtle researchers used the location to observe breeding activity on the beach. After nesting season, the area was empty and forgotten. The platform wasn't visible from the buildings, and no one would go near it on a day like this. Our stealth was assured. Hopefully.

The rear gate to the LIRI complex was locked, as expected. Sunday was an off day so the shuttle ran only at noon and dusk. Few worked, usually those with patients requiring care. We'd arrived a little past nine, hoping to find the complex empty.

Despite the ghost-town appearance, one of two souls was certain to be present. Sam and Carl, security guards extraordinaire, alternated weekends. One or the other would be manning the security booth, perhaps with one eye on the monitors. Perhaps with both shut.

In any case, we knew how to avoid detection. At least, we

thought we did. This caper was the first time we'd put theory into practice.

Breaking in *should* be easy. We were about to find out.

Our target was Lab Six in the rearmost building of the cluster. Hi had overheard his father griping that Karsten had closed the building several weeks earlier, giving no explanation. The doors were now locked at all times.

Odd, that. The Loggerhead labs usually ran at full capacity, with waiting lists. The closure would burden operations, cause logjams for equipment, and rankle staffers.

Whatever Karsten's reason, I wasn't questioning our luck. I wanted a name from that dog tag and intended to get it.

Sneak in, sneak out. Don't get caught.

Hi read my mind. "We can still back out. My parents will flip if we're busted. My mother may even drop dead."

"We don't need another reaming from Karsten," Shelton said. "He'd ban us forever."

"We won't get caught." I tried to sound firm. "Our plan is solid."

Though Shelton and Hi radiated apprehension, neither would back down in front of the other.

Ben looked stoic. As usual.

Dropping the binoculars to my chest, I turned to bolster my troops. Captain. Squad leader.

First, my entry-man. "Shelton, you can pick locks in a heartbeat." I patted his shoulder. "You know you can. I've seen you practice hundreds of times."

Uneasy nod.

"Ben, the digital recorder for the security cameras is broken, right? You said your dad is bringing the replacement next week." Temple tap. "That means no tape."

This was key. There wouldn't be a recording for Karsten to review. We just had to avoid *live* detection.

Ben gave a tight smile, mocking my "master criminal" imitation. I nodded back.

Raising the binoculars, I ran a quick recheck of the compound. Nothing stirred.

"The ferry's not due for two and a half hours. The island is deserted, except for security, and those bozos *never* pay attention. We're only in the open a few seconds, tops." I squared my shoulders. "Our plan will work."

Rain ticked the rocks, the leaves, and branches overhead. Still sensing doubt, I attempted the Jedi mind trick, willed them to agree.

"I could watch the boat?" Hi suggested hopefully.

"We need you." Shelton was back on board. "You've been inside Lab Six. We haven't."

"Once," Hi whined. "One time. My dad grabbed something and we left." A raised hand waved off my response. "I know what you're going to say! I'm the only one who can work the sonicator. Lucky me." Big sigh. "Fine. I'll sonicate."

"Then let's go," I said, allowing no time for a wimp out.

"I should've written a will." Hi dropped to a squat, tightened his sneakers, then bounced into a sprinter's pose. "Okay. Just yell 'go.'"

"Don't crowd me at the fence." Shelton was gripping his tools so tightly I thought he might break them. "I need space to work."

I turned to Ben. "Ready?"

Ben nodded. Had he spoken since we'd set foot on the island? Maybe not. But I was damn sure he was ready.

One last peek up the trail. All clear.

"Go!"

We shot along the path, water pluming from our sneakers.

Twenty seconds to the enclosure.

The chain-link fence was covered with green nylon sheeting and topped with razor wire. Climbing it wasn't an option. The gate consisted of a pair of fence sections hinged and set on wheels. A stout padlock secured the segments when closed. Basic, but effective.

Shelton dropped to one knee to assess his target.

Being the smallest, yours truly was the designated lookout. Pressing one eye to the fence, I peered into the enclosure. Ben and Hi took cover behind a stand of bushes.

Shelton unwrapped his kit, purchased months earlier on eBay. He practiced with the tools daily, boasted he could pick any lock in under thirty seconds. Faced with the actual task, he looked a tad less confident.

Chewing a thumbnail, I watched Shelton insert and jiggle a small, L-shaped torsion wrench until it fit. He then pushed a half-diamond pick into the lock and gently applied pressure with the wrench.

Though the rain eased back to a sprinkle, the temperature showed no such mercy. Sweating from heat and trepidation, I promised myself a dozen showers.

I could hear a clock ticking in my head. Someone could spot Shelton or me at any moment. Or Sam/Carl, in an uncharacteristic burst of responsibility, could glance at the security monitors. We'd be dead ducks.

"Hustle!" I whispered. "You're over one minute!"

Tongue between his teeth, eyes half-closed, Shelton focused on his task. I watched him wiggle the wrench, then push back on the lock. Wiggle. Push. Wiggle. Push.

Click.

Shelton smiled. "Got it!" He yanked downward and the lock popped free.

I eased open the gate. Hi and Ben materialized from the shrubbery and bunched behind me. I hung the padlock from the chain-linking, ready for re-locking on our way out.

Next came the dangerous part.

Deep breath.

After a thumbs-up, I raised my fingers and mouthed the words. *One. Two. Three.* We shot through the breach and darted left along the fence line.

For five terrifying seconds we were on wide-open grass, exposed to security cameras and to anyone in the main yard. Unavoidable. No cover. Like frightened mice, we scurried toward safety.

Adrenaline pumping, we rounded the corner of the building containing Lab Six, and squeezed behind it.

Hearts pounding, we listened for sounds to suggest that we'd been spotted.

Silence.

After counting to sixty, we bumped fists, pleased with ourselves for clearing the first hurdle. We were off the camera grid.

Taking the lead, I crept along the rear of the building until a small alcove came into view. The service door.

Phase two.

Shelton kicked into gear. Though the door lock was cake, the deadbolt was tricky. Wrench. Pick. Shelton raked the pins, coaxing them into proper alignment.

Minutes ticked by.

"Bingo." Shelton slid back the bolt.

The door swung inward, revealing blackness beyond.

CHAPTER 12

Cool air oozed from the darkness, bringing with it the smell of disinfectant and air conditioning.

We slipped inside and closed the door behind us.

"Hit the freakin' lights!" Shelton does *not* love the dark.

"Shh. Hold on," I whispered.

I groped the wall, finally found a panel of switches. Flipping several, I activated halogens overhead.

We stood in a windowless concrete chamber, empty but for a short staircase leading to a sturdy wooden door.

I bounded up the three treads, tested. The knob turned.

"Let's go." I motioned Hi to lead. The others followed.

"No talking until we get to the lab."

My warning was unnecessary. No one was feeling chatty. We'd just committed a felony.

Emerging, we found ourselves in a small tiled lobby. Directly opposite was the building's main entrance. In the rear left corner, a narrow staircase rose to a second floor. Gray light arrowed through dusty window blinds, throwing diagonal slashes across pale green walls, plastic trees, and a row of connected metal seats. The motif was corporate drab, as inviting as a lost baggage claim office.

Hi pointed to open double doors to our right. We scuttled through them, down a short hallway, through another set of doors, and into Lab Six.

The room had no windows, so we risked the lights. Ceiling fluorescents revealed a chamber the size of a large classroom. In the center were six workstations floor-bolted in two rows. Each station overflowed with equipment.

A stainless steel counter jutted from three walls of the room. Above it hung glass-fronted cabinets filled with beakers and other scientific apparatuses. Microscopes. Circular lenses. Gadgets whose functions were a mystery to me.

A Plexiglas enclosure occupied the right quarter of the room. Housing the more expensive technology, that section was locked and alarmed. Luckily, we needed nothing from there.

"Okay, hit it." Shelton nudged Hi into action. "Find the sonicator."

Moving to the third workstation in the second row, Hi removed a plastic cover from a small machine. "*My precious*," he rasped in his best Gollum impression.

The contraption consisted of a small white sink backed by an LCD control panel. About the size of a microwave, it resembled a tiny top-loading washer with the cover removed.

"Sweet, eh?"

Hi's father, Linus Stolowitski, was the mechanical engineer in charge of all LIRI scientific equipment. A technophile, he'd transmitted his love of gadgets to Hi.

"Sonicator is actually shorthand for ultrasonic cleaner." Hi spoke in his very best church voice. Temple voice?

"What's it do?" Shelton asked.

"The device uses ultrasound to clean objects." Hi worked as he talked, filling the basin with fluid. "We'll clamp the specimen an inch underwater."

Shelton's nose curled. "Whoa. That stuff smells like mega-strength Windex."

"It's cleaning solution," Hi said. "I've set the machine's frequency for the type of object we're trying to clean, and for the type of substance we're trying to remove. In this case, metal and dirt."

Shelton looked lost. Ben looked bored.

"It's like a sonar washing machine," Hi explained. "The ultrasound enhances the cleaning solution's effect." He paused. "Do you guys know what 'cavitation bubbles' are?"

Nope.

"A sonicator has a transducer that produces ultrasonic waves in the fluid. That creates compression waves, which rip the fluid apart, leaving behind millions of microscopic 'voids' or 'vacuum bubbles.' That's called cavitation."

Okay. That was pretty cool.

"In our case, the cavitation bubbles will penetrate microscopic holes, cracks, and recesses in the dog tag. Then they'll collapse, creating energy pockets. The reaction should remove even deeply embedded particles."

"So when the mini-bubbles burst they blast away the gunk?" I summarized.

"Exacto." Hi was enjoying his lecture. "Like tiny scrubbing dynamite."

"Why's the thing here?" Shelton asked.

"Sonicators are used for cleaning glasses, jewelry, and metal stuff like coins and watches. Even cell phone parts. Dentists, doctors, and hospitals use the gizmos to clean instruments."

"And scientists." Shelton had his answer.

Satisfied with the settings, Hi extended a hand in my direction. "The ring, Frodo?"

I pulled a plastic baggie from my pocket and removed the dog tag. Seeing the cement-like crust, my confidence faltered.

"This thing better work," Shelton said. "We're risking our butts to use it."

"How long?" Ben asked, already restless.

"Fifteen minutes. Get out of my hair and it might go faster."

Ben checked his watch, then wandered off the way we'd come in. Shelton settled into a chair to wait.

Knowing we'd need something to view the tag once it was cleaned, I scanned the lab for optical equipment.

One counter had a Luxo lamp clamped to its top. The movable-arm magnifier lens was surrounded by a circular fluorescent bulb. Perfect. In a drawer I found several hand lenses and a penlight and placed them beside it. Viewing station complete.

"Five more minutes," Hi chirped. His love of experiments had overridden his fear of capture.

"I'll get Ben," I volunteered.

I checked the hallway and lobby, but found both empty.

"Ben?" I hissed, as loudly as I dared.

No answer.

I considered yelling up the stairs, decided against it. Not wanting to stumble around in the dark, I returned to Lab Six.

A series of beeps was announcing the end of the cleaning cycle.

"All rriiighty then!" Hi removed the tag and ran it under cold water. I watched over his shoulder.

Much of the grime was gone. For the first time, I could make out indentations on the tag's surface.

Hi wiped the tag with a paper towel and handed it to me. Excited, I placed it on the counter, thumbed the light switch, and positioned the Luxo.

"I can read something!" I confess. It was almost a squeal.

"What do you see?" Shelton crowded so close I could smell his deodorant.

"The bottom lettering is clearest. Hold on." I adjusted the lens. Characters swam, then crystallized into focus. "*C-A-T-H*. Then an *O*, I think. I can't get the rest."

"Catholic," Shelton guessed. "A soldier's religion was stamped on the last line. What else?"

I squinted through the lens again. "Above that, more letters: *O P-O-S*." *Aha!* "His blood type, right? O positive?"

"Gotta be." Shelton thought for a moment. "Can you make out any numbers?"

"I think so. On the next two lines. But they're really hard to see. Looks like the first string is nine digits long. Above that is a second sequence, looks like both letters and numbers." Quick count. "Ten characters. Why?"

Shelton grinned and raised both hands to the sky. "Good morning, Vietnam!" he whisper-screamed, elongating the final word by a dozen syllables.

"How can you tell?" Hi asked. "You haven't even looked."

"Now it's *my* turn to teach, sucker!" Beaming, Shelton threw an arm around Hi's shoulders. He started to arm-wrap me but stopped short, self-conscious about my gender. The spontaneous move morphed into a head scratch.

Boys.

"We've got a nine-digit social security number *and* a ten-digit military service number. That's rare." Releasing Hi, Shelton pointed at the tag. "In the late sixties the armed forces switched from military ID numbers to social security numbers. But for several years they printed both, just to be safe." Dramatic pause. "That occurred *only* during the Vietnam War."

"Incredible," I said. "We caught a big break there."

"True," Hi agreed. "Call me crazy, but couldn't we solve this in an easier way?" He adopted a pensive look. "How about . . . oh, I don't know, maybe just reading the guy's name?"

Good point. Back to the magnifier.

As much as I raised and lowered the arm, I couldn't bring

the letters into focus. "There's too much damage," I said. "The lettering is obliterated."

I flipped the tag indented side up. Vague symbols wavered under the lens.

"The reverse side's a little easier to see. But the letters are backward. I can only make out an *F* on the next line up."

"Focus on the top row," Shelton urged. "That's the soldier's last name. Get that, we could investigate online."

Using the penlight, I angled a beam across the tag. Letters appeared as shadows in the metal. "This is working. I see an *N*. Then a *C*. No, it's an *O*." I increased the angle of the penlight. "Then a *T-A-E*. The last is an *H*."

I reversed the string in my mind. "Heaton."

"Well, that's a start." Hi flicked a salute. "Nice to meet you, F. Heaton."

I summarized aloud. "F. Heaton. Catholic. O positive blood. Served during the Vietnam War era."

"Not bad," Shelton said.

Not bad? I was psyched. We'd accomplished our goal. But our discovery only led to more questions.

Who was F. Heaton? Why was his dog tag buried on an uninhabited island? Where was he now?

I didn't know. But I was determined to find out.

And it was time to go. Our luck couldn't last forever.

We were repacking the sonicator when Ben burst through the double doors.

"Ben, the name was—"

He waved me off. "I found another lab upstairs. Locked, but I think it's in use." Ben was speaking to everyone, but looking at me. "You'll want to see."

"We got what we came for. We should leave before we're nabbed."

"Something's in there. Something alive."

"Why do you say that?"

"I heard barking."

CHAPTER 13

A windowless steel door barred our path. Thwarted us. If thoughts could destroy, it would have become a smoldering ruin. I wanted past that door in the worst way.

The thing looked shiny-new and had a ten-digit electronic keypad entry system. Billions of combinations. Unbreakable.

This was not a door that made friends. Its sole purpose was to make you go away. I could feel it sneering. Aggressive. Cocky. Intending to stay closed.

After Ben's bombshell, I'd flown up the stairs, the others trailing behind. At the top, a dingy hallway cut across the building, leading to this monstrosity. Stopping me cold.

"Ben, are you sure, *absolutely* sure, you heard a dog?" My nerves were firing like automatic weapons.

A firm nod. "I know what I heard."

"Okay," I said. "Shelton, do your magic."

Shelton worried his right ear. "Sorry, Tor, but this one's out of my league. I can't crack a keyless system."

Think! Find another way.

"We need the code." My mind raced for a solution. "Who put this thing here, anyway? I've never seen a door like this in the other buildings."

Hi pointed at the keypad. "That monster is *waaay* more advanced than the keyless systems in the main building. The others aren't even electronic, just old push-button jobs." He shrugged. "I could probably get past one of those, they all have the same . . ."

Hi trailed off. His eyes narrowed. He opened his mouth, closed it. He scratched his head. Shifting his weight, he started to speak, shut down once more. Shifted again.

"Quit dancing," Ben commanded. "If you've got something, out with it."

Hi shrugged. "It's a long shot, but try 3-3-3-3."

I punched the numbers and pressed enter.

Green light. Beep. Pass Go. Collect two hundred.

"Hi, you're a genius!" My second near-shriek.

"How in the world?" Shelton looked perplexed.

"It's the default." Hi grinned. "When a person moves to a new office, that's the original code. They're supposed to change the settings, but half the time they don't bother."

Hi rubbed the doorframe. "This baby is new. I figured, maybe the same workers install *all* the new doors and use the same default code. So then I thought, whoever ordered the fancy lock might have forgotten to adjust the sequence." A wink. "I was right!"

"Great work," Shelton said. "You get the fruit cup."

"I'm going in," I said. "Still with me?"

Ben snorted. "Sure. What's one more B and E?"

Not exactly reassuring. Using the palm of my hand, I pushed the door wide.

Colored lights blinked in the darkness. Screensavers danced across monitors. Machines hummed. The room possessed an energy that spoke of recent use.

Ben flipped the light switch.

Racket erupted across the room. Everyone jumped. The noise separated into recognizable parts. Barks. Whines. The scratching of paws.

A dog! I rushed forward to locate the source.

A far corner of the lab contained a sealed glass chamber resembling a phone booth. Inside sat a medium-sized cage.

Crouching, I scrutinized the miniature prison, trying to spot its inmate.

"Careful!" Shelton cautioned. "Don't open the glass—it looks like a quarantine."

I heard nothing. My eyes had locked onto a pair of blue eyes I'd seen before. The world receded. Thunderstruck, I stared, unable to comprehend the terrible scene.

"Coop," I whispered.

Then I shouted. "Coop! It's Cooper in this cage!"

The others crowded close, disbelieving. But there was no doubt. Speechless, we stared at the inconceivable. Coop was the subject of some twisted medical experiment.

Through the bars I could see tubes protruding from Coop's right leg. He wore a bell collar to prevent him from pulling out the needles. His side was shaved and bandaged.

Emotions tumbled inside me. Anger. Fear. Horror.

Forcing myself calm, I examined the contents of the glass compartment. Beside the cage was an IV stand with hanging fluid bags, their tubes running downward into the enclosure. The pen itself was constructed of closely spaced metal bars, and was latched, not locked. It contained a soiled mat and scuffed water dish.

And Coop. Captive.

Fury won out. Fighting tears of rage, I scanned the bright orange tag affixed to the cage. In bold, black letters the label read: **SUBJECT A—PARVOVIRUS XPB-19.**

Oh no.

Parvovirus. Deadly, especially for a puppy.

Coop now lay quiet on the enclosure floor. My heart broke. I laid a hand on the glass.

Seeing me, Coop tried to raise his head. Exhausted by his initial outburst, he could no longer muster the energy. He whimpered softly. My heart broke again.

How did you get there? Who did this to you?

In a flash, I understood why the pack hounded the complex each night. Some monster had stolen their baby.

A clipboard hung from a hook beside the glass partition. I snatched it, read furiously. The attached papers resembled a hospital chart, largely incomprehensible. My eyes dropped to a line of handwritten notes scribbled at the bottom.

"Subject A not responding to experimental regimen for parvovirus XPB-19. Scheduled for immediate termination."
The form was signed: *Dr. Marcus E. Karsten.*

Anger exploded through my veins like the Incredible Hulk.

That bastard Karsten was planning to put Coop down!

I won't let this happen! No chance! No way!

"I'm getting Coop out of here," I said, in a tone that brooked no argument. "I'll understand if you don't want to help."

Shelton tapped the clipboard. "It says he's infectious." His voice cracked. "It's not safe."

"The dog must be in that box for a reason," Ben agreed.

I shook my head fiercely. "Coop has parvo. I've heard of it. The virus is bad, but not infectious to humans, only other dogs. It's no threat to us."

Hi jumped in. "Look, normally I'd be with you. I hate this crap too. But if that dog's gone when Karsten comes back, all hell's gonna break loose." His voice became a plea. "We'll get caught."

Breathing deeply, I met their eyes. Which, frankly, were unconvinced.

"We won't get caught." My mind groped. What to say? Taking in the scene, I considered what we'd stumbled upon.

Intuition flashed.

Of course!

But how to convince them?

"Karsten is breaking the rules." I spoke slowly, carefully

ordering my thoughts. "Everyone thinks this building is shut down, right? But inside we find gorilla security and a hidden lab. *Shady.*"

As the words hit the air, I started to believe my own theory. Nothing else made sense. "And this secret experiment? Karsten is testing on freaking *dogs*. Dogs to be *euthanized*. Ever hear of trials like that on Loggerhead?"

Hi chewed his lower lip. Ben and Shelton looked, if not persuaded, at least like I'd created a crack.

"Karsten's running something secret," I pressed, convinced. "Off the grid. I doubt he'll ever report Coop missing. Coop's not supposed to be here in the first place."

"Where would we take him?" Shelton asked. "If he's got some doggy disease, we can't release him on the island or he'll infect the whole pack."

I'd thought of that. "The bunker. No one knows about it. We can nurse Coop there."

No response.

"We can at least give him a chance. Parvo isn't always fatal."

True, but without veterinary treatment the virus killed more times than not. I didn't say that. Caring for Coop wouldn't be easy, and there was no guarantee he'd pull through. Parvo had no known cure. I didn't say that, either.

Still nothing.

"I'm going to try." I crossed my arms and braced for opposition. "Will you help?"

Seconds passed. Five. Ten. Twenty.

"Okay." Ben first. Unexpected.

"Fine," said Shelton. "But I hope you're right, Tory. I'm not cut out for prison."

Hi muttered to himself. "Stupid, stupid, stupid!" Then, glancing up, "All right, but if we get caught, I'm blaming the whole thing on you three. I'll even make stuff up."

Tears welled. Thankfully, I kept control. "You guys are the best. I mean it."

"True," said Shelton. "But it's time to bounce."

Raiding the shelves, I shoved medical supplies into an empty plastic bag. Then I opened a small refrigerator and appropriated bags of intravenous fluid. I noticed three vials of antibiotics and swiped those as well.

Last, I grabbed a small animal carrier and lined the bottom with a spare lab coat. Best I could do to make the crate more comfortable.

Satisfied, I approached Coop's cell. The glass enclosure wasn't locked. When I pulled the handle the door released with a soft hiss.

I unhooked the drip bags from the stand, making sure not to disturb the lines. Coop would need fluids; best not to remove the tubes from his leg.

Finally, I opened the cage. Odd smells seeped from within. I switched to breathing through my mouth, reminding myself that Coop couldn't infect me.

As Ben lifted the dog, I arranged his collar and tubes. Together we placed him inside the carrier. Ben would be our pack-mule and carry Coop off the island.

Eyes closed, the puppy sprawled inside the crate, too tired to resist.

"Ready?" I asked.

"Ready." All three.

Right then, the alarm sounded.

CHAPTER 14

An ear-splitting wail pulsed through the building. I slammed the cage door and froze, hoping against hope the sound would stop.

No such luck. Blasts screamed at three-second intervals.

"We're screwed!" Hi sounded close to panic.

"Hold it together!" I snapped. "No one's seen us yet. We just have to get out!"

The alarm shrieked on and on.

"Move!" hissed Ben. "Quick and quiet, back the way we came."

Shelton streaked down the hallway. Ben followed, clutching Coop's carrier to his chest. I could have kissed him. I raced close behind, lugging the supply bag.

Last out, Hi pulled the metal door shut.

The blaring ceased.

My head whipped around.

"The electro-lock triggered the alarm," Hi said, chagrined. "We should've closed the door."

Too late for that now.

Hurrying to the staircase, I risked a quick glance out the second floor window. Rain was still falling. Water ran down the glass in tiny rivers and stood puddled in the courtyard.

My heart froze in my chest.

The alarm had registered in the security booth. Three-hundred-pound Carl was lumbering our way, sky-blue uniform already drenched.

"Carl's heading for the front steps!" I hissed.

"We're screwed," Hi repeated.

Ben took charge. "He'll check the main lab downstairs first. We hide on the stairs, wait till he passes, then bolt out the back." He looked at each of us in turn. "No noise. Got it?"

We did. And it worked. Carl waddled right by us, shedding water like a duck.

Out the back door, we skimmed the rear of the building. At the corner, I peeked around to check. The yard was empty.

Ben tied his jacket over Coop's crate to shield him from the downpour. We exchanged glances, bracing for a suicide sprint.

"Now!" I commanded.

We charged.

I slogged through ankle deep puddles, nearly losing my balance more than once. Lightening bolts slashed the sky, cutting bright streaks across my vision. I heard someone go down with a splash.

Arriving at the Turtle Beach gate, I spun and waved the others through. Hi. Ben and his cargo. Shelton, covered in mud. The boys snaked into the woods.

With shaking hands I closed the gate and slammed home the lock.

A loud bang cut through the drumming of raindrops. A door?

Panicked, I dove for the nearest cover, a thin strip of holly just short of the tree line. Rolling to my belly, I looked back through the chain-linking.

Carl emerged from the building and scanned his surroundings. His gaze landed on the back gate. Standing in the deluge, he looked wretched but determined.

My camouflage wouldn't survive close inspection. Movement would give me away. Only the driving rain had protected me this far.

As Carl stepped toward the fence, the clouds pulled out all stoppers. Rain fell in torrents.

Carl looked up, reconsidered. Shaking his head, he retreated toward the dryness of the inside world.

Miracle. Thanking various deities, I rose to a squat and crab-scuttled into the forest.

The ole bunker had never looked so good.

Commandeering the back room, I stripped and wrung out my sopping clothes. Fail. Soaked stayed soaked.

I rejoined the others in the main chamber and together we constructed a makeshift recovery ward for Coop. After, Ben sat on the bench, a bundle of beach towels before him. Coop lay inside, alternating between dozing and halfheartedly licking rain from his fur.

The ride back had been a horror. Rain and seawater drenched us as *Sewee* struggled over head-high breakers. Seasickness claimed more victims than Hi.

Huddled in the stern, I'd tried my best to keep Coop dry. Everyone had been nervous. When we finally slipped into the bunker's cove, I'd whispered a quiet prayer of thanks. To whom, I wasn't sure.

"What now?" Hi was ruffling Coop's outrageously oversized ears. "I know squat about caring for a sick pup."

"Re-hang his IV bags," I instructed. "We'll need to change them when they run out." The pilfered supplies were lined up on our table. "Until then, we keep Coop warm and hydrated and try to get him to eat."

And hope.

It was the best we could do.

Coop lay on his side, looking miserable. I hated keeping him in the bell collar but had no choice. Without it he'd rip out the IV tubes.

I proposed a plan. "We'll take shifts. I'll watch Coop today. Let's meet here before school tomorrow and set up a rotation. Bring any dog supplies you can find at home."

"No blabbing," instructed Hi. "This fiasco stays secret or we're all screwed."

Shelton raised a hand. "What happens when Coop's better?"

"If he beats the virus, he'll be immune," I said. "We can find him a normal home." I couldn't keep the dog. Kit was opposed. And knew him. But we'd craft Coop a good life somewhere.

"I'm dead serious." Hi wouldn't let up. "Secret. Undisclosed. Covert. Let's swear a blood oath or something. Lock it in."

Shelton chuckled. "Fine." He took a knee. "I swear on my life, I'll never breathe a word about the dog."

"Ditto," said Ben. He caught a sharp look from Hi. "Okay, okay!" Air quotes. "I swear. Happy?"

"Somewhat. Tory?"

"I promise, Hi. Not a word."

I looked down at Coop, sleeping in his improvised burrow. "I'll take care of you," I whispered. "Just get well."

Outside, thunder rolled.

CHAPTER 15

Dr. Marcus Karsten went cold.

Standing just inside the door to his secret laboratory—the entry upon which he'd misplaced so much faith—he could see that his fears had been realized.

Subject A was gone.

Impossible!

One hour earlier, Karsten had been at home reviewing papers. The phone rang. Annoyed at the interruption, he'd answered.

Carl from the institute. Someone had broken into Lab Six. The esteemed professor had dropped the receiver and raced to his car, panicked.

Karsten sped to the marina, running red lights. Wrangling a boat, he'd ordered the captain to take the short way to Loggerhead Island, tide notwithstanding. Paid double. Speed was everything.

Karsten had talked down his nerves during the rain-soaked

crossing. No one knew about the upstairs lab, he told himself. His secret was safe.

The guards couldn't even open the electronic lock he'd special-ordered. No one else had the combination. Once he determined what had triggered the alarm, he'd slip off to double-check the hidden room.

Slowly, Karsten's fear turned to anger. Some lazy tech must've needed supplies and didn't want to fill out the paperwork. Typical. Whoever tripped that alarm would get both barrels.

Upon landing, Karsten hurried directly from the dock to Lab Six. The downpour did little to improve his mood.

Carl waited outside on the steps. Now sporting a massive black raincoat, he resembled an enormous bowling ball on legs. A nervous one.

Karsten scowled upon seeing the guard. *This buffoon is the best we can do for security?*

"Out with it," Karsten demanded. "Was there a break-in? Was anything taken?"

"Uh . . . we, uh . . . I mean, I don't know."

Despite his bulk, Carl stood barely five feet tall. Karsten towered above him, glowering.

"Doctor. Sir." Carl added, just to be safe.

"Check. The. Video. Tape." Slowly. Karsten had no time for fools, and considered Carl one short step above.

"That's just it, sir." Carl wished he were anywhere else on the planet. "We can't. The recorder broke last week, and the replacement is still on backorder."

Karsten closed his eyes, willing self-control. He vaguely remembered a memo to that effect. "Did you examine the locks?"

"Oh yes, sir!" Safer ground. "The gates were closed and locked. And both of the building's outer doors remained secure."

Carl scratched his head, stumped. "I even went inside. Nothing missing, nobody there." A pause. "Of course, I couldn't sweep the back part, upstairs."

"Not your concern!" Karsten spoke more sharply than he'd intended. "That area is safe, I assure you. No one can get in there."

Carl blanched. "But sir, that's the sector that was breached."

Karsten froze. "What?"

"The alarm that activated," Carl mumbled. He could tell Karsten was taking this news badly. "The signal came from the new electronic lock, upstairs."

Karsten's mind rifled the terrible possibilities. He'd assumed only the first floor had been violated. The building entrance wasn't alarmed, but two inner doors were.

Think, he chided himself. Gates, locked. Doors, locked. No signs of forced entry. Yet something had tripped the most secure alarm in the complex.

"Who else is here?"

"No one," Carl answered quickly. "I checked everywhere. Not a soul. Mr. Blue's first shuttle won't arrive for another hour."

"The steel door was closed when you arrived, yes?"

"Yes, sir. Doctor."

The alarm malfunctioned, Karsten told himself. Nothing else made sense.

"The storm must've tripped the sensor. Go finish your report. I'll verify upstairs."

Carl wavered. "I'm supposed to look myself, for the report, or—"

"Guard." Karsten's voice was granite. "You are dismissed. I will let you know if further services are required."

That was enough for Carl.

Karsten watched the guard waddle off before entering the building.

The subject, he thought, racing up the stairs. *The subject must be secure!*

One look sent Karsten's hopes crashing.

The wolfdog was gone.

Karsten struggled to process the magnitude of the calamity.

Professionals, he thought. *Burglary specialists.* No one else could have breached the gates, the doors, and the keypad lock. No one else could have evaded capture so seamlessly, left no trace of a crime.

Karsten had always suspected there were factions who wanted to steal his research. His findings could one day be worth millions, perhaps billions. But how had they discovered *this* lab?

Particles of an idea coalesced with a jarring shock. The intruders must have known the cameras were down!

Dear God! An inside job!

They've no idea what they've done.

Horror flooded Karsten's mind. Subject A was infected with the *experimental* strain of parvovirus. Though he'd told no one, he had a terrible suspicion about XPB-19.

Karsten picked up the phone and dialed with trembling fingers. "Dr. Marcus Karsten here. My business is urgent."

Karsten listened to dead air as his call was transferred. A click. Two long beeps. A voice answered.

"Yes."

Karsten forced his voice calm. "We have a problem."

◇   ◇   ◇

Minutes later the professor stood with gut clenched, receiver still clutched in his hand. Thinking one thought: *I need a drink.*

His instructions were clear.

Find the dog.

Or else.

And he'd held back the worst of it, even from him. Hell, *especially* from him. That news was far too dangerous to share. His sponsor was far too dangerous a man.

Karsten rummaged through his pockets, found a key ring, and unlocked a desk drawer. Yanking papers and scattering files, he finally located a document at the bottom of the stack.

Karsten recognized his own handwriting at the bottom. He examined the record again, wishing it read differently.

It didn't. His words screamed from the page. Accusing.

"The highest caution must be employed. Due to its radical structure, Parvovirus strain XPB-19 may be infectious to humans."

CHAPTER 16

I sat in the Bolton Prep library, researching on my lunch hour. After a dozen Googles, I knew my adversary. Nasty. Heartless. A serial killer that fought dirty. But my investigation confirmed that the enemy could be beaten.

Parvo. The puppy plague.

Unvaccinated dogs are virtually defenseless against it. A remorseless assassin, parvovirus often kills within days of invading its host.

Not on my watch.

I vowed to deprive the microscopic murderer of yet another victim.

Monday morning. A new school day had me back in uniform. Dull plaid tie and matching pleated skirt. White button-down shirt. Black knee socks.

Blech.

I shouldn't complain. Without the dress code the Bolton Prep hallways would host a yearlong fashion show, one in which I could never compete. Unlike some girls, I play the outfit straight and don't slut it up at every opportunity.

The information I'd downloaded wasn't pleasant. My memory had been correct: no cure exists for canine parvovirus. But the survival stats provided a glimmer of hope. I clung to it like an anaconda.

A voice sounded from directly behind my chair. "Hey, Tory, shopping for prom dresses?"

I spun, defenses slamming into place. All year I'd been the target of ridicule. I knew the drill.

But it was only Hi, strolling to the neighboring computer station, his Bolton Prep jacket inside out to expose the blue silk lining. Hi claimed that if he wore the required attire, he met the dress code. Period. The administration disagreed, but after a year of defiance, Hi had prevailed. Teachers seldom tried to make him conform anymore.

I wondered why Hi kept poking the powers that be in the eye. Civil disobedience was out of character for him. Factoring in Ruth Stolowitski, his rebellion was downright astonishing.

When asked, Hi simply claimed to be the "Fresh Prince of Bolton Prep." To each his own.

Gripping a half-eaten meatball sub in one hand, Hi flipped through my printouts with the other.

"Good idea, finding a proper gown." Typical Hi sarcasm. "The Prom Queen has to look sharp. Vera Wang, perhaps? Or maybe something in a Lauren Conrad?"

"Thanks," I responded dryly. "You'll still be my date, right? Or will you have a playoff game that night? I'll understand; we need our star quarterback on the field."

"I'll let you know," Hi replied breezily. "I may be dining with Kristen Stewart. Or Bill Compton. Some vampire, I'm not sure which."

Despite the ribbing, I was glad to see Hi. We had identical schedules and spent most lunches together. Joking with someone about being cool was more fun than being unpopular alone. Safer too.

Hi skimmed a few of my pages. "This doesn't sound great," he noted, less jocular than before.

He was right. Coop faced an uphill battle.

Hi read a bit more, then put the papers down. "Have you found any good news?"

"Not much," I admitted, referring to my notepad. "Canine parvovirus is the most widespread infectious disease in dogs. The worst, too. Puppies are at highest risk. Vaccines exist, but living wild on Loggerhead, the pack was never inoculated."

Hi plopped into a chair. "Of course not." Chomping on his hero, he nodded for me to continue.

"The most common form of parvovirus is intestinal, known as enteritis." I skimmed as I spoke. "Coop's symptoms suggest that's what he's got. Loss of appetite, lethargy, vomiting, diarrhea, and fever."

"How does the little bugger work?" Garbled through meatballs, cheese, and marinara.

"The virus invades the lining of a dog's small intestine, preventing absorption of nutrients into the bloodstream. Also, look here." I pulled up a veterinary website. "Enteritis lowers a dog's white blood cell count. As the animal weakens, the virus tears through its digestive system, opening the way for secondary infections."

I paused before adding my least favorite part. "Some sites place the mortality rate from untreated parvo as high as 80 percent."

Neither of us spoke for a moment. Not much to say, really.

"How'd Coop get parvo in the first place?" Hi's tone reflected the anger I felt.

"My question exactly."

I'd gone over it a dozen times. I didn't want to trust my gut. Karsten wouldn't have infected Coop *intentionally*, would he?

Shelving that thought, I continued. "We need to be careful. The most dangerous thing about parvo is how easily it spreads. The virus can survive on stuff like bedding or cages for up to six months. We need to bleach *everything*. Our clothes, shoes, anything that contacts Coop."

"Does the germ go airborne?" Now Hi sounded anxious.

"No. Parvo spreads through direct contact with dog feces."

"Great. A dog poop bug. Just what we need." The rest of Hi's sandwich sailed into the trash. I'd lost my appetite as well.

"On that note, I'm gone." Hi pushed to his feet. "I didn't study for the Spanish quiz." He sauntered out whistling the *South Park* theme.

"Remind Shelton we're meeting after school." Bolton Prep had two lunch periods; Shelton and Ben ate later. "We still need to track down our soldier."

I hadn't forgotten about F. Heaton. I hoped an after-school trip to the public library would solve the case. Ben could cover Coop while Hi, Shelton, and I investigated.

Without turning, Hi gave a thumbs-up. He'd pass the word.

I ran a mental check of our sick ward setup. We needed to bleach all of Coop's things and every spot where he vomited or pooped. Pretty much anything he contacted, even our hands, clothes, and shoes.

After Coop recovered—and he *would* recover—we'd scrub the whole bunker, top to bottom.

Nursing Coop wasn't going to be easy. The experts were unanimous: dogs suspected of contracting parvo should be taken to a veterinary hospital for immediate in-patient treatment. Unfortunately that wasn't an option. Unless we wanted jail time.

So, contrary to web advice, I hunted for home-care tips. Initial treatment seemed to be geared toward keeping the dog hydrated and preventing secondary infections. I was thankful for our pilfered medical supplies. With the IV bags and antibiotics, we were nearly as capable as a vet.

Every site recommended encouraging the dog to eat, though most advised against solids at first. Some suggested a cooked hamburger-rice mixture once the patient could keep food down. I decided to try the recipe that night.

Our game plan *had* to work. It was the best we could do.

Tears threatened as I thought of Coop's chances.

Stop. You won't *be that girl crying in the library.*

I gathered my printouts and shoved them in my backpack.

While closing the web browser, a thought struck: Coop was half-wolf. How would parvo affect a wolfdog? Would being partly feral change his diagnosis?

My fingers flew over the keys. Five minutes of searching killed any optimism I might have felt. Parvo was equally deadly for wolves and wolfdogs. Coop's mixed heritage changed zilch.

Disheartened, I pulled up images of wolfdog puppies. The playful little rascals put a smile on my face in no time.

Which is how they snuck up on me.

CHAPTER 17

"What's with the doggy show?" The voice was inches from my ear. "Is *this* why you skipped the party?"

Twice! Never sit with your back to the door!

I remained eyes-forward until my voice-recognition software identified the speaker. A huge pit opened for business in my stomach.

I turned.

Jason Taylor crouched behind me, examining the web page I'd been viewing. He wore the standard Bolton male regalia: griffin-crested navy sport coat, striped "power" tie, blue button-down shirt, tan slacks, loafers. Everything neatly ironed, tucked, knotted, creased, and polished. And right side out.

Fast as a synapse, I closed Firefox. Too late.

"Seriously, Tory, you should spend less time ogling pooches and more time rocking the boat. In this case, literally."

My mouth opened but nothing came out. What was he talking about?

"The yacht party, Victoria." The corners of Jason's eyes crinkled. "Saturday? Text message? Ring any bells?"

Of course.

One day, I won't be so dense. Please?

"Sorry, I'm a bit spacey right now. Thanks for the invite." I tried for witty. "Did you manage to stay afloat?"

"I guess. It wasn't that sweet, actually. You didn't miss much." Then, mock-stern, waggling a finger. "But you still should've come."

"The marina's a bit of a hike for me."

"I know. How's Gilligan's Isle these days?" Jason dropped into the seat recently vacated by Hi.

Jason's style tended toward flippant. I reminded myself he was one of the nice guys.

"A nonstop thrill ride," I said. "How's Mount Pleasant?"

"Same old."

The Taylor clan inhabited a house in Old Village, one of the classiest neighborhoods in the pricey burb. The estate had a private dock directly accessing Charleston Harbor. Not too shabby.

Pointing at the screen, Jason changed the subject. "Why the wolfdog photo album? Wait. First, what's a wolfdog?"

Nice job, genius. Not a "criminal mastermind" move.

Had reporters already broken the story of an island wolfdognapping? I had no idea. Yet, there I was, browsing wolfdog images on a public computer.

Dumb. Unlike Jason, who could put two and two together.

"Oh, nothing." I sounded way too casual.

Get it together!

"Honestly, I don't know *what* that was," I lied. "I'm looking for information on wolves. For an English paper."

Pure babble. My improv sucks.

Jason lost interest. "Too bad it's not for bio. We could've worked together." A mischievous grin.

Uh-oh.

Though Jason was a sophomore, we had AP biology together. I'd been assigned to his workgroup my first day. Being a freshman in an upper level course was no picnic. Lucky for me, Hi and Ben were also in the class.

In some ways, Jason was my most important ally at Bolton Prep. He seemed to like me, and that kept some of the other jerks off my back. At least in his presence.

But lately he'd taken a more direct interest. I wasn't sure why, but the attention made me nervous. Jason was great, but he just didn't do it for me.

Now, his buddy Chance . . .

Jason interrupted my thoughts. "What will you write about your four-legged friends? Growl poetry?"

My search for a comeback was cut off by new arrivals.

Ugh. Frying pan to fire.

"Jason, are you coming?" Courtney Holt was blonde, skinny, and impossibly dumb. I was amazed she could even find the library. Courtney wore her cheerleading uniform, though no game was scheduled that day. Classic.

Courtney wasn't alone.

"We're going to scope out Madison's new Beamer." Ashley Bodford had a Prada bag draped over one tan arm. With her free hand she fussed her perfect black hair. "Her dad finally stopped being a jerk about grades."

Beside Ashley was Madison Dunkle, blonde only by diligent and expensive effort. I guessed Madison's earrings cost more than my townhouse.

The three formed an ongoing tableau of carefully manufactured perfection. I'd nicknamed them the Tripod of Skank.

The Tripod smiled at Jason, my presence not registering on their limited gray cells.

"Sure," Jason said. "Madison hasn't gotten a new car in, what, a semester?" Turning to me, he did the unthinkable. "Tory, want to come check out MD's new ride?"

The Tripod froze, expressions equal parts shock, distaste, and annoyance. Jason may as well have farted as invite me.

Fighting the urge to crawl under the desk, I repeated my vow to keep my back protected at all times.

Think quick.

"Oh, no thanks. See . . ." I floundered. "I need to finish. Wolf stuff. I have to figure out where they sleep. And what they eat."

Silence.

"For food," I clarified.

I closed my mouth. Rarely have I failed so spectacularly.

The Tripod stared.

"Wolves?" Courtney snickered. "Are you, like, one of those

hippy chicks who lives in the woods and doesn't shave?"

"No, no, she lives on an island," Ashley snorted. "Your dad's a shrimp boat captain or something, right?"

"Marine biologist," I corrected, face red with embarrassment. "He works for CU."

Ignoring their scornful looks, I spoke directly to Jason. "Thanks, but I really need to finish up here."

"If you say so." Jason leaned toward me and spoke behind one hand. "I don't want go either."

"Come along, Jason." Madison smiled sweetly. Mannequin fake. "The freshman has a project. We should give her space."

"Thanks," I responded dumbly. "I like your shoes."

"Of course you do. They're Ferragamo."

Ouch.

Another unwelcome voice piped in.

"It seems we're all in the library." Chance Claybourne's amused Southern drawl was unmistakable. "Can someone please explain? I thought Maddy had a new auto to parade?"

My heart pole-vaulted. With Chance present, I stood in the eye of Bolton's social hurricane. With no storm doors.

Chance wore the same uniform as the others. Most looked like little boys wearing daddy's lame tie and jacket. Not Chance. Not even close.

Darkly handsome, Chance Claybourne was night to Jason's day. Black hair, expertly tussled. Deep brown eyes under curving brows. Captain of the lacrosse team, young Mr. Claybourne was built like a racehorse.

In a word, Chance smoldered.

The son of state senator and pharmaceutical magnate Hollis Claybourne, Chance was Bolton's most connected student. Old-money Charleston aristocracy, the Claybournes had owned a Meeting Street mansion for over two centuries. Their ancestors numbered among the region's mayors, governors, even a vice presidential candidate. Oh, yeah. The Claybournes were blue bloods squared.

Chance's own story was legendary. His mother, Sally Claybourne, died in childbirth, leaving her husband to raise their son alone. The term *stern* was too soft for Hollis. Rumor had it the old man rode Chance mercilessly.

Most girls at Bolton heard only two words: *sole heir.* At his next birthday Chance would inherit the Claybourne family fortune. Almost eighteen, Chance was a rocket ship set to blast off.

"Jason's talking to the brainiac girl from the boats." Courtney sounded way too eager to please. "Something about werewolves."

Sweet Lord.

I was grateful for the arrival of Chance's girlfriend, Hannah Wythe. Long auburn hair. Bright green eyes. A real stunner. Oddly, Hannah seemed unaware of her beauty. I liked that about her.

Chance arm-wrapped Hannah's waist, pulled her close, and kissed her cheek. All the while he eyed me, like a jogger sizing up a stray.

Hannah was the most popular girl at Bolton. And, for once, the award was deserved. Southern sweet, she never bad-mouthed anyone. In class Hannah tended to stay on task, so we didn't chat much, but she was always friendly.

Hannah and Chance had been together for three years and were unmistakably Bolton's royal couple. Their future was the subject of much gossip, with people laying bets on engagement dates.

"My fault, Chance." Jason, always the diplomat. "I was just saying hello. Tory has bio with Hannah and me. We're in the same study group."

"Not to worry. I recall you invited Miss Tory last weekend, yes?"

Jason nodded.

Chance dipped into a bow, typical of his mock-formal style. "A pleasure, Tory. Sorry you couldn't attend. Will you be joining us this afternoon?"

The Tripod went rigidly silent. Nobody argued with Chance Claybourne. But their unfriendly eyes drilled lasers at me.

"Thanks," I replied. "But I'm swamped. Maybe next time?"

"Next time?" Ashley sniped. "How late do the barges run?" Madison and Courtney snarked viciously.

"That's enough," snapped Jason. "Quit being rude."

The spiteful smiles vanished. I knew later they'd cut me to pieces amongst themselves. Bitches.

Chance frowned, but otherwise seemed indifferent. He glanced at his watch, clearly ready to leave. Hannah looked sympathetic, but remained silent.

"Sorry about that, Tory." Jason sounded sincere; I think he felt responsible. "See you in class tomorrow."

"Sure thing." I flicked a wave. Lame. "Bye guys! Have fun."

Madison and her sidekicks moved off, not deigning to acknowledge an inferior. Chance and Hannah smiled as they left. In seconds I was alone.

I put my head on the desk.

The final bell couldn't ring quickly enough.

CHAPTER 18

Three o'clock found me sitting on Bolton's front steps, impatiently waiting for Hi and Shelton. As usual, they were late. Two granite lions kept me company, guarding the gothic stone building with hulking menace.

I hummed, aimless. And tuneless. I'm tone deaf.

The weather was pleasant, with clear skies and temperatures in the low eighties. The courtyard was abuzz with the song of sparrows and cardinals.

Bolton's landscapers toil year-round seeding, pruning, and sculpting the grounds into postcard-pretty settings. Paths meander through tree-speckled commons, rock gardens set with stone benches, and around a small pond. The place is visually stunning. Tuition-paying parents expect nothing less.

The campus occupies a full block of Charleston's southwestern waterfront, near the peninsula's tip. Pricey turf. A ten-foot brick wall surrounds the school, complete with ornate cast-iron gates adorned with copper griffins.

Broad Street cuts straight east behind campus, through the heart of old Charleston. It's a short stroll to the Battery where decommissioned guns provide climbing opportunities for resident schoolchildren. The city's grandest estates are right around the corner.

Just north lie the city marinas. Yacht central. Moultrie Park and Colonial Lake are mere blocks away. Tucked in its corner, gazing across the bay toward James Island and Charleston Country Club, Bolton's address can only be described as "premier."

The boys finally appeared, Hi pleading that he'd misplaced his iPhone. Whatever. Truth be told, I'd enjoyed my brief sojourn with the marble kitties.

Given weather conditions, we decided on the scenic route. Broad Street.

Charleston is one giant garden in spring, each block striving to outdo the next. Live oaks and oleanders overhang shady streets, their perfumes mixing with the scents of azaleas, begonias, and yellow jessamine. Flowering dogwoods and redbuds shade lawns and parkways. Colors and scents bombard from every angle.

"I can't get over these goofy houses," I wisecracked as we walked.

"Darlin', don't knock my city's sense of style. " Hi mimicked a deep drawl. "She has her own special flavor."

"Special flavor?" I exclaimed. "Who puts a house sideways?"

Old Charleston homes are built long and narrow, with the

short end parallel to the sidewalk. Street-facing doors open onto the side of long porches, called piazzas. Usually two to three stories high, most houses have multilayered balconies facing inward, overlooking a courtyard or garden.

Locals say the architectural style emerged to save money, since property taxes were calculated based on street frontage. The more likely truth? The Lowcountry is hot. Southwest-facing houses capture harbor breezes, and piazzas protect windows from the scorching sun.

Personally, I prefer the tax story.

At Meeting Street, I glanced to my right. Just south, near the Battery, loomed the Claybourne mansion. Chance's mail was delivered to one of the poshest addresses in town. Big money country.

Turning left, we passed City Hall and the white spire of St. Michael's Episcopal Church. Our route sliced through the heart of Charleston's shopping district. Expensive storefronts displayed high-end clothing, and aggressive restaurateurs called from doorways, urging us to feast within.

Continuing up Meeting, we skirted the old market, often called the slave market, though slaves were never sold there. It's now a world-famous open-air bazaar.

Gullah women wove sweetgrass baskets on the sidewalk, hoping to score bucks from out-of-towners. Tourists in visors and sneakers examined trinkets and crafts spread across tables. Further up, outside Hyman's Seafood, a line of would-be diners snaked from the front door.

Eight more blocks brought us to Calhoun Street and the main branch of the Charleston Public Library. Built in 1998, the building is modern brick and stucco.

We entered and crossed a brightly lit atrium to a help desk manned by a small, rat-faced guy. Skinny, maybe thirty-five, he had black hair, oiled and razor-parted. His brown sweater-vest covered a tan shirt hung with a yellow paisley tie. Brown corduroy pants completed perhaps the most boring ensemble ever conceived.

"Can I help you, children?" Annoyance pinched Rat Face's already pinched features. A dog-eared copy of *Battlefield Earth* was pressed to his chest.

Time for some buttering up.

"Yes, sir," I chirped. "I certainly hope so. We've got a research problem. My teacher said that only public library people are smart enough to help."

Rat Face puffed at my largesse, so I plowed ahead. "I know your time is precious, but could you spare a moment to mentor us?"

The weaselly face brightened. "No trouble at all! My name is Brian Limestone." He laid down his book. "What's yours?"

"Tory Brennan. These are my friends, Shelton and Hiram."

"A pleasure. Now, what do you fine young scholars require?"

"We found an old dog tag," I explained. "We'd like to return it to its owner. Seems like the right thing to do."

"Wonderful! What thoughtful, special children!" Limestone hopped from his stool and scurried around the desk. "I have an idea. Please follow!"

Limestone bustled toward a staircase, leaving us to keep up. We climbed to the second floor and entered a chamber labeled *The South Carolina Room.*

"I suggest you start here," Limestone instructed. "See if your soldier was a citizen of Charleston County. We have directories dating from 1782, phonebooks from 1931." He pointed across the room. "If that proves unsuccessful, most of the city's newspapers are on microfilm. The oldest dailies were first published in 1731."

I surveyed the large room. This wouldn't be easy. But Internet searches had generated an overwhelming number of *F. Heaton* hits. Slogging through local records seemed a reasonable plan.

"Thank you *so much*, Mr. Limestone." I laid it on thick. "You're a genius. We'd have been totally lost without you." Big smile. "Looks like we have our work cut out for us!"

"Call down if you need anything," Limestone offered. "Such sweet kids," he remarked, tiptoeing from the room.

The door had barely closed before Hi pounced.

"Oh, Mr. Limestone, thank *God* you were here! I would have *wet* my *pants* without you!" Hi fake-swooned into Shelton's open arms. Both started laughing, drawing frowns from the other patrons.

"Zip it," I responded, giggling. "It worked, all right?"

I looked around, searching for a place to begin.

It was going to be a long afternoon.

CHAPTER 19

Two hours later, frustration reigned.

We'd gotten nowhere with the directories and phonebooks. Ditto for birth certificates and marriage licenses. I began to accept the fact that F. Heaton wasn't local after all.

Hi tried more online sources, but found squat. Shelton was searching newspaper obituaries, looking for a needle in a haystack. Our confidence was in the basement. The name Heaton was simply too common without more information.

The only thing left was the longest of long shots. Sighing, I starting thumbing through records of the Charleston Orphan House. A long shot was better than no shot at all.

Formerly the oldest orphanage in America, the state of South Carolina demolished the Orphan House in 1951. By law, records remained sealed for seventy-five years, meaning the files in the library stopped at 1935. I wasn't holding my breath.

So my find came as a total shock: a musty file labeled *Francis P. Heaton.* Snatching the weathered folder, I rushed to a table.

"Guys! I've got something!" No need to worry about lowered voices. We were the only people left in the room.

Shelton and Hi crowded close as I opened our first lead of the day.

The contents were underwhelming. Two documents. The one on top appeared to be a standard intake form. I reviewed the scant information provided:

Name: Francis P. Heaton

Born: 1934

Parents/relations: unknown

Date accepted as ward of state: July 15, 1935.

Manner of acceptance: left on doorstep of Charleston Orphan House

"They left him on the freakin' doorstep?" squawked Shelton. "That's cold!"

"It *was* the Great Depression," Hi countered. "That's greatly depressing."

"Enough," I shushed. "There's more."

Below the typed information, someone had penned a few lines in an old-fashioned hand:

The infant was left outside the orphanage gates during the night of July 15, 1935. A note attached to the child's swaddling provided only a name. Investigation failed to unearth any information regarding the child's natural parents. The Board has therefore assumed responsibility for Francis P. Heaton as a ward of the state of South Carolina.

"Do you think it's our boy?" asked Shelton. "Francis P. would've been in his thirties during the Vietnam War."

"Could be," said Hi. "What's the other page say?"

The second document was a standard sheet of loose-leaf paper. I flipped it over, revealing a handwritten message in the form a journal entry.

The date scrawled on top read November 24, 1968. Although shakier, the penmanship matched that of the first document. The message had been written by the same person who'd completed the intake form thirty years earlier.

Terrible news for Thanksgiving. Frankie Heaton was killed in action last month fighting in the Mekong Delta. I'd not heard from him in years. A Gazette story reported that Frankie fought valiantly as his entire squad was overcome.

Biting my lip, I forced myself to keep reading.

What a wretched war! My heart breaks to think of Frankie's daughter, Katherine. Only sixteen, and with her

mother gone, now an orphan herself. May the Good Lord
bless Frankie's soul, and watch over his child.

The note was signed with an illegible name.

We all stared at it mutely.

Shelton spoke first. "What's the *Gazette*?"

"A Charleston paper that went out of print in the early seventies," Hi said.

"I think Frankie's our guy." Shelton sounded as downcast as I felt. "But if he died in the Mekong Delta, how did his dog tag end up on Loggerhead Island?"

"His daughter was fifteen in 1968." Hi calculated in his head. "She'd be fifty-seven now."

"Then the tag belongs to her," I said vehemently. "We've got to find Katherine and give it back."

Hi nodded. "Let's try Google. We have a full name. It might work this time."

Shelton and Hi moved to the computer bank, anxious to distance themselves from my emotional orbit. I didn't follow. A tremendous sadness had enveloped me, more powerful than expected.

Across the span of decades, I empathized with Francis Heaton's daughter. Like Katherine, I knew how it felt to lose a mother. She'd lost her father, too. The world could be very cruel.

And Francis himself? The child abandoned on a doorstep had grown into a man who fought for his country. And paid the ultimate price. Unspeakably sad.

"Tory!" Shelton sounded wired. "Oh man, check this out!"

Reading Shelton's screen, my shock doubled.

Worse and worse.

Shelton's keyword search had brought up a crime site exploring missing person cases. According to the information, sixteen-year-old Katherine Heaton disappeared in Charleston, South Carolina, in 1969, leaving no trace.

Vanished. Gone.

"This can't be legit," I studied the screen. "The Stab Network? What ridiculous blog is this, anyway?"

"Not exactly CNN," Hi agreed. "Hit the sources page."

Though the entry listed references, none of the links worked. But the story cited quotes from the *Gazette.*

We flew to the microfilm reader. Shelton located and spooled the reel containing *Gazette* issues from 1969. For the next hour we huddled together, absorbing the saga of Katherine Anne Heaton.

Katherine's disappearance had captivated Charleston. On August 24, 1969, the young woman left home, headed for the docks at Ripley Point. She was never seen again. For weeks the police scoured the region, found nothing. In mid-September the search was called off.

During the investigation, the *Gazette* published several background pieces. Katherine grew up in West Ashley, a modest neighborhood east of the peninsula. She attended St. Andrew's Parish High School, achieved excellent marks, even won a merit award for science. Friends said Katherine planned to attend Charleston University after graduation.

I skimmed through weeks of newspapers, desperate for a happy ending. Nothing. Katherine's story simply ended.

Then, a bombshell.

In October of 1969, the *Gazette* ran a front-page story profiling Charleston County citizens killed in Vietnam. Among them was Francis "Frankie" Heaton. The reporter noted that Frankie Heaton was the father of still-missing Katherine Heaton, in whose disappearance police continued to have no leads.

"Guys, listen! According to an aunt, Katherine Heaton wore her father's dog tags to honor him."

"That's it." Shelton whistled. "We've got the right Heaton. I bet she dropped the tag on Loggerhead."

"But why would Katherine be out there?" I wondered aloud. "Her bio suggests she wasn't the party-island type."

"Did they ever find her?" Hi asked.

"Not in 1969." Shelton replaced that reel in its box. "Should we move ahead to 1970?"

"My word, you've been diligent! Any luck?" We all turned at the sound of Limestone's voice.

"Yes, sir. We discovered quite a bit, but have more questions."

"Splendid. The library closes soon, but perhaps I can be of additional help?"

Shelton took charge. "Have you ever heard of a girl named Katherine Heaton?"

Something flickered in Limestone's eyes. Was gone. "What did you say?" The whiney voice had raised an octave.

"Katherine Heaton," Shelton repeated. "Local girl, went missing in the sixties? Her pop was a soldier in Vietnam. Ever heard of her?"

"I'm sorry. I can't help you." A different Brian Limestone stood before us. The encouragement was gone. The man now seemed anxious. "I've got to close this room now, if you'll please excuse me."

"Sorry to be a pain," I soothed. "We'd just like to know what happened to Katherine. We got caught up in the old newspaper articles. Can you show us where to find more of her story?"

"No, I cannot. I'm very busy. I thought you were doing schoolwork." A bony finger pointed to the exit. "Please leave. You'll have to return another time."

We exchanged glances. Limestone was shutting us down. Bewildered, we gathered our things and hustled from the building.

Outside, I glanced back at the library. Limestone stood inside the door, watching us intently.

"What was that?" I asked. "An evil twin? The guy couldn't cut us some slack?"

"For real," agreed Shelton. "The minute *I* ask for something, he's a grade-A dick."

"Librarians," remarked Hi. "Always hatin' on the brothers. Good thing I didn't open my Jew mouth."

"No doubt." Shelton chuckled. "Probably donning his bedsheet and hood as we speak, saluting a Nazi flag! Racist."

I grinned. "He's not a big fan of women, either."

We were joking, of course. Whatever had gotten into Brian Limestone, it wasn't bigotry.

When our amusement faded, anxiety settled in its place. The librarian's sudden change of attitude was unnerving.

I remembered Limestone's face just before he'd morphed into a jerk.

His expression.

Had that been . . . fear?

CHAPTER 20

M y body dozed on the boat ride home.

Not so my brain. It kept a half-open eye on my surroundings, and on my bench position between Hi and Shelton.

We'd barely caught the last ferry. Thankfully, Ben's dad had waited an extra ten minutes before making his final run from the city.

Dusk gave way to night as we bounced across the chop obscuring the shoreline, the harbor, and Fort Sumter.

My sleeping psyche meandered through visions and memories. Dreaming, but aware at the same time.

In my dream I wandered deep woods at night. Alone. The midnight air infused me with a bone-deep chill.

I wasn't afraid, but felt an urgent compulsion to search. Though undefined, the drive was all-consuming. A massive, essential *something* was missing, and everything depended on my finding it. I *needed,* but didn't know "what."

Knee-high fog wafted among the trees, thick and soupy. Pale moonlight struggled, but failed to penetrate the gloom. Direction-blind, I lurched through the vapor, eyes probing my surroundings, sifting for clues. Nothing.

The formless urge grew stronger—to trace, to determine, to ask. But what was the question?

After stumbling a few more yards, I halted. Recognized the terrain. I was in Y-7's clearing. Right where we'd found the dog tag.

My mind wandered the heart of Loggerhead Island.

Something called out from deep in my subconscious. Saying what? I couldn't catch the message.

Instinctively, I scanned the ground. Dense, rolling fog hid the forest floor. I needed to see beneath, to inspect the earth.

I can't find anything in this soup.

As if on cue, the mist parted and rolled from the clearing. I froze, confused. Then comprehension dawned.

I'm dreaming. I can do anything I want.

I considered exiting the fantasy. Knew I could. Some instinct told me to remain, hinted that my unconscious was trying to tell me something.

My mind searched the dreamscape. The field looked as I remembered it. I crisscrossed the open space, seeking anything that might spark my interest. Nada.

The clearing itself?

I launched myself skyward. Fifty yards up I pivoted to face the ground. Perched upon nothing, I hovered in midair, gazing down.

Too dark.

I summoned daylight. Bright sunshine scattered the shadows. Bathed in glowing rays, the ground now looked as it had during our weekend visit.

This was fun.

Like a bird of prey, I scanned the terrain, hoping for dots to connect in my brain. But what was I looking for?

I ramped up my concentration. Details registered. The shape of the ground. The varied greens of the vegetation. Y-7's agitation.

My mind circled, clutched. What did these things mean?

Abruptly, gravity reasserted control and plunged me earthward. I flailed, flapped my arms. Useless. I dropped like a rock. The ground hurtled up to greet me.

A scream echoed in my ears. Mine?

Hi danced backward, yanking his hand from my shoulders.

"Jeez, Tor! We're here."

My head snapped up. Disoriented, I glanced around.

The Morris Island dock. Shelton. Hi. A very startled Mr. Blue.

"Sorry, Hi. I passed out a bit."

"No problemo. You hit like a girl."

Hi dropped his voice so Ben's father wouldn't overhear. "I'm going to relieve Ben. I'll let you know how Coop's doing." He lumbered down the plank. "Toodles!"

Shaking cobwebs, I said goodnight to Shelton and Mr. Blue, who motored off to collect the last stragglers from Loggerhead. Kit included, I assumed.

I trudged toward my house.

◯   ◯   ◯

Hours later, sleep wouldn't come. Over and over, snatches of the dream replayed in my head.

The clearing. Why did I keep seeing the clearing?

Restless, and Red Bull–awake, I powered up my Mac, accessed Google Earth, and pulled up satellite photos of Loggerhead Island. An aerial survey took time, but eventually I identified a likely spot.

Zooming in, I recognized the tree Hi and I had used for cover during Y-7's smackdown. Excitement fizzed in my chest. I had the right location.

By maxing the magnification, I got picture clarity that was spectacular. Even more amazing, the image mirrored the setting of my dream.

What is it that bugs me?

I cataloged the scene. Circular clearing, roughly twenty-five yards in diameter. My stalwart oak standing alone on the left. Ground grassy, with a slight depression at center.

So why the mental *Psst*?

The depression?

I studied it. The indentation was roughly six feet in diameter and appeared to be overgrown by vegetation darker than the surrounding grass.

Or was that merely shadow?

Okay. So what? The ground dipped. Water pooled at the low point. Higher moisture in the soil attracted different plants.

I rubbed my eyes, preparing to forget the whole thing.

Wait!

The subliminal message fired into my conscious inbox.

Ground slump. Vegetative change. Six foot radius.

Oh my God.

For a hot moment I forgot to breathe. Then I sucked in six or seven deep gulps, hyperventilating.

Could it be? What to do?

Obvious. Go find out.

I opened Twitter and buzzed my crew: CHAT ROOM NOW!

Then I logged on to our webpage and stared at the screen, waiting.

Come on. Come on.

My fingers drummed the desk. Five minutes. Ten. Finally, the gang was convened.

I posted: Back to Loggerhead tomorrow afternoon. Highest importance! Will explain at school.

The boys responded quickly, succinctly, and in total accord with each other. Ben typed that returning to the scene of our crime was wildly risky. Foolhardy. Shelton and Hi agreed, Hi using all caps to drive the point home.

I hadn't wanted to share my fears online, but their opposition left me no choice. I launched a flurry of posts, firing my suspicions into the ether.

Finished, I sat with eyes glued to the monitor, awaiting reactions. I needed their support. This was too big to handle alone.

For a good half minute, zero response. Then Ben and Shelton said they'd think about it. Following an impressive string of profanities, Hi consented to sleep on it.

Logging off, I felt confident my team would come through. At least I hoped so. What I suspected was simply too terrible to ignore. They'd require more details, sure, and some cajoling, but, in the end, they'd trust my judgment. After all, I was the niece of Dr. Temperance Brennan. I knew certain things.

In the dark, under the covers, the implications of my theory horrified me.

Don't be right!

Had I ever wished that before?

But we had to go back.

Had to dig.

Had to check for a grave.

CHAPTER 21

B rian Limestone was anxious.

Though puzzling, his instructions had been clear all those years ago. So far back he'd almost forgotten. Almost.

He'd advanced in the hierarchy since that day, his first on the job. Indeed, Limestone felt he had a decent shot at head librarian when old lady Wilkerson hung up her bookmark.

The old biddy must be two hundred by now, he thought wryly. *Surely she'll kick it soon. Then me. My chance.*

The library was closed and locked. Limestone had just finished re-shelving materials dislodged by the day's scholars.

Time to follow orders.

Descending three flights, Limestone used an old brass key to let himself into a small basement office. The room was dusty from disuse, empty but for a single filing cabinet. He unlocked the rusty relic and pulled a folder from the bottom drawer.

Fifteen years earlier, Brian Limestone had sat in this room with the man he'd been hired to replace. Fenton Dawkins was a strange old coot, possessive and distrusting. Limestone had sensed the reluctance with which Dawkins had revealed his secret.

The deal was simple. An unknown benefactor paid a yearly, thousand-dollar stipend to the research librarian of the public library's main branch. Should the fact of this bonus ever be disclosed—to anyone—it would cease to exist.

A single duty came with the money: vigilance concerning a specific name.

Katherine Heaton.

Should anyone ask about Ms. Heaton, Limestone must obstruct the party in any manner possible. In addition, should such inquiry occur, he must return to this office and open a sealed envelope for further instruction.

That's all.

Limestone had agreed without hesitation. Free cash was free cash.

So there he sat, holding the magic packet. With a firm hand Limestone tore open one side and removed a single slip of paper.

Nine digits. Typed, not handwritten or computer printed. Recognizing the obvious, Limestone returned to the main desk and dialed the number.

A male voice answered on the third ring.

"Yes."

"My name is Brian Limestone. I'm research librarian at the Charleston Public Library."

Limestone waited.

Dead silence.

"Years back I was tasked with calling this number should a certain event ever transpire. Today it happened."

Still no response.

Limestone glanced at the phone's display, assuring himself that the call hadn't disconnected.

Get it over with, he thought. *No big deal.*

"Three students visited the library, one a young lady named Tory Brennan. I failed to catch the other names. The children were asking about a Katherine Heaton."

Limestone laughed nervously. "Does that make any sense to you?"

Another pause, then a soft click.

Dial tone.

"Hello?"

Limestone waited a beat, then slammed the receiver. "Nuts!"

Having fulfilled his obligation, Brian Limestone trashed the phone number and headed home to his cats.

CHAPTER 22

The next day, school seemed endless. I couldn't shake my suspicion that something was buried on Loggerhead. I tried to concentrate, but time and again my thoughts circled back to the ghastly possibility.

Before catching the morning ferry, I'd checked on Coop. He still looked dreadful, the proverbial "sick as a dog." I told myself to stay positive. But I had to admit. Things didn't look good.

We were down to our last IV bag and had no hope of obtaining others. Antibiotics were also running low. Everyone had tried, but the puppy continued to vomit what little he ate. Coop needed to turn a corner, and soon, before he weakened beyond his ability to recover.

Mind burning with worry, I was thoroughly distracted during biology. Jason and Hannah were quiet, but I could tell their patience had worn thin. I tried to shake the negative vibes. We had work to do.

"Sorry guys," I mumbled, "I'm out of it today. What were you saying?"

Jason snorted. "Out of it? You've been staring at nothing for the last half hour. If you didn't usually do 90 percent of the work, I'd be outraged."

"It's okay," said Hannah, understanding as always. "But we need to get through this. We have to present our results next week."

"I know. My bad. Where do we stand?"

Our project was to compare human DNA to that of several animal species to determine which are our closest relatives.

"Neck-deep, by my count." Jason sighed. "Let's face it. We're going to have to work . . ." His eyes closed in dramatic agony. ". . . On the *weekend.*"

Hannah giggled. "Looks like it. Let's exchange phone numbers."

It felt strange, storing Hannah Wythe's digits in my cell. She was popular, cool, admired by all. Strange, and oddly like trespassing.

Self-confidence at an all-time high, eh Tory?

"I'll take the cystic fibrosis gene," said Jason. "That section compares humans to chimps, gorillas, and orangutans. My money's on the chimps."

"I can handle the bone-growth protein sequences," I said. My menagerie would be pigs, rabbits, and sheep.

Hannah nodded agreeably. "That leaves me with Leptin counts for cows, dogs, and horses."

The bell rang, sounding our release.

"My house on Sunday?" Jason was already headed to the door.

"We can go over results and plan the presentation."

"Okay." Hannah and I responded as one. *Jinx.*

The day continued to drag. At lunch Hi and I met at our usual spot, out the cafeteria's back door and across the lawn, on a small stone bench. I ate a cucumber and cream cheese sandwich. Hi worked on a veggie panini.

I was bagging my wrapper when I saw Jason walking our way.

"What the hey, Tor?" Hi murmured under his breath. "Popular jock approaching. I doubt he's looking for me."

"Relax."

"Tory, I just thought of something!" Jason called.

"First time for everything," whispered Hi.

"Shh. Jason's nice."

"*Nice.* Right. Watch, he won't even acknowledge me."

Flopping to the grass in front of the bench, Jason cocked his chin at Hi. "What's up, man?"

"Nothing, bro." Hi, playing it cool. "Chillin'." He leaned back, hands laced behind his head.

Jason refocused on me. "You've got an iPhone, right?"

I nodded, curious where this was going.

"Great! Download iFollow." He displayed the icon on his own cell. "It's a free GPS communications app."

"Okay." Sounded easy. "Do I need to join anything?"

Jason nodded. "Join the group: *Bolton Lacrosse.* Password: *state-champs.*"

I installed, and joined. With me, the group had seven members.

"Hit *Locator*," Jason said.

I did. A city map appeared, with seven glowing circles bunched together at the school's address.

"See those dots?" Jason asked. "That's us. When we're logged in, our orbs will appear on the map wherever we go. Pretty slick, huh?"

"Definitely," I agreed.

I meant it. I intended to start a separate circle for my crew. But why did Jason want me to join his lacrosse group?

Jason pulled up the features page. "Now that you've linked in, we can text, chat, share documents, that kind of stuff. Exchanging project info will be a snap. Hannah's already in."

Ah. Schoolwork.

"Tory, not you too!"

Chance Claybourne could move so quietly it was almost creepy. I hadn't heard him approach.

"Not another information junky?" Chance stood behind Jason, a *tut, tut* expression on his perfect face. "Why do people persist with this 'new app' madness? Privacy is dead."

"You've got a cell too," Jason retorted.

"True." Chance produced a mobile probably hot during the Clinton years. First term. "My father wants me at a moment's notice, so I'm cursed with this vulgar device." A wink came my way. "Three missed calls this morning."

Chance's phone clearly lacked Internet capability, computer functions, or even an MP3 player. Hell, the thing didn't even have a liquid crystal display. It belonged in a museum.

"The current phone obsession is a disease," Chance said. "Everyone's gone mad, typing to themselves all day long like mindless robots."

Guilty. If I misplace my iPhone for fifteen minutes, I get the shakes. Call me a technology addict, but I feel naked without it. Hi looked downright offended.

"I've heard this rant before," Jason cracked. "You prefer painting messages on the walls of caves."

The bell ended further debate on the pros and cons of modern communication.

"Until the next." Chance rolled a wave as he and Jason ambled off.

"You're beginning to attract some real whack-jobs, " Hi said when the two were out of earshot.

"Mm-hm." On their own, my eyes followed Chance.

"At least they didn't blow me off. Gotta give them credit."

"*Bro?*" I teased.

"He caught me off guard." A touch defensive.

Heading inside, I shook the scene from my mind. We had a job to do soon. Perhaps a gruesome discovery to make.

Focus. Forget Chance Claybourne.

Just a few more hours to kill.

CHAPTER 23

Disembarking the Charleston-Morris ferry, we raced to our homes to change. The temperature and humidity were cranking again, and I looked forward to sliding into a T-shirt and shorts. Besides, ties and blazers aren't *haute couture* for digging up graves.

By the time the gang regrouped on the common, Mr. Blue's ferry was fast disappearing across the harbor. Coast clear. We hopped into *Sewee* and headed to Loggerhead.

The tide was out, so we couldn't take the shortcut through the sandbars. That added fifteen minutes, but Ben wouldn't risk grounding the boat. Not after his mishap in Schooner Creek.

Today we anchored off Dead Cat Beach. Shelton's idea. A western landing put us closer to Y-7's clearing. Equally important, we avoided any potential encounter with Karsten at the main dock.

I waded ashore, canvas duffel balanced on my shoulders. My

second gift from Aunt Tempe. Admittedly, excavation tools are a peculiar present to a newfound niece. But my aunt, by all accounts, is a peculiar woman.

The gift scored a direct hit with me. Tempe seemed to get me without even trying. Better than Kit, that's for sure.

Once on land, we hunted for the main trail exiting Dead Cat. The boys were being helpful, carrying the buckets and other bulky gear. But I detected an undercurrent of impatience. They didn't want to be on Loggerhead, were taking me largely on faith.

At school I'd laid out my theory, referencing the satellite photos. The guys granted that I wasn't crazy, but I suspected they were mainly humoring me. Fair enough. They came. That's what mattered.

"There," was all Ben said before disappearing into the trees. We hurried to follow him onto the path.

Minutes later we located the smaller, north-bearing trail. We hiked in silence through dense forest until spotting the clearing. Y-7 and her troop were nowhere in sight.

From the field's edge, the signs that had roused my suspicions were barely noticeable. The ground slump, visible as a subtle shadow in the center of the clearing, was no more than six feet in diameter. Small wonder it hadn't registered on our first visit.

Moving close to the depression, I saw other indicators of decomposition. The vegetation was thicker and composed of multiple plant species. The rest of the clearing was nothing but grass. Some leaves appeared more waxy than normal.

"I wish we had a cadaver dog," I said.

"A what?" Shelton asked.

"A dog trained to alert on the smell of human decomposition. Some body dogs are expert at locating skeletons, even really old ones."

"Gross," Ben said.

"While you're at it, wish for ground penetrating radar, surface probes, and a metal detector," said Hi. "Back order on those toys, too."

"Then we do it old school." Shelton flexed one twig arm. "Manpower!"

I examined the depression to determine how big our excavation needed to be. Then, after a visual scan, I removed all surface debris from a ten-foot square.

Next, I created a simple grid by pounding four wooden stakes into the ground and running string between them, forming an outer perimeter. After unfolding a portable sifting screen, I pulled collapsible shovels from my bag and handed them to my reluctant recruits.

"You macho men can offload topsoil into buckets," I instructed. "I'll screen. At the first sign of staining we'll switch to trowels."

"Staining?" asked Ben.

"Any change in soil color, texture, or composition could mean a body's nearby. If you spot any discoloration, call out."

Hi raised a hand.

"Yes?"

"This sucks."

"Got it. Dig."

We removed the first eighteen inches in roughly an hour. The guys scooped, I sifted through quarter-inch mesh screening, watching closely for bone fragments, bits of clothing, jewelry, anything not native to the earth.

The conversation went something like this:

"This blows." Shelton.

"I said that." Hi.

"You said it sucks." Shelton.

"Same concept." Hi. "When can I work the screen?"

I didn't bother responding.

They shoveled.

I sifted.

Two more hours took us down another two feet. Nothing.

I started to feel foolish. The boys grew crankier.

The heat and humidity weren't helping. Nor was the fact that a call had gone out to every biting insect native to the Lowcounty. Maybe some outsiders.

I was slapping a mosquito when I heard something odd: silence. Looking up, I confronted three grumpy faces. Interest in excavation had dropped to zero.

Hi spoke first. "I don't want to bitch, but this isn't working. Three and a half feet down and we've got zilch."

"There's nothing here," Ben said.

"It was a good gamble." Shelton braced to climb out of the pit. "No shame in that."

"Fifteen more minutes?" I implored. "Please? I have this gut feeling. We could be close."

"Fifteen. One-five." Ben picked up his shovel.

Shrugging, Shelton followed suit.

Hi shot an *are you kidding?* look my way.

"Hi, switch with me," I said. "You sift; I'll dig."

He nodded and we exchanged places.

We'll go to four feet. That's it.

As I dug, emotions kaleidoscoped inside me. Relief? Disappointment? Embarrassment?

While a part of me wanted to be right—to show the others I wasn't insane—another part wasn't totally unhappy that I'd struck out. Yes, I wanted to solve the mystery of Katherine Heaton. But I had no desire to unearth a murdered human being.

Then I saw it. A dark oval materializing in the soil by my feet.

Switching to a trowel, I dropped to my knees and began slicing thin layers of dirt. The oval darkened. Grew.

More slicing.

Sensing my excitement, Ben and Shelton stopped to watch.

Slice.

Slice.

Tick.

My trowel nicked something solid.

I grabbed a brush and, moving ever so gingerly, swept overlying dirt from the surface of the object.

A musty scent rose from the earth. Ancient. Organic.

A chill traveled my spine.

I brushed gently. Shapes emerged. Tiny cylinders arranged in a familiar pattern.

Heart hammering, I stared.

"Okay, that's fifteen." Hiram dropped the bucket he'd been sifting. "I'm bushed."

Still I stared. So did Ben and Shelton.

"Tory?" Hi ventured. "You upset? No one's blaming you or anything. If I'd read more about bodies, I might've thought the same thing."

Still I was speechless.

"Hey, Victoria Brennan!" Hi shouted. "What's what?"

A cloud crossed the sun, casting shadow over the small space in which I knelt. Crickets chirped from hidden places. Sweat glued my shirt to my back.

Nothing penetrated. My mind was locked onto the tiny brown objects before me.

I forced myself to acknowledge the truth.

I'd uncovered the delicate bones of a human hand.

CHAPTER 24

I snapped out of my trance.

My head whipped up.

"I've got bones here."

"Where?" Ben dropped his shovel and peered over my shoulder. "Holy crap! You were right."

Shelton's response was less manly. Spotting the gruesome discovery, he yelled, "Grave, grave!" and scrambled from the pit.

Hiram took one look and promptly upchucked.

Both dropped to the grass, flushed and panting.

Only Ben kept his head. "They're human, right?"

"Absolutely," I confirmed. "I'm positive." And I was. I'd seen enough diagrams of the human skeleton to recognize human carpals, metacarpals, and phalanges.

"Then we call the cops." Ben's tone was decisive. "Now."

Practicality tempered my roiling emotions. "Yes. But first we have to be sure."

Ben nodded. "How?"

"I want to see more than hand bones." I took a deep breath. "I want to know exactly what's buried here."

"We find a freakin' *dead body*, and y'all want to keep on digging?" Shelton's alarm was escalating by the second. "That's crazy!"

"It's a police matter now," Hi whined. "They'll be pissed if you mess with a crime scene. Especially if that's the Heaton girl."

"Don't say that!" I snapped. "We've no proof it's her." Inexplicably, I wanted to punch Hi like a speed bag.

"Silly me." Hi held up both hands. "Let's dig a little more. Maybe it's someone else."

Shelton and Ben eyed me, clearly surprised. I'd jumped on Hi for stating the obvious.

Easy. What did you think you would find?

I took a deep breath. Admitted to myself. As illogical as it was, I didn't want to accept that Hi was right. Not yet.

"I'm sorry, Hi. That wasn't fair. I just need to be sure."

"No sweat," Hi replied. "I don't think before I talk." But he still looked wary, like a cat circling a sleeping dog.

Ben and Shelton said nothing. But I could read their faces. They, too, were convinced we'd found Katherine Heaton.

"I know what you're all thinking," I said. "Just let me examine the bones."

Skeptical looks.

"The cops won't believe us without proof," I said. "Not those Folly Beach yokels. We need pictures of the grave, the skeleton, everything we find."

"We can't mess anything up," Shelton said.

"We'll be careful," I promised. "We'll document as we work. That way we preserve the evidence in case monkeys disturb the site after we leave."

Reluctantly, the boys agreed.

I formulated a plan. Ben and I would dig inside the pit. The 'fraidy cats would stay topside, Shelton hauling dirt, Hi capturing images on his iPhone.

Two more hours of steady, painstaking excavation exposed a fully articulated skeleton. Darkened to the color of very strong tea, the bones looked like relics from another time.

One glance extinguished any lingering doubts.

The remains were human, and buried over four feet down.

I squatted for an up close look at the skull.

"Oh Jesus!"

I pointed at a small hole centered in the forehead. The defect was sharp-edged and circular.

"Holy shit. Is that a bullet hole?" asked Ben.

"I think so." My voice trembled slightly.

The boys watched as I eyeballed the skeleton from top to bottom.

"There's no trauma on any of the other bones. I'll try to determine gender."

"How?" Hi asked.

Lying sideways in the dirt, I observed the right pelvic blade. "The overall shape is broad." I twisted my head so I could see the belly side of the bone. "The pubic portion is long, and the angle below, where the right half meets the left, is shaped like a U, not a V. Those are all female traits."

Recalling a tip from Aunt Tempe's book, I searched for the sciatic notch. Without displacing the bone, I stuck my thumb inside. It had plenty of room for wiggling.

An emphatic groan from the boys.

"Don't be babies," I said. "Sometimes you have to touch the bones."

"Well?" Ben asked.

"Female."

"How old was she?" Shelton was sounding maybe a hair calmer.

Crawling to the skull, I noted the sutures, the thin, squiggly lines between the individual bones. The ones I could see were wide open.

I peeked into the mouth.

"Healthy dentition. Wisdom teeth not fully erupted."

I moved back down the torso. "Little caps at the ends of the long bones solidify as growth is completed. It's called epiphyseal fusion. The cap of her femur hasn't fused completely. Same with the clavicle."

"The what?" Ben aked.

"The collarbone." Shelton and Hi, in unison.

"From what I can see without moving anything," I said, "she was young."

"How young?" Hi.

"Less than twenty years old." I felt numb.

"Like Katherine Heaton," Shelton whispered.

Attaching a name to the bones made the tragedy real. This wasn't an experiment, an adventure for a group of high school science junkies. I was kneeling in the lonely, unmarked grave of a young woman.

A teenager long ago murdered, buried, and forgotten.

"It's time to call the cops." Hi's voice held not a trace of humor.

I nodded. "The sun is setting. Take as many pictures as you can before dark."

Ben, Shelton, and I started gathering equipment. I was pulling a trowel from the earth when I heard a soft clink.

And knew right away.

Sifting dirt with my fingers, I discovered what my blade had struck.

"Holy Hell."

The others turned to look.

"This should close the loop." I held my find high. It glinted in the long ginger rays of the setting sun.

A second dog tag, twin to the one in my pocket.

Legible.

Francis P. Heaton.

The last light of day faded to gray.

I wanted to cry. To open the floodgates and unleash a torrent of sobs. But I wouldn't. Not in this lifetime. Not ever.

Clamping my jaw, I backhanded a tear from my cheek. I added the newly unearthed tag to my Ziploc, and started shoving tools into the duffel. Stakes. String. A shovel. A trowel.

The boys were uncomfortable in the way males are when confronted by female emotion. Unsure how to react, what to say, they simply ignored me.

Sorrow coursed through my body. Katherine Heaton was dead. I'd uncovered her bones. There would be no magical happy ending.

Inevitably, the sorrow congealed into fury. Then hardened into resolve.

The crime was official: murder most foul. Now it was time to expose the murderer.

I vowed silently, speaking to Katherine. Someone will pay for this outrage. Four decades of time will make no difference. Justice will prevail.

My promise was cut short.

Men with guns had come to kill us.

CHAPTER 25

"You guys hear that?" Shelton asked.

"Hear what?" Hi froze, iPhone extended toward the pit. "Listen."

Everyone went still, ears sifting the forest sounds. Night had fallen. My eyes weren't ready. I could barely see beyond my hand.

At first, nothing but crickets, frogs, the whine of a mosquito.

Then a familiar riot of hoots and barks.

As my vision adjusted, I noticed movement among the branches at the clearing's edge.

"Something spooked the monkeys," Ben said.

The primates scurried through the trees, panicked, uncertain of the source of danger. Young males barked and lunged in our direction, then turned and performed for the forest at their backs.

"They seem confused," Hi noted.

"The males are giving threat displays," I said. "But they don't know where to direct them."

"Threatened by what?" Ben asked.

"Can we please get out of here?" Shelton had definitely had enough. "It's pitch dark, monkeys are screaming at us, and we're standing next to an open grave."

"Calm down," Ben said. "I brought a flashlight—"

Clank. Clank.

"What was that?" I whispered.

The noise was not natural to the forest. Somewhere close by metal had struck metal.

"The dogs?" Hi sounded almost as hyper as Shelton. "Somewhere nearby?"

"No," I whispered. "We'd never hear the pack moving through the trees. And what could they clang?"

Swish.

Thwak!

A string of curses followed.

My heart jumped a gear. *Someone* was out there. And we stood, tools in hand, over the recently uncovered skeleton of a murder victim.

Instinctively, the four of us knotted close.

The startled primates disappeared into the foliage. Whoever was out there had accidentally driven them to our location, warning us.

The woods went silent.

"What should we do?" mouthed Shelton. A three-quarter moon

was rising and I could just make out my companions. Beyond them, nothing but black.

I gestured for silence. We needed to pinpoint the source of the noise. Pulse thumping, I held my breath and listened.

Pop!

My head swiveled.

Pop!

One-eighty from the first.

Shit! More than one!

Questions winged in my brain.

Why no lights? Why two directions? How many? Who?

LIRI personnel never prowled the island at night. Sneaking through the woods without a flashlight was *not* normal behavior.

Hi was on the same page.

"This is wrong! Let's bail!"

"Quiet!" Ben hissed.

Too late.

"Over there!" A male voice. Deep. "In the clearing!"

Branches crashed. Feet pounded. Three beams flared to life, probed the darkness. A motor fired up.

The beams closed in.

"Run!" I shout-hissed. "To the boat!"

I didn't know where the path was or how to find it. But I understood one thing with bone-deep certainty. Capture wasn't an option.

With only a vague sense of where Dead Cat lay, I pounded for the tree line.

Three figures emerged from the trees, black cutouts against the blacker forest. No way these men were scientists.

One figure raised a hand and pointed in my direction. Then he froze, arms straight out and clasped in front of his face.

Crack! Crack!

Overhead, a branch exploded. A lone monkey screamed and bolted in panic.

GUN! GUN! GUN! GUN!

My brain, understanding bullets, surrendered the Tory Machine to its primitive instincts. Spurred by a massive dose of adrenaline, I sprinted into the night.

○　　○　　○

Though I never finished the story, you know what happened next.

My blind flight succeeded, and I found Dead Cat Beach. Shelton, Ben, and I crouched inside *Sewee* praying for Hi to appear.

Terrified, my thoughts went nasty places. A thousand questions jockeyed for attention.

What were armed thugs doing on Loggerhead? Why did they shoot at us? Did they know about the body? Did they know who we were?

One thought dominated: *Someone just tried to kill me.*

Murder me. Dead.

A murderer shot a gun at my head, trying to end my life.

The reality threatened to trigger my panic button.

You escaped. You're okay.

But not everyone had made it to the boat. Where was Hi? Seconds ticked by. I barely dared to breathe.

"Start the motor!" Shelton was trembling.

"They'll hear it," said Ben.

"They've already got Hi!" Shelton sounded near hysteria. "Hi's been shot!"

I shook Shelton by the shoulders. "Get it together! Hi will come to the beach. He knows where the boat is." To Ben. "Can we at least pull the anchor?"

Ben did as I requested, then hopped into chest-deep water to steady the boat.

"Where the hell is he? He always gets lost!"

Shelton had a point. Hi could be anywhere. The longer we waited, the more uncertain our fate.

And another thing worried me.

I'd left my archaeology kit by the grave.

I searched my memory. The bag was not monogrammed and contained only equipment. There was nothing to tie it to me.

Minutes dragged by. Five. Seven. A thousand. We couldn't stay there forever. Sooner or later, we'd have to go.

As I was losing hope, Hi appeared, his pale face barely discernible in the moonlight. He darted from the undergrowth, eyes frantically seeking the boat.

Despite Ben's efforts, *Sewee* had floated some distance offshore. We splashed our hands in the water to get Hi's attention. His head whipped seaward as he dropped to a crouch, prepared for fight or flight. Shelton and I waved madly in the dark.

Relief spreading his face, Hi crossed the sand and launched into the surf. Ben pulled himself aboard, then reached down to drag Hi over the gunwale.

"You didn't leave!" Hi gasped and spit seawater. "Oh thank God! Thank God, thank God, thank God!"

"No way, buddy," said Shelton. "Never considered it!"

"You're lying, but I don't care!" Hi flopped onto the deck. "You guys are the best. I was sure you'd be gone."

Ben turned the ignition and the engine gunned to life. Anyone close would have heard.

We watched, terrified.

No one emerged from the woods.

Ben dropped the hammer and we shot from the island, leaving pale ribbons of froth in our wake.

CHAPTER 26

"We should go to the police right now!"

Hi said it for the third time. He sat with his arms crossed, back pressed to the bunker wall. "We're in way over our heads."

"With what?" Shelton asked. "You lost the only evidence we had."

For a beat, Hi just stared. Then he spoke slowly. "I just ran through pitch-black woods, at night, while killers shot at me. Then I had to dive into the ocean and swim to the boat." He spread his hands wide. "I'm very sorry that, *somehow*, I lost track of my phone!"

"I know, I know," Shelton said. "But you had the pictures. Now we don't have anything to show the cops."

"There's a freakin' human skeleton in the woods!" Hi exploded. "I think that'll work, don't you?"

After our escape, Ben had steered *Sewee* straight to the bunker.

We had a *lot* to discuss, and needed privacy.

I sat on the floor stroking Coop's back. The last saline bag was dry, so I removed the needle from his paw and took off the bell collar. He began gnawing the hated thing with relish.

Coop looked better, had even eaten some solid food. His energy level was up. I tried to stay detached but couldn't. Coop's improvement helped balance the horrors of the evening.

"Why tonight?" Ben asked. "Tomorrow's fine. I don't want to bother my Dad this late for no reason."

Hi pulled a face. "For no reason? Did you miss the human bone display?" He looked around, incredulous, expecting support. But on this point I agreed with Ben.

"Ben's right," I said. "If we confess tonight, our parents will make us go over everything a hundred times. Then we'll have to ride down to Folly Beach and convince the cops as well. I'm too exhausted to answer a barrage of questions right now. The morning will be okay."

"Does anyone even work a night shift at Folly PD?" Ben asked. "They're a small department."

No one knew. Folly Beach was a sleepy town.

"Those guys aren't exactly CSI," said Shelton. "Without proof, they might not believe us. Even with our parents."

I nodded. "They'll be more receptive in the morning."

"Fine," said Hi. "I guess Heaton's not going anywhere."

The instant the words were out, Hi cringed, regret clear on his face. I waved off the impending apology. Everyone was tired.

"We need to get our stories straight," I said. "We should tell the truth as much as possible, but steer clear of the lab break-in. Let's just say the first tag was legible when we found it."

The dog tags!

I rifled my pockets. Empty. Where could they be?

Oh no.

I remembered. I put them in my duffel. Which was still out in the woods.

"Shit! I left the dog tags with my tools."

"So what?" said Ben. "They'll use DNA to ID the bones."

I shook my head. "If the police see the first tag, they might notice that someone has cleaned it off. Karsten *definitely* would."

"Did we clean the sonicator before we split?" asked Shelton. "If not, that could lead to some bad connections."

"Tomorrow, we'll have to guide the police to the grave," said Ben. "When we get to the clearing, go straight for your bag. The adults will all be gaga over the dead body. You'll have a free moment."

"Good idea," Shelton said. "The cops don't need both tags anyway."

"One minor thing." Hi's finger tapped the bench. "Who the hell just tried to *kill us*!?!"

The subject I'd been avoiding.

"Take it easy," Ben cautioned.

"Take it easy?" Hi's voice hit an all-time high. "A death squad just tried to *off* me! I'm not 'taking it easy.' What the hell were they doing there?"

"Were we followed?" Shelton asked. "Seems impossible. We took our own boat."

"Maybe the encounter was random," Ben said. "Monkey poachers?"

I hadn't considered that. There must be a black market for stolen monkeys. Could the answer be that simple?

Shelton shook his head. "One guy yelled, 'Over there!' like *we* were the target."

"Not necessarily *us*," I said. "Maybe he meant the clearing itself. That field could be a monkey hotspot."

"*Or . . .*" Hi drew out the word. "They knew the body was there. And why *we* were there."

Scary. But was it possible? How could anyone have known about our plan? My brain was running in circles.

"Let's deal with this tomorrow," I said. "I'll tell Kit at breakfast, then come get the rest of you."

Three nods.

"Remember." Ben ticked off his fingers. "We found the dog tag, visited the library, and noticed the satellite photos. Got it?"

Everyone did.

But Hi wasn't finished. "For the record, you guys seem *way* too comfortable with the fact that someone just tried to murder us."

"Shut it, Hi!" I'd had enough for one night. "Tomorrow. First thing."

Hi frowned but went silent. Finally.

With nothing more to say, we headed down to the runabout. I hoped I'd be able to sleep.

The next morning promised to be wild.

CHAPTER 27

I ambushed Kit before his morning coffee. No choice. It was already seven o'clock. The others would be waiting.

Kit sat speechless, Frosted Flakes forgotten. When I'd finished he tried to process my words. After many long seconds, he found his tongue.

"Someone *shot at you*, last night? On Loggerhead Island?"

I nodded.

"You found a *dead body*?" Incredulous. "You dug it up?"

Nod number two.

Another pause. Then Kit rubbed his eyes. "Tory, if this is about me not spending enough time with you, I'm sorry. I know I haven't been the best—"

"I'm not making this up! We uncovered a skeleton. Then thugs stormed in shooting. Maybe to kill us, maybe to chase us away. I don't know. But it happened."

"Okay. Okay." Kit scratched his temple, thinking hard. "Did you see who they were?"

"No. They wore black and it was pitch-dark."

"And the body you found, you think it's this missing Keaton girl?"

"Heaton. Katherine Heaton. I *know* it's her." I didn't say how. First I needed to recover the incriminating dog tag.

A third interlude while Kit's mind fought to catch up.

"So we go to the police," Kit finally decided. "Right now. You get ready; I'll go talk to the other parents. Then we'll drive down to Folly Beach. You'll explain everything to me on the way."

The next hour was a blur.

Kit started with the Stolowitskis. Ruth didn't take the news well. After grilling Hi, she was convinced that masked executioners would soon be storming Morris Island.

Shelton had already told Mr. and Mrs. Devers. Lorelei agreed to accompany Kit and Ruth to the Folly Beach station.

Kit caught Ben's father on the dock, preparing his boat for the day. When informed, Tom Blue looked askance at Ben, but agreed to meet the group on Loggerhead after his morning ferry run.

Folly Beach stretches for six miles along a barrier island fifteen minutes from downtown Charleston. Far from high end, the area is a haven for young hipsters seeking good surf and cheap flats by the sea.

Since Morris Island's sole road runs through the tiny community, the FBPD is responsible for law enforcement out our way. Loggerhead Island is private property, so jurisdiction there is less clear. But Folly seemed the best place to file our report.

We found FBPD headquarters on the first floor of City Hall, a pink stucco building with blue-and-white shutters. The place looked more vacation rental office than government epicenter.

The department takes up very little space. In the offseason things are quiet, but come summer, tourists roll in and the phones start ringing. There are only a handful of full-time officers.

Eight in the morning. Wednesday. Late spring. We were the only citizens present.

If Tom Blue had been skeptical, Sergeant Carmine Corcoran was downright suspicious. And far from happy to see us.

Corcoran was a big man, probably in his mid-forties, with mutton-chop sideburns and a bristly black moustache. His large frame wore his bulk like a sack of wet hay.

Kit and Corcoran shook hands. The sergeant gestured to a metal chair facing his desk, then unfolded two more for Lorelei and Ruth. The three adults took their seats.

The boys and I lined up by the back wall. To an observer it would have been unclear whether we'd reported a crime or been accused of one.

As concisely as possible, Kit explained our adventure of the last few days and the bones we'd discovered.

Sergeant Corcoran glanced at his half-eaten Egg McMuffin, sighed, and shook his head.

"Mr. Howard," he drawled. "That's one *incredible* tale."

"*Doctor* Howard," I blurted. "And it's not a *tale*. It's the truth."

Kit hand-shushed me. "Sergeant, we didn't come to waste your time. These kids found something, and someone fired a weapon at them."

"So they claim." Corcoran settled his considerable derriere into his too-small chair. "*Doctor* Howard."

Okay. My input hadn't moved this along.

"Children are often mistaken." Corcoran said. "We get crazy calls like this all the time. They never pan out."

"All four tell the same story," Kit said. "Question them if you like."

Corcoran gave a half smirk. "Don't take this personally, but I've found academics and their kids to be particularly unreliable. Prone to exaggeration, shall we say."

"No, we shall not." Kit's tone was glacial.

Corcoran ignored him. "While this office is technically responsible for policing Morris Island, we don't have the funding or the personnel for goose chases on Loggerhead. That's Charleston University property. Campus security should deal with the situation."

Kit opened his mouth, closed it. Changed tack. "I'm reporting a possible murder. Are you refusing to investigate?

"Don't twist my meaning, Dr. Howard." For the first time I noted hesitation in Corcoran's manner. "Covering Morris strains departmental resources enough. It drains my time and manpower. Policing Loggerhead is out of the question."

"Strains your department!?" Ruth's voice cut the air like a cleaver. "Your people never set *foot* in our neighborhood! Our own community watch is the only protection we have!"

Shooting to her feet, Ruth grasped the edge of Corcoran's desk. The sergeant flinched, regretted it, squared his shoulders.

"My bubby says a man shot at him." Ruth's voice was shrill. "You will move your tuchus and *investigate*, or, so help me, I'll be down at the mayor's office faster than you can say Deputy Dawg."

We were cruising on a police boat ten minutes later.

CHAPTER 28

The rest of the morning was a disaster.

The ride from Folly took thirty minutes. Sergeant Corcoran stayed inside the pilot's cabin, avoiding Ruth. We Morris Islanders crowded together on the bow.

Slowly, Loggerhead materialized before us. And with it, a serious problem.

"Oh boy," Kit groaned.

Marcus Karsten was pacing the dock. Spotting the police boat he stopped, laced his fingers on his chest, and waited. A bird of prey, preparing to strike.

And Karsten had company. Linus Stolowitski, Nelson Devers, and Tom Blue. It was obvious the fathers had already informed the agitated professor. The trio stood in silence at a safe distance.

"What is this nonsense?" Karsten demanded, before we'd even tied down. "These *children*"—he spat the word—"claim there are dead bodies on *my* island? Ridiculous!"

Kit's face hardened. My heart went out to him. This wasn't going to be pleasant. But I knew he'd soon be vindicated.

"Dr. Karsten," Kit answered, soft but firm. "The kids insist they found a human skeleton in the woods. If so, a crime may be involved. They also report that someone chased them firing weapons. We had no choice but to inform the police."

Karsten's face grew so red I thought he might explode.

Again, I jumped in unbidden. Dumb, but that's what I do.

"Just let us show you the damn grave!"

"Tory!" Kit's eyes whipped to me, then back to his boss.

Karsten pointed both index fingers in my direction, preparing to rip me a new one. Then he paused, seemed to reconsider.

"Very well." His tone was ice. "Lead on, Miss Brennan. But you'd better be right. For your sake."

We headed back to the dig site. Third time's a charm.

My gang led, followed by Karsten and a heavily sweating Sergeant Corcoran. The gaggle of unhappy parents brought up the rear.

Soon Ben spotted the field.

That's when things bottomed out.

As per our plan, while the group congregated at the grave, I slipped to my duffel. Inside, my tools lay haphazardly, still covered with soil. A quick rummage failed to turn up the dog tags.

"Oh my God!" wailed Ruth Stolowitski. "There *are* bones down there!"

Linus offered an arm to his wife.

In grim silence, the others peered into the hole. We hadn't tarped the site, and gusts of wind had covered the remains with a thin layer of dirt.

"Human? No BS?" Corcoran's entire demeanor had changed.

Told you so, I thought. Then felt bad. What was the point of smug satisfaction?

I refocused. Where the flip were those tags? I was sure I'd put them in the bag, which sat exactly as I'd left it.

"All right." Karsten's nose and eyes were pinched, as though he were conducting an unpleasant experiment. "Dr. Howard, please enter the excavation and verify the find."

Kit hopped into the grave, careful to avoid stepping on the remains. As he landed I shot a quick headshake at the boys. Questioning looks flew back. I shrugged. *How should I know?* The tags were just gone.

Seconds passed before Kit passed verdict.

"Uh, kids, I think you've made a mistake." He looked . . . was that . . . *embarrassed*?

"A mistake?" *Impossible.* I bit back the last word.

"I'm sure it was too dark to see clearly." Kit avoided my eyes. "It's easy to get confused."

"Confused? What? The skeleton is right there!"

Kit sighed. "Honey, these are primate bones."

I rushed to the pit. The others followed.

If eyes really can bug, ours did it.

The human skeleton was gone. In its place lay a jumble of old monkey bones. Anyone could see the stuff wasn't human.

"What the hell?" squeaked Shelton.

"That's *not* what we found!" I cried. "We dug up a young female with a bullet hole in her skull. I've never seen these bones before!"

Hi and Ben nodded like bobbleheads, equally astonished.

"Dear lord!" Sergeant Corcoran shot me a wicked look. "Monkey bones on a monkey island. Imagine that." He wagged his head in disgust. "Kid scientists."

Karsten snorted. Like Corcoran, he seemed to be enjoying our disgrace.

Hi's mother was uncharacteristically speechless. Shelton's parents looked relieved. Tom Blue just shook his head. Our credibility had dropped through the floorboards.

Someone switched the bones!

"The gunmen!" I sputtered. "They snatched the skeleton and planted animal bones in its place!"

"Gunmen?" Corcoran scoffed. "You're sticking to that crazy terrorist fantasy?"

"Tory," Kit said, "it was pitch black, right? Maybe you got overexcited after reading about that missing girl, and—"

"Bullets!" I gestured at the trees. "The shooter hit a branch. The slugs will still be there."

I sprinted for the tree line. The boys followed. The adults didn't.

Frantically we scanned the canopy.

No damage. No bullets. In the background I could her Kit trying to placate Karsten and Corcoran.

"Tory, look! Eleven o'clock." Shelton pointed. "See, near the trunk? Someone sawed off a branch and covered the spot with sap."

Shelton was right. I wanted to scream with frustration.

"The shooters took the dog tags," Ben said quietly. "That's why you can't find them."

"Then they replaced the skeleton with monkey bones. Making us look like fools." Hi whistled. "I'm going to catch hell."

"Not another word until we figure this out," I ordered. "Got it?"

The boys agreed. Someone clever was working against us. We couldn't walk blindly into any more traps.

Dejected, we rejoined the adults.

"Find anything?" Kit asked.

I shook my head.

"I'm sure you were frightened," Lorelei empathized. "In the forest. In the dark. Any loud noise could sound like a gunshot."

Shelton nodded meekly. No point arguing.

"Hiram Moshe Stolowitski," Ruth rumbled. "You're in *big* trouble, young man!"

Hi rolled his eyes, reconciled to his fate.

"Go easy," said Kit. "It was an honest mistake."

"Honest mistake or not, this little escapade killed my morning." Corcoran turned to Karsten. "In the future, doc, keep your own house in order."

"I did not invite you here," Karsten seethed. "But I *am* inviting you to leave. Now."

Sensing he'd overplayed his hand, Corcoran lumbered off down the trail. The rest of us fell in step behind him.

"There is another matter," Karsten called to our retreating backs. "A break-in occurred at Lab Six last weekend."

We all turned, clearly apprehensive. Except for Ruth, each parent worked in some capacity for LIRI.

"I'll be conducting an investigation," Karsten continued, an inquisitor confronting wicked souls. "I expect everyone's *full* cooperation."

"Of course," Kit answered. The other adults nodded.

"For openers, I want to know why these children are here so much. What they do. Where they go."

I started to protest. Kit's hand clamped my shoulder. Firmly. I got the message.

"For now, I'll only add this." Karsten smiled without warmth. "If *I'd* done something foolish, like, say, *stolen something*, I might try to misdirect the authorities."

Karsten's eyes drilled into me.

He suspected. And he wanted me to know.

"And what better way to divert suspicion," Karsten said, "than to fabricate a tale of masked marauders with firearms rampaging across the island?"

With that, Karsten pushed past us and strode down the trail.

CHAPTER 29

On the return trip, my mind spun wheelies. I couldn't believe what had happened. The skeleton was gone. We'd been humiliated.

What had we stumbled upon? Who were we up against?

Hi had it the worst. Ruth grilled him nonstop, firing a barrage of pointed questions. He bobbed and weaved with his answers.

Lorelei Devers was convinced that, due to nerves, we'd imagined the whole thing. Rolling with his mother's theory, Shelton emphasized how "chaotic" and "alarming" the night had been. Lorelei ate it up.

I felt a sharp pang of sadness. Where was my mom, to comfort me? Why did I always have to take care of myself?

Tears welled behind my lids. The sudden grief spread, threatened to overwhelm. I gave my head a quick shake, tried to dislodge the thoughts. I didn't want to go there. Not with others around.

Ben sat next to me. Kit had remained on Loggerhead and Tom was driving the boat, so we were alone. For now. A bit of luck on a day having none.

After Karsten's revelation, Kit had seemed less receptive to my version of events. Not outright suspicious, but definitely wary. He'd said that we "needed to talk" when he got home. I wasn't looking forward to that conversation. At all.

"We looked like idiots," Ben muttered.

"Total morons," I agreed. "And now Karsten suspects we're responsible for the break-in. Talk about bad mojo."

"They must've come for the remains," Ben said. "To dig Heaton up. We were in the way."

"I think so, too. They confiscated the skeleton and the tags, then planted monkey bones to discredit us." I sighed. "The bastards erased all traces of Katherine from that grave."

But the timing mystified me.

"After what, forty years?" I asked. "Why now? Why remove Katherine *yesterday*, just twenty-four hours after we learned about her disappearance?"

Ben shook his head. No answers.

I considered the last few days. I don't believe in coincidence. Something bothered me.

Synapses fired in my brain. Images. Sounds.

A seed of suspicion sprouted. Sent out roots.

Maybe.

I kept the theory to myself. I needed proof.

It was mid-afternoon by the time we arrived back at Morris.

We'd missed an entire day of school. I stretched, tired. A nap beckoned.

But the gang needed to dissect today's fiasco. To tease meaning from the melodrama that had just played out.

How? Sneaking off to the bunker would be impossible.

"I'm texting Shelton and Hi. Download iFollow." I told Ben about the app Jason had shown me. "Load the program onto your laptop, too. iFollow has real-time videoconferencing. After dinner tonight, we can meet online."

"Will do."

As Ben worked his mobile, I fired my message into cyberspace. It only took a moment.

Hi glanced at his current phone, an older model he'd dug from a desk drawer that morning. His iPhone was still missing, no doubt lining the ocean floor below us. Ten seconds. Then, careful not to alert his mother, he flashed me a thumbs-up behind his back.

Shelton read my text from his pocket. Staring into space, he nodded, seemingly at nothing.

I leaned back, mentally poking and prodding my theory. I needed to be sure.

From now on, I wasn't going to play the fool.

◇   ◇   ◇

At dinner I danced around Kit's questions. Telling the truth was pointless. He'd never believe it.

"I made a mistake. Got scared."

"A mistake?" Kit's eyes narrowed. "About bones?"

Two-shoulder shrug.

Distracted by his own problems, Kit didn't press. His face looked drawn. Getting chewed out by your boss will do that, I guess.

"We'll discuss this again," Kit promised.

The meal ended in silence.

Safely locked behind my bedroom door, I booted my Mac. Two mouse clicks launched iFollow with a flourish of colors and dance beats.

When the GPS function opened, seven glowing circles dotted the Charleston map. One hovered over Mount Pleasant.

Hel-lo, Jason. How's the water?

I changed my online status to *away*. No time for sparring with Jason tonight. My island crew had urgent business.

I switched from *Bolton Lacrosse* to *Bunker*. We really needed a better group name.

The GPS screen now showed four dots stacked over Morris Island. Even online, our neighborhood looked sadly alone.

Ping. Ping. Ping.

One by one, the gang checked in.

"Go to video," I typed.

My screen split into quarters.

A face filled each square, Brady Bunch style. My own was on the upper right. Embarrassed, I smoothed corkscrew curls gone wild.

"Stop primping, Miss America," said Hi.

"Maybe you should start," joked Shelton.

Hi was top left, wearing Chuck Norris PJ's buttoned to his chin. His bedroom light was off. He was flying under Ruth's radar.

Ben's face hung below mine. He was in his bonus room beside a dilapidated pool table.

Shelton gazed from the final square, backdropped by his bedroom Star Wars posters. His hair was wet and he looked tired.

I cut to the chase. "Someone at the library spied on us."

Shelton's eyes widened. Hi and Ben nodded.

"Makes sense," said Ben.

Hi agreed. "We know about Heaton for *one* day, and someone snatches her bones? Can't be a fluke."

"How'd the spy know we planned to dig?" Shelton asked. "Or where? We never said that in the library."

Good questions. I had no answers.

"Maybe someone copied our research?" I offered. "They could've shadowed our work in the library."

"The killer," Hi said. "Get that straight. We're talking about the killer. Who else would know about the grave? Whoever followed us probably murdered Katherine Heaton."

That stopped the conversation.

Impressions flashed in my mind. Dark shapes in a very dark forest. Two loud bangs.

"The librarian?" Shelton offered. "He got weird, quick."

"Heaton disappeared in 1969," I said. "Limestone's too young. Besides, my gut says he's too much of a weenie."

But Limestone's behavior bothered me. Filing him away for later consideration, I shared my second theory.

"Karsten was furious today."

"He's always mad," Ben pointed out.

"True," I agreed. "But he was over-the-top out there. Like he was hiding something. And he seemed almost distraught that we brought a cop."

"Karsten has controlled Loggerhead for years." Hi was following my line of thought.

"He keeps everyone out of those woods." So was Shelton.

"The guy's running secret experiments." Ben was catching on.

"Three gold stars," I said. "Think about what he did to Coop. And Karsten has access to monkey bones."

"Who else could move heavy equipment in and out of the woods so fast?" Hi asked.

An uncomfortable silence followed. Shelton broke it.

"So you think *Karsten* is the killer?"

"He's a prime suspect," I said. "We need evidence."

"This is pointless." Hi ticked points off on his fingers. "We don't know who followed us. We have no evidence against Karsten. And we're in enough trouble as it is." His hands dropped to his desk. "Plus, I'm not looking to get myself shot."

We'd come down to it. The reason I'd called this meeting.

Hi was correct, every single word. But I didn't care. I felt a connection to Katherine Heaton that I couldn't ignore. She needed an advocate. Me.

"I'm not giving up," I said. "Katherine lost her mother, just like

I did. Then she lost her father. I won't abandon her."

She was tough like me. She'd never quit. I feel it in my soul.

"I'm in," Ben said. "Heaton was murdered. No one's fighting for her. We should do it."

Simple. To the point. Ben Blue in a nutshell.

"I hate being the non-heroic, practical guy, but we can't just quit." Shelton tugged his earlobe. "The killers may know who we are. We need to nail them before they nail us."

Hi's head dropped to his desktop. Pounded out three thuds. Then, without looking up. "Fine. Who wants to live forever?"

"We're a team, guys." I felt a rush of pride. "We're smarter than the creeps who did this. We can beat them."

"What next?" Hi was once again upright. "We've got no leads."

I smiled. "What do you gentlemen have planned for tonight?"

Three groans.

My grin widened.

CHAPTER 30

"Why do all your brilliant ideas involve felonies?"

Hi looked ridiculous in his long-sleeved black shirt, black pants, and ski mask. I could tell he was sweating up a storm.

The four of us were crouched in azalea bushes bordering the alley behind the Charleston Public Library. It was 12:42 a.m. If Kit learned I was out, he'd ground me for the summer.

Earlier, before logging off, I'd outlined my plan. Before the boys could object, Kit knocked on my door. I'd slapped my Mac shut, jumped into bed, and feigned sleep.

I heard Kit hesitate, then retire to his bedroom. Bearlike snores soon echoed down the hallway.

I felt bad deceiving my father. For his sake, I hoped we wouldn't get caught. And for mine.

Shelton's whisper came from right at my back. "The library

has to be wired for security, right?" Fifth time he'd said it. "It's a relatively new building."

"We won't know until you pick the lock," I repeated. "If something goes off, we bolt."

The night was hot and sticky. Of course. Clouds blocked the moon and fog cloaked the city. Perfect conditions for a break-in.

A police cruiser lazily circled the block, then turned east up Calhoun Street. We'd watched it pass three times.

"Move!" Ben hissed. "Now's our best chance."

We darted toward a secluded alleyway door. I'd hoped the alarm system wasn't more than we could handle, but both the key lock and deadbolt looked new and formidable.

"Guys." Hi pointed ten yards down at a ground-level window.

A *cracked-open* window.

We scuttled along the wall.

Inserting two hands, Shelton pried up the sash. We held our breath.

No bells, alarms, or whistles. Big break for the felon squad.

One at a time, we shimmied through the gap. Ben lowered the window behind us, then thumbed a flashlight to life.

We were in a square room lined with empty shelves. In the center stretched a single long table. On it laid a dozen books and a half-empty cup filled with sodden cigarette butts.

"Thank you, Mister Nicotine," I breathed. The sneaker of cancer sticks had forgotten to close the window. Spitefully, I hoped it was Limestone.

I refocused on our mission. Someone had looked at the files

we'd examined on Monday. How else could they have learned our intentions?

How to prove it? Maybe even ID the jerk?

Fingerprints.

The plan was a shot in the dark. But if we had an enemy, we needed to know. Especially if that enemy had a gun and was willing to use it.

We followed Ben's beam upstairs, all the while watching for security cameras. Spotting none, I grew more confident. What we needed would take only minutes.

Entering the South Carolina Room, we beelined to the microfilm reader. Rarely used in the Internet age, it was unlikely anyone had operated the antique since our visit two days earlier.

No one but our stalker, I hoped.

"Here goes nothing." I switched on the ultraviolet light I'd lifted from Kit's toolbox and moved it over the controls, searching for a miracle.

Not so much as a glimmer.

"What good's this going to do us?" Ben asked.

"Fingertips have microscopic ridges and valleys to provide extra grip." Hi's voice was muffled by his mask. "The pattern is unique on every person."

"I know that much," Ben said. "What I mean is, how do you pick the buggers up?"

"Fingers get sweaty and oily, so they leave prints on almost everything." I was rescanning the controls.

Still zilch.

"You can see some with the naked eye, but that's unusual. Invisible prints are referred to as 'latent.' That's really what I'm looking for."

The microfilm reader was made of dark, glossy metal that was ideal for capturing latents. I ran the little blue spot over its surface.

Zip.

Moving to step two, I removed a bottle of fine gray powder and a magnetic brush from my pocket. "If a print is present, the tiny particles in this powder will cling to the oil and sweat," I said. "That will make the ridges visible."

I gently dusted the controls. No prints. I tried the machine's outside surface. Nope. The screen. Zero. We'd struck out.

"Let's bounce," said Shelton. "We'll think of something less likely to land us in jail."

Sudden thought.

"Where are *our* prints? On this surface they should have lasted several weeks."

"Maybe the janitor cleaned the machine," said Hi.

"Or someone wiped it down," said Ben. "To remove their own prints."

Crap.

We'd broken into a government building for nothing. I was about to concede defeat, then had one last idea.

"Let's check the *Gazette* film before we leave. No one else would've pulled that reel."

Hi groaned, but hurried to retrieve it.

"Don't touch it yourself!" Loud whisper.

Using his cat burglar mask to cover his hands, Hi teased the correct volume from the shelf and set it on the table.

Touching only the edges, I crisscrossed the reel with the light. Nothing.

Disappointed, I scanned the opposite side.

Bold as high noon, an oval glowed white.

Repressing a squeal of delight, I dusted with the powder. The print emerged in spectacular detail.

"I'll be damned," Ben muttered under his breath.

"Let's bag her and scram." Shelton handed me a roll of scotch tape and an index card.

Moving cautiously, I pressed a section of tape over the powdered print. Then I pulled it back and stuck it on the card. A gray swirly pattern transferred to the paper.

Finally something went right.

For a nanosecond.

Thunk.

A car door slammed.

Hi raced to the window.

"Damn!"

Flashing blue-and-red light bathed his face.

"Outside!" he yelped. "Cops!"

CHAPTER 31

I hit the deck, crawled to the window, and peeked over the sill.

Two police cruisers were parked outside. Three officers stood in a group, flashlights probing the library grounds.

"How?" I couldn't muster more. It didn't seem real.

We were in major trouble. Those were real-deal cops, and this was a no-joke breaking and entering. Our parents couldn't bail us out of this one.

"Silent alarm?" Hi's head was buried in his hands. "Motion detectors? Psychics?"

"Oh man, we're the worst burglars ever!" Shelton lay on the floor, defeated by the roller-coaster ride of the last few days. "Forget it. I give up!"

Ben popped Shelton on the head, conveying his opinion of surrender. Then, hunched over, he scuttled to the door to check the main lobby.

"Two more cops out front. We can't go that way."

He moved to a fire exit at the back of the room. Found the door unlocked.

Like rats fleeing a cage, we scurried down the stairs. Back on the ground floor, we slipped into the room through which we'd entered the building.

From the direction of the front entrance, I heard keys rattle. Hinges creak. Voices.

I pulled the door closed.

"5-0 in the alley!" Shelton hissed. "Down!"

I dropped like a boulder.

A cruiser was slowly rolling up the alley, its radio sputtering static. It stopped outside our window. A powerful beam shot through the glass. Red and blue lights swirled on the walls.

I lay on the floor, motionless, barely breathing. Thanking every deity I knew that we'd closed the window coming in.

The spotlight sniffed the corners of our hidey-hole. My heart banged like a kettledrum. My cheek pressed deeper into the musty old carpet. My nose inhaled decades of library grime.

An eon passed. I was sure we'd been spotted. The room seemed far too small to hide four teenagers.

Finally, the cruiser edged forward down the alley.

No one budged.

A knob rattled. Close. Footsteps clicked and echoed in the hallway. Adrenaline did another loop of my body.

Cops. Inside. Hunting room-to-room.

The door had no lock. I waved frantically at the others.

They got the message.

The blue and red lights faded. The alley went dark as the cruiser turned the corner.

Ben sprang to his feet and threw up the window. I scrambled out, flew across the alley, and dove into the bushes on the far side.

Hi followed. Shelton. Ben emerged last. I watched him struggle to shut the window. The sash inched downward, jammed a hair short of closed.

My pulse went bonkers.

Move! Get out of there!

Ben gave up and ran for the bushes. He was halfway across the alley when another squad car rounded the corner, spotlight slicing the darkness.

Ben blasted through the azaleas and kept on running. Shelton, Hi, and I followed. No one looked back.

⬡　　⬡　　⬡

Heedless of the dark and the fog, we ran through the night. Even Hi, whose fear of arrest trumped his physical imperfection.

Two blocks from the library, we heard a siren wail, then saw a squad car zip by. The fog? Who knew. The cops failed to note the frazzled teens bombing through the streets.

We pumped on. A shame no one recorded our sprint times. Personal bests were undoubtedly set.

Ten minutes later we were aboard *Sewee*, gasping and puffing, sweat coating every inch of our bodies.

Ben started the engine, Shelton untied the lines, and we nosed into the misty harbor. The water was as still and flat as glass. Hushed. Unruffled. A welcome offset to the turbulence of the last hour.

I was enjoying the serenity when Shelton snorted, then cackled.

"We may suck at breaking *in* to places, but we're money at sneaking *out!*"

Shelton's laughter was contagious. Hi chuckled, then lost his breath and ended up coughing.

This only made things funnier. I started to giggle. Even Ben got caught up, hooting into the wind as he steered. Pent-up tension evaporated into the night.

I slid next to Hi.

"You okay?"

When Hi looked up, his eyes were pinched, and his jaw was skewed at an unnatural angle. He started to speak, but his lips froze. For a second his pupils glinted in the moonlight. Then his eyes rolled backward into his head.

"Hi!" I screamed.

Hi slumped forward, unconscious. I lunged to catch him before his head smacked the deck.

"Ben!" I yelled. "Something's wrong with Hi!"

Ben cut the motor and hurried to join me in the stern. Though Hi was out, he was breathing normally.

"Did he crack his head on something?" I struggled to remember how to treat a concussion.

"Hiram, wake up man!" Shelton slapped Hi's cheeks, then

rubbed his arms. Not exactly Web MD stuff. I gently eased Shelton back.

Hi's lids rose slowly, revealing eyes that looked very wrong. His soft brown irises were gone, replaced by golden orbs split by dark, black pupils.

Driven by instinct, I backpedaled, stumbled. Hit the floorboards.

What was that?!?!?

"Something happened to his eyes!" I said.

Ben and Shelton stared in my direction. Neither had been close enough to see. They moved to Hi, expecting the worst.

Hi blinked. Sat up. His irises were their normal chestnut brown.

"That felt weird." Hiram shook his head, trying to realign his thoughts. "Did I black out?"

"Yep," answered Shelton. "You okay? Your eyes working all right?"

Hi raised and lowered his lids. "Of course." Then his voice went high. "Wait, why? What's wrong? Is one hanging out or something? Tell me!"

Shelton and Ben glanced my way.

"Nothing, Hi, my fault," I said. "It must've been a trick of the light. Sorry! I didn't mean to scare you."

It was true. His eyes looked fine. Whatever I saw was gone. Or never existed.

"This is what happens when a jellybelly tries sprinting a mile," teased Shelton.

"I don't see you on the track team, pal."

"Let's get home." Ben moved to the wheel. "It's past two, and we've got school tomorrow."

"Everything's okay, right Tory?" Hi needed reassurance. I'd frightened him badly.

"You bet. We got a fingerprint and didn't get caught. Pretty damn okay, I'd say."

Hi leaned back and closed his eyes. "Weird," he said. "I've never fainted before. And now I feel great."

I tried to block it, but the image came unbidden. Golden irises split by black pupils. Bottomless. Primordial. Reminiscent of a different creature.

Suddenly I felt drained. My mind slurred, seemed to bend, then snapped back into shape. Energy coursed through me.

I struggled to move. Couldn't. Helpless, I slouched against the seatback. My lids sought each other.

Deep within my body, links shattered, fell together, were reborn.

My eyes flew open. Something was different. I could sense it in every fiber of my being. What? A change had occurred. I ran an internal check, trying to understand the alteration. Found nothing.

I felt light. Powerful. The weariness of the day washed away in a flood of visceral strength.

The boat skimmed the placid waters. An almost-full moon floated high overhead. I stared, rapt, entranced by the lunar beauty. Hearing a call I'd never heard before.

I glanced at Hi. He was gazing skyward, as I had, eyes glowing. I understood. He felt the same pull.

Unbidden, a name sprung to my lips.

"Whisper," I said, not knowing why.

"Whisper."

The name hung for a moment, then dissolved in the darkness of the soft summer night.

PART THREE:
INCUBATION

CHAPTER 32

The alarm blasted for ten minutes before I stirred.

Beep! Beep! Beep!

Kit pounded on my door, a reminder that missing school two days straight wasn't an option.

"Up!" I lied.

I lay motionless beneath the covers, still exhausted from the previous night's adventure, plotting schemes to stay in bed. My joints ached. My head weighed a thousand pounds. I hoped I wasn't getting sick.

Thunk. Thunk.

"Tory! Get moving!"

Ugh.

One foot on the carpet. Two. Sluggish, zombielike movements. My eyes refused to stay open. I plodded through my morning routine, then had to sprint to catch the shuttle.

The boys didn't look any better. Ben and Shelton moped,

churlish, in no mood for conversation. Hi snored, occasionally slumping on Ben's shoulder until shoved away.

At school, time moved in slow motion. Usually I enjoy my classes, but today I wanted a fast-forward button. I needed to talk to Jason about the fingerprint.

During biology class? No. My request was unusual, and borderline illegal. Not a topic for the group. Plus I had to do some prep work first.

Shelton and Hi met me in the library during lunch. Ben wasn't there when we used the microfilm reader, so he was excused.

"We need our prints as a control," I said.

Snagging an ink pad, I rolled my first finger, pressed it to an index card, and jotted my initials. Shelton and Hi did the same.

"Remind me why we're doing this?" Shelton asked.

"To be sure the mystery print didn't come from one of us," I said. "We don't want to chase ourselves."

"Do you have any idea how to analyze prints?" Hi asked.

"I read up. There are three types—looping, whorling, and arching." Using my hand magnifier, I studied the cards. "You're both loopers. Shelton, your ridges run from the left toward center of the fingertip, then back to the left."

"Mine don't." Hi was squinting over my shoulder at his card.

"Yours still loop, but the ridges go in the opposite direction."

"Long lost brothers?" Hi asked.

Shelton snorted.

"Nope, just commoners," I said. "Two-thirds of the population are loopers."

"I want whorls," Hi said. "They sound cooler."

"Whorlers have a full circle at the center of each print." I lifted my card. "That's me. Less than a third of the population has that type."

"So the last pattern must be pretty rare," Hi said.

"Yep. Less than 5 percent of the population has arches. The center of that print resembles a tiny heap of stacked hills."

"And last night's winner is—?" Shelton voice sounded a drum roll.

I placed the mystery print under the lens.

"An archer!" Hi crowed.

"Which excludes us," I said.

Hi arranged the four cards side by side. "And it's huge! Way too big for any of our fingers."

"A print this perfect has to be recent," I said. "Shelton, you're certain you replaced the reel yourself? You didn't leave it on a cart to be re-shelved?"

"Positive—110 percent sure."

"Then this print was left by our stalker."

I snapped a picture with my phone, then checked my watch. Twenty minutes to the end of the lunch period. Time to find Jason.

But Jason was AWOL.

I looked everywhere, the corridors, the lawn, the gym, the cafeteria. No dice. Though students aren't supposed to leave campus during school hours, the guards often looked the other way. For the connected kids, anyway.

Figuring Jason had slipped off to Poogan's Porch for some crab cakes, I decided to grab him after last period. We had trigonometry together.

The afternoon dragged like a death march. During trig, the sandman hit me with everything he had. Twice my face nearly smacked the desktop. I counted the seconds to the final bell.

Ring!

I shot from my seat as if spring-loaded.

"Jason!" I hurried to catch him in the hall. "Wait up!"

"Yes ma'am!" Big Jason smile. "Anything for a lady."

"Got a minute?"

"Practice starts in ten. Until then, I'm yours."

Bolton's lacrosse team was defending state champion, and deep in the playoffs again that season. Jason was the team's leading scorer.

Target acquired. Go.

But to my horror, I couldn't think how to phrase my request.

Jason waited, a bemused expression on his face. Words were fluttering inside my head when Ben appeared.

"Will he help?" Ignoring Jason.

"I just caught him," I replied.

"I assume we're talking about me?" Jason said. "You're Ben, right?"

"That's right." No smile, no return inquiry.

Jason's brows climbed in surprise.

What the flip? I tried to warm the chilly atmosphere.

"Do you two know each other?"

No response. Jason's eyes remained locked with Ben's. The atmosphere grew more and more uncomfortable.

But Charleston's highborn sons are bred to gentility. Jason's upbringing kicked in. "Pleasure to meet you," he said, not meaning a word.

Niceties completed, Jason retuned his attention to me. Ben no longer existed.

"I have a problem," I said quickly. "I was hoping your dad could help."

Following his graduation from the Citadel, to the Taylor family's dismay, Jason's father had turned his back on tradition and joined the Charleston PD. After years as a beat cop, he'd risen to detective, eventually being assigned to homicide. He now headed up the violent crimes unit.

"My dad?" Jason's voice registered surprised. "Did you shoot someone?"

"Nothing like that." I launched into my fake story. "My laptop was stolen. My fault, I'm a dope. I left it on the front steps while I ran around back to grab the mail. When I returned, gone-zo."

"Any suspects?"

"No, but the thief left a clue." I whipped out the microfilm fingerprint. "I pulled this from a soda can. It was lying where my Mac had been."

This was sounding *so* lame. I forged ahead.

"I was wondering if your dad could run it?"

"You lifted this yourself? Seriously?" Jason looked amused. "Who are you, Jack Bauer?"

I shrugged. "Family talent."

"Most people just learn to fish or something." He thought a second. "Did you file a police report?"

"Here's the thing." This part was tricky. "I was hoping to check the print *first*. The thief must be a neighbor."

"Awkward."

"Yeah. I'd prefer to get my computer back without having anyone arrested. We're pretty tight out on Morris."

"That's a tough one." Jason frowned. "My father could submit a request, but the form requires a case number. Even legit, it'd take weeks."

"For side jobs?" I asked.

Jason shook his head. "The lab guys only do favors in emergencies, and they expect something in return. I don't think I can help."

Ben rolled his eyes. Jason cut him a look I couldn't interpret.

Did I miss something with these two?

"Thanks anyway," I said. "I guess I'll just—"

"Wait!" Jason snapped his fingers. "I know who can help." Before I could react he bellowed down the hall. "Chance! Come here a sec!"

My blood pressure spiked.

"No, no," I sputtered. "Don't bother Chance. It's no big deal!"

"Relax," Jason said. "He's the man for the job."

Chance joined us, Hannah perched on his arm like an exotic bird.

"Harassing Tory again?" After shooting me a wink, Chance

turned to Ben. "I don't think we've met."

"That's Ben," Jason said. "He's the best. Bit of a talker, though."

Ben glowered.

I jumped in to defuse. "This is my good friend Ben Blue."

"Chance," Jason interrupted. "We need someone with pull. That would be you."

As Jason described the fictional robbery, Chance seemed, what? Bored?

"That's terrible." Chance picked nonexistent lint from his jacket sleeve. "I hope they catch the guy."

Jason nudged me. "Show him."

Reluctantly, I displayed the fingerprint card, hoping the scene wasn't as weird as it felt.

"I suppose I could have someone at the SLED take a look," Chance muttered. "I golf with the director's son. I think my father sponsored their club membership."

Chance referred to the South Carolina Law Enforcement Division, the state's version of the FBI.

"But is this really worth the fuss?" He could have appeared less enthused, but only on heavy medication.

"Chance!" Hannah admonished, sounding all magnolias and juleps. "If you can help Tory, you must. It wouldn't be a big deal, would it?"

"Of course not. A friend of Jason's is a friend of mine." Chance snapped off his patented wink. I was sure he practiced it every morning while knotting his tie. "But let's not tell my father about this, shall we?"

"My lips are sealed." I couldn't believe it. "Thank you so much!"

"No problem," Chance said. "And don't seal those pretty little lips. Hopefully we'll hear more from you, now that we're co-conspirators in a secret plot." He cast mock-suspicious glances over both shoulders.

I stared, completely thrown.

Hannah giggled.

"Ignore him." She gave Chance a girly knuckle-punch. "He's a *hopeless* flirt."

"Guilty as charged." Chance chuckled, then spoke to Jason "Headed to practice?"

Jason nodded, turned to me. "Later, Tor."

"Later."

"Ben." An insincere afterthought. Jason and Chance ambled out the front doors.

Ben fumed.

"Silver-spoon jock morons," he muttered when the trio was out of earshot.

I held my tongue. I'd learned not to argue when Ben was in one of his funks.

But Chance stayed on my mind.

His eyes. Had they lingered on me? And the winks. Were they just for show? How many winks before they start to mean something?

Enough. Daydreaming about the most popular guy in school? How pathetic.

"Come on, tough guy," I teased Ben. "Let's find that mythical stolen computer."

Ben's frown remained fixed. "Whatever."

Okay then.

The ride home was a blast.

CHAPTER 33

The next morning I woke up smiling.

Friday. Always good. And summer vacation was just two weeks off. Soon I would finally shed the freshman label.

But my grin had little to do with the calendar.

Last night I'd witnessed a marvel: Coop, scampering about, tail wagging. Happy. After ten minutes of bouncing off the walls, he'd cleaned his bowl and nudged me for more.

A strong appetite meant the dog was recovering. Coop's immune system had beaten the virus. Elated, I'd fed him seconds then thirds.

But not everything was rosy on the fitness front. Unlike Coop, I felt weak and listless. Worried about the flu, I popped a Zicam doused with echinacea. Preemptive strike.

That wasn't my only concern.

Karsten had summoned the four of us for an "interview" with

Loggerhead security. The potential blowback was too appalling to contemplate.

School that morning was business as usual. We had a lecture in bio, so I didn't meet with Jason or Hannah. Good thing. I hadn't run my DNA comparisons. Note to self: finish before meeting on Sunday.

At lunch the gang assembled by the dock as ordered. Mr. Blue hurried us aboard, then pushed off for Loggerhead. We gathered by the rail, too anxious to sit.

All morning I'd avoided thoughts of the upcoming interrogation. But now I started to get the jitters.

Hi had *very* strong feelings on the matter.

"Does everyone understand that we can't screw this up? Our stories have to match. Exactly. To the letter."

"I got it." Shelton rolled his eyes. "We found a dog tag. Went to the library. Learned about Heaton. Tory noticed some weird stuff about the ground, so we dug up what turned out to be monkey bones. Easy."

"Then we 'got scared' like idiots." Even Ben's air quotes were sarcastic. "And we 'imagined' gunshots and human skulls."

To avoid taking heat, we'd decided on a strategy of playing dumb. No one would believe what had really happened, so telling the truth was useless. *Au contraire.* Full disclosure would create *more* suspicion.

I nodded my agreement.

Hi smacked his forehead in frustration. "No, no, no!"

"What's wrong?" I asked. "That's all we can say."

"Details!" Hi barked. "To make a lie believable you need specifics. The more vague you are, the less credible you sound."

We all looked at him.

Hi sighed. So patient.

"First, we need an alibi for Saturday. On top of that, we have to convince Karsten we made an honest mistake at the gravesite."

"We'll be fine," Shelton said. "The man's not psychic."

"Really?" Hi locked his hands behind his back, pivoted, and loomed over Shelton. "You!" Thundered like a drill sergeant. "Where is the dog tag you found?"

"What?" Shelton yipped. "We . . . lost it."

"Where?"

"In the woods. After we ran."

"Where in the woods? Ran from what?"

"Oh, uh . . . Tory dropped the tag when we ran from . . . whatever."

"From *whatever*?" Hi hammered. "Did you see men with guns or not?"

"Um, no, I guess not."

"You guess?"

"It was dark." Shelton struggled. "I realize now that nobody was there."

"Then what *did* you hear?"

"Uh, er . . . pops. Like sticks breaking?" Shelton's responses were growing increasingly feeble.

"How many? From which direction?"

"Lots. Like, from everywhere."

Hi's eyebrows shot up. "You heard 'lots' of 'pops like sticks' coming from everywhere? *That's* your story?"

"Wait, no, not everywhere. From the . . . left?"

Hi honed in like a Patriot missile. "How many men chased you?"

"Three dudes." Shelton replied without thinking.

Hi pounced. "But I thought you *imagined* the shooters?"

"Oh, no, I mean, I thought I saw men, but actually . . ." Sweat dampened Shelton's hairline. "Okay! Enough!"

"You!" Hi pointed at Ben. "What'd you find in the pit?"

"Bones," Ben answered.

"How many? Which ones?"

Ben opened his mouth, closed it.

"The bullet hole," Hi said. "Which bone?"

"Skull."

Hi leaned into Ben's face. "But the monkey skull had no bullet hole!"

"Right . . . I thought the skull had a hole but I was wrong."

"You thought? You can't tell if there's a hole in something?"

Ben paused. "Yell in my face again, buddy boy, and I'll put a hole in *your* skull."

Ignoring him, Hi turned on me.

"Where were you at nine o'clock Saturday morning?"

"What?" I hadn't thought about Saturday. "I was at home. Sleeping."

"Your father can verify that? He was home too, right?"

Oops.

"No, I forgot, I was at the bunk—"

Can't say that either.

"With Ben in his boat," I finished lamely.

"Alone?"

Crap. What the others would say?

"Maybe."

"Maybe!?!" Hi threw his hands skyward.

"We're screwed," Shelton muttered.

"Okay, Hi," I said. "I'm convinced. Lay it out."

"Details are *key*." Hi gestured for us to gather close. "We lock in the critical ones. Then, if Karsten asks something outside the box, either you don't know, or you make up something the others don't have to corroborate."

He pointed at Shelton. "No one saw anybody in the woods. No lights, no voices, none of that."

"I hear you."

"Let's say we heard exactly two bangs," Hi said. "Like a whip cracking. Got it? 'Whip cracks.'"

"Got it," Shelton said. "Could have been a monkey in the trees. Maybe a branch breaking, who knows?"

"Right! But let *them* draw conclusions. We just act stupid. And the whip cracks came from 'the other side of clearing.' Nothing more specific than that. Okay?"

Everyone switched to memorization mode. Luckily, we were good at this kind of thing.

"And Tory lost the tag, so she can handle that however she wants. The rest of us say what?"

"I don't know." Shelton and Ben, together.

"Bingo." Hi checked his watch. "We've got about thirty minutes. You guys are lucky I did some research."

For the rest of the crossing we huddled, tweaking the alibi.

Please don't let me foul this up!

CHAPTER 34

"**M**r. Stolowitski." Karsten glanced at a clipboard. "You first."

Hi rose and entered the conference room. Inside, three chairs circled a folding table. Karsten sat next to Carl on one side. Hi took the chair opposite them.

Karsten wasted no time. "Where were you Saturday morning?"

Carl leaned on his forearms in an attempt to look menacing. The posture failed.

"Saturday morning? Let me think." Hi glanced at the ceiling. "Oh, right! I went to the canine festival with Shelton, Ben, and Tory. We took Ben's runabout down to the marina and walked to Marion Square."

Hi propped his chin on his fists.

"I remember because it was drizzling, and the dogs were

howling like mad. A massive Doberman slipped his leash and tripped Ben. He landed in a *huge* puddle. It was hilarious! Ben had to buy a new shirt from a stall that only sold animal prints. He was so mad—"

Karsten interrupted. "What time did you get to the park?"

"Hmmm. Must've been around eight thirty that morning. Tory wanted to buy dog pastries from a vendor selling designer animal treats. The guy had run out, but said his partner was bringing white chocolate bars at nine.

"I know what you're thinking. White chocolate. Bad for dogs. But the vendor said only the cocoa is dangerous, and white chocolate doesn't contain any."

Karsten opened his mouth, but Hi was a boulder rolling downhill.

"Anyway, we bought a bunch to give to the rescue dogs. We couldn't adopt one ourselves, but we figured we could at least—"

"Stop!"

Karsten's hand shot up to block the torrent pouring from Hi's mouth. Carl had long since given up taking notes.

"How long were you at this dog festival? And before you answer, know that I *will* double-check everything."

"No problem." Hi leaned back, fingers laced behind his head. "I think we left around noon, when the last of the greyhounds was adopted. This huge woman from North Carolina—"

"I don't care about that!" Karsten's nostrils flared. He paused, as though debating something internally. "Out of curiosity, how have you been feeling lately?"

Hi's face registered surprise. "What? Fine. Why?"

"No reason." Karsten's eyes returned to his clipboard. "When did you return home?"

Hi shook his head, resumed his excruciatingly detailed account.

"Maybe twelve thirty. Just after the large lady left with her pooch. We went to the dog show. A toy poodle won best in breed." He smiled. "You have to hear about this dog!"

○　　○　　○

"So you left the dog festival at eleven?" Karsten asked. Coy.

"No, sir."

Shelton tugged his earlobe, eyes on the tabletop. "It was at least noon. Like, twelve thirty. I remember because it was after the fat chick in the Tar Heel shirt took the greyhound, but before the dog competition."

Carl yawned, snapped his mouth shut at Karsten's disapproving glance.

"Who won?" Karsten feigned only minimal interest.

"Poodle," Shelton said. "Best in breed."

Karsten changed topics. "You saw three men in the woods on Sunday night, yes?"

"Honestly, I was so scared I'm not sure *what* I saw." Still Shelton did not look up. "I remember some monkeys running around."

"But you reported being chased by *armed men*." Karsten was

clearly annoyed. "You claimed they shot at you."

"I heard two loud sounds, *crack crack*, like a whip." Shelton shrugged. "I don't know what made the noise. I just started running."

"What nonsense is this?" Karsten snapped. "You saw *no one* that night?"

"I'm sorry sir." Shelton did meek exceptionally well. "I'm afraid of the dark. Ask my mom. I'm always jumping at shadows."

"Why would you run if no one chased you?" Karsten pressed.

"We found the bones at sunset. Tory said they were human, how scary is that? Then we heard noises coming from across the clearing." For the first time, Shelton made eye contact. "What can I say? I got spooked. I'm a wuss. I took off."

"No armed men? No gunshots?" Karsten raised frustrated palms. "You're now saying that *no one* chased you? It didn't happen?"

"Sorry," Shelton muttered. "I guess my mind was playing tricks. After all, no one found any bullets, right?"

◇   ◇   ◇

"Where did you dock your boat?" Karsten asked.

"Charleston City Marina," Ben said. "Slip 134."

"Do you have a receipt?"

"No. It's prepaid for the shuttle."

"The institute pays for that slip?"

Ben shrugged.

Karsten was silent for a long moment. Ben waited. Bored, Carl fidgeted with his badge.

"Have you been ill?" Karsten asked.

"No." Surprised.

"Nothing at all?"

"No." Now Ben sounded suspicious.

Karsten changed course. "You claimed you saw a human skull."

Ben said nothing.

Karsten slapped the table. "Well?"

"Was that a question?"

"Don't get cute, Mr. Blue. Did you find a skull or not?"

"It was dark."

Karsten glared. "Was there a bullet hole in the skull, as you said before?"

"I never said that. Tory did."

"Was there a bullet hole or not?"

"It was dark."

Karsten drew two long breaths through his nose. One nostril whistled.

Ben waited.

Carl asked his first question of the day. "When you arrived at the dog festival, what's the *first* thing that happened?"

Karsten looked annoyed, but listened.

Ben paused, eyes narrow.

"Well?" Carl demanded.

"A dog tripped me. I took a header and ruined my shirt. I had to buy a dorky new one from a vendor."

"What was *on* the shirt?"

Ben hesitated.

Karsten leaned forward, eager for a misstep.

Ben smiled.

"Some dog."

"That will be all," Karsten hissed.

◯   ◯   ◯

"Tory Brennan."

Karsten had saved me for last. To mess with my head, I was sure. Make me nervous. Advantage Karsten. But I was determined to hide it.

"Nice to see you. Sit down."

I parked on the hot seat. I felt prepared. We'd practiced like mad.

Do your worst, jerk.

"Before we begin, let me be clear." Karsten removed his glasses and wiped them on his tie. "I *know* your friends are lying."

Gulp.

The long knives were out. This wasn't just "information gathering." This was an interrogation, pure and simple.

"Their stories were . . ." Karsten chose his word carefully. "Perfect. Airtight." He replaced his spectacles. "Rehearsed."

"I don't understand." Innocent as Bo Peep. "We enjoyed the rescue festival, if that's what you mean."

Karsten stared lasers through his now smeared lenses.

"Carl, leave the room."

The command caught Carl by surprise. "My supervisor said I'm supposed to observe."

"Now!" Karsten pointed at the door. "Or you'll be mucking out monkey cages the rest of your career!"

Shaking his head, the guard shuffled out.

Oh boy.

I prepared for the onslaught. By sweating. Thanks glands, glad you could help out.

When the door closed, Karsten spoke softly.

"I'm not jumping through the same hoops with you, Miss Brennan. I'd be wasting my time."

"Dr. Karsten, I made a mistake." I tried to sound embarrassed. "I was confused. It was frightening, finding something dead in the dark. I panicked."

"I don't believe for one second you *confused* anything."

The gloves were off.

"Do you know how I'm acquainted with your Aunt Temperance?" Causal as water-cooler gossip.

I shook my head. This wasn't what I'd expected.

"We worked together in Sudan. Five years ago. Excavating Tombos, a colony of ancient Nubia." Karsten pressed both palms to the table. "Dr. Brennan is an expert with ancient skeletons. You idolize her. You read her books."

Karsten leaned close. I could smell the starch of his lab coat, see the enormous pores on his nose. "You'd *never* mistake monkey bones for human remains."

I cast about for a response. My mind was quicksand. I hadn't prepared for a direct attack.

"You've felt unwell lately." Karsten's voice was hard. "Haven't you?"

"Unwell?"

"Fever? Headache? Disorientation? Fatigue?"

"Not at all."

Karsten exploded.

"*Where is the dog!?*"

Adrenaline fired through me.

Coop! He knows!

"What?" My voice cracked.

"Where. Is. The. Dog?" Karsten slammed both fists on the table. "Enough games! I want him back. Now!"

"I don't know what you're talking about," I whispered.

The denial rang false, even to me. I considered bolting, decided it was pointless.

"Did you steal him by yourself?" Karsten hissed. "How did you gain entrance to that lab?"

I didn't answer. For a terrifying moment, I thought I might faint.

"Who told you to look for a body *there*?" A bony finger jabbed the table. "At that precise spot." Something malevolent danced in Karsten's eyes. "I know you're working with someone."

Silence.

Karsten sat back, squared his shoulders, and breathed deeply. When he spoke again, his voice was cool and modulated.

"If you think I'm a fool, Miss Brennan, you've picked the wrong man. I will catch you. And I will recover the animal."

I found the icy calm more unnerving than the fury. But anger kept my fear in check. Given the chance, I knew Karsten would execute Cooper.

Suddenly I pushed forward, craning over the table. The move caught the old bastard by surprise.

"Bring it on," I hissed, inches from Karsten's face.

Before he could react, the door burst open and Kit stormed in.

"Why is my daughter being interrogated alone?"

"We're done here." Karsten rose. "Feel free to take the children home."

With that, the old bastard strode past Kit and disappeared down the hall.

"You okay, kiddo?" I could see that Kit was livid. He glared down the hallway Karsten had just vacated. I suspected Kit was verging on a career-threatening move.

"I'm fine. We were chatting about the dig stuff. No biggie."

"Are you sure, Tor?"

"Absolutely. Karsten's not so bad!" The lie turned my stomach, but I didn't want Kit taking action he'd regret. "Let's go home. I've got tons of homework."

Kit hesitated a moment, then, "Fine. We'll talk about this later."

Gathering my things, I hurried outside on shaky legs. And managed to keep it together the entire ride home.

Barely.

CHAPTER 35

The director of LIRI was angry. And more than a little scared.

Dr. Marcus Karsten sat in his office, absently stroking the chimp skull he used as a paperweight. He'd acquired the artifact years earlier while researching Ebola in the jungles of Zaire. Its solid presence reminded him of past successes. Gave him confidence during times of turmoil.

Like now.

Karsten lifted the cranium and gazed into the empty orbits. My life has revolved around killer viruses, he mused. What's one more in the collection?

He stroked the polished bone, trying to calm his jangled nerves. Without success.

No way to sugarcoat things. The interviews had been a disaster. The kids had been prepared. He'd learned nothing.

Karsten returned the skull to his desk, still agitated. He, the adult and intellectual superior, had lost his cool. Worse, he'd failed to trip up the little delinquents. Their stories matched, down to minutiae.

A blasted dog festival? No way. They were lying.

And they'd uttered the name Katherine Heaton.

A chill traveled Karsten's spine. What had these bubble-gummers learned about Heaton?

Karsten's fingers drummed the desktop. In the large bay window at his back, afternoon sunlight faded to evening.

Their audacity astounded him. Did they request authorization to dig? Not a chance. They'd just gone ahead with their plan. On his island!

They knew I'd say no, so they simply ignored me. Impertinent punks.

But why dig *there*? That spot and no other? Someone directed them. Who? I must find out, before they cause more trouble. Real trouble.

Tory Brennan.

Karsten's fingers started drumming adagio. He returned them to the soothing cool of the skull.

The Brennan girl was the key. Insolent. Know-it-all. And, yes, brilliant. He had to admit. Her intellect was astounding for one so young.

And she is tough. The cheeky brat *taunted* me.

The memory enraged him. He pressed trembling palms to the chimp's parietals.

I lost control back there, tried to intimidate a teenage girl.

Foolish. And sending Carl from the room? Lunacy. Attempting to bully Brennan had been a colossal mistake.

Dr. Howard can make waves. From now on, I must be more careful.

The University will ask questions, learn of the hidden lab. Inevitable. I can't keep Carl quiet forever.

I have to proceed with caution. Keep away prying eyes.

And I must find that cursed dog.

Karsten watched a tangerine sun slip below the top of a green-black forest. Breathtaking. But he couldn't shake the anxiety, the feeling of impending doom.

He kept remembering the Brennan girl's eyes after his outburst. Something lurked there. Not fear. Not confusion. Not panic.

Something more dangerous. And very familiar.

Rage. Brennan had been furious.

What could trigger such anger in a teenage girl?

Fear for something she loves.

Karsten's palms squeezed the skull.

The dog.

Brennan knew the whereabouts of Subject A. She'd practically admitted it.

Karsten had no choice. He needed that animal back as quickly as possible. His benefactor was neither forgiving, nor afraid to use force.

In the game Karsten played, there were no second chances.

CHAPTER 36

"Carl said I talked too much. What a joker."

Hi sat on the floor, locked in an intense tug o' war with Coop. The puppy rolled and growled, giving it his all.

"Yuck it up, pal." Shelton spooned dog food into a bowl. "Karsten harassed me the whole time. I almost blew it."

Catching a whiff of Science Diet, Coop padded over to investigate.

"He suspects us," Ben said.

Parked in my usual turret groove, I debated sharing what had taken place during my interview. Ben was right. Karsten had accused me directly.

"Playing dumb worked," Shelton said. "My parents don't suspect a thing."

"We still have Dr. Dumbass to worry about." Hi, ever the poet.

We'd met up after dinner. The adults usually left us to our own devices on weekend evenings. While they thought we were on the beach, we'd gathered at the bunker.

Shelton smiled. "Your advice was good. Karsten asked about little things. Ben's pratfall, the fat lady, even the poodle. I could tell he was pissed."

Hi bowed without rising. "BS is my specialty. If you lived in *my* house, you'd be a pro, too."

"The old fart even asked where I parked the boat," Ben said. "Weirder, he asked if I'd been sick. Trying to throw me off, I guess."

The tinniest alarm sounded in my brain.

"What exactly did he say?" I asked.

"Just that. 'Have you been sick?' Now that I think about it, he asked me twice."

"Funny, I had the same question," Hi said. "Caught me off guard. But I lied and said no. I wasn't going to mention my blackout after running from Charleston's finest."

"Me too." Shelton mimicked Karsten. "Have you been unwell lately, Mr. Devers? Flu-ish? Anything at all?" His eyes rolled. "What's his angle, anyway?"

"Karsten must have a reason," I said. "He brought it up with me, too."

An accusation, not a question. I didn't say it.

"Why would he think we don't feel well?" Shelton cleaned a glob of dog chow from Coop's whisker.

"Or care?" Ben added.

"I don't know." Not totally true. "The break-in took place during a storm. Maybe he thinks the burglars caught cold."

The others looked at me like I was nuts.

"To be honest, I *haven't* been feeling great." Hi sounded a touch nervous. "And why *did* I faint on the boat?"

"Don't worry, I'm feeling run down too." I forced a chuckle. "We've had a big week."

I wasn't ready to mention my own little fit.

"All right." Shelton spoke with reluctance. "I wasn't going to say, but something strange happened to me yesterday."

We all waited.

"My legs just gave out. I was showering, then I was lying on the tile and couldn't move. I felt incredibly hot. Then, poof. I was normal again."

Oh boy. Shelton's attack sounded similar to mine.

"How have you felt since?" I asked.

"Fine. Not sick in the slightest."

"That's what happened to me!" Hi squawked. "I dropped like a rock, scorched up inside, then it all went away. But I've felt run down ever since."

"Ben?" I still wasn't ready to share.

"Nothing. Strong like bull."

Could be coincidence. Don't start a panic.

"It's probably just the flu," I said. "We *were* out in the rain all day."

Shelton and Hi nodded, but looked uneasy. That clinched it. I'd keep my own blackout secret for now.

Ditto for Karsten's accusations. No need to stir up pointless worry.

Change the subject.

"If Karsten had evidence against us, he'd have used it. So long as we keep quiet"—I glanced at the puppy—"and Coop out of sight, we'll be safe."

There. That sounded confident.

As though on cue, Coop scampered over and nudged Shelton for an ear scratch. When Shelton obliged, the puppy rolled tummy-up and wagged his tail. He was so adorable I could throw up.

"What's next for the wolfpup?" asked Ben.

"We start looking for a home." Though I hated giving Coop up, he was a smoking gun. If Karsten spotted him, we'd wind up in juvie.

"We need someone trustworthy," I said. "Outside the city. Somewhere Karsten will never stumble across him."

"What about Heaton?" Shelton asked. "I don't have plans for tomorrow, but I'd like a heads-up if we're going to rob a bank or something."

"Hilarious," I said. "You should write for *The Simpsons.*"

"I'll think about it," Shelton said. "Heaton?"

"The fingerprint is our only lead. If that bombs, I'm out of ideas."

"Relying on Chance Claybourne." Ben shook his head. "Great."

"He's not so bad," Shelton said. "For a trust fund baby."

"Goodbye." Hi stood. "I'm hitting the rack before I feel worse. I'm paranoid enough as it is."

I was on the same page.

The boys ruffled Coop's fur as they trooped outside. He whined, but curled on his cushion. In moments he was sleeping.

We'll need a door soon, I thought. Any day now Coop will be bounding through the dunes. A good problem.

"Sweet dreams, little guy."

I followed the others out into the night.

CHAPTER 37

Saturday arrived with heavy storm clouds. I waited for Kit to leave, then vaulted from bed.

And found a note taped to my door. Kit wanted to "chat" right after work.

Great. Fun times ahead.

Whatever. Today I'd enjoy some quality time with Coop. We'd have to ship him off soon. I planned to soak up as much puppy love as I could.

A light drizzle began as I pedaled to the bunker. Picking up the pace, I rounded the last dune, dropped my bike, and scampered toward the entrance.

From nowhere, a gray blur shot from the bushes and tangled my legs. I tripped and landed in a patch of myrtle. The shape streaked into a stand of sea oats and disappeared.

Heart hammering, I looked around. Through the silky stalks,

I could see a small gray snout pointed at me. Skinny legs. Floppy ears.

Seconds later, Coop pounced on my ankle, snarling and tugging.

"How did you get out?" I scratched his head. "You're *supposed* to be resting!"

Coop nuzzled my hand, ears flapping all wrong, eyes twinkling with spirit. Yipping a mock threat, he dropped his head onto his forepaws and raised his rump in the air.

"Did Uncle Hiram let you run free? Or did you go walkabout all on your own?"

I pushed Coop inside the bunker and followed. No sign of Hi, though he'd promised to help disinfect.

"Okay, little buddy. Looks like it's just you and me."

Coop rolled to his back. I rubbed his tummy, delighted all signs of illness appeared to be gone.

"Time to sterilize this joint."

Coop's body would shed virus for another week. Since he'd be contagious, we had to make sure the disease didn't spread.

Using a bleach solution, I doused the walls and wiped down the furniture. Then I bagged Coop's blankets for laundering.

Outside, I poured bleach on Coop's "potty patch." Not eco-friendly, but parvovirus can survive in soil for up to six months. I didn't want some dune-walking beagle picking up the disease.

Coop lay curled in the corner, ignoring my Clorox binge.

I'd just finished swabbing the floor when dizziness swept through me. I leaned against the wall and closed my eyes.

The vertigo worsened.

I began to cough. Slowly at first, then in rapid, choking hacks. The spasms sent pain firing through my skull. My eyeballs throbbed. Hot tears poured down my cheeks.

Must be the fumes. Get fresh air.

I lurched for the entrance.

Consciousness wobbled. The room tilted like a ship at sea. I felt a curious lightness, then something hard against my face. A small corner of my mind understood I'd fallen to the ground.

Seconds passed. Hours?

Reality drifted back into focus.

I became aware of a giant pink slug attached to my nose.

"Bleah!" I swatted weakly. "Enough!"

Coop withdrew his tongue. Retreated. Barked.

Food now. Can.

"Okay. One sec."

My head was still spinning and my mouth tasted like metal. Ignoring ladylike decorum, I hawked a loogie on the floor. The sour tang remained.

I struggled upright, my brain feeling like twisted spaghetti.

Gasp.

My breathing was all over the map.

The second attack struck.

A cerebral boom dropped me to my knees. I felt pressure. Pain. Cold sweat.

I went flat again.

Eventually, the fit passed and my wits returned.

"What the *frick*?"

I braced for a third wave.

Nothing.

I rubbed my temples, then probed my body for damage.

All my parts were where they belonged.

And I felt perfectly fine. Energized even. Stronger. Sharper. Like I'd chugged a double espresso.

Same as on the boat. What the hell?

Coop yapped, loud and insistent, then stood on his hind legs and pawed my side.

"I know." I scratched his ears. "You want the canned food."

Feeding Coop was easier than thinking, so I opened a can and spooned the contents into his bowl. I was about to place the food on the floor when a message clicked home from my crazy detector.

"Holy crap!"

I stared at Coop.

Coop stared at me.

No way.

"Did you talk to me?"

As soon as the words escaped, I felt ridiculous. Coop didn't know English, hadn't spoken out loud. A dog doesn't have the vocal cords needed for human speech.

But the puppy had done . . . *something.*

True, my memory was cottage cheese. But a gut feeling persisted: Coop and I had connected on some level.

Coop cocked his head, whined, then nose-nudged my hand.

My delay in serving was unappreciated.

I set the bowl aside, cupped Cooper's head between my palms. Spoke slowly.

"Did you place a lunch order? In my head?"

Whine. Slurp.

Stop acting loony. You passed out. It was a dream.

Shaking my head, I gave over the bowl. Coop pounced. Tail wagging, he inhaled his lunch in hungry gulps.

"Sorry, boy," I cooed, stroking his back. "Mommy's hallucinating."

○　　○　　○

Hi's no-show worried me. It wasn't like him. Could he be sick again, too?

Belly full of brown glop, Coop conked out. Minutes later I was bouncing up the Stolowitski's front steps.

Two knocks. No answer.

I waited, knowing Ruth's routine of checking the whole planet before opening the door.

A curtain flicked. Chains rattled. Locks clicked.

"Bubbala!" Ruth's hug pulled me through the door. "Would you like something to eat?"

For a moment I tensed in Ruth's embrace. Thoughts of Mom flashed through my head. When was the last time I'd been hugged? Kit and I certainly weren't there yet.

I ducked that train of thought. Now was not the time.

"No thanks," I said, quickly disengaging. "Is Hiram in?"

"Tsk." Ruth was a world-class tsker. "He's lounging in his room. Such a slugabed." Loud, directed up the staircase. "Get him to do something *productive* with his Saturday. For a change!"

"Will do."

Hi's door opened before I could knock. Motioning me inside with sharp, quick gestures, he closed it and flopped into his barcalounger, breathless and pale.

My stomach tensed at seeing his condition.

"You look terrible," I said.

"Trust me, I *feel* worse. My head's pounding like a Lady GaGa song."

"Me too." I told him about my breakdown, leaving out the canine telepathy. I needed answers, not stares.

"Did you faint again?" I asked.

"No." Hi dodged my eyes. "I've had . . . other problems."

I motioned for him to continue.

"Let's call it 'plumbing,' and leave it at that. Don't tell my mother. You know how she gets."

"No problem. But I'm worried we caught a bug."

"Have you checked with Shelton?"

I shook my head. "Next stop."

"We've probably got the plague," Hi moaned. "Should we bite the bullet and see a doctor?"

"Let's see how the others are first. Stay online."

"I'll be here." He pointed at his bathroom. "That toilet's the center of my universe."

Ugh. TMI.

I rang the bell at the Devers house, two doors down.

No response.

I rang again.

No one home.

I was texting Shelton when I noticed Ben on the dock, fixing *Sewee*'s lines. I walked down to him.

"Hey," I called. "You still feeling okay?"

"Yep. Why wouldn't I?"

I told Ben about my fainting spell and Hi's discomfort. He stepped back and covered his mouth with one hand.

"I'll keep my distance. I've got enough problems."

"Thanks. Your sympathy is underwhelming."

But Ben's lack of symptoms reassured me. If he was okay, what was affecting Hi and me could be routine.

"Just tweet if you start feeling bad," I said.

"Fine. Now scram, carrier monkey. I'm not shopping for swine flu."

"I hope you get what Hi's got," I shot back, then turned toward my house.

Nap time.

CHAPTER 38

My nap wasn't to be. Kit hadn't gone to Loggerhead after all. When I returned, he was lurking in the living room, armed with questions that couldn't wait.

"Tory. Sit." Patting the sofa cushion beside him.

Game face. I couldn't reveal my condition. Paranoid about his lack of parenting skills, Kit might overcompensate with medical attention. I wasn't getting shipped to a doctor today. Too tired.

Ignoring his gesture, I crossed to a wing chair and sat, cross-legged.

Kit allowed my small rebellion to slide. "The last few days have been crazy," he said. "Truth now. What's going on?"

The question irked me. Why the sudden interest in my life?

"I already explained. If you want the details, ask your pal Karsten."

Low blow, but I didn't care.

"I don't like what happened any more than you do." A flush spread Kit's face. From anger? Embarrassment? Who knew?

Awkward silence. Then, "I'm trying to help."

"Why?"

"I'm your father."

"Thanks, *Kit*"—emphasis on the name—"but you're a bit behind schedule. The interrogation was *yesterday*. Too late to play super-dad now."

Kit looked as though he'd been slapped. I felt awful. Why was I being such a bitch?

"Tory, I apologize." He sounded genuinely sorry. "I wasn't aware you'd be grilled like a suspect. I wouldn't have allowed it."

That seemed to require no response, so I gave none.

"I know I can't replace your mother. I'm doing the best I can."

Silence. This time, because I didn't trust myself to speak.

"I'll file a complaint on Monday," Kit said. "Dr. Karsten's actions were totally inappropriate."

"No!"

My stupid mouth might get Kit in trouble.

"It's no big deal. I promise." I moved to the couch, gave my best plastic smile. "I'm just being a brat. Please don't make waves at work."

"You looked petrified in that conference room. Karsten should *not* have questioned you alone."

"I overreacted." Nonchalant shrug. "Karsten's done with us anyway."

"It's up to you, Tory."

"Really. I'd rather just move on."

Kit's face relaxed, and his usual self-deprecating humor returned. "Just as well. I'd probably cause more problems than I'd solve."

I smiled for real. Kit was pretty likeable when just being himself. And, to be fair, *I* was the main reason he rarely could do that.

"But you *will* explain your whereabouts these last few days." Kit assumed a parental tone. "Spill. Start with this dog festival."

I tiptoed through the past week's events, sticking to the gang's agreed upon version. It was hard to believe that seven days earlier I'd never heard of Katherine Heaton.

Kit listened, asked a few questions, seemed to accept my story. He shook his head when I'd finished.

"Sounds like you've had a rough patch. And I missed it, always being at work. I'm sorry I let you down. I promise to be more available in the future."

"Hey, no sweat."

"As soon as I complete these salinity tests," he said, "we'll do something together. Deal?"

"Deal." Like what? "I'm just tired now. I'm going to catch a nap."

"Fine. Whitney's coming for dinner, so don't disappear."

Great. The last thing I needed.

"Maybe tonight isn't the best—"

He waved off my objection. "I've already invited her; I'm not canceling now." Kit's eyes grew almost plaintive. "She not *that* bad, right?"

"She's not trying to train *you* like a dancing bear."

"Ha!" Kit snorted. "Shows how much you know."

⬡   ⬡   ⬡

Except for the chink of utensils, dinner progressed in silence. I made no move to break it, knowing her ladyship would start in on me eventually.

I wondered how she'd go about it. Obliquely, by casually mentioning some new dresses she'd seen? Or directly, with a pass hurled straight at the numbers.

One thing was certain: Whitney would take aim. I was her new Barbie doll. She wanted to dress me up and star me in her games.

And I was definitely sick. Headache. Fever. Runny nose. Nausea.

Survive the meal. That's all.

Whitney had prepared our dinner at home. As I ate, I fantasized her drive to Morris from Tradd Street. I imagined slammed brakes, a slopping kettle, shrimp and grits splattering her immaculately detailed Mercedes and Laura Ashley sundress.

Uncharitable? Sure. But the image tickled me.

Normally I eat like a heavyweight in training. That night the thought of food turned my stomach.

The nap hadn't gone well. As soon as my head hit the pillow, the room started spinning. My gut roiled. Every few minutes, I'd crawled to the porcelain god in terrible anticipation. After the final purge, I'd gone fetal in bed until Kit summoned me to dinner.

So I rearranged the contents of my plate without eating, hoping that Whitney would spare me out of some cosmically transmitted pity.

No such luck.

"Tory! Good news!" Whitney's drawl was pure Southern belle.

My heart sank.

"The committee has agreed to consider your application for next season's cotillion. You're as good as in!"

They *already* agreed? She hadn't even asked my permission!

Whitney continued, oblivious to the dismay on my face.

"Even better, you can attend this year's functions as a junior debutante. Isn't that just the best?"

They will never find her body.

"That sounds wonderful," Kit said. "You can hang out with your classmates." His next words came in a rush. "I went ahead and signed you up."

Signed me up? What the hell was he thinking? I opened my mouth to protest, but my body had other plans.

Points of light exploded behind my eyelids. Invisible centipedes crawled over my skin. My muscles burned. Then froze. I felt my body topple, my head strike the hardwood.

Then Kit was at my side. "Tory, what's wrong? Talk to me!"

My mind was wrapped in fog. I fought to clear it. I had to escape before I crashed for good.

"I'm fine." Shaking Kit off, I got to my feet. "What a klutz. I slipped off the chair. Stupid, huh?"

Kit's eyes were round. Whitney's were rounder.

"Should I call a doctor? Or Lorelei?"

"No!" I shooed Kit away. "Too much sun, that's all. I'll just lie down."

Whitney threw an *I told you so* look at Kit. "The poor thing needs feminine activities. Too much running wild through the dunes with boys."

Kit raised a quieting hand. "Now's not the time—"

But Whitney on a mission is an unstoppable force. Her sights were trained on me.

Stepping around Kit, she grabbed my hand in hers. "Just attend Wednesday's dance, sugar. No strings. I know in my heart you'll adore it." Honey dripped from her voice. "It will do you oodles of good."

I hadn't the strength to fight her.

"Whatever. But now I need sleep."

"Okay, kiddo, go take it easy." Kit ruffled my hair, a rare display of fatherly affection. "I'll check on you later."

"I hope you feel better, darling." Whitney's smile was triumphant. "You're going to love the party. I promise!"

I climbed the stairs on trembling legs, anxious for escape.

CHAPTER 39

I tried to flee, but my feet were lead.

My pursuers thundered closer, faceless monsters determined to make me their lunch. My legs flailed uselessly, giving up ground.

Desperate, I dropped to hands and knees. My hips and spine realigned. Bones bent and shifted. My arms and legs thickened with muscle.

On all fours I took off like a shot, leaving the demons behind. I tore across the grass, wind whistling past my ears.

The ecstasy of pure speed ripped a sound from my throat.

I awoke with a start.

Had I howled in my sleep?

I stretched. Rubbed my eyes. Slowly, the images faded.

Even my dreams are insane.

The digits on my clock said 11:00 a.m.

Impossible. I checked my phone. Yep. I'd slept straight through the night and most of the morning.

I took stock of my body. Worse. Much worse. All systems under attack.

Head throbbing.

Stomach churning.

Lungs congested.

It was official: I'd caught something bad.

Throwing back the covers, I slipped out of bed.

SNAP.

Light exploded inside my head. My knees buckled.

Then. What? Nothing.

No aches. No flashes. No pain.

"Whoa."

A sudden, cloying smell nearly overwhelmed me. I looked around in confusion.

The odor was rolling in waves from my bathroom. Not a pure scent, but a cocktail of fat, lavender, mint, and rose.

Strange. I'd never noticed the noxious muddle before. I hadn't bought any new products or changed my routine. But the reek was overpowering. Shutting the door, I vowed to scrub my bathroom top to bottom.

Later.

Now, caffeine.

I shuffled downstairs.

As I passed through the living room, another smell assaulted my nostrils. A sickly funk floated from beneath the coffee table. I shuddered, covered my nose.

Had something died? The source of the odor had to be potent

for me to notice from across the room. Steeling myself, I slid the coffee table six inches left.

On the floor lay a brown piece of lettuce. I scooped it, sniffed. The smell of rot made my eyes water. My gut clenched.

Gross.

It didn't make sense. A single lettuce leaf creating such a stink? How was that possible?

SNUP.

Sparks exploded in my brain. I wobbled, caught myself.

"Jesus!"

My nose shut down. The aroma of decay disappeared like a snuffed candle flame.

What the what?

I raised the veggie to my nose. Nothing. On impulse, I hurried upstairs. The soap-cleanser-flower bouquet was gone as well.

Perplexed, I descended again and plopped on the couch. My head was ringing anew. Closing my eyes, I let my mind drift.

SNAP.

Blast of light.

Burst of pain.

Air exploded from my lungs.

I heard a tapping sound, quiet at first, then joined by a pulsating whine, like a lawnmower kicking to life.

I turned my head left, right, trying to pinpoint the source. The racket was coming from the kitchen.

My eyeballs tingled as I stared down the hallway. Suddenly, every detail crystallized into extraordinary clarity.

I sat rock still. It was as though I were seeing the kitchen through a telephoto lens. I could read the Cheerios ingredients from twenty feet out.

The tapping and whining grew more frenzied. Then new acoustics, a sucking, dripping sound.

Eyes wide, I laser-scanned the kitchen. Zeroed in. The noises were coming from the window.

Zip!

My vision zoomed to an even higher level of sharpness. I spotted a housefly patrolling the windowsill. Dark lines crisscrossed its cellophane wings. A thousand tiny red bumps formed its eyes.

The insect was exploring with small hairy feet. Its proboscis sucked and probed. Wings vibrating, it tried to solve the riddle of the glass.

I swear my jaw actually dropped.

I can hear a fly from across the house. I can see specks of dirt clinging to its feelers.

SNUP.

My vision flickered, shrank back to normal. After the clarity of the last few moments my usual 20/20 seemed fuzzy and imprecise.

I listened. No whining or tapping.

I sprang up and hurried to the kitchen window. The fly was there, but its movements were now barely audible. Its wings and eyes just looked like wings and red spots.

Numb, I raised the sash. The insect darted free, oblivious to my confusion.

Don't flip out. You're clearly sick.

Smell. Sight. Sound. All out of whack.

What could possibly cause such sensory delusions?

My operating system had crashed and I didn't know the reboot command. I decided to contact the gang. Pronto.

Coughing and perspiring, I ran upstairs and logged on to my Mac. Two icons glowed. Hi and Shelton, online.

My fingers flew over the keys: **Are you guys feeling weird? I'm slammed.**

Shelton replied first: **Sick as a dog. Pukesville.** ☹

Hi's icon popped up: **Dying. Give my things to the poor.**

OhmyGod. It wasn't just me.

I typed: **Switch to iFollow. Conference mode.**

I changed programs and waited. Minutes passed. Clicking back, I found two unread messages.

Shelton: Too tired. Going back to bed. Maybe later.

Hi: Stuck in the can. You don't want to know. Bye.

Crap balls.

I closed my computer. Perhaps a shower? That seemed normal. Safe.

I didn't make it.

Full body pins and needles. Grimace. Primal whine. Then, as before, all symptoms vanished.

I sat on my bedroom floor. Hugged my knees. Dripped sweat.

What the flip?

A tiny suspicion popped into being. Unfolded in my mind with ruthless logic, indifferent to the unease it created.

You know, it whispered. *You unleashed it.*

The break-in at Karsten's lab. The parvo experiment.

Cooper.

No. Canine parvovirus can't infect humans. The dog posed no danger to us.

Coop was the subject of a secret experiment, the suspicion hissed. *Who knows what he was carrying?*

Was that it? Had the virus changed? Mutated? Was Coop's infection more sinister than I suspected?

"Stop," I ordered myself aloud. "Quit being paranoid. The timing is coincidental."

But I don't believe in coincidence.

Why did we all get sick at once? Was Coop the only common factor? What were these insane reactions?

But Ben *didn't* get sick. He carried Coop from the lab, had as much exposure as anyone.

Cut the dramatics. You've got better things to do.

From nowhere, a different thought rocked me.

Study group! I was supposed to meet Jason and Hannah at noon.

Time check. Eleven forty-five. No chance I could make it. Worse, I hadn't done the work. The assignment had completely slipped my mind.

Not that it mattered. I was in no shape to see anyone. I had to cancel.

I composed a text, hitting hard on contrite:

Jason, So sorry, but I've been beaten down by the flu.

In a rout. Can't meet today. Please apologize to Hannah for me, and I'll get my work to you on Monday. My bad for canceling late! Tory.

Send. Minutes passed. My eyes remained glued to my phone. Finally, a return message beeped in: **Okay, get better. Later, J.**

After crunching every possible nuance of the message, my brain punched out.

I closed my eyes and slept.

○   ○   ○

Two forty-five.

Great. Thirty minutes of wakefulness so far that day. Not my most productive Sunday.

I staggered downstairs, realized I was ravenous. No breakfast. No lunch. No surprise.

I pawed through the fridge, but had no appetite for my usual yogurt, veggies, or fruit. As though moving on their own, my hands grabbed a package of ground beef.

SNAP.

My nerves fired like jumper cables. A gong clanged in my head.

Without thinking, I ripped off the wrapper and sank my fingers into the beef. My salivary glands went wild. I scooped a red, meaty handful and stuffed my mouth.

For a moment, pure ecstasy. Then my taste buds clocked in.

"Ech!"

I spat the half-chewed glob into the sink.

Raw meat? Disgusting!

But, for one brief flash, I'd wanted to devour the whole half pound. Fiercely. More than anything else in the world.

Okay. You've lost it. It's a fact.

Like some shadowy creature, my dark idea taunted me from the depths of my mind. I drew a breath, tried to regain control.

Easy. Easy.

When I finally looked up, a twisted version of my face reflected back from the faucet. The gleaming chrome warped my features like a funhouse mirror.

Only no fun here. My eyes glowed a deep, primal gold.

"No!"

I slid to the floor, squeezed my lids tight. Tears trickled down my cheeks.

Don't be real, my lips mouthed silently.

SNUP.

One body-shaking tremor, then the shockwave passed.

I opened my eyes. Then I bolted to the bathroom mirror.

Green irises stared back. Normal. I allowed the breath to ease from my lungs.

But my relief was short-lived.

Something was wrong. Something serious, perhaps deadly.

My mind circled back to the odd connection I'd felt with Coop. That instant of kinship and understanding. Of communion.

"What's happening to me?" I whispered.

My question was answered by silence.

CHAPTER 40

Monday morning dawned really, really early. I stumbled into first period half-dead.

Jason and Hannah were already waiting by our workstation, laptops booted. I dreaded delivering the bad news.

"Guys, I'm so sorry, but I don't have my data." I slumped into my chair. "I know I promised it today, but I've been sick all weekend."

Hannah frowned but said nothing.

Jason shook his fists in mock indignation.

"Outrageous! We count on you to make us look smart."

"I'll get it done ASAP, I promise." I blew stray hairs from my forehead. "If you'd endured the weekend I had, you'd understand."

"Don't worry," Jason said. "The presentation isn't until Friday. We'll put your part last, and you can present the findings however you want."

"Just get better." Hannah's concern sounded genuine. "That's most important."

I smiled my thanks. Academic slacking isn't my style. Guilt is. My conscience had been eating at me since I woke up.

"What's on tap today?" I asked.

"We're observing the effects of olfactory cues on gerbil activity," Jason said. "We've been assigned two scents."

Hannah read the instructions. "One: Place an aroma canister inside the cage. Two: Wait five minutes. Three: Time the gerbil's use of its exercise wheel. Sounds easy."

"Bring on the rodent," Jason said.

I loaded the first scent: wild lavender. A soothing spa-like fragrance floated into the air.

Our test subject, whom we nicknamed Herbie, sniffed the canister, then promptly curled up and checked out.

"Lavender works like Ambien on the Herb-man," Jason said.

We checked our watches. Again and again.

"Time's up," Jason said. "New aroma, please."

Hannah made the swap. The new scent was grapefruit.

"Citrus oils are supposed to promote energy," I said.

"He hasn't expended much so far," Jason said. "Come on, Herbie, kick it up for the g-fruit."

Herbie and I were on the same page. I hadn't slept well in days. My eyelids drooped, almost met.

Mistake. The room began spinning in a now familiar manner.

No! Not here!

SNAP.

Pain split my frontal lobe. Heat radiated from my chest to my limbs. My vision blurred.

I rubbed my temples, desperate to keep it together. Sweat dotted my forehead.

"Tory? You okay?" Hannah's brow was furrowed.

Lame laugh. Talking was difficult. "Just post-flu fatigue."

I rose, trying to stop the room from whirling. But my brain felt loose, as though slipped from its tether and floating free.

The scent of grapefruit became overpowering, bombarding my nose and tickling my throat.

Nausea threatened. No time for excuses. I had to haul ass.

As I began a fast break to the bathroom, movement flashed in the corner of my eye. Herbie was working out on his wheel.

My symptoms dissolved.

Suddenly, I saw nothing but gerbil.

I crouched beside the cage, eyes fixed on the little brown body chugging like mad. I could smell fur and wood chips and a secretion like musk.

A flood of saliva bathed my gums and tongue.

"Tor?" Jason placed a hand on my shoulder. "What's wrong? You need to see the nurse?"

All my senses stayed focused on the rodent.

Who suddenly noticed me.

Something deep in Herbie's brain screamed out a warning. Abandoning the wheel, he scampered to his nest.

My hand shot out, knocking the cage off kilter. Jason grabbed it before it crashed to the floor.

"Whoa! Tory, what are you doing?"

SNUP.

A cerebral door slammed shut.

The smells receded.

I shook my head, hoping to clear my thoughts.

Reality reasserted itself.

The class was staring, some openly, some pretending not to. Then the sniping began.

"Boat girl. Panic attack." Madison's whisper drew giggles from her entourage.

"She's afraid of mice," Ashley said. "They must have *armies* of mice on her dirty island."

It's a gerbil, you moron.

"She's just a spazz," said Courtney. "Little girls are like that."

The Tripod laughed at their own wit.

My cheeks burned with humiliation.

The heat spread from my face to my brain, triggering a second bout of nausea. I covered my mouth. Too dizzy to run, I braced, waiting for my stomach to redecorate the floor.

Hannah came to my rescue. Clasping my hand, she wrapped a protective arm around my shoulders.

"Let's splash some water on your face."

I closed my eyes and let Hannah guide me. With each step I concentrated on not puking.

"Mrs. Davis?" Hannah called. "Tory is feeling faint. I'm going to help her to the ladies room."

Without pausing, Hannah whisked me from the bio lab, up

the corridor, and into a bathroom stall. She maintained a polite distance as I heaved and spat. At one point, she slipped a box of tissues under the door.

Eyes teary, nose running, I finally emerged.

Hannah waited by the sink, small bottle of mouthwash in hand.

"Better?" she asked.

"Much. I can't thank you enough. I'd never have made it without you."

"There's nothing to thank." Hannah patted my wrist. "You're not well. Those girls are critical enough as it is. No need to give them a show."

As I executed a quick swish and spit, Hannah plucked and offered more tissue.

"They don't like me much, do they?" Blotting my chin.

"Don't mind them. Jealousy brings out the worst in people."

"Jealousy?" Hannah's choice of noun shocked me.

"They don't appreciate the attention Jason pays you." She giggled. "They'd prefer you weren't his favorite."

Ugh. Jason was a tangle I'd yet to sort out. He was intrigued by me, but I was into Chance. Awkward. Double awkward. I doubted Hannah would be so nice if she knew I was infatuated with her boyfriend.

Hannah sensed my discomfort, though not its source. Thankfully.

"Ignore them," she said. "Those three are narrow and petty and rarely meet anyone outside their own privileged circle. They're *dreadfully* immature."

"But not you. You've been great. And believe me, I appreciate it." I hesitated. What the hell? "This year has been tough."

"I hope I'm not like them!" Hannah laughed, flashing perfect teeth. "But it's easier for me. I have Chance."

"He seems very nice." Neutral as Switzerland.

"We're in love. Someday we'll marry." Again, the flawless pearly whites. "Chance and I are meant to be."

"I'm happy for you both." Most of me meant it. Ninety percent. Seventy-five.

The bell rang.

I made a few more dabs at my hands and face.

"How do I look?"

"Beautiful." Hannah took my arm. "Let's leave together. The terrible trio won't start in again."

We walked out side by side.

And smack into Jason and Chance.

"Tory, you all right?" Jason pushed off from the wall.

The day had already been too much. I couldn't control my body, had no idea when it might betray me next. The last thing I needed right then was Jason Taylor.

Disengaging from Hannah with an arm-squeeze of thanks, I lowered my head and set off down the hall.

"I'm good! Thanks!"

I didn't look up until I hit the nurse's office.

CHAPTER 41

Nurse Riley viewed my tongue. Checked my pupils. Stuck a thermometer into my mouth.

Though she poked and prodded her best, none of my symptoms reappeared. My vitals came up perfectly normal. Baffled, she gave me two Tylenol and released me back to class.

Her failure wasn't surprising, since I didn't tell her the truth. I couldn't share what had really happened. How I'd lost control.

Second period was in full swing. AP British Literature. Handing over my pass, I took my seat between Hi and Shelton. Both looked relieved to see me.

Mr. Edde, a tall and gangly Hispanic man with an eight-inch Afro, was discussing the merits of iambic pentameter. I tried to concentrate on the lesson.

"Tory." Whispered. "Tor!"

I slid my eyes right. Hi's new phone lay nestled between the pages of his book. Without looking down, he typed a message.

Oh so casual, I slipped my cell from my purse. Powered it on.

Hi's text held a link.

Click. A chat room flashed onto my screen.

I glanced up. Mr. Edde was death on cell phones. He'd already confiscated a dozen that semester.

The gods were smiling. After instructing the class to read a chapter on seventeenth century poetry, Mr. Edde rounded his desk. A moment of scrutiny, then he sat, tipped his chair back, and focused on a crossword puzzle.

The room quieted. Feigning absorption in John Milton, I turned my attention to cyberspace.

Two avatars lurked. The image of Napoleon Dynamite was Hi. Shelton was represented by the Abominable Snowman eating a giant robot. Don't ask.

My own avatar—a gray wolf done in black and white—was the only other character present.

Hi had already posted.

Napoleon: Where did you go? You freaked me out!!!

Moving ever so discreetly, I replied.

Wolf: Nurse. Kept quiet, but something's wrong with me. Bad!

Napoleon: Me too! Not just flu. Weird things.

Snowman: I'm worse. Going crazy!

I glanced to the left. Shelton's foot was tapping like he was playing Rock Band on expert.

To the right. Hi's jacket was off, his top button undone. He was wheezing like an ancient and scratching his arms.

Hope packed up and headed out the door. My illness wasn't isolated. We'd caught something together. Something nasty.

I typed fast, watching Mr. Edde with one eye.

Wolf: Need to meet. Today. Bunker. Not a word until then.

Fingers danced on both sides of me. Willing Mr. Edde to stay engrossed in his puzzle, I dropped my eyes.

Snowman: Too sick. Getting scared. May tell Mom.

Napoleon: No bathroom in the bunker. Problem.

I felt a prickle of irritation. Didn't they realize the source of the illness? We *couldn't* tell our parents. Not with Karsten watching.

My fingers flew across the screen.

Wolf: Must talk first, sick or not! In private. Bunker. After school. Super important.

Wolf: Say NOTHING! Not even to each other!

Mr. Edde lowered the front legs of his chair, a sure sign he was retiring the crossword. Conversation over.

I dropped my cell into my purse. Hi slipped his into his front pocket. I raised an eyebrow. *Well?*

Hi ran both hands through his hair, pretended to pull it out. Then nodded.

Shelton squirmed, frowned, dipped his chin curtly.

All aboard.

Now to get through the day. One class at a time.

◇   ◇   ◇

A light breeze meandered the marina, carrying with it the scent of salt water, hydrangeas, and diesel fuel. On the harbor, sails flashed white in the afternoon sun.

The heat and humidity both hovered around ninety. Not a day for the great outdoors.

Upon boarding the shuttle, Hi and Shelton had headed straight for the semi-air-conditioned cabin. We hadn't talked since second period, wouldn't until we reached the privacy of the bunker.

Neither seemed happy, but they hadn't rebelled. Yet. I'd get an earful later, no question about that.

I chewed a thumbnail, repeatedly scanned the dock. Where was Ben? I hadn't seen him since biology. He'd missed both of the afternoon classes we shared.

Ben's continuing good health was my ace in the hole. If he succumbed, hello panic.

As if on cue, Ben came loping down the dock. Mr. Blue shoved off the second his son's shoes hit the deck.

"Welcome aboard, sir. Shall I show you to your cabin?"

Ignoring my joke, Ben dropped onto the stern bench, stretched his legs, and leaned back.

I waited. There was no rushing Ben.

Finally, he spoke. "I feel like three-day-old spit."

Crap.

"What's wrong?"

"Everything. My head hurts, my lungs, my feet, even my *teeth*. It makes no sense."

It made terrifying sense.

"And that's not the worst of it."

As he talked, Ben watched our wake vee back toward the city. Above it, gulls swooped and bobbed, anxious for scraps.

"My body's out of whack. I keep going in and out of some kind of trance.

"Yesterday, in my garage, my heart went apeshit, and I felt flames race through my veins. I started to fall, so I grabbed some metal shelving nailed to the wall."

Ben avoided my eyes. "My dad has an old Z28 engine he's using to restore a Camaro. Anyway, the shelving came loose and the engine started to fall on me."

Ben's eyes finally met mine. "That thing weighs a ton. I could've been killed."

"What happened?"

"I caught it." Disbelief. "The heat flashed, I reached up, and I caught the frickin' engine. I even placed it back on the shelf." Ben sounded as though he'd replayed the scene again and again in his mind.

"That's impossible, right?"

"No," I said gently. "I have a *lot* to tell you."

CHAPTER 42

Coop nipped my fingers, wanting to play. Not a good time. I'd just spilled my guts. About everything.

Well, almost.

"So that's what happened. At least, that's what I remember."

"You could see patterns on the fly's wings?" Shelton asked. "From across the house?"

"And a billion little lenses making up its eye."

"That beats my attack." Shelton's sport coat rested on his lap. I'd been afraid of losing the boys if they went inside to change. "My vision blurred, so I took my glasses *off*. Whammo: 20/20. For a few seconds, anyway."

"I felt normal until yesterday," Ben said. "Then it hit me like a freight train. No sonic hearing or super-smells, just weird cravings. Impulses. And my mind scrambles."

"Anything else?" I asked.

"At times, my limbs feel like they're on fire. When the burning fades, I'm strong, like I could blast through walls." He shook his head. "Then I throw up, pass out, it all goes bad."

"I'll take that over my symptoms," Hi said. "I can't leave the throne for more than a few minutes. And I must've fainted at least twenty times." He pointed at me. "You talk about smells? I got slammed while eating cream cheese. I'll never touch the stuff again."

Without question, Hi had been the sickest. He'd suffered every misery imaginable.

"It's like I was food-poisoned while suffering from malaria and poison ivy," Hi grumbled. "And brain fever. And get this. From my roof deck, I watched a mouse creep through the grass on the common. I could see his earwax from fifty yards out. Worst part was, I wanted to *eat* the little bugger." Hi rubbed his forehead. "Just for a second, though! I swear!"

"I understand. Raw hamburger, remember?" I shuddered. "And you saw me try to snatch Herbie."

Hi nodded.

Though I kept a brave face, inside I shivered. Hi's story reminded me of the one thing I *hadn't* disclosed.

I wasn't ready to talk about golden eyes.

"Sometimes I hear the smallest noises." Shelton tugged one earlobe. "Yesterday morning, the freaking power lines woke me up. I could *hear* the electricity. And the fits burst on and off without warning. Just a pop in my head, then bang!" Pause. "I'm getting tired of blacking out."

Silence crammed the bunker.

I pushed to my feet. Resolved to put it out there.

"We've caught a disease."

Hi and Shelton slumped. Ben tensed, fingers curled into fists.

"There's no point kidding ourselves," I went on. "Each of us had different experiences, but our symptoms are too similar to ignore."

I ticked off points by raising fingers. "Fatigue. Headache. Nausea. Fever. Congestion. Hot flashes. Cold sweats. Spiking pains."

"Blackouts," said Hi. "It all comes back to the blackouts."

Ben and Shelton nodded.

"Blackouts," I agreed, only one finger still curled to my palm. "And what they trigger. Our senses go into overdrive. It's like our minds snap briefly, then get . . . confused."

Can't say crazy. Or primal. Not yet.

"I've never heard of anything like this," said Ben.

"And whatever it is, we can't control it," said Hi.

I hesitated. Once spoken, the next words could not be withdrawn.

"I think we caught something from Coop."

Silence. Then, three voices at once.

"How is that possible?" Ben.

"You said we *couldn't* catch parvo!" Shelton.

"We're screwed!" Hi.

"I don't know what happened. But Coop must be the vector; he's our only common link." I turned to Shelton. "Canine parvovirus *can't* infect humans. I double-checked. It has to be something else."

"What?'

"I don't know. But we won't panic." I tried to sound confident. "It may not be serious."

"Do you even have a guess?" Shelton asked.

"No," I admitted. "I won't lie. I've never heard of anything resembling our condition. Whatever we've caught must be extremely rare."

"Great," Hi said. "A magical *mystery* virus. Lucky us! The very first Virals."

"Karsten's experiment." Ben frowned. "The secret tests. We don't know what he was doing."

I nodded. "But we're going to find out."

The boys stared.

I soldiered on. "We should lay low for a few more days, get stronger. And keep our condition secret. I don't think we're contagious."

"Why not?" Shelton looked skeptical.

"No one else has gotten sick, at home or at school. But let's keep to ourselves just in case. If this thing *is* contagious, we don't want to spread it."

"Keep it secret?" Shelton's voice rose even higher. "We could be dying!"

Gulp. *Here goes.*

"Karsten knows we stole Coop."

"What!?" In chorus.

I told them about my interview. All of it. Karsten's accusations. Why he'd questioned our health.

Three shocked faces.

"So we can't see a doctor," I said. "Karsten will be looking for that."

"Why didn't you say anything?" Ben sounded angry.

"I'm sorry. I didn't want to cause panic. Besides, Karsten has no evidence." Lame. I knew it.

Hi dropped his head.

Shelton opened his mouth.

I cut him off.

"Just hold out a few more days. If we don't improve, we'll get medical help. Promise."

Shelton flashed a peace sign. "Two days. That's it. Then I'm telling my mom."

"Good enough."

"Say we do recover." Hi was looking from me to Shelton to Ben. "What then?"

I spoke with grim determination.

"Then we find out what the hell Karsten is up to."

CHAPTER 43

I slammed my locker door.

Lunchtime.

Shelton and Hi intercepted me en route to the cafeteria. We trudged down the hall, a sorry-looking group.

The morning had begun with a school-wide assembly. Speakers had droned on about the need for energy conservation. I thought I'd qualify for Medicare before they finished.

The four of us had huddled near the back, breathing only on ourselves. Nervous. Hoping to avoid infecting the entire student body.

Because of the program, both lunch periods had been combined for a special buffet menu. Organically grown vegetables. Free-range chicken. For the first time that year I hadn't packed a lunch.

Shelton still felt lousy. So did Hi. No new reactions, but the lingering sickness did nothing for their spirits.

I felt crappy too, but kept it to myself. At least I hadn't attacked another rodent.

Ben was waiting at the cafeteria entrance. We entered as a group.

The line was long, but moved quickly. After purchasing our selections we commandeered a table in one corner, near an emergency exit.

I dug into the veggies. Carrots. Snap peas. Buttered asparagus. If this option became standard, I'd never brown bag again.

I was chasing a pea across my plate when a strangled whine interrupted my thoughts. I looked up just as Shelton dropped his fork. His hands flew to his head and his lids slammed shut.

"No," he muttered. "Not here."

"Shelton, are you—"

The clatter of Ben's fork caused me to turn.

Ben's eyes were vacant. Spit bubbles foamed at one corner of his mouth.

"Ben?" I said softly.

No response.

"Hey! Blue!" A little louder.

Across the table, Hi dropped his utensils.

"Chicken," he whispered. Then his hand shot out and swept veggies from his plate. Zucchini and squash splattered the tabletop.

"Hi? Hiram?"

Oblivious, Hi grabbed a chicken leg and stripped off the flesh. Shoved it between his jaws.

Beside me, Ben gnawed a drumstick, grinding both meat and bones with his teeth. I watched juice dribble down his chin and dampen his shirt.

Horrified, my eyes scanned the room. So far, no one seemed to have noticed the drama playing out at our table. That wouldn't last. Hi and Ben were making a mess.

I was debating a course of action when Shelton clamped a chicken breast with his teeth and shook it savagely.

My eyes dropped to my own plate.

SNAP.

Boiling oil rushed through me. My brain jumped the tracks.

Oh no.

The odor of poultry overrode all other sensations. On instinct, I stuffed a piece of chicken into my mouth. The taste was indescribable. Drool covered my tongue.

Stop! STOP!

Closing my eyes, I dug my nails into my palms. Hard. Until it hurt. Willing my higher centers to regain control.

Blinking away the haze, I looked around.

The boys were shredding meat with their hands and teeth, all manners forgotten. Then I saw it.

Shelton's irises glowed deep saffron yellow.

I checked Hi, then Ben. My heart thudded madly. Their eyes shone with the same golden radiance.

Dear God in heaven!

The boys continued gorging, unaware of the *Lion King* scene they were making. I had to do something. Our table was a disaster of strewn utensils, shattered bones, and smeared veggies. Someone would spot us at any minute. We'd be the joke of the school forever.

My mind blanked. The fingernail trick worked for me, but I didn't know how to call the others back. Without a better idea, I did the one thing I knew would clear the room.

Against every principle, everything I knew to be right, I pulled the fire alarm.

A piecing wail blasted from the PA system.

I jumped away from the little box, already feeling guilty.

The false alarm continued to scream out, blaring, refusing to be ignored.

Still slammed, my ears were hypersensitive. The pain was almost unbearable. A moan rose from my throat. The boys pawed their ears in agony, food forgotten. Shelton fell to the floor and curled in on himself.

The other students jumped to their feet, aware of the Bolton routine and knowing this wasn't a drill. With a clatter of trays and a few screams, the anxious mob rushed the front doors. In their hasty retreat, not a single person glanced our way.

In seconds we were the cafeteria's only occupants.

"Let's get out of here!"

I blasted through the emergency exit, desperate to escape the mind-splitting sirens.

SNUP.

Midway across the yard my knees buckled as if gunshot. I fell to the grass, rolled twice, and lay still.

Slowly, awareness reasserted itself. Running teachers. Huddled students. My friends lying nearby, panting, speechless.

Gradually, my body returned to normal. For long moments no one moved.

I spoke first.

"Did you guys like the chicken?" I asked. "Mine was a bit dry."

Dead silence.

Then nervous laughter rose around me.

It was music to my bruised ears.

CHAPTER 44

No way I was going to school the next day.

I turned on the shower, rattled bottles, made getting ready noises. Kit bought my act. He rushed off to work early, oblivious to my plan. When the front door closed, I flopped back into bed.

The boys weren't so lucky. Sorry, guys.

The four of us had agreed to wait another day before presenting ourselves to an ER. Or a psych ward, whichever made more sense.

But school was the least of my worries.

A cotillion dance, my first event as a junior debutante, was taking place that evening. With Kit and Whitney so fired up about it, I couldn't back out. Aside from Mom's funeral, I'd never dreaded a gathering more in my life.

I slept all morning and a good chunk of the afternoon. I awoke still sluggish, but free of the overwhelming fatigue. Maybe I was recovering.

I tried to distract myself, even went to see Coop at the bunker. But my thoughts turned repeatedly to the dance. What was I supposed to wear to this thing?

The other girls would feature expensive designer gowns. Stunning red-carpet numbers. I owned nothing even close. A fact that Madison and her coven would be sure to point out.

At 3:27 p.m. I opened my closet door. And found that I'd underestimated Whitney.

The dress practically jumped from the hanger to spin a pirouette. Marchesa. Light pink, strapless, with gold accents. It must've cost a thousand bucks.

To my horror, it was my size. Below the dress sat a jewelry box containing two items. A silver David Yurman cable bracelet with pearl tips, and a diamond solitaire necklace.

I stared at the ensemble. Appalled.

Whitney *was* dressing me like a doll. One with questionable taste.

Pink? I glanced in the mirror, noted my red hair, green eyes, and pale complexion. Had she never met me?

Blarg.

This was not a *blend into the background* getup. This combo said, "Look at me," loud and clear. Exactly what I *didn't* want.

Dual dilemma. I owned nothing else. Ignoring the dress would hurt Whitney's feelings.

I had no choice.

Double blarg.

◇   ◇   ◇

The car ride from Morris Island was torture. Whitney's endless pointers. Kit's awkward compliments. I was anxious to get to the dance just to escape them.

"The jewelry's mine of course. I borrowed the dress from a friend who owns a boutique on King Street." Whitney was in her element. "We'll return it to her next week. Daisy said she'd loan us as many outfits as your sweet little debutante heart desires. Isn't that just the most generous thing ever?"

I tuned out her babbling excitement. The whole thing was a nightmare. A big pink one.

Fenworth House is classic Charleston, all shutters and piazzas and twisty wrought iron. The grand old dame sits on Queen Street near the Powder Magazine and the Gibbes Museum of Art. At my insistence, Kit dropped me at the curb. No way I'd walk in on his arm.

Butterflies fluttered in my stomach as I entered through the carved oak doors. I felt like a giant strawberry cupcake, wobbling in heels, clanking with Whitney's high-priced jewelry.

Panic thought. *What if everyone else wears jeans?*

I needn't have worried. The debs were decked out as if Brad Pitt might drop by looking for a date to the Oscars.

But no one else wore pink.

Oh joy.

The ballroom was straight out of *Gone with the Wind*. Brocade drapes framed floor-to-ceiling windows, and enormous crystal chandeliers hung over acres of gleaming oak. Small linen-clad tables surrounded the dance floor.

Musicians tuned their instruments on a stage at one end of the room. Saxophones. Trumpets. Trombones. Cymbals clanged and horns tooted as the acoustics were perfected.

A long table hugged the room's right-hand wall, spread with vases of lilies, china, punch bowls, and appetizers mounded on elegant silver trays. Crab cakes. Mini beef Wellingtons. Bacon-wrapped scallops. Not a bad spread.

"Tory?"

Jason stood beside the buffet. In his black tux and cummerbund, he looked like James Bond. The Daniel Craig version.

"Hi." I kept it short.

"Wow. You look ridiculous."

My cheeks burned.

Stupid cupcake dress! Stupid Whitney!

Jason whistled. "Fantastic! Please dress up more often. I'm stunned." He called across the room. "Chance, look who's here."

"Tory, my God!" Chance wore a white tuxedo with tails. On anyone else? Dopey. On him? Yes, please.

Chance snagged a crab cake, all the while appraising me like an art collector evaluating a painting.

"You're a brave woman," he said. "It takes great courage to walk in here like that."

"Like what?"

"Hands down the prettiest girl in the room. All the other ladies will be furious."

Wait for it . . . There! The wink.

"Don't let Hannah hear that," I said without thinking. "You're spoken for."

My stomach performed a back flip. Flirting with Chance? Was I insane? Why not grab the mike and sing "Macarena." Complete the lunacy.

Chance's brows floated an inch up his forehead. Then his lips curled in amusement. "Lucky for me, my princess hasn't arrived. In fact, I'd better meet her coach outside. Excuse me."

With that he was gone.

"I didn't know you were a deb," Jason said.

"Junior deb," I corrected. "This is my first event. I have no idea what I'm supposed to do."

"Then, Mademoiselle, I shall be your guide this evening." Jason bowed from the waist.

My face must have betrayed my confusion.

"Tonight we practice our dance steps for the big ball. You need a partner. Please allow me the pleasure of being your escort?" Formal.

"Oh! Then, kind sir, I accept."

Where was I getting this stuff? I'd never taken a dance lesson in my life. This could be a disaster.

Whispered voices intruded.

"Maddy, look! It's the boat girl."

Ugh. Courtney Holt. Where one skank lurked, two others couldn't be far.

"What's she doing with Jason?" Ashley whispered.

I didn't turn, didn't let on that I heard. Jason was grazing the appetizers, completely unaware.

"Poor thing. We should rescue him." Madison's giggle was pure malice. "What's she doing here anyway?"

"She's a junior deb now, can you believe it?" Ashley whispered. "My mother's on the committee. She told me that Dubois woman got her in. I have no idea how."

"She looks . . . good." Courtney sounded surprised. "Very good, actually. I never noticed she was pretty."

"So the child has a dress," Madison said. "Big deal."

"Pretty gutsy wearing pink," Ashley said.

"And she's pulling it off," Courtney added. "Nice bracelet, too."

I was astonished. The unholy trinity thought I looked good? The world was officially upside down.

The glow was quickly extinguished.

"If the tramp makes a move on Jason, she's roadkill." Madison's resentment was unmistakable. "The little girl's definitely out of her league."

Nonchalant, I scanned the room. The Tripod was huddled by the stage, at least twenty yards off. Nowhere near me.

No! Please God. Not here.

I ran a check for signs of an impending attack. Prepared to bolt.

Oddly, I felt fine. Good even. My hearing had gone superhuman, but nothing else seemed altered. Yet.

The band struck up Sinatra's "I've Got You Under My Skin." Irony there.

Around the room, debs paired up with their escorts.

"Ready to fox-trot?" Jason offered an arm.

Holy moly.

"Sure." I most certainly was not.

At that moment, Hannah floated into the hall wearing an elegant white dress with a simple blue sash. I conceded the title of prettiest in the room.

Madison sauntered over, cleavage fighting to escape her Vera Wang dress.

"Shall we, Jason?"

"Sorry, Maddy." Leading me out onto the dance floor. "Tory's new. I promised to show her the ropes."

Madison's overly mascaraed eyes fluttered in surprise. "Sure. No problem."

But it was, in fact, a problem. Mine.

Jason and I paused a moment to catch the beat. Then we were off.

At first I stepped all over his shoes. Zigged when he zagged. Floundered when he tried to spin me. Madison smirked over the shoulder of her second-choice partner, amused at my clumsiness.

But soon my natural sense of rhythm kicked in. Before long I was following Jason's lead.

Against all expectations, I began to have fun.

Halfway through our third number, Jason twirled me faster than before. I flowed with the move, curling back into his chest. He reversed the spin and we ended up side by side with arms outstretched. As if on cue, Chance swooped by.

Jason released my hand and captured Hannah's in one smooth motion. My momentum carried me into Chance's arms.

Turning on instinct, I managed to fall into the proper tempo with my new partner.

"Let a girl know next time!" I laughed.

"And spoil the fun? No can do."

Chance was an even better dancer than Jason. And held me much closer. No complaint there.

Halfway through the song he led me into a new sequence.

"I don't know this one," I squawked.

But Chance directed our movements with ease. I followed his lead, even added a closing flourish of my own.

"Never doubted you'd nail it," said Chance. "You're the best dancer here."

Another spin. Our bodies drew together.

"And still the prettiest girl in the room," he whispered.

Yikes.

This was beyond friendly flirting. Right? I had no frame of reference.

The music reached a crescendo, then stopped.

Chance bowed, winked, and walked off to collect Hannah.

I hurried to the food table and downed a cup of punch. Grapefruit-melon. Blech. But I needed something. My cheeks were hot and my pulse was still speeding.

"You're sure you've never fox-trotted before?" Jason had come up beside me.

I nodded, not trusting my voice.

"Well, you're a natural." He popped a chocolate ball into his mouth.

The band started into "My Favorite Things." Couples reengaged and headed back out.

"Let's see how you waltz." Grabbing my hand, Jason pulled me toward the dance floor.

A little too fast.

A little too hard.

SNAP.

Fire shot through my body. Divided into a million shards of ice. The pain was intense.

I jerked free.

Pressed my palms to my cheeks.

"You okay?" Jason squeezed my shoulder. "Do you need water?"

"Don't touch me!"

My hands slammed Jason's chest with a will of their own.

Jason flew backward and cracked the wall with his head. I stared in shock as he slumped to the ground.

SNUP.

My mind cleared.

My stomach dropped.

Holy crap!

"Jason!" I rushed to his side. "I'm so sorry!"

Jason rubbed the back of his skull, clearly confused. "What happened?"

"I pushed you." Think fast. "I had a migraine attack. It was a reflex."

Escape!

"I'm so sorry Jason, but I have to go."

"No, wait, don't leave." Jason's words were slurred.

"You're pretty strong," he noted, struggling to his feet.

I glanced around. We were the only couple not dancing. No one had seen me knock a 180-pound star athlete back five yards. With ease.

"I'm sorry, but I really do have to go."

"Okay." Jason smoothed his hair. "I'll walk you out. Drive you. Home."

The song ended. I looked across the room. Chance, Hannah, and Madison were now watching. No way I could leave with Jason. The rumor mill would eat that one up.

"Thanks, but I'm good. See you later."

Before he could object, I scurried for the door.

Out on the front steps, I considered my plight. How the hell would I get to Morris Island? No car. No shuttle. A cab would cost fifty bucks.

Kit and Whitney were at a movie, expecting to pick me up at eleven. Their phones would be off.

I checked my watch: 9:20.

Great. I was stuck for almost two hours.

A limo idled by the curb at the foot of the stairs. As I mulled my limited options, the driver's door opened and a black-suited man climbed out. He was speaking into a cell.

He looked at me. I looked at him.

In the lamplight I could see that the man was short and

compact, with pale blue eyes and gray hair buzzed to his scalp. A white scar traced the right side of his jaw.

The phone snapped shut. "Miss Brennan?"

"Yes?" Surprised.

"Mr. Claybourne requested that I assist you."

"Mr. Claybourne?"

"The younger Mr. Claybourne." Buzz Cut opened one of the limo's rear doors and stepped aside. For a moment I thought he might click his heels.

Chance must have called the moment I left. Ergo, he'd been thinking about me.

"I'm sorry. Your name sir?"

"Tony Baravetto." Gruff. "Chance Claybourne's personal driver."

I paused. This man was a complete stranger. I'm suspicious by nature and wasn't going to jump into the limo on his word alone.

"I'm sorry, sir, but may I see your phone for a moment?"

Puzzled, Baravetto handed over his cell. I checked. The last call received was Chance Claybourne.

What to do?

Duh. You got another way home?

"Thank you, Mr. Baravetto. A ride would be greatly appreciated."

⬡   ⬡   ⬡

I slipped inside the house and relocked the door behind me. Then headed straight for my room.

Kit and Whitney were entangled on the living room couch. On hearing my footsteps they flew apart, smoothing hair and clothing.

Gross. Who's the teenager here?

"How was the movie?" I asked.

"Sold out." Kit was clearly embarrassed, tried to play it off. "You're home early. Did you get a ride?"

I nodded.

"Was it grand?" Whitney chirped. "I must hear every scrumptious detail."

"It was fine. I'm going to bed. Night!"

Ignoring their pleas, I scampered upstairs as fast as my dress would allow. Performed a cupcake dive onto my bed. Relaxed. For the first time in hours.

Then I rolled to my belly and screamed into my pillow. What a night.

During the long ride to Morris, I'd dissected my cotillion attack. That's how I labeled them now. By context. The boat attack. The fly on the wall attack. The cafeteria attack. The cotillion attack.

What caused them? Were they random? Or was there a trigger?

Tonight's episode had been different.

I'd felt my brain snap, but no blackout followed. There'd been just one sensory symptom—my ears turning up the juice. Then I'd exhibited a burst of raw physical power. Like Ben catching the engine in his garage.

All things considered, tonight's change had been minor. Manageable. Hell, even useful.

Was the pattern changing? How? Why?

Something incredible had happened to our bodies. Something new to the world, I feared. Whatever we'd contracted had warped us.

In our brains? Our DNA?

I didn't know. But I knew that we were transformed.

Twisted, to the core.

Viral.

I resolved to understand. To get answers.

One way or another.

CHAPTER 45

That night, the storm raging inside me broke.

My dreams were peaceful, free of disturbing images.

I woke energized for the first time in a week. No headache, congestion, fever, or pain. All systems go.

Yahoo!

The gang had agreed to meet before school. I hoped the others had good news, too.

Twenty minutes after rising, I ducked inside the bunker. The mood was light years distant from our last meeting.

Hi and Shelton stood in opposite corners, tossing a tennis ball back and forth. Cooper raced between them, trying to snatch it. Ben sat by the table, watching Coop's acrobatics.

"Hi, guys!"

"Glad you could make it," Hi said. "Only five minutes late."

Shelton dropped the ball. Coop pounced, then rolled to his

back to gnaw his prize. Healthy. Content.

"How's everyone feeling?" I asked.

"I'm great!" Shelton's eyes no longer looked haunted. "No problems at all."

"What about you two?"

"Strong," Ben said. "Whatever it was, I beat it."

"I feel like two million bucks," Hi said. "Thank God."

"Even Cooper Dog's tip-top." Shelton tickled the puppy's belly. "Isn't that right, you little fugitive?"

Coop wiggled to his feet and charged Shelton's chest. The two began to wrestle.

Hi, back to his old self, provided color commentary on the Man versus Dog bout taking place on the floor. Even Ben was jovial. A sort of half grin curled the corners of his mouth.

I hated to spoil the good vibes, but decisions had to be made.

"I'm glad everyone's recovered," I said. "I think the worst is behind us."

"Better be," Hi said. "My sweet cheeks can't take any more throne time."

"The worst part?" Shelton pushed his glasses up the bridge of his nose. "That implies there are other parts."

"We need to be sure our recovery is real," I said. "To be certain, we have to know what happened in the first place."

"Why?" Ben asked. "Done is done."

"It may not be over."

I described the cotillion attack. They listened without interrupting.

"The snap came without warning," I finished. "But I didn't black out."

"What's your point?" Hi asked.

"We don't know if these fits will keep happening." I searched for the right words. "The side effects. Reactions. Whatever. I'm not sure what to call them."

"For me," Shelton said, "it always kicks off with a jolt in my head."

I nodded. "I'm not sure if I hear it or feel it, but something snaps in my brain. The weirdness comes after that. Then there's another snap and I'm back to normal."

"That's right," Hi said. "My vision went crazy again last night. The opener was just what you describe."

"These flares must have a trigger," Ben said. "Something that sets them off."

Flare. Perfect description.

"Bottom line, we need answers," I said. "And there's only one place to look."

"Crap." Hi closed his eyes. "We're going back, aren't we?"

"Just Ben and me," I reassured him. "We can't all go. Too suspicious."

"Fine by me." Shelton and Hi spoke in unison.

"Where are we going?" Ben asked.

"Loggerhead. After school." I waved a hand. "No biggie. Just breaking in to Karsten's office and searching his files."

"Pff." Ben pooched air through his lips. "I thought you meant something dangerous."

"You're nuts. Suicidal." Shelton was ear-tugging double-time.

"Maybe," I said. "You and Hi also have an assignment."

"What now?" Hi sounded resigned. "Steal a car? Invade Russia?"

"The Internet didn't provide enough information about parvovirus. According to everything we found, we weren't supposed to be at risk. We need to know more. You two are going to dig up as much as you can at the CU medical library."

Hi and Shelton looked relieved that their task was legal.

"We'll cover it, top to bottom," Shelton promised.

"And I'm not giving up on Katherine Heaton," I added. "I'm still waiting for Chance to get back to me on the print."

The others nodded, committed to seeing the investigation through.

"Ten-hut, Virals!" Hi barked like a sergeant ordering new recruits. "We have missions to complete!"

CHAPTER 46

An hour later I paused on Bolton's front steps, dreading what awaited me inside the doors.

Jason was in my first period class. Last night I'd ditched him, with all his friends watching. Not to mention that I'd knocked him silly.

Would he be furious? What would he say? The encounter promised to be super-awkward.

Bolton's hallways always hum with gossip. Normally I manage to avoid the limelight. Not likely this time. The story of the Pink Monster was sure to top the playlist.

I caught a break. Lecture in biology. Our lab group wouldn't meet. Lucky. Given Chance's flirtatious comments, I wanted to see Hannah even less than Jason.

And I *still* hadn't completed my DNA comparisons. Due tomorrow.

Jason's attention strayed to my desk several times. I kept my head down, eyes glued to my laptop. My lecture notes were detailed enough to sell to a publisher.

At the bell, I shot out the door. For the rest of the morning, I kept a low profile.

During lunch I hid in the computer lab, working on my part of the presentation. Comparing the sequences took most of the hour. When I'd finished, I emailed my results to Jason and Hannah.

You've got mail! See, I'm not avoiding you.

Passing through the halls, I picked up whispered comments. Noted hidden smiles. My flight from the dance hadn't gone unnoticed.

Inevitably, my luck ran out. After the final bell Jason spotted me scooting out the main doors.

"Tory! Hold up."

Run? Bad form.

I waited, trying to act natural.

"Where have you been all day?" Jason said. "I looked all over."

"Sorry! I had to finish the DNA project. I sent the results to your Gmail account."

"Oh? Great." Jason ran a hand across the back of his neck. "But I wanted to talk about something else."

Here it comes.

"Chance needs to see you, says it's serious. He got a hit off that print you gave him."

That's it? I didn't know whether to be relieved or offended.

Jason seemed puzzled by my silence. "You still need the fingerprint, right?"

"Yes. Absolutely. Thanks." Before I could stop myself. "I thought you wanted to talk about the dance."

Cringe. *What in the world was I thinking?*

"Now that you mention it, you did split early." Jason laughed. "Sorry I'm such a klutz."

"*You've* got nothing to apologize for." What was he talking about? "*I'm* sorry. I pushed you."

"I didn't know you got migraines," Jason said. "I shouldn't have grabbed you; those things can be a killer."

"Mm."

"I can't believe I tripped. I have a knot on my head the size of a kiwi." He snickered. "I'm telling everyone it's a lacrosse injury to save myself the embarrassment."

My breath caught. Jason didn't realize what really happened. If no one else saw, I was in the clear.

"Anyway," Jason said, "Chance wants to meet before practice tomorrow to give you the info. That work?"

"Definitely. Tell him I really appreciate his help. And thank him for the ride last night. Mr. Baravetto was a godsend."

"No problem. And don't worry about the gossip girls."

Ahh. So I hadn't escaped.

"Oh?" Feigned indifference. "What's the word on the street?"

"It's nothing." Jason had assumed I already knew. "Those chicks just like to pick on people. Makes them feel better about themselves."

"Tell me. I can take it." Lie.

"It's nonsense." Jason sighed, clearly uncomfortable. "A few of them said you pulled a Cinderella. That you had to return your outfit before the stores closed."

I felt my face flame. How humiliating. Worse, it was kind of true.

I wanted to crawl under a rock. To transfer. To die. But anger pushed aside the embarrassment.

"Who said that?"

"Forget it. You looked great. They were just jealous."

"Jason, please. Who?"

"Madison and company. Courtney and Ashley."

The Tripod again. No matter what I did, those three had it in for me.

I'm not letting this one slide. Game on.

"Whatever floats their boat, I guess. Thanks for telling me." I forced a smile. "Tell Chance I'll meet him right here, if that works."

"Will do. Take care." Jason walked a few paces, turned. "And don't worry about Maddy's BS. No one believes it."

"Thanks," I said.

Walking toward the marina, I vowed to take action against the Tripod. I was done being badmouthed.

But not today.

Today I had a crime to commit.

CHAPTER 47

Hi and Shelton hurried along Beaufain Street. They the passed crew teams rowing on Colonial Lake, a man-made oval stretching a full city block. Ducks paddled in noisy clusters of two and three. Intent on their task, the boys barely noticed.

Near the shopping district, single-family homes gave way to townhouses arranged in orderly rows. Window boxes overflowed with petunias, marigolds, and lantana. Honeybees worked overtime in the warm afternoon sun. The beauty of the day was lost on them.

Hanging a left on King, Hi and Shelton finally reached the CU campus, three square blocks of Gothic stone and ivy rubbing shoulders with modern brick and glass. Beneath ancient oaks and magnolias, dogs chased Frisbees hurled by college kids.

A sign directed the boys to a massive stone building on the eastern edge of the common.

"Any blackouts today?" Shelton asked as they hurried along the path.

"Nope, but I had a flare. For few moments I could read the answer key on Mr. Hallmark's desk. I was in the back row."

"Mine was auditory," Shelton said. "In the bathroom I heard a ripping noise, like a power saw. It was Kelvin Grace, unzipping his fly. Ten feet away, outside the stall. Crazy, huh?"

"Barking mad."

In the bio-med library, the boys asked and were directed to the veterinary wing. There, they divided topics and set to work. Two hours later, they compared findings.

"I scoured a billion medical journals," said Shelton. "No disease matches our symptoms. I couldn't even *find* some of them."

"Here's what I got on parvo," Hi said, shuffling papers. "They're tiny buggers, some of the smallest viruses in nature, with only a single strand of DNA. *Parvus* means small in Latin."

"Fascinating," Shelton deadpanned. "How does that help?"

"Different species have different strains. Dogs, cats, pigs, even minks. And listen to this." Hi read from his notes. "Parvoviruses are specific to the life forms they infect, *but this is a somewhat flexible characteristic.*"

"What does that mean, *flexible*?" Shelton asked.

"It means the viruses aren't *completely* species-specific. Canine parvo usually affects only dogs, wolves, and foxes. But certain strains can infect other animals, like cats."

"So if the dog version can jump to cats, why not to people?"

Hi shrugged. "Beats me. But Tory was right. Canine parvovirus isn't supposed to affect humans."

"Then that's a dead end." Shelton sighed. "We'd better keep looking."

Shadows deepened, lengthened, eventually shot like dark arrows across the wooden tables centered in the room. Shelton had almost given up when he stumbled upon a new lead.

"Hi. Look at this."

Hi leaned over to read the page under Shelton's pointing finger.

"Humans can't be infected by canine parvo, but they *can* catch viruses from the same family." Shelton sounded excited.

"Really?"

"There are three types: dependoviruses, bocaviruses, and erythroviruses. The last type has a bug called Parvovirus B19."

"Parvo B19." Hi rubbed his forehead. "Why does that ring a bell?"

"B19 was discovered in 1975." Shelton continued picking out facts. "It was the first parvovirus proven to infect people. There's still no vaccine. The last epidemic was in 1998." Shelton looked up. "Kids get it, mostly. Outbreaks are usually in nurseries or schools."

"What does B19 do?"

Shelton returned to the journal, again skimmed. "It leads to something known as 'fifth disease' or 'slapped cheek syndrome.'" Shelton's eyebrow rose. "Those names sound made up. Anyway, it looks like all B19 does is cause a bad rash for a few weeks."

"That's definitely not what happened to us."

Shelton continued reading. "B19 spreads via infected

respiratory droplets. Coughs, I guess. Infected individuals can experience fever and fatigue."

"Now *that* sounds familiar."

Shelton nodded. "Once inside a host, B19 invades the red blood cell factories in the bone marrow. Symptoms begin a few days after exposure and last a week. Those infected are only contagious *before* showing symptoms."

"We caught our virus from Coop," Hi said. "Can dogs get B19?"

Shelton scanned the page. "No. B19 only infects humans."

"Then this is another dead end."

"I don't know. This seems important. We must be missing something."

"Let's copy the article then check out the references cited."

The shadows faded to gray, then black as Shelton and Hi pulled every source they could find. Loops led to loops and more loops. Nothing else jumped out at them.

At ten o'clock, the intercom clicked on and a prim voice informed patrons that the library was closing.

"I think we're onto something," Hi said. "I'm just not sure what. Let's bounce this off the others."

"Good idea."

A second warning was broadcast, somewhat chillier than the first.

The boys headed for the exit.

CHAPTER 48

Ben and I stood outside the doors of LIRI. Deep breathing. Trying to calm our jangling nerves.

The last thing we needed was a flare.

Only a zillion things could go wrong. But I saw no alternative. Karsten had answers. We needed them.

"If the old goat's still here, we're toast." Ben, always the optimist.

"He won't be. Karsten's due at the aquarium right now. And if he *is* here, we fall back on our excuse and leave."

I sounded confident, but Ben had a point. Tossing Karsten's office would be difficult with him sitting in it.

Hopefully we'd taken care of that.

"What if Karsten recognized my voice?" Ben hadn't wanted to make the call.

"The caller had to sound like an adult. Could I have pulled that off? Besides, you speak so rarely he probably has no a clue what you sound like."

I'd struggled with step one of the plan. To have any chance of success, we had to lure Karsten off the island.

My inspiration came from his online biography.

Dr. Marcus Karsten was director emeritus and veterinary consultant to the South Carolina Aquarium. Armed with that knowledge, tricking him had been a cakewalk.

Despite his nervousness, Ben smiled. "Karsten will be livid when he learns there was no penguin emergency."

Oh yeah. We had to move quickly. Already paranoid, Karsten might guess he'd been lured away on purpose and hurry back to Loggerhead. By then we had to be long gone.

"Ready?" I shook out my arms, hopped on my toes.

"Ready," Ben said.

We pushed into the main building and walked to the security office. Sam was manning the desk. Break there. Sam was less moody than Carl. And physically his polar opposite. Scarecrow thin and bald as a cue ball, he looked more like a cadaver than a guard.

Dragging reluctant eyes from his magazine, Sam acknowledged our presence. "Great. The troublemakers. Here to burn down the building?"

"Hello." I hit him with my most engaging smile. "We need to give my father some documents."

"Leave them in the box." Sam's eyes returned to his *Guns & Ammo.*

"I can't. These have to be faxed in the next thirty minutes. If not, we can't go."

Sam sighed, extended a hand. I handed over the forms.

"Math camp?" Chuckle. "You need shots for *math* camp? Better question: Why go?"

"Ha ha. Can we please just do this? We'll be out of your hair"—oops—"your way in no time."

Sam hesitated, perhaps wary of Karsten's recent foul temper. Finally, he nodded.

"Ya'll are in luck. Dr. K's out for the moment." Handing the papers back, he waved us though. "Don't sign in, and step on it. I don't want to get chewed out because of this."

"Thanks." We scurried down the hall before he could reconsider.

"No log in," Ben whispered. "Numb nuts just did us a favor."

"Time for some larceny."

We took the stairs to Karsten's office, all four flights. Kit's an elevator guy. Couldn't risk running into dear old Dad.

On four, the stairwell opened onto a short hallway. At the opposite end, a pair of frosted-glass doors closed off the director's suite.

Our last roadblock lay ahead: The Dragon.

Karsten's intolerance for noise is legendary. His secretary, Cordelia Hoke, is the only employee who works inside the inner sanctum. If we could dodge the Dragon, we'd have a chance.

For the moment we needed a hiding place.

Ben nudged me and pointed to a supply closet. We ducked inside and peeked out through the tiny window.

One minute passed. Five. Ten. I started to sweat. Of course.

Finally, Hoke pushed through the doors and waddled to the

elevator. So predictable. An incurable chain smoker, the Dragon slipped out at ten past every hour. Two cigs, plus a call to her trucker boyfriend. We'd have at least fifteen minutes.

Funny. The Dragon's routine was known to everyone at LIRI but her boss.

As the elevator clicked shut, we dashed into the suite and entered Karsten's office.

Countdown. Twelve minutes.

"Where do we start?" Ben whispered.

"Look for files, records, anything with a roster of projects."

The office was positively Spartan. Corner bookcase, stacked with reference materials. Desk. File cabinet. Hat stand.

Karsten clearly stored most of his papers elsewhere. But we couldn't gain access to the secret lab. We had to find something in here. And fast.

I sat at Karsten's desk and started with the computer. When I right-clicked the mouse, a password screen filled the monitor. Of course.

I tried the file cabinet. Found it locked.

"Ten minutes left," Ben warned.

I rifled the desk drawers. Three contained office supplies. Pens. Post-its. A three-hole punch. Another held power cords and computer cables.

Across the room, Ben was working the bookcase.

"Nothing so far," he said. "Eight minutes."

"We need the file cabinet key," I said. "His papers must be in there."

Ben spread his hands, a *this is doomed* look on his face.

Ignoring him, I inventoried Karsten's desktop. Monitor. Mouse. Printer. Metal cup filled with pens and paperclips. Small clock.

Chimpanzee skull.

Huh?

I lifted and rotated the skull. Heard a rattle. I tilted Mr. Chimp, then shook him from side to side. A small key dropped from the hole at the cranial base.

"Booyah!"

I set down the skull, inserted and turned the key in the lock. The cylinder popped and the drawer opened.

Ben dropped to a knee beside me. Together we flipped through files as quickly as possible.

"Six minutes." Ben's voice was beyond tense.

I checked folder after folder.

Equipment. Expenses. Employee evaluations.

"Hello!" Ben held a file labeled *Active Projects—LIRI.* Inside was a spreadsheet, its latest entry dated this week.

I speed-read the contents. Lab Six had its own column. Within that section was printed: *Closed—out of service.* The closure stretched back to mid-February.

"I knew it," I whispered. "Karsten's project isn't registered. The University doesn't know about the parvo experiment."

What was Karsten's game?

Ben opened the bottom drawer. The files it contained were unlabeled. We tore through them, ears alert for signs of the Dragon.

"Three minutes," Ben hissed. "We need to bail."

"What's this?" I held a folder containing bank deposit slips. The name on the account was Dr. Marcus E. Karsten.

"*Wow.* This one's for fifty thousand dollars!" I flipped through the stack. Dozens. Each for the same amount. "Every check is from the same company, Candela Pharmaceuticals."

"Look." Ben lifted the bottom slip. "The first deposit took place six months ago."

"The checks are made out to Karsten, *not* to the University," I said. "They must tie in somehow."

The outer door opened, clicked shut. The Dragon's humming drifted from just outside Kartsten's door.

I stuffed a slip into my pocket, then, moving as quietly as possible, locked the cabinet and slipped the key back into the skull.

Ben and I snuck to the door and peered out.

Hoke's desk was directly between us and the outer doors. She sat behind it, unwrapping a box of Godiva chocolates.

We were trapped.

We couldn't wait an hour. Karsten would return. Catch us. Call the cops. My pulse raced at the prospect.

Suddenly I felt heat. The sensation of falling through a long dark tunnel.

SNAP.

Bolts of light flashed in my brain.

I heard Hoke's fingers thundering through candy papers. I smelled chocolate, walnuts, and caramel. Sweaty polyester. Chantilly cologne.

My eyes focused to laser points. I saw lacy dust particles riding the air. Mites clinging to the wooden desk. Tiny grooves embedded in the chimp's skull.

Ben was beside me, flexing and un-flexing his hands. Our eyes met. His irises gleamed gold. Like mine.

Suddenly, I knew what to do. Ben nodded, right there with me.

I cracked the door. Crouched.

Ben coiled at my back, ready.

Finally, Hoke bent and reached for something beneath her desk.

Like desert wind, we shot from Karsten's office. Blew past the Dragon. Slipped soundlessly into the hall.

Out.

Free.

◇　　◇　　◇

Puzzled by the sensation of moving air, Hoke glanced toward the suite's entrance. The double doors were slowly drifting shut.

Odd.

The Dragon lumbered to her feet and stuck her head out into the corridor.

Empty.

Shrugging, she returned to her desk and resumed the serious business of snacking.

CHAPTER 49

Leaving the library, Hi and Shelton began the fifteen-minute hike to the marina.

"I hate walking through town at night," Shelton said. "There's hardly anyone else out here."

"It's barely ten o'clock and we're in the tourist district," Hi replied. "You afraid of getting mugged by a granny from Jersey?"

"It's dark. I'm just saying."

"I'm not worried." Hi gestured to the storefronts. "I think it's safe between Abercrombie and Lacoste."

A half block up the streetlights died, drowning the sidewalk in gloom.

"Okay," Shelton whispered. "How about now?"

"Keep moving, wimp."

Hi picked up the pace. Seconds later, he spotted two men idling at the corner of King and Hasell. Both wore tight black clothing. Neither spoke.

Without a word, both boys stopped.

"Shelton." Hi's silent alarm was blaring. "Something's not right here."

"So not right."

"Let's go another way."

"Another way sounds great."

They crossed King and headed east up Hasell Street. The wrong direction, but neither minded the detour.

"My temple is up ahead," Hi said. "We can cut over on the next block."

At K. K. Beth Elohim, they turned and checked the murky darkness at their backs. The street was empty.

"That's what I get for making fun of you," Hi said. "Now I'm spooked for no reason."

Shelton laughed. "Yeah, we're not exactly Jason Bourne, are we?"

Feeling foolish, the boys turned right. Two blocks south, they arrived at the old marketplace. In the dark the structure looked like a giant sea serpent running down the center of Market Street, creating narrow alleys along both sides.

"Crap," said Hi.

The two men now stood on the opposite side of Market. One was smoking. Both were watching Hi and Shelton.

"Holy buckets," Shelton whispered. "Haul ass!"

The boys fired down the alley to the north of the market. After they turned, the structure blocked the shady duo from view.

"We're going the wrong way!" Shelton's voice wobbled with the effort of speed-walking.

"I don't want to pass those guys. Do you?"

Shelton didn't bother to reply.

They continued east past the market's older portion, now dark and abandoned for the night. At the next cross street, they stopped to look over their shoulders.

And nearly wet their shorts.

The men were in the alley skirting the market's south side. Watching like predators tracking a meal.

"Move," Shelton whispered. "Keep going."

"Bay Street," Hi said. "We'll go all the way around."

Footsteps bounced off the cobblestones. Both boys turned.

The men had crossed to the north alley and were moving toward them. The distance was closing fast.

Hi and Shelton looked at each other. Fight or flight? No contest. They tensed, ready to bolt.

The world receded.

Darkness.

Falling.

SNAP.

Voltage slammed through Shelton and Hi. Their surroundings sharpened into crystal clarity.

The footfalls quickened to a trot. Their pursuers were closing in for the kill.

"Run!" Shelton screamed.

The boys streaked like greyhounds. Feet hammered behind them. The chase was on.

Hi's eyes now pierced the darkness like night vision goggles.

Inside the market, he noticed a darker patch among the shadows.

Grabbing Shelton, he veered right. Shelton changed course with ease. As one, they slipped into the pitch-black structure. Crouched behind an overturned table. Held their breath.

Their pursuers paused just outside the opening. Their panting sounded to the boys like roaring wind. They could smell sweat, sense agitation.

"Where the hell are they?"

"Damn! I'll cover the street; you check in there. Don't let them get away!"

The footfalls divided. One pair pounded east. Receded.

The other pair crept toward them, gravel cracking beneath leather soles like exploding popcorn.

Then silence.

Hunkered down, Hi and Shelton saw their pursuer stop. To allow his eyes to adjust to the dark?

"Come on out." The voice was high and whiney. "We just want to talk."

The man moved one foot forward.

A soft click cut the stillness.

The boys' hyper-human ears registered the noise.

Their eyes met. Gold haloed their pupils.

They knew.

A gun had been cocked.

"I'm not going to hurt you." The voice now came from the darkness to the right. They could see its owner clearly. Tall, arms and legs sinewy inside the tight black fabric.

The man inched forward, unsure of the footing. One hand was outstretched, feeling its way. The other clutched a gun.

Shelton and Hi shared the same understanding. *Our enemy can't see. We can.* They scanned their surroundings, eyes shining. Looking for weapons.

There.

Two brooms stood angled against the wall behind them. Each had a stout wooden handle.

Moving silently, the boys armed themselves.

Wait.

Wait.

Finally, the thug drew level with their hiding place. His gun swept back and forth in front of his body. Amateur. Foolish.

Shelton edged closer, not needing to be told. His broom handle arrowed between the man's legs. The man stumbled, but somehow kept his balance.

Fast as lightning, Hi smashed down on the man's outstretched hand. The gun hit the cobblestones and ricocheted into the shadows.

Shelton didn't hesitate. Slipping forward, he jabbed his broom into the man's rib cage.

"Hmmmph!" The thug doubled over.

Hi reversed his grip, whipping his broom handle 360 degrees and slamming it across the back of their assailant's head.

Wood cracked on bone.

The man dropped. Lay still.

No time for celebration.

The warriors bolted from their hiding place.

Raced the darkened streets.

Didn't slow until they hit the water.

CHAPTER 50

"Where have you been? We've been waiting for hours!" Venting felt good. I still had adrenaline up the wazoo.

"Sorry," Hi said. "The research took longer than we expected. And the hit men slowed us down."

"Right." I rolled my eyes.

"Two dudes tried to cap us!" Shelton was wired higher than I was. "We took one out, gave the other the slip."

Hi and Shelton bumped fists.

Ben held up a hand. "Stop. Explain."

They stepped all over each other telling the story.

"Who'd be after you?" Ben asked.

"The same fools from Loggerhead," Shelton said.

"Why?"

"We know about Heaton's murder, so now they want us dead. Right?"

"Maybe." I wasn't so sure. "Seems like a lot of trouble over a forty-year-old crime."

"Tory, we *used* our flare this time," Hi said. "The change gave us powers. Super senses and super strength."

Shelton concurred. "It was amazing."

"You're not the only ones." Ben shared our adventure at LIRI.

"So Karsten is banking cash to run secret experiments?" Shelton whistled. "And we walked right into it."

"Whatever he's doing, records of the project aren't in his office," I said. "Must be in the lab. Did you guys learn anything useful?"

"Could be."

Shelton and Hi took turns explaining the findings.

"So some parvoviruses *do* transfer between species," Hi summarized, "and there *are* human-infecting strains. But the human form doesn't infect dogs, and the canine form doesn't infect people."

Something bothered me. What? The answer stayed hunkered deep in my brainpan.

"What's the human form called again?" I asked.

"Parvovirus B19," Hi said. "The scientist who named it found the first example in his nineteenth petri dish."

"B19," I repeated, more to myself than to the others. Was that the message that was nagging? Why? The name was as generic as mud.

Still the answer refused to surface.

I closed my eyes.

Think. Think.

No go.

Just then Coop bounded into the bunker. Now that he was stronger and more spirited, we were allowing him free run of the nearby dunes.

The puppy wormed figure eights around my legs.

"Coop, whoa!" I barely kept my feet.

Tucking his tail, the puppy crawled beneath the table and whined softly.

I rubbed his back and made comforting noises. I hated when he got scared. He'd suffered enough at Karsten's hands.

I was scratching Coop's ears when the subliminal message finally broke through.

B19.

That's it!

"Guys!" I yelled. "I know what happened! Karsten must have—"

Hackles rose into a prickly ridge along Coop's spine. He growled, eyes fixed on the bunker's entrance.

I whipped around.

From outside came scratching, then the unmistakable sound of someone squeezing through the opening.

A shadow appeared on the floor.

We drew back into one corner, shocked that someone had found our secret hideout. Whoever it was had us trapped.

A form emerged from the crawl. Straightened. Glared at us with undisguised malice.

It was the last person I expected to see.

CHAPTER 51

"Tory Brennan."

Karsten spat my name as though it were something bitter on his tongue.

I gaped, thunderstruck.

Our bunker was practically invisible. How had Karsten found it?

The boys stared in dejected silence. Game over. We'd lost.

"So this is where you plot your little larcenies." Karsten smirked, amused by his own wit. "How quaint."

Karsten's eyes suddenly widened, then narrowed to slits. I followed his sightline.

To Coop.

The puppy was planted before me, legs splayed, ears flat, fur bristling. His lips were curled, revealing glistening white teeth.

Coop's eyes stayed on Karsten as a low snarl rose from his throat.

"It's true." Karsten's voice trembled with rage. "You took him."

"Yes," I said evenly. "We did."

I stroked Coop's head. He remained tense, alert to Karsten's every move. Ready to strike.

"Who told you to do it?" Karsten glanced about, dropped into a chair. His yellow sneakers were splattered with mud. "Who are you working for?"

"What are you t-talking about, m-man?" Shelton stuttered with nervous agitation. "We d-don't work for an-anybody!"

"Bullshit!" Karsten's outburst shocked me. I'd never heard him use profanity. "How did you get through the doors, the locks? Don't insult my intelligence by claiming you acted alone."

"Sorry, but it's the truth." I crossed my arms. "We weren't even there for the dog. But when we found him, we had no choice."

"Then why did you break in? And how did you do it? Tell me everything. Now!"

Seeing no other option, I did.

I explained the mad-bomber monkey. The crusted dog tag. The sonicator. Stumbling upon the secret lab. Discovering the story of Katherine Heaton. Finding the skeleton. Being shot at in the dark.

Karsten was quiet for a very long time. When he spoke again, his voice was calmer.

"You actually found a body?"

"We did," Ben said.

"Katherine Heaton." I watched for a reaction. "But gunmen chased us away. On *your* island."

Karsten's eyes went far away.

"Katherine Heaton." Barely audible. "All my years on Loggerhead, she was there all the time."

I was surprised. His sadness appeared genuine.

Nevertheless, I pressed.

"You were angry we brought the police. And you have access to monkey bones. That makes you a suspect."

"Stupid girl!" The acid was back in his voice. "Katherine and I were classmates at St. Andrew's High. She was a friend, a fellow lover of science." A bony finger jabbed the air in my direction. "I was devastated by Katherine's disappearance. Don't speak of things you know nothing about!"

"I'm sorry." I was. Karsten's words rang true. "But *someone* buried Katherine Heaton on Loggerhead Island. That someone stopped us from revealing that we'd found her remains."

Karsten's eyes drifted. For a moment he seemed to debate with himself. Then he refocused.

"I have no idea. Katherine's death is a very cold case. One unlikely ever to be solved." Karsten stood. "You children have committed a serious crime. More serious than you know."

"We're not the only ones," Hi shot back. "Your twisted experiment was unauthorized."

Karsten straightened his glasses. "Is that so?"

"It is. We found proof this afternoon." I couldn't help myself. "Did you enjoy the aquarium?"

Karsten stiffened.

I poured it on.

"You don't list your sick tests on the official register." I pulled the deposit slip from my pocket. "And you've been taking money on the side. How's that work, Dr. Karsten?"

Karsten's face went ashen. His hands trembled, curled into fists.

For the first time, I felt fear. Was the man crazy? Desperate? We were alone out there, miles from help.

Instead of lashing out, Karsten removed his glasses and rubbed his eyes. When the thick lenses were repositioned, a different man peered through them.

"You're right," he said quietly.

Excuse me?

"My project *was* secret. Illegal." He inhaled deeply. Exhaled. "I pray I haven't caused irreparable damage."

"Like torturing an innocent puppy?" I demanded.

Karsten glanced at Coop. Coop growled.

"Why'd you do it?" Ben asked.

Karsten shook his head. "You wouldn't believe me."

"Try us."

"To save millions of canines from untimely deaths. To create a cure for parvo, not just a vaccine." The thin lips drew up in a humorless smile. "And yes, to make a fortune doing it."

As before, Karsten's demeanor changed without warning. His fist slammed his palm.

"I took every precaution! That door was supposed to be impenetrable. No one knew of that lab but me."

"If that was your goal, why not get approval?" Shelton asked. "Why sneak around?"

"I know why."

Eight eyes shifted to me. I could feel Karsten trying to read my mind.

"Dr. Karsten created a new virus. A dangerous experimental strain. A hybrid of canine parvo and Parvovirus B19."

Karsten appeared to shrink in on himself. "How could you possibly know that?" he whispered.

"We saw the clipboard by Coop's enclosure. You infected Coop with something called Parvovirus XPB-19." I glanced at Shelton and Hi. "Tonight we learned about a human strain called *Parvovirus B19.* Doesn't take a genius to do the math."

Defeated, Karsten didn't bother to protest.

"The names could be coincidence," I went on. "But that's not how I know."

"Then how?" he asked quietly.

"Because we caught it, Dr. Karsten. We've been infected." I spread my arms wide. "You turned us into Virals."

CHAPTER 52

"**Y**ou've been sick?" Karsten blanched. "Describe your symptoms."

He moved one yellow-sneakered foot in my direction. A growl from Coop drove him back into his chair.

"What are you experiencing?" He studied me like a bug on a pin. "Tell me! Leave nothing out."

No one spoke.

"I'm the only one who can help you," Karsten pleaded. "You must believe me. I never meant to harm anyone. You know how hard I tried to maintain security."

Right," Hi snorted. "Try changing the default code next time."

"Default? What? That code was supposed to be randomly generated!"

Ignoring him, I looked a question at the others.

"How can we trust him?" Shelton was skittish.

Karsten answered. "You're infected with a dangerous variant of parvovirus." He held up his hands. "What I did was stupid. I admit it. We're past that now. We need to make sure your lives aren't at risk."

Shelton still looked dubious. I couldn't read Hi or Ben.

Fingers steepled, Karsten spoke in a lecturing tone.

"Tory guessed correctly. I inserted DNA from canine parvovirus into the genetic code for B19. I was searching for a mechanism to weaken the canine form."

Karsten looked from face to face.

"I'll never know if the approach would have been successful. I destroyed the new strain immediately after the dog was stolen. The paperwork, too."

"Why destroy it?" I asked.

"Testing indicated the virus might have the potential to infect humans. I hadn't followed proper protocols. When I lost containment, I panicked. My credentials were at stake."

"Your credentials!?!" Hi exploded.

"Let me make this right!" Karsten practically begged.

"Let's tell him," Ben said.

A beat, then Hi and Shelton nodded.

I told Karsten about the blackouts. The nausea. The fatigue. The chills and sweats. All of it. His shoulders drooped more with each new detail.

"The blackouts have passed?" Karsten asked when I finished.

"Yes," we said.

"The flu-like symptoms? Gone as well?"

Nods all around.

Karsten let out a breath. Relieved.

I changed that.

"There are side effects."

"Side effects?"

"We call it flaring."

I explained the powers. How our senses would expand, our perceptions sharpen. The flashes of strength and speed. The glowing golden eyes.

Karsten almost slipped from his chair. We managed to catch him.

"Amazing." Karsten's head wagged from side to side. "Amazing," he repeated.

"Okay, doc," Hi said. "We're amazing. But what do we do?"

"Can you call on these abilities at will?"

"No," I said. "The flares come and go randomly."

"Probably not," Karsten said. "From your descriptions, the episodes seem to be triggered by strong sensory input. And by stress."

"What does that mean?" Shelton asked.

"I believe your powers are activated by stimulation of the limbic portion of your brains."

"Meaning?" Ben asked.

"Neuro-anatomy is very complicated." Dismissive.

"So am I."

Recognizing the menace in Ben's voice, Karsten paused to organize his thoughts.

"The limbic system contains a structure called the

hypothalamus, which regulates the autonomic nervous system via hormone production and release. The ANS affects heart rate, digestion, respiration, salivation, perspiration, pupil diameter, among other things."

"So?" Ben asked.

"I suspect the virus altered your DNA. I think that alteration caused a change in how your brains work."

My heart leapt to my throat.

Karsten continued, oblivious to the anxiety his words were creating.

"Instances of great stress set off hormonal reactions within the human body," he explained. "That's normal. But for you there seems to be a whole new level. When threatened or frightened, you experience sensory and physical capabilities consistent with the natural abilities of wolves." Karsten swallowed. "Somehow, my hybrid strain of parvovirus inserted canine DNA into your genetic blueprint."

Silence filled the room. An unearthly stillness that floated up from the bunker's subterranean passages, and rolled in from the sky, the sea, and the dunes. Our hearts hammered in unison.

When able, I spoke with what voice I could muster.

"Can you cure us?"

"I don't know," Karsten said quietly. "But you have my word. I will never stop trying."

Suddenly, Coop growled, low and menacing.

I moved between the dog and Karsten. Coop ignored me. His eyes were again locked on the bunker's entrance.

"What's up, boy?"

Coop's head whipped to me, back to the opening. His ears were flat, his muscles tense as steel. He barked three times, loud, aggressive.

Everyone froze.

Voices drifted in from outside.

Lots of them.

CHAPTER 53

"Shh!" I whispered. "Hold Coop."

I slipped through the opening and inched down the crawl. What I saw outside chilled me to the bone.

Dark figures, one holding a gun. The group stood twenty feet from the bunker, locked in heated debate.

I scuttled back inside.

"We've got company. Three. At least one is armed."

"Friends of yours?" Hi asked Karsten.

"No. I followed you"—he pointed a shaky finger at Shelton and Hi—"from the Morris dock. I have no idea who these people are."

"There's no back door." Ben clenched his fists. "No way out. We'll jump them as they crawl in."

"Are you crazy?" Shelton grabbed his ear. "They could *all* have guns!"

"What choice do we have?" Ben snapped. "We're trapped."

"What about the window?" Karsten asked.

I shook my head. "The drop-off is way too far, with nothing but rocks below."

Karsten cocked his chin toward the entrance to the back chamber. "What's in there?"

"Another window and a collapsed tunnel," Hi said.

"Tunnel?" Without hesitating, the professor disappeared through the opening.

We followed.

Karsten crossed to the abandoned passage and waved a hand over the loose planks blocking the opening.

"I feel moving air," he said. "Have you ever entered this shaft?"

"No way," Shelton said. "It could cave any time."

A male voice bellowed outside.

"All right, kids." Raspy, like gravel sliding down a drain. "Don't make us smoke you out!"

Coop growled. I looped my arm around his neck, worried he'd bolt.

"No cell reception." Shelton was frantically punching keys. "I can't keep a signal."

"If we flare, we can take these guys." Ben grabbed a plank.

"Don't be absurd! These men may be professionals." Karsten's brows crimped in thought. "Into the shaft. Now."

"They'll follow us," Ben objected. "The front entrance is a choke point. They have to enter one by one. We should ambush them there. It's our best chance."

"No arguments!" Karsten pushed me forward. "I'll stop them

here while you escape through the passage. Quick now."

I wondered why the killers hadn't stormed in yet. Perhaps they'd had the same thought as Ben. Whatever the reason, their hesitation wouldn't last long.

As Shelton and Hi pried loose and tossed aside boards, Ben rolled rocks from the tunnel's mouth. A quick minute's work created a two-foot gap.

Beyond it yawned absolute blackness.

"I'm not going down there." Shelton looked petrified. "No chance!"

"It's the only way out," I said.

"We don't know where it empties." Shelton was practically in tears. "*If* it empties. The passage could be blocked. A dead end!"

Crack!

"We're armed, little piggies," a voice bellowed. "Come out, *now*, or we'll huff, and puff and shoot your little asses!"

"Into the passage!" Karsten barked.

"What about you?"

"They don't want me." Karsten avoided my eyes. "I'll be fine."

"Thank you." I didn't contradict him. It was easier that way.

"Go," he said. "Now."

Ben wriggled through the gap. Hi followed, then Shelton. Pushing Coop in front of me, I shimmied through last.

The passage angled sharply downward. Overhead, there was barely a six-inch clearance.

I glanced behind me. Karsten was refilling the opening with debris.

"Forgive me, Tory."

The entrance went black, enveloping us in eerie gloom.

Five yards down the passage, a massive boulder blocked our way. Ben strained as he tried to muscle it aside. With Shelton and Hi's help, he managed to grind it several inches sideways.

Raised voices carried into the tunnel. Coop growled. I clamped my fingers around his snout.

Crack! Crack!

Thud.

I almost screamed.

"Over here!" Raspy Voice shouted. "There's some kind of shaft!"

I scraped past the boulder. Behind me, debris crashed as it was pulled free and tossed aside. I started to panic.

SNAP.

The darkness separated into particles that slowly drifted apart. My head throbbed.

I looked over my shoulder. Two silhouettes were straining to lift a boulder at the tunnel's mouth.

My ears picked up a faint ripping sound. I rotated my head, trying to locate a point of origin.

The noise was coming from overhead.

I looked up.

My heart went into overdrive.

Cracks were slowly spiderwebbing the roof.

Suddenly, the ripping became a rumble.

"Guys, run!"

Ahead, eight golden eyes gleamed in the darkness. Ben. Shelton. Hi. Coop.

All understood. As one, we bounded down the tunnel, clawing past fallen beams and scrambling over rocks.

The rumble exploded to a roar.

Dirt rained down in clods. Dust blinded my eyes and clogged my lungs. Tears streamed down my cheeks.

Hand cupping my mouth, I scrambled forward.

Something crashed behind me. I dropped to my knees, hacking, gasping, desperate to breathe. Dank air blasted my body as the tunnel went black.

CHAPTER 54

Blinking to clear my vision, I looked behind me.

A solid wall of earth sealed the tunnel just paces from where I knelt. We'd barely escaped the impact zone.

Utter blackness. Even flaring, I could see nothing.

"Everyone okay?" I called out.

The boys sounded off. Even Coop gave a short bark.

"Keep moving," I said. "It's one-way now."

We stumbled forward, totally focused on footing and breathing, refusing to consider the horrifying possibilities.

What if there was no way out? Would our pursuers be waiting when we emerged? What was the thud that followed the gunshots? What happened to Karsten?

Concentrate. Get out.

The tunnel forked.

"Which way?" Shelton's voice carried from the left.

"I sense fresh air coming from the right," Hi said. "I think I smell grass."

I raised my nose. Sniffed.

Hi was right. New scents had joined the mix of dust and mildew and rotting wood. Grass and wet sand.

My heart pounded against my ribs.

I was about to speak when I heard movement, a bark, then, "Oof."

"Coop votes to go right, too," Hi said. "At least, I think that's why he knocked me over."

"Do it," Ben said.

The darkness hid obstacles until they were just inches away. We picked our way along, tripping over rocks, beams, and a host of unidentifiable objects.

Triple doses of adrenaline pumped through me. My head felt too small for my brain. I reached out with my senses, probing for a way through the darkness.

Never should've listened . . . knew the roof would cave . . . can't breathe . . .

What was that?

"Shelton, did you say something?"

"No." His voice was shaky.

Puzzled, I searched for the thread I'd lost.

No use. Gone.

It *had* sounded like Shelton. I attempted to refocus.

Balance. Breathe.

Ambush at the entrance . . . could have taken these bastards . . .

I shouldn't be able to smell anything but dust . . .
Grass? I'm a freak of nature . . .

OhmyGod!

I was hearing the other Virals.

In my head.

No. Way.

I tried again. Couldn't reconnect. Couldn't reopen whatever had closed. I strained to hear their voices, came up empty. Nothing.

You're losing it, Tor.

Focus. Feet. Lungs.

Bad smell . . . danger . . . rip, tear . . . save pack . . .

Coop! I was sure of it! He wanted to protect us.

I stumbled forward, grabbed the puppy, and hugged him to my chest.

Warm . . . mother-friend . . . shield . . .

As powerfully as I could, I willed a message from my brain to his.

I'll protect you, little one. We'll be safe. I promise.

Coop yipped and nuzzled my face. I kissed the top of his head.

"What was that?" Ben had stopped moving.

"Protect who?" Shelton asked.

"Tory, that was weird." Hi. "Where are you? Are you talking to me?"

"I'm here," I said.

Had everyone heard me? I floated a test message.

I'm here, too.

"Whoa!" Shelton and Hi.

"You're in my head!" Ben sounded shocked. "Get out!"

I couldn't believe it. They could hear me! The Virals could hear me!

Then the feeling passed.

I struggled to regain it. Useless, like trying to hold onto a dream.

I floated another message.

No link up. Damn.

"What did you just do?" Hi asked.

"I don't know."

"Do it again."

"I can't."

I released Coop. He darted forward through the murk. From up ahead, I heard barking. We wove toward it like rats in a maze.

Minutes later, the darkness lifted ever so slightly. The promise of light drew us like a beacon.

Ben called out. "Ladder!"

We all rushed forward.

Above the ladder hung a square of night sky speckled with stars. A pale shaft of moonlight oozed through the opening.

A way out. I almost cried with joy.

Shelton tested, one, two, then shot up the rungs. Hi followed.

Slinging Coop over one shoulder, Ben went next. I was right on his heels, ready to catch the dog should Ben stumble.

The ladder ended in a bunker so small the five of us barely fit. Its window slit faced north, toward the harbor.

My flare was still burning.

I drank in the night air, senses blazing, terror slowly receding.

"Where are we?" Hi asked.

"Across Morris, on the Schooner Creek side." Ben was scanning the terrain. "This must be one of the sand hills."

We were perched high above the waterline, overlooking the northern tip of the island. Big pie-faced moon. With my canine vision, the landscape was lit up like high noon.

"Look!"

Shelton pointed northeast toward our clubhouse. Two hundred yards away, just off the shoreline, four men struggled to load a bundle onto a skiff.

"Jesus. Look at that bag." Hi's voice cracked.

The shape. The bulk. The way the men strained.

My front teeth clamped onto my lower lip.

As we watched, the skiff rose on a wave and the bundle lurched sideways. The men struggled to regain control. One corner of the wrapping slipped loose.

A bright yellow sneaker popped into view.

My breath caught in my throat.

Dr. Marcus Karsten.

The shots.

The dead weight hitting the floor.

No! It couldn't be true.

Karsten was the one person who had understood. The one person who might've reversed the changes that had altered our bodies.

I almost cried in despair. Karsten's death closed a door. Our last hope had been murdered.

But why? What threat did he pose? And to whom?

The men finally hauled their gruesome cargo onto the boat. An engine kicked to life. Our attackers put to sea.

We watched until the skiff disappeared over the horizon, our eyes glowing gold in the darkness.

PART FOUR:
INSIGHT

CHAPTER 55

I returned to my workstation. I'd blown it in stunning fashion.

Jason said nothing, but his jaw was tight. Hannah avoided my eyes. Across the room, Team Madison snickered and whispered.

My presentation had been a disaster. I'd stumbled through explanations, confused figures, forgotten the significance of my findings.

Even Mrs. Davis was looking at me sideways.

It was a world-class foul-up, but I found it hard to care. After the previous night's catastrophe, everything else seemed trivial.

Karsten was dead. Murdered. There was no one alive who could help us now.

Concentrate on class work? I was a mutant freak. And masked men were *hunting* me. I'd only come to school because I was afraid to stay home alone.

I hadn't said a word to Kit. How could I? We didn't have Karsten's body.

Just as we hadn't had Heaton's body.

The Virals had agreed not to repeat our earlier blunder. We were tired of adults looking at us like we were nut jobs. Or liars.

But the fact remained. Someone wanted us dead.

The knot in my gut tightened.

Why?

You know why. You found Katherine Heaton.

But why would the killer persist? The skeleton was gone. Not a soul believed our story. We had no evidence. We could identify no one.

The murderer had nothing to worry about. The Heaton case wasn't in danger of being cracked.

And yet we were targets.

I'm missing something.

Who would risk shooting four kids? It was crazy. A quadruple homicide involving Bolton Prep students would make the headlines for months. Every resource would be thrown at the investigation. The risk of capture would be enormous.

We must be forcing the killer's hand. Which meant we were getting close.

But how? We had zilch. Zip. Nada. Bupkes.

My thoughts flashed back to our confrontation with Karsten. His answers had unlocked the secret of our illness. I finally understood why my body was out of control.

A designer virus had mangled my genetic code.

Shudder.

Deep in my core, inside my cells' nuclei, wolf DNA intermingled with my own. The idea terrified me. What would come next? What if I completely lost control?

But I have powers, I reminded myself. *I can do things others can't. I can* flare.

Except I didn't understand how to turn those powers on and off. Didn't know how to use them. And Karsten could never fulfill his promise to help. Would never have a chance. He'd sacrificed his life to save ours.

We Virals were on our own.

Flying solo.

Only one course of action made sense. We had to solve Heaton's murder. Find the evidence. Expose the killers before we became their next victims. Perhaps then we'd find the answers that died with Karsten.

But time was running out.

$$\hexagon \qquad \hexagon \qquad \hexagon$$

After the final bell, I waited for Chance on the front steps. He was late.

I paced, edgy. The fingerprint was our only lead. If Chance had struck out, I was uncertain what to do next.

It was a very helpless feeling. Our pursuers were out there. Could return at any time.

Minutes dragged by. The stone lions watched, impassive.

Finally, Chance emerged from the building. A tight frown was standing in for his usual easy grin.

"Tory, I found something." He nodded to a bench down on the lawn. "Let's talk over there."

Despite my anxiety, I noted that Chance looked good. His lacrosse uniform displayed his muscles to perfect effect.

Eyes front and center. Your life might depend on his information.

"I heard back from the SLED," Chance said. "They got a hit off your print."

"Who is it?"

I flipped to a page in my spiral and poised a pen over it. Nervous sweat made the thing slide through my fingers.

"A man named James Newman. According to the SLED, Newman is a local thug with ties to crime syndicates throughout the southeast."

Chance laid his palm over my pen hand. "He's bad news, Tory. Very bad."

His touch thrilled me, but I stayed on topic. "Does the SLED know where Newman lives, or what he's been up to lately?"

"No. But apparently Newman's jacket is as thick as a phone book. Over the years he graduated from petty thefts and assaults to robbery, drug trafficking, maybe even murder." Chance's fingers tightened on mine. "This isn't someone you want to mess with over a stolen laptop. Or anything else."

"I'll just file a police report," I said. But my mind was already searching for ways to find Newman.

Chance glanced at my notes. "I won't pry into your personal

business, but I advise you to stop whatever it is you're doing. From what I've learned, this guy would never just cruise around looking for stray computers. If he was out on Morris Island, he was out there for a reason."

Too true. But I can't tell you.

"You're right," I said. "I'll forget the whole thing. No point poking a hornet's nest."

Chance gazed into my eyes, as if taking my measure. Flustered, I looked away first.

Oh-so-gently, Chance began stroking my hand. His caresses left little burn tracks on my skin.

"Please don't mess with this guy, Tory. I like you. I'd be upset if something bad happened to you."

I didn't trust myself to speak.

"I can tell you're not the type to back down. But Jimmy Newman is bad news." Chance leaned close, voice earnest. "You could get seriously hurt."

My pulsed raced.

"I promise, Chance. I'll let it go."

A smile spread across the beautiful face. God, he was gorgeous.

Before I could react Chance pulled me close, buzzed my cheek, released me.

"Smart as always."

With that, he rose and walked away.

I couldn't move.

Chance Claybourne had kissed me.

Holy smoking buckets.

CHAPTER 56

I glanced around, making sure I had the right universe.

And spotted Hi, jacket inside out, sneaking back up the steps.

Frick.

"Hold it!"

Hi straightened, slowly turned, and trudged down to my bench.

"Oh, hey." Feigned nonchalance. "Didn't see you there."

"Come *on*, Hiram." My hands found my hips. "Why the embarrassed face? What is it you *think* you just saw?"

"Not you and Chance canoodling like newlyweds, if that's what you mean." He smiled, then tsked. "Shame, shame! When good girls go bad!"

"It wasn't like that." My face burned to the tips of my ears. "Or maybe it was. I don't know." I covered my eyes and peeked through my fingers. "He started it!"

"None of my business," Hi said. "And don't worry. It's in the vault. Forgotten."

"Thank you. FYI, I'm not out to steal anyone else's boyfriend. *He* hit on *me*." Pause. "I think."

"Sure." Hi winked. "Whatever you say, TB."

Grrr.

"What did loverboy have on the print?"

I looked at my notepad, thankful to change subjects. "It was left by a guy named James Newman, a local meathead with ties to organized crime."

"Organized crime?" Hi's eyebrows plunged into a V. "That sounds unpleasant. Where does he hang?"

"We've got to find him."

"Right. The cops can't but we will."

"We have to. The guy was scoping out our activities at the library. That makes him our only lead in the Heaton case."

"I've been thinking about that." Hi dropped down beside me. "We may be going about this the wrong way. This Newman guy probably works for someone, right? *That's* who we have to find."

"Okay. How?"

"Motive," he said. "We need to find out *why* Heaton was killed."

That tracked right. And seemed safer than chasing a dangerous felon across greater Charleston.

"Then we should investigate Katherine's disappearance," I said. "Find something the cops missed back in '69."

"We already checked the newspapers," Hi said. "Where else could we look?"

I had a sudden thought.

"What about Katherine's family?"

"Her father was an orphan. And her mother died in childbirth."

"Katherine was only sixteen when Frankie Heaton was killed in Vietnam. She must've been living with someone while he was overseas."

"Maybe her mother had family?" Hi sounded dubious.

"Whoever it was, if that person's still alive, they might remember details of the day Katherine vanished."

Hi scratched his chin. "Back to the public library?"

"I've got a better idea."

○   ○   ○

"What is the DOE Network?" Hi asked.

"An organization that investigates old missing person cases." We were once again in Bolton's computer lab. "Cold ones. It's a long shot, but they might have a file on Katherine Heaton."

After logging on, I navigated to the website and entered Katherine's name. A link popped up the screen.

"Yes! She's on here."

I double-clicked to open the file. A case synopsis appeared. Barely breathing, I read the report.

"Someone named Sylvia Briggerman submitted the original missing person report."

"On it."

Hi walked to the next terminal and ran a search. "There's one Briggerman listed in the Charleston area. Centerville address, on James Island. Shall I give her a ring?"

I nodded.

Hi dialed, listened, disconnected.

"It's a retirement home. I can't get through to her room without an access code."

I looked at the clock: 3:45 p.m.

"The city bus would get us to Centerville in less than thirty minutes."

"I'm supposed to help Shelton with Cooper," Hi said. "The little guy's all alone at the new bunker we found."

"Shelton will be fine. This is more important," I said. "Briggerman might be the last person to see Katherine Heaton alive."

CHAPTER 57

The bus dropped us near James Island Park, a sleepy tangle of tree-lined paths meandering through salt marsh. We continued a quarter mile, turned south onto Riverland, then left onto a private access road.

Bordered by enormous willows, the laneway was shady and pleasantly cool. We passed slow-moving creeks and reed-covered banks, silent but for the gurgle of water and the whine of insects.

A pair of herons watched from deep in the spartina grass, long stick legs disappearing into water, avian eyes unblinking. Though Hi called to them, he got no response.

The terrain was classic Lowcountry—placid, serene, and muggy as a sauna. Despite the brackish marsh smell, I was enjoying the exercise. The insanity of the past two weeks had completely derailed my running routine. I hoped to get back on track soon.

If no one shot me first.

In minutes we reached our destination, a cluster of condo-like residences sandwiched between green-yellow swamp and the Stono River. The Shady Gardens retirement community definitely lived up to its name. The Spanish moss overhead kept the grounds in perpetual dusk.

When we drew close, the front doors slid open with a hiss. The smell of air conditioning and hand sanitizer rolled over us.

We approached a desk and asked for Sylvia Briggerman.

Roadblock.

Roberta Parrish wore a white nurse's uniform and brass nametag. Her hair was a shade of orange straight out of a bottle. Drugstore lashes crawled her lids like hairy little centipedes.

On seeing us, Parrish flashed a false smile.

"Visiting hours just ended," she said. The centipedes fluttered. "I'm afraid you'll have to come back tomorrow."

"Is there any chance we could see Sylvia today?" I asked. "I hate to be a bother, but we took the bus all the way from downtown."

Parrish shook her head, lips locked in the up position. "As you know, Ms. Briggerman suffers from dementia. We mustn't disturb her routine."

"I completely understand, ma'am." Very polite. "But we only need a few minutes."

"Are you family?"

Hi cut in. "Yes ma'am. And we *never* get to see Great-Auntie Syl." He turned to me. "I *told* Dad she should be closer to the city. It's too hard to visit out here."

That got Parrish's attention.

"Now, now! No need to fret. I just had to make sure you were kinfolk." She glanced at the clock. "I'm sure we can squeeze in a quick visit."

"Gee, thanks!" Hi beamed. "I can see why our parents picked this place."

Parrish led us from the main building to a row of suites facing the river. I could tell she was trying to hide her annoyance.

"We're going to hell for this," I hissed. "What if *Great-Auntie Syl* blows our cover?"

"She's got dementia," Hi whispered. "She won't know the difference."

"That's horrible."

"People in these places love to have visitors. Even from fake relatives."

"Like I said. To hell."

"We'll do something nice. Fill her ice trays, or fluff her pillows." Hi shrugged. "We're trying to solve a murder, for Pete's sake. I think she'll forgive us."

"Here we are." Parrish knocked on a bright blue door. "Sylvia, dear! Visitors!"

The door opened.

Sylvia Briggerman stood no more than five feet tall and wore an outfit that would have made Lucille Ball proud. I guessed her age at somewhere north of eighty.

"What's that?" Sylvia's eyes looked enormous behind thick bifocals. "Guests?"

"Your grandniece and grandnephew are here." Parrish spoke

slowly and loudly. "They've come to visit. From the city."

"I don't have a nephew."

Great. We were sooo busted.

Then Sylvia's face brightened. "Katherine?"

Oh, God. No.

This was too cruel. I couldn't do it.

Hi nudged my back. Nudged again. Toe-kicked my heel.

"Yes, Aunt Sylvia." I burned with shame. "I'm here. You remember me, don't you?"

"Of course. Silly!" Sylvia turned to Parrish. "Don't keep my niece on the doorstep. Show her and her little friend in."

Parrish waved us forward.

"I'm sure she'll know you," Parrish whispered as Hi passed her. "Her memory comes and goes."

Hi nodded solemnly. "Thanks. You're doing a wonderful job. I'll let my parents know."

It was official. We were terrible people.

"I'll return in a few minutes." Parrish closed the door quietly.

Sylvia's living room was an eye-stunning canary yellow. Bookcases lined one wall and a reading machine occupied one corner. Standard come-as-a-group sofa and chairs. Coffee table. TV, probably built when Lucy was big. Fake flowers on every horizontal surface.

The old woman sat on the plastic-covered couch and arranged her skirt. When she looked up, her eyebrows rose in surprise.

"Hello? Can I help you?"

"Hello, Ms. Briggerman." No more lies. "My name is Tory

Brennan. This is my friend Hiram. We came about your niece, Katherine."

"Oh." Sylvia tugged down the sleeves of her gown. "Where is Katherine? I haven't seen her today."

"We're not sure," I said carefully. "We're also looking for her."

True, as far as it went.

"She stays busy, that one." Sylvia smiled. "Always on the beach. She plans to go to college, you know. To study ecology. I'm not sure what that is, but I'm certain Frankie would have been proud."

"Frankie is your brother?" Hi half-asked. "I thought he grew up at the Orphan House?"

"Well of course he did, young man. So did I."

Sylvia pointed to a black-and-white photo hanging over the bookcase. A boy and girl stood by a swing set, dressed in worn but well-patched clothing. The girl was slightly older, and held the little boy's hand. Both smiled like it was Christmas morning.

"Frankie and I aren't blood-related, but we grew up together just the same. That was good enough for us. Katherine *always* calls me Aunt Syl."

"What was Katherine doing when you last saw her?"

"She's working on her science project," Sylvia replied. "The one she and Abby have to do for school." A frown deepened wrinkles crossing the bridge of her nose. "I hope Katherine arrives soon. She shouldn't miss dinner."

"Who is Abby?" I hoped Sylvia's mind hadn't tiptoed into another time.

"Abby Quimby is Katherine's best friend. Haven't you met her?

They do *everything* together."

Hi tried a new tack. "What beach did Katherine like? Might she have gone there for her project?"

The watery blue eyes seemed to lose focus. Several seconds passed. Finally, "Hello? Can I help you?"

"Hello, Ms. Briggerman." I smiled brightly. "We were talking about Katherine."

"Katherine's not here."

I looked at Hi. Time to go. He nodded.

"Thank you so much for your time, ma'am." I said. "Is there anything you need before we leave?"

"Could you do one thing for me?" With surprising agility the old woman rose and shuffled from the room. Hi and I exchanged glances. He shrugged. Moments later she returned carrying a light blue sweater.

"Please give this to Katherine when you see her. It's her favorite. I don't want her to catch cold."

What to do? I couldn't take the sweater. But how to give it back?

I felt terrible lying to this woman. She couldn't recall that her beloved niece had vanished years ago. The whole thing broke my heart.

My gut clenched. Tears threatened.

I needed to escape.

Now.

SNAP.

Electricity fired through me. My eyes watered, burned, flashed golden. My senses kicked into hyperdrive.

Hi noticed my eyes and stepped forward to block Sylvia's view.

"Ms. Briggerman, how are you set for ice cubes? We'd better check your trays."

"Ice cubes?"

Hi guided a confused Sylvia into the kitchen.

A clock ticked a thundering metronome. The refrigerator roared from the next room

On instinct, I held Katherine's sweater to my nose. Inhaled deeply.

At first, just wool and dust. Then, from deep within the folds, a delicate blend of aromas. Shampoo. Perspiration. Clearasil.

A vague image formed in my brain.

Dissolved.

I filed the impressions away for later consideration.

Knock knock.

"Okay, kids." Parrish was at the door. "Time for Sylvia to rest."

SNUP.

The flare passed. My head cleared.

But the distinctive smell of Katherine's sweater had burrowed into my brain.

I caught Hi's eye, tipped my head toward the door.

"Bye, Auntie Syl!" he said loudly. "We'll come back soon!"

Sylvia resumed her seat and spread the long, satin skirt out around her. Without acknowledging our departure, she leaned back, closed her eyes, and began to snore.

I left the sweater beside her.

○   ⬡   ○

On the bus ride home, I searched for Abby Quimby on my iPhone, found two listings.

I keyed in the first number. Disconnected.

I tried the second.

A woman picked up on the third ring.

"Abby Quimby?"

"Yes." More curious than wary.

I wasted no time.

"Katherine Heaton?" Quimby sounded shocked. "I haven't heard that name in forty years. Dear God, has she been found?"

"I'm sorry, no." I hated lying, but had to be careful. "I'm updating cold cases for the DOE network. I thought you might have information we could use."

"I'd love to help, but I told the police everything I knew. The day she disappeared, Katherine and I were supposed to meet for lunch. She never showed."

"Sylvia Briggerman told me you were working on a science project together."

"Yes." Quimby paused. "You know, I don't think I mentioned the science project in my statement. No one ever asked, and it didn't seem important."

"Please tell me what you remember."

"Our assignment was to do an ecological survey," Quimby said. "Simple stuff, really. But Katherine and I wanted to study an endangered species. It was 1969, and the whole conservation movement was just picking up steam. Katherine was scouting the beaches, looking for possibilities."

"Do you know where she'd planned to go the day she went missing?"

"Oh my goodness!" Quimby's voice rose. "The Morris Lighthouse. I'd forgotten that. I can recall it so clearly now. I'm not sure if I told that to the officer who interviewed me or not. At the time, I was very upset."

My pulse quickened. The Morris Lighthouse wasn't mentioned in the missing person report.

"Wasn't that lighthouse decommissioned by '69?" I asked.

"Yes. It had been replaced by the one on Sullivan's Island. Katherine wanted to see which bird species were nesting there."

I thought a moment. The Morris Lighthouse stood on a sandbar, which, even at low tide, was a short distance offshore.

"How did Katherine plan to get out to the lighthouse?"

"She kept a little kayak in the back of her van." Pause. "That's what made her disappearance so suspicious. If she'd capsized and drowned, her van should still have been parked wherever she left it."

"It wasn't?"

"No. And it was never found."

I waited, hoping she'd elaborate. She did.

"Wait." The excitement drained from Quimby's voice. "It's all coming back. The police checked the lighthouse during the search. They found nothing."

"Do you know if Katherine actually went there?"

"No."

Silence hummed across the line.

"You know, Katherine *did* find a species that interested her. Not that it matters now, bless her heart."

"What species?" I asked.

"I have no earthly clue. Katherine left a message with my mother, but no details. Then she vanished."

"Might anyone else know?"

"I doubt it." Quimby gave a self-deprecating laugh. "We were going to be famous biologists. We kept our big ideas secret." Pause. "After Katherine vanished, I was excused from school for a few weeks. The project never crossed my mind again."

More silence. Then, "I wish someone had found Katherine's notebook."

"Notebook?" My ears perked up.

"Katherine always recorded her thoughts. She took her journal everywhere. If she'd found something, she'd have written about it in her notebook."

I'd run out of questions.

"Thank you, Ms. Quimby. We'll add this information to Katherine's file."

"Sorry I couldn't tell y'all more." Quimby sighed. "The police searched *everywhere.* Never found a thing."

"You've been very helpful," I said. "Thanks again." I gave her my number. "Please call if you remember anything else."

"I will. And let me know if there are any new developments."

"Of course."

"Well?" Hi asked when I'd disconnected.

I recapped the entire conversation.

"The science project stuff is new," I said. "The police didn't know about it back in '69."

"It's pretty thin." Hi scratched his chin. "We know Heaton was searching the beaches for endangered species. The police may not have known that, but according to news reports, the search focused on marshes and shorelines anyway."

"I know. But it's the only information the cops didn't have. They didn't know Katherine was looking for something specific."

"So what's our next move?"

Quimby had given us a single lead.

"The lighthouse," I said. "Maybe we'll stir up a ghost."

CHAPTER 58

"Why go out there now?" Shelton, as usual, was nervous. "The thing is falling apart."

We'd gathered aboard *Sewee*, at the Morris Island dock. Our bunker was out. Too risky. Ben and Shelton had settled Coop into the ladder bunker, the best we could do for now. I hoped he wouldn't wander too far.

"Katherine might've gone to the lighthouse," I said. "That could be where she was attacked."

"But her body was buried on Loggerhead," Ben said. "*We* know that, even if no one believes us. Who cares if she stopped by the old lighthouse?"

"According to Abby Quimby, Katherine recorded everything she did. If we recover her notebook we might get the answers we need."

"We're going to find a forty-year-old journal?" Ben was way

beyond dubious. "You can't be serious. Anyway, the police checked the lighthouse."

"They didn't know about Katherine's plans," I argued. "Maybe they didn't look very hard. Maybe they missed something important."

"Weak," Shelton said. "This lead is way slimmer than a needle in a haystack."

"It's the only idea I've got, " I said. "Unless you want to chase down a trigger-happy ex-con."

"We should go to the police," Shelton said. Again. "Tell our parents about Karsten's murder. They'll have to believe us when he turns up missing."

"The cops don't trust us," Ben said. "We cried wolf once, remember? And while we screw around debating this, the killers could find us again."

"We can be to the lighthouse and back in a hour," Hi said. "Why not just cross it off the list?"

"Sold." Ben fired up the engine.

The Morris Lighthouse rises like a decrepit old sentinel off the island's southern tip. The sandbar on which it stands is often submerged, so the sea occasionally floods its ground floor. Wind and rain have stripped away most of its paint.

It was high tide, so Ben motored directly to the base of the tower.

I ran my eyes up 160 feet of crumbling stone, a bleak, solitary spike surrounded by ocean on all sides. Dark and empty, the structure seemed to brood. Resentful at being abandoned? At losing its battle with the elements?

It's the most depressing thing ever, I thought.

"It's big," I said. My understatement of the year.

Hi nodded. "When did they build this monster?"

"1876." Shelton had a book on Carolina lighthouses. Of course. "This lighthouse replaced an older one destroyed during the Civil War. And *that* one replaced an even older one constructed in 1673."

"Does the light still work?"

"Nope," Shelton said. "They shut it down in '62. When they originally built this baby, it was on dry land, but the water level has been creeping up ever since."

"So now she stands alone in the sea." Hi whistled. "Freaky."

"There used to be a keeper's residence. They tore that down in the thirties when the light became automated."

"Who owns it?" I asked.

"The state," Shelton said. "Some non-profit is hoping to restore the whole thing, but for now it's closed to the public."

"Which means we make this quick," Ben said. "I'm not getting busted for trespassing."

Conservationists had recently installed a steel cofferdam around the lighthouse to protect it from rising tides. The circular barrier looked like a giant metal coffee filter sticking eight feet up from the sea. Inside, the water had been drained to its previous level.

Ben anchored *Sewee* alongside the cofferdam. We pulled ourselves up onto the rim and followed the single catwalk to the base of the lighthouse. Up a short brick stairway, and we reached the entrance.

A large sign read: Danger: No Trespassing.

Big bold letters. Not an inch of wiggle room.

The wind whipped my hair and clothing as I stood watching Shelton pick the padlock. I wished I'd brought a jacket.

Finally, the prongs popped free and we trooped inside.

The ground floor looked like the bottom of a birdcage. One that hadn't been cleaned in ages. Sticks. Feathers. Gallons of bird poop. The harsh stench of ammonia was almost overwhelming.

"What's that?" Shelton was eyeballing a pair of gray cable boxes attached to the tower wall. Wires ran from their ends and branched to cover fissures in the stonework.

"Strain gauges. Probably monitoring cracks to make sure they don't grow." Hi pointed out two more of the devices. "They're also monitoring how much the tower leans. An early warning system in case the whole shebang decides to topple."

"Comforting," said Ben.

A rusty metal staircase spiraled up the tower's interior. Tipping my head back, I looked straight up. The stairs cut through the ceiling, a hundred feet above me.

"Let's climb," I said.

"Is it safe?" Shelton pushed with both hands against the wall. "It feels like I could shove the whole thing over."

"This lighthouse has been standing for a century," Hi said. "I think it can handle a few teenagers. Even a fat one like me."

"Come on, we don't have all day," Ben said.

He began climbing. His shoes made soft clanging sounds. Particles of rust cascaded to the ground.

The rest of us followed in single file: me, Shelton, Hi.

Circling upward, I passed long narrow windows without any glass. Birds darted from the weathered sills, startled by the invasion.

By the time I reached the top, I was sucking wind.

Note to self: break out the running shoes.

The stairs ended inside a small round chamber. This floor was heaped with old bird's nests, broken eggshells, and windblown debris. Several inhabitants cawed loudly before winging out the window.

"It stinks like a chicken coop in here," Ben complained.

"This is the watch room." Shelton's hand covered his nose. "Machines in here used to rotate the lantern above."

"Where does this lead?" Hi had crossed to a staircase on the chamber's far side.

"The lens room should be one level above us." Shelton pointed to an opening halfway up the stairs. "You can reach the main gallery through there. Not me though."

Three blank looks.

"The gallery is a steel balcony that circles the tower," Shelton explained.

"Cool!" I climbed to the opening and stepped outside.

My breath caught in my throat.

The sun was low, throwing pink and yellow rays across a blue-green ocean. Below me, the coast met the sea like a crumbled linen tablecloth. I could see our tiny community on Morris, beyond that Fort Sumter and Sullivan's Island.

To my left, the town of Folly Beach looked like a string of Monopoly houses crawling the beach. Here and there, a window or porch light glowed yellow in the rosy dusk.

I glanced up over my shoulder. The lighthouse was topped by a giant metal birdcage rising into an iron dome. The space inside was vacant. Gulls watched from the ironwork, wary of my unwelcome presence.

I imagined the powerful beam that had once sliced the darkness, guiding sailors safely to Charleston Harbor. It must've been an awesome sight.

Hi and Ben emerged onto the walkway.

"Whoa." Ben gazed down at his runabout bobbing far below. His face lost its color.

"Shelton, check this out," Hi called.

"Thanks, but I'm not falling to my death today."

"Your loss."

I circled the tower, taking in the panorama. Trespassing or not, I could've stayed forever.

"We should go." Ben's forehead was damp. He avoided looking down. "There's nothing here, and another boat could cruise by any time."

"One more area to check," I said.

Ducking inside, I hustled up to the lens room. Smaller than

the one below, this chamber had barely enough footage to turn around. The iron framework rose above me, glassless, open to the sky.

No furniture. No equipment. Dozens of angry gulls. I didn't linger.

"Time to give up?" Hi asked.

I nodded. We'd looked carefully. The tower was an empty shell. This trip was a failure.

With exaggerated groans, the boys began the long descent.

What a waste, I thought. We were no closer to solving Katherine's murder than when we started. The killers were still in the clear.

I paused, watching the tops of the boys' heads spiral down the stairs.

It was stupid to think we could make a difference. That a bunch of teenage brainiacs could outsmart a murderer. Our adversary had probably been laughing the whole time.

Score another win for bad guys everywhere.

My fists clenched as my frustration boiled like a kettle. I was angry enough to spit.

SNAP.

The bird stink almost knocked me off my feet. I couldn't think, couldn't breathe. Gagging, I held my breath, desperate for fresh air.

Without thinking, I scrambled back out onto the gallery, desperate to escape the noxious fumes.

Outside, I gulped oxygen in huge gasps. Too quickly. Spots

danced before my eyes. My vision expanded, then retreated down a long, black tunnel.

Terrified of falling, I sat down on the balcony, hands clamped on the railing.

Deep breath. Two. Three. Four.

Slowly my mind unscrambled. My head cleared, and the darkness receded. I glanced out over the water.

"Wow."

The world lay before me in immaculate detail. I could see the smallest objects with laser precision. Particles of vapor making up clouds. Water droplets hanging above foam-topped waves. A worm wiggling in the mouth of a sparrow. My own bedroom window.

My gaze flew across the harbor to Charleston itself. Lights now twinkled everywhere. Soft yellow rectangles in the homes along the Battery. Neon orange and blue strips near the old market. A stoplight changing from yellow to red.

Through the acrid ammonia, my nostrils picked up millions of other scents. Salt. Algae. Rotting vegetation. Diesel fuel.

And something else. New. Familiar.

I raised my chin. Sniffed.

There. That direction. Trickling from the watch room.

I crawled to the opening, poked my head inside, and sniffed. The odor flickered in and out, barely perceptible beneath the cloying stench of refuse.

With a jolt, I recognized the newcomer. Something I'd smelled only once before.

Excited now, I drew air through my nostrils. The reek of bird poop watered my eyes. I wiped away tears, tracing, hunting, pinpointing.

The smell was coming from the floor beside the small balcony staircase. If I hadn't sat right where I was, I might never have noticed.

I scurried inside and began clawing away leaves and turds. Bird crud coated my fingers and jammed under my nails. I fought the urge to puke.

Six inches down, I uncovered a steel grate in the floor, clogged with years of debris.

A noise startled me.

My head whipped around.

"Tory, what are you doing?" Ben was panting and his face was red. "I had to climb all the way back up."

SNUP.

I blinked. Shook my head.

"Shoot. I lost my flare."

"You were *flaring* up here? Why?"

"It just happened. Help me lift this. I smelled something underneath."

Ben didn't argue. Together we pried the grate loose. Beneath was more garbage. I dug with my hands, sifted through God-knows-what.

My fingers closed on something solid. Heart pounding, I dragged the object into the light.

The remains of a knapsack. Faded green. Caked with years of salt and dried slime.

Half the canvas had rotted away, but I could make out letters embroidered on the flap: K. A. H.

"How 'bout that, Blue?" I leaned back against the wall.

"I'll be damned." Ben shook his head in wonder. "You did it, Tory. You found Heaton's pack."

CHAPTER 59

All the way home, I was totally jazzed.

I'd done it! Against all odds, I'd found Katherine Heaton's backpack.

All it took was a little flare.

I giggled at my own wit.

Finding something of Katherine's had lifted my spirits. It felt impossible, like I'd reached back through time. If you thought about it, that wasn't far from the truth.

The sun slipped from sight as we cut across the waves. The sky faded to indigo and the stars ventured out for a peek. A lone pelican took wing, either preparing to bed down or heading into the night for one last snack. On evenings like this, I love the Carolinas.

I drank in my surroundings, heady with confidence. *We can do this*, I thought. *We can solve this mystery.*

Despite my euphoria, I'd shown self-control. I hadn't so much as peeked inside the backpack. We had to be careful. Katherine's bag hadn't been opened in over forty years. Who knew what condition the journal was in?

Or if it was even there.

Of course it would be there. I didn't climb a gazillion stairs, gag, sift through filth, and uncover something lost since the first moon landing, only to come up short. No way, José.

We reached the Morris dock just as full night took charge. I stood with Katherine's stinky bag hugged to my chest, waiting while the boys fixed the lines. Growing impatient. It was time to unwrap this bad boy.

"Where to now?" I asked.

"My place," Shelton said. "Pops converted our garage into a workshop. He takes computers apart, so he's got tweezers, gloves, that kind of stuff. Plus my parents went to see *La Bohème* in town. They won't be back for hours."

Ben glanced at my scum-covered arms. "Does it have a sink? A hose?"

Ha ha.

"Perfect," I said. "Lead the way."

"Not a chance," said Shelton.

"Clean up," said Hi.

"Now," said Ben. "We'll wait."

I stuck out my tongue, but hurried home to scrub up.

Each unit on Morris has a single-car garage. Neither of the senior Devers ever parks in theirs. The walls are lined with metal shelving. Plastic containers cram every inch, carefully labeled, holding an oddball assortment of screws, wires, plugs, cables, adapters, and circuit boards. Nelson's workshop looks like a RadioShack jammed into a phone booth.

Ten minutes later I joined the boys there, freshly showered, neatly changed, and raring to go. They were clustered around a drawing table. True to their promise, the backpack lay untouched.

My dirt-free attire got a round of applause. Ben whistled.

"Much better," Shelton proclaimed.

"I don't know." Hi pooched out his lips. "The avian excrement added a certain *je ne sais quoi.*"

"Very funny," I said.

"Sir." Shelton stepped aside with a bow. "I yield to your superior skills with scientific protocol."

"Why, thank you," said Hi. "Now let's please open this thing."

Hi positioned a magnifying lamp over the parcel. Fluorescent light bathed the tabletop.

"You *smelled* this bag?" Shelton still couldn't believe it. "Under a floor grate? Through a half foot of bird crap?"

"What can I say?" I shrugged. "I sniffed Katherine's sweater in Sylvia's apartment, then picked up the same scent in the tower. I was flaring both times."

"Amazing," Shelton said. "I wanna try that. Sounds awesome."

"Believe me, it didn't *smell* awesome. Bird funk nearly killed me." But I had to admit, my bloodhound act excited me. These flares might be useful after all. *Very* useful.

"Ready?" I asked.

"Ready." Pulling on a pair of latex gloves, Hi reached inside the crusty pack. A smile spread over his face. He carefully removed a crumbling notebook.

My heart leapt. Success! Unbelievably, we'd found a clue the police had missed.

I'd found it, thank you very much.

The journal's cover was cracked, its pages rippled and swollen. When Hi lifted a corner, dirt poured from its spine.

"Careful," I scolded. "The paper is disintegrating."

"You think I don't know that?" Hi set the notebook down, gently raised and jostled the bag. Out came a pencil and a barrette. Nothing else.

"Can you read it?" I crowded close, anxious to see if the journal's pages were intact.

"Back it up!" Hi shooed me with gloved hands. "I can't work like this."

Reluctantly, I retreated a step. Inched forward again.

Using tweezers, Hi teased the front cover open.

Nature had taken a devastating toll. Rainwater. Salt spray. Bird droppings. The abuse had rendered the entries indecipherable.

Hi leafed carefully, a page at a time. Nothing was legible.

The air slowly leaked from the room. It seemed impossibly cruel, that we could locate Heaton's notebook after forty years, yet be unable to read a single word she'd written.

"Here's something." Hi sounded excited. "Look!"

He'd reached the very back of the notebook. The last two sheets were better preserved than the overlying ones.

Hi was pointing at what appeared to be a sketch of a bird. The caption underneath was too smeared to read.

"What *is* that?" Shelton was tipping his head from side to side. "Robin? Woodpecker?"

"Eagle," Ben said with conviction.

"How can you be sure?" I squinted at the wavy lines, barely visible on the stained page. It looked like any old bird to me.

"The body is uniformly shaded, but the head and tail are white," Ben said. "And look at the beak. The talons. That's a bald eagle."

"Why was Heaton drawing eagles?" Shelton asked.

"Who knows?" Ben said. "Maybe she was super-patriotic."

"There's writing on the back of the page." Hi squinted. "I think I can make it out."

Peering through the magnifier, he read aloud:

I found them! A bald eagle colony! Three enormous nests, way up in a stand of longleaf pines, just off the Stono River. Who would've guessed that bald eagles were living on Cole Island? An endangered species, right on our doorstep! This is perfect for our science project. Abby will be thrilled! The University will probably send people to study—

The rest of the entry had washed away.

"Bald eagle." Ben pumped his fist. "Told you."

"Cole Island?" Shelton's face scrunched in thought. "There aren't any bald eagles on Cole Island. Hell, there aren't any *trees* on Cole, much less eagles. The only thing out there is a factory."

"This was written in 1969," Hi reminded him. "Things have

changed since then. Some moron probably clear-cut the trees."

Data bytes connected in my brain.

"Oh no." My hands flew to my mouth. "Oh damn!"

"What's wrong?" Hi asked.

Ben and Shelton just stared.

"Don't you guys see?" It all made sense. Brutal, tragic sense.

"See what?" Ben asked.

"I know why Katherine Heaton was killed."

You could have heard the proverbial pin drop.

For a moment I was overwhelmed by the terrible truth I'd discovered. I couldn't speak.

"Well?" Hi crossed his arms. "Enlighten us, Agent Scully."

"Katherine found an endangered species on Cole Island," I said. "And not just *any* species. She found bald freaking eagles! The symbol of America."

"So?" All three at once.

"Heaton's discovery would've been a *big* deal," I said. "It was the hippie sixties. Everyone was suddenly into saving the Earth. Protecting habitats was a hot topic."

"But that's a *good* thing." Shelton was clearly perplexed. "I don't follow."

I paced, thinking out loud. "Maybe someone was unhappy to learn that an endangered species was living on Cole Island."

"An eagle colony would cause problems if the owners wanted to develop the land," Ben said. "Displacing or killing the birds would cause mucho bad press."

"Or maybe the birds were being raised illegally," Shelton

suggested. "It's against the law to own or sell a bald eagle without a permit."

"And killing an eagle is a crime," I said. "The law even protects their nests."

"Guys," Hi interrupted. "I found more writing. Last page. There's an entry at the top, then some chicken scratch at the bottom."

I tapped Hi's shoulder. He screwed his mouth sideways, but stepped back. I moved to the table and read to the group:

Only two more places to survey. Maybe I'll find more eagles? That'd be groovy! But then I'm done. Some guy has been showing up everywhere I go. I've never seen him before. He gives me the creeps. Maybe I've spent too much time on remote beaches! Kiawah Island, then the Morris Light. Then, sayonara!

"Oh, Lord." Hi looked sick. "Oh, God. That's awful."

"She was being followed," I whispered, overwhelmed by sadness. "Why didn't she go straight home?"

"What about the last part?" Ben asked. "At the bottom?"

"It's harder to make out." I repositioned the lamp. "Looks like the same hand, but shakier."

I read the short entry to myself. Read it again.

This time I couldn't stop them. Tears overran my lower lids and rolled down my cheeks.

"And?" Hi asked.

I didn't reply.

"Tory?" Shelton's hand found my shoulder. "What does it say?"

I stepped aside. The others watched me, confused. Then Shelton moved to the table and read aloud:

I think someone is below. I don't know who it is, but I'm afraid. No one should be out here but me. I'm going to stash my journal just in case. Maybe I can hide.

My mind went numb with grief. I closed my eyes. No good. I kept seeing those final words written by that trembling hand.

I heard Ben punch the wall. Hi shift his feet. Shelton lift a hand to his earlobe. I was aware of these things, but apart. Adrift.

I imagined Katherine's final moments as she scribbled that last terrified entry. I saw her rush to hide the journal, then turn to face her stalker. I felt her despair as she realized she was trapped high atop a deserted lighthouse. Alone. With no way out.

Katherine Heaton was murdered in the loneliest place on earth.

I palmed tears from my face, devastated, revolted. The scene in my head was so real, it seemed I was there.

I didn't want to cry. I wanted to cry forever.

Then, I got angry. White-hot furious.

Okay. Go with it. Rage will work better than grief.

I despised whoever had done this. A soulless monster walked the streets free, thinking he'd gotten away with it. Callous. Smug. Untroubled by guilt.

I renewed my vow to Katherine. To myself. *I will catch this killer. Expose him. Bring him to justice.*

Make him pay.

CHAPTER 60

I woke early the next morning, on fire with an idea.

First things first.

Cooper.

A ten-minute hike brought me to Morris Island's western shore. I checked my bearings, located the ladder bunker, and climbed inside.

Coop yelped when he saw me, tail wagging out of control. Popping up on his back paws, he tried to lick my face.

I snuggled his head, drank in his warm puppy smell. Then I grabbed his rope and challenged him to a tug o' war. He accepted with vigor.

For a few minutes, my problems receded. Coop was bigger now, strong enough to roam free. Thankfully, he restricted himself to the uninhabited western side of the island. No one in our neighborhood had reported sighting a stray wolfdog. Yet.

Coop needed a permanent home, pronto.

"Soon," I promised. "You won't be stuck out here forever."

I wanted to stay longer, but there wasn't time. I slipped out while the puppy was wolfing down his breakfast.

It was going to be another hot one. Halfway back to the compound, I was sweating up a storm.

I buzzed the other Virals as soon as my phone caught a signal. We met on the front lawn.

"Whose parents aren't home?" I asked.

Hi raised a hand. "Mine went to temple. They'll be gone until noon."

"Then we'll use your computer."

"What do we need to research?" Shelton asked.

"Who held title to Cole Island in 1969. Maybe the owner knew about the eagles, or at least can tell us who had access to the island. It's a start."

"Good idea," Shelton said. "We can use the PIS."

"PIS?" Hi asked. "What's that? Online dating for nerds?"

"Hilarious. I'm talking about the county's Property Information System. Land records are accessible there. You can get information about deeds, property lines, whatever. The owners of Cole Island should be listed."

"Then the floor is yours," I said.

We hustled up to Hi's bedroom.

"Hold on a sec." Hi pushed aside books, dishes, and piles of dirty clothes, trying to make room for all of us to sit. "Make yourselves at home."

"You're a pig." Ben held up a greasy plate. "This pizza must be nine weeks old."

"I've been looking for that!" Hi winged the slice into his wastebasket. "It's probably still good, but why take a chance?"

"Gross." Ben moved to the other side of the room.

"Sir, I apologize. I wasn't expecting company this morning. You're free to find other accommodations."

"Come on," I said. "We don't have all day."

"Yes, ma'am." Hi saluted. "Right away, ma'am."

Hi booted his Mac, then moved aside.

Shelton pulled up the Charleston County home page and selected "View a parcel." A black-and-white map appeared on the screen.

"This is a blueprint of the Charleston area," Shelton explained. "It shows every property line."

"Cole Island is southwest of Folly," I said. "On the Stono River Inlet."

"I'll zoom that area." Shelton magnified until individual parcels appeared. Cole Island remained one undivided block.

"Cole is a single piece of real estate," Shelton said. "I'll access the owner data."

He clicked and property information appeared on the right side of the screen.

"Bingo!" Then Shelton whistled. "You're not going to like this, Tory."

"Won't like what?"

"Cole Island is currently owned by Candela Pharmaceuticals,

Inc." His eyes found mine. "Ring any bells?"

"That's the outfit that funded Karsten's experiment," I said. "Someone at Candela wrote the checks to him."

"What could Karsten's secret parvo research have to do with bald eagles?" Hi asked.

"Or Katherine Heaton?" Ben added.

"Candela must own the factory out on Cole Island," Shelton said.

"Why would I not like that?" I asked.

"I wasn't finished," Shelton said. "I paused for dramatic effect."

"Out with it," Ben said.

"Guess who sold Cole Island to Candela?"

"Who?" I asked.

"Hollis Claybourne." Shelton tapped the screen. "And it looks like he made a bundle."

"Claybourne?" Ben scowled. "Are you talking about Chance's father?"

"The very same," Shelton said. "State Senator H. P. Claybourne, father of Bolton Prep's golden boy. And it gets worse. Guess *when* Hollis made the sale."

"When?" I had a bad feeling.

"January 4, 1970. Just a few months after Katherine Heaton disappeared."

"Shady," Hi said. "Heaton drops off the map, then Hollis sells the island."

"That proves nothing," I said. "It could be coincidence."

Damn. That word again.

"It's suspicious," Shelton said. "Last night I searched the net, and didn't find a single mention of eagles ever living on Cole Island. Obviously, they were never reported."

I scrambled to make sense of things.

Chance Claybourne's father, Hollis, owned Cole Island at the time Katherine Heaton was doing her school project. Katherine found bald eagles nesting on Cole. Soon thereafter, Katherine vanished. Months later, Hollis Claybourne sold Cole Island to Candela Pharmaceuticals. For boatloads of money.

What did it all mean?

"Can we learn more about Candela?" I asked.

"I'll check the corporate records database." Shelton's fingers flew over the keys. "Bull's-eye! Candela is registered in South Carolina. I can pull the filing documents."

"That one." I pointed to a PDF file. "Article of Amendment, dated January 5, 1970. That's one day after Candela purchased Cole Island."

Hi clicked to open the record. "Wow. This adds Hollis Claybourne as an officer and puts him on the Candela board of directors. They made him a vice president."

"So Hollis sold Cole Island to Candela, and the next day they gave him a management job," Hi said. "Sweet deal."

"And no one ever reported the eagles," said Ben.

"The eagles which are now gone," I said.

"Replaced by a stupid factory." Shelton's lip curled in disgust. "What a bunch of jerks."

Ben crossed his arms. "The Claybournes are involved in Heaton's murder somehow."

"Chance wasn't even born yet." For some reason I felt compelled to defend him. "And we can't prove that the land sale connects to Katherine's murder."

"I sure hope Chance doesn't know anything," Hi said. "Because he analyzed our fingerprint. He could be playing us."

Frick. Good point.

I put my hands to my temples. "Let me think this through."

The boys rolled their eyes, but clammed up. They'd seen my concentration trick before. Eyes closed, I shut out the world. Focused on the variables. Ran the data.

Slowly, my brain gave me output.

I didn't like it, but the logic was inescapable.

"Ben may be right."

He raised the roof. I ignored him.

"So . . . Hollis kills Katherine to stop her from reporting the eagles," I mused. "Then he sells Cole Island to Candela for a ton of cash and a cushy new job. Heaton is buried where no one will find her. No one ever learns about the birds."

I poked at the theory. Prodded. Turned it this way and that in my head.

Then I nodded. "It's logical. But this all happened a long time ago. Chance wouldn't know anything."

"Don't forget about the checks to Karsten," Hi added. "Hollis is a bigwig at Candela. He might know about the secret parvo experiment."

"So you guys think Hollis Claybourne is the one trying to kill us?" Shelton asked. "That those were his men at the bunker?"

"It all adds up," I said. "Everything we know points to him."

"But he's a millionaire. A state senator." Shelton removed his glasses and wiped them on his shirt. "Why would he need to kill anybody, then or now?"

"No idea," I said. "But this all started when we found Katherine's bones. Only her murderer would be after us. And Hollis *does* have the resources to hire goons for his dirty work."

I didn't want to believe it. Chance's father as our prime suspect? Madness. But the facts only pointed in one direction.

"Why would Hollis kill Dr. K?" Shelton asked. "If he was funding the parvo experiment, he'd want to keep the doctor alive."

"To cover his tracks?" Ben suggested. "Karsten's experiment was illegal. Maybe Karsten threatened to expose him."

"Or maybe Karsten was just in the wrong place at the wrong time," Hi said. "Collateral damage."

"Enough." I was tired of being jerked around. "We finally have a suspect. Now we need proof, not more speculation."

"I doubt Hollis is going to confess," Ben said. "He's skated four decades so far."

"Then we'll find the evidence ourselves," I said. "Today."

CHAPTER 61

The boys agreed to wait at the Charleston marina. They didn't like it, but there was no other way. My cover only worked if I went in alone.

"This is *way* too risky," Shelton said. "What if you run into Chance? Or worse, Hollis?"

"I'll say I dropped by to chat. Chance thinks I like him, so he won't be suspicious."

Hi grinned ear to ear, but made no comment.

"Anyway," I added quickly. "Chance will be in Greenville all weekend for the lacrosse finals. And with the legislature in session, Hollis should be in Columbia. Today's our best shot."

"We don't know if Bolton won last night," Hi said. "If the team lost, Chance might already be back."

"They're still there." I pulled up iFollow on my phone. "The GPS puts Jason's lacrosse group in Greenville. *All* of them. The team must still be alive in the tournament."

"Go Griffins!" Hi quipped.

"Chance isn't part of your iFollow group," Ben pointed out. "We don't know where *he* is, and can't track him."

True. With his Stone Age cell phone, Chance couldn't run the app if he'd wanted to. Which I'm sure he didn't.

"But *Hannah* is still in Greenville, too." I tapped my screen. "She wouldn't be there without Chance."

Ben frowned, but nodded.

"*Someone* is going to be inside that house," Hi said. "Claybourne Manor has forty freaking rooms! The place will be knee-deep in ninja butlers."

I'd thought of that. "Hollis is rumored to be cheap. Jason once said there's very little staff present on the weekends. The place should be almost empty."

"Almost doesn't mean completely," Ben said.

"I know, but I have to chance it. We're out of options."

I shouldered my backpack. Inside were Katherine's notebook and Karsten's deposit slip. If I got arrested, I wanted the evidence with me. I had no illusions about winning a credibility battle with Hollis Claybourne. I'd need all the proof I could muster.

"Be careful," Shelton warned. "If someone stops you, pretend you thought it was a museum."

"If Chance catches you, act love-struck." Hi winked. "That'll work."

"Love-struck?" Ben's brow furrowed. "What's he talking about?"

"Nothing. Wish me luck." Stupid Hi.

I took Broad Street and turned right on Meeting, toward the

Battery. South of Broad. Enormous mansions lined both sides of the street. The air stank of old money and blue blood. Privilege. I felt like a trespasser.

I reviewed my game plan as I walked. Sneak inside, poke around, get the hell out. Easy, right? This time, if I found something incriminating I'd go straight to the police. No more games. The stakes were too high.

I couldn't stop thinking about Katherine's journal entries. Imagine, finding bald eagles right there on the South Carolina coast. Remarkable.

But Katherine never had a chance to share her discovery. Someone silenced her. Permanently. Soon afterward, Cole Island was sold and the trees were destroyed. Bye-bye eagles.

Someone *must've* known about those birds. But there were no news reports. No articles. No photo spreads. Katherine's journal was the only record of their existence.

If Hollis Claybourne knew about the eagles before he sold the island, he was a prime suspect in Katherine's death. I needed something to prove he had that knowledge.

The thought of what I was about to do made me cold all over. Whoever murdered Heaton probably killed Karsten, and was trying to kill me. It could be Hollis.

And I was about to break into his home.

Something else worried me. The million-dollar question. Did Chance know about any of this?

I drew level with *chez* Claybourne.

Showtime.

Claybourne Manor is a registered historic landmark, even has its own website. Before departing Morris, I'd combed through online slideshows, trying to get a feel for the layout.

Built just after the Civil War, the house is styled after a nineteenth century Italian manor. Every inch is handcrafted. Crystal chandeliers. Carved wooden mantles. Elaborate moldings. A home fit for royalty. And a Claybourne has always sat on its throne.

I reviewed the stats I'd found on line. Three stories high, the house contains forty rooms, two dozen fireplaces, sixty baths, and a fifty-foot-long entrance hall.

And I planned to pop in and search the place by myself. Tremendous.

A ten-foot wall surrounds the two-acre property. Spikes top it, and ornate iron gates block access to the driveway.

I studied the gates as I walked by. A tourist, intrigued.

Centered in the scrolly wrought iron was the Claybourne family crest, a gray shield with three black foxes surrounded by black and red vines. The family motto arced above the crest: *Virtus vincit invidiam.* Virtue overcometh envy.

Please.

I peered through the bars.

A guard hunched inside a booth beside the drive, attention focused on a small black-and-white TV. Without breaking stride, I continued down the block.

Twenty yards past the gate, the wall turned a corner and shot back the length of the lot. The next-door neighbors had planted sumac to block their view of the brick. A narrow trail ran between the Claybourne's wall and the shrubs.

I took a deep breath, looked both ways, then scurried down the trail. Fifteen yards from the sidewalk I reached a small service gate.

Right where it's supposed to be.

I dropped to my knees and wiggled the bricks underlying the gate. One felt loose. A sharp tug and it lifted. A key lay in the dirt.

I smiled ear to ear. Cheshire cat style.

The things you can learn in class, if you listen. Thanks, Jason.

As quietly as possible, I swung open the gate. Ahead lay the manor's formal gardens. Replacing the key, I stepped inside.

No turning back now. I was trespassing on private property. Again.

Dogwoods lined a cobblestone walk directly before me. To both sides of the trees stretched neatly trimmed lawn. Statues dotted the grass, unsmiling witnesses to generations of Claybourne picnics, garden parties, and croquet matches.

Lacking a better plan, I followed a branching path toward a naked cherub rising from a colossal stone fountain. Water arced from its oversized horn. A leaf covered its genitals. Classy.

The fountain was centered in a small courtyard from which paths led toward the four compass points. I'd entered from the east. The path to my left cut south, back toward the front door. I scurried north, toward the rear of the house.

So far, no alarm. I was still operating below the radar.

The path wound deeper into the grounds. Six-foot hedges

cropped up, creating a narrow walking lane. Smaller paths intersected mine, giving the garden a mazelike feel. I soon lost my bearings.

My heart kicked up a notch. Yes, I was hidden. But I couldn't see a thing. I could blunder into someone at any turn.

I reached another fountain. Three dolphins, water shooting from their mouths, koi swimming below. Stone benches faced in from three sides. A towering hedge surrounded the whole deal.

Which way to go?

I turned left, hoping I was still moving toward the back of the manor. The path widened, then ended at small lawn bordering the rear of the house.

Bingo. Door. Dead ahead.

I paused to look around. The coast was clear.

I scampered forward and pressed my back against the warm brick of the main building. I quickly tried the knob, which turned.

Deep breath.

I slipped inside Claybourne Manor.

CHAPTER 62

It took a moment for my eyes to adjust.

I stood at the end of a narrow service hall. Shelves and storage closets lined both sides.

I hurried forward, ears on high alert. No Claybourne would use this corridor, but their servants would. Explaining my presence would be tricky, to say the least.

The passage ran thirty feet, turned right, then ended at a four-foot-high entryway.

Feeling like Alice, I cracked the tiny door and peered out. Before me lay the famous entrance hall.

Sunlight glinted off the white marble floor, and prismed from the crystal chandeliers hanging twenty feet up. Gold gilt tables lined the walls, holding statues, vases, and sculptures, each probably worth more than Kit's portfolio. The open space was enough to accommodate a family of Wookiees.

To my left loomed the front doors, gigantic oak behemoths that could survive a missile strike. To my right the white marble shot the center of the house like a four-lane highway.

I closed the undersized door behind me. It sealed with a click, blending seamlessly into the wall. I couldn't tell how it opened.

According to the website, the main staircase stood at the far end of the entrance hall. To reach the second floor, I first had to navigate the marble interstate.

Here goes nothing.

I crept forward, passing a formal dining room, a drawing room, and an observatory containing a Steinway grand piano. The walls were hung with portraits of dead Claybournes, each looking more dour than the next.

My heart hammered and my eyes never stopped moving. This was definitely the danger zone.

The hall ended in a circular foyer topped by a magnificent stained glass dome hanging seventy feet above me. Rainbow colors danced the marble. Murals adorned the walls, bordered by painted frescoes and carved molding. The room looked like something out of the Vatican. For a moment I gaped like a tourist.

An eight-foot statute stood centered beneath the dome. Milton Claybourne, the manor's architect. Milton frowned, face bandaged, musket in hand.

"You're a fun one," I whispered. "Modest, too."

At the far end of the hall, a Versailles-sized staircase swept upward between polished wood banisters. I scurried to it.

The second-floor corridor ran parallel to the hall below. Doors lined both sides.

The passage was deep night compared to the bright daytime below. Mahogany-paneled walls. No windows. Dim lights, spaced far apart. Shadows hid the corners and lay thick on the dark red carpet.

My target was specific. Hollis Claybourne's private study. My instincts told me it was up there somewhere.

A door opened somewhere down the hallway.

I scrambled, heart banging, frantic for cover.

The first place I tried was a linen closet. No room to hide.

The unseen door closed.

I yanked a second knob.

Creak!

The hinges sounded like a scream in the stillness.

I barreled inside and shut the door. Froze. Shaking hands covered my mouth.

I heard movement in the hall. The clank of china. Then, far off, another door opening, closing.

Air exploded from my chest. Close. Too close.

I turned to examine my sanctuary. Relief turned to alarm. Then excitement.

I was standing in Chance's bedroom.

No doubt about it. The walls were covered with pictures. Chance in London, Paris, Venice. Chance suited up for baseball, tennis, golf. Hannah and Chance on a blanket at the beach.

A massive bookcase held trophies and memorabilia. A framed

picture enjoyed pride-of-place on the dresser. Hannah, in a white dress, holding a single rose. It looked like a gift. She looked stunning.

Blech.

I peeked in the closet. Bolton Prep uniforms hung from a jumble of mismatched hangers. Italian leather shoes lay heaped on the floor. Expensive silk ties sat balled on a built-in shelf.

"Chance," I whispered. "Quite the slob. Surprise, surprise."

Next, I poked through the books. Mostly nonfiction.

I stayed out of the dresser. Even I have limits. And if the door swung open, the last thing I wanted to be caught holding was Chance Claybourne's underpants.

Finally, I arrived at the desk. Disconnected cords awaited the return of a laptop. Papers and books lay haphazardly tossed. A printer sat next to a scanner, neither plugged in. A Citadel mug held pens and highlighters.

A manila envelope caught my eye. Originally sealed with red tape, one end was sliced open. I noted a logo with the acronym SLED.

South Carolina Law Enforcement Division.

The fingerprint report.

I pulled a single sheet from the envelope. A handwritten note was clipped to the front. It read: "Here's the info. You owe me! See you on the links, Chip."

I frowned. Why hadn't Chance given me the actual report? Was he holding back?

Relax. He'd probably promised not to let it out of his possession.

And he didn't want me chasing a dangerous crook like Newman. It's not surprising he didn't share the hard copy.

Curious, I scanned. Saw a photocopy of the fingerprint I'd lifted from the microfilm reader. Next to it was a mug shot.

I almost dropped the paper in shock.

That face! I knew it. The buzz-cut hair. The scarred jawline.

I read every word twice.

The report didn't identify any James Newman. He wasn't mentioned anywhere in the document. The print belonged to someone else.

Someone I'd met once before.

Tony Baravetto. Personal chauffeur to Chance Claybourne. The man who drove me home the night of the disastrous cotillion.

My mind raced. What did this mean?

But I knew.

Chance lied to me.

One by one, links connected.

Baravetto followed us to the library.

Baravetto learned that we knew about Katherine Heaton.

Baravetto worked for Chance Claybourne, son of Hollis Claybourne, our prime suspect in Katherine Heaton's murder.

Then, one awful, inescapable connection.

Chance Claybourne might be trying to kill me.

CHAPTER 63

Chance had played me like a xylophone.

And I'd fallen for it. Hook, line, and one-ton sinker.

Like a love-struck moron.

Chance was only interested in protecting his father's secret. He'd toyed with me, distracted me from the truth. And I'd been suckered.

Shame burned my face. How could I have been so stupid? Chance probably thinks I'm wrapped around his little finger.

We'll see about that. You messed with the wrong *girl, Claybourne.*

I knew what I had to do. Find the evidence. Bring the Claybournes down.

I shoved the print report into my bag.

Livid. Furious at Chance. At myself.

I let the anger build. Multiply. Reminding myself again and

again how dense I'd been. How gullible. How juvenile. The rage blossomed in an instant.

Something flashed in my brain.

My lips curled.

A low growl rose from my throat.

SNAP.

The flare rushed through my veins. Energizing me. Filling me with deadly purpose. My senses sparked. Soared.

Golden light shone from my eyes.

I eased the door open and sniffed the hallway. Burnt tobacco, one thread among many. I honed in, tracked the scent back toward the main staircase.

Hollis Claybourne smoked cigars—the odor would lead me to his study. I slunk down the corridor, eyes boring through the gloom.

Swish.

I froze. Cocked my head. The sound was faint, but growing in intensity, coming right for me.

To my left stood a towering armoire. I shrunk into its shadow and pressed myself to one side. Waited.

Seconds later, a maid passed, skirt swaying with the movement of her body.

My heart returned to my chest.

Yikes. Without my flare, I would never have heard in time.

I continued toward the staircase, sniffing all the while. The olfactory trail led to the third floor. I followed.

Leaving the last riser, I entered a long passageway set at intervals with small brass sconces. Dark murals covered the walls—men killing game, men in battle, men in wigs signing documents with feather pens.

The smoke smell was coming from the second door on the right. I slipped inside.

The chamber was massive, its opposite side an expanse of floor to ceiling windows framed by red velvet drapery drawn back by gold cords. Bookcases climbed the remaining walls to a wood-beamed ceiling twenty feet up. A wrought-iron catwalk circled the room three yards above the floor, accessed by a spiral staircase tucked into the far left corner.

In the room's center, four leather-bound chairs formed a semi-circle around a low coffee table. The arrangement faced an enormous stone fireplace. Behind the seats, a desk the size of Kansas sat with its back to the window. On it were pictures of Hollis smiling or shaking hands with famous people. Souvenirs from a life in the upper crust.

Now what?

Hollis Claybourne's study made the Colosseum look small.

I rummaged the desk, found nothing suspicious.

I tried a wooden bureau standing beneath a tapestry of General Custer at Little Big Horn. The drawers held Civil War era clothing. Reenactment garb.

I circled the room, probing with my laser vision. Under different circumstances, I might've enjoyed myself.

Hollis Claybourne was a collector. Along with books and pictures of himself, the shelves were jammed with African tribal masks, Inuit carvings, Indonesian puppets, and sculptures from every corner of the globe. The collection was refined, the work of a man with a discerning eye.

But it held nothing I could use.

My fists clenched in frustration.

What'd you expect? A folder labeled Incriminating Evidence Here?

I closed my eyes, desperate for a plan. I was alone in Hollis's study. I'd never have this chance again.

My nose picked up a trickle of loam, an earthy smell out of place in the immaculate office. And something else. Non-organic. Chemical.

My lids flew apart. I knew that smell. Dirt. Metal. The sharp bite of cleaning solution. Like Windex.

The dog tags! They were somewhere in this room.

I went still. Sniffed. My nostrils recaptured the scent.

Up.

I hurried for the spiral stairs and climbed to the narrow catwalk. Skirting the shelves, I paced the length of the inside wall, then turned left, toward the windows. The catwalk ended in the corner directly across from the room's entrance.

Built into the wall, deep in the corner, was a small wooden cabinet. The smell was coming from inside.

I tried the little silver handle.

The cabinet was locked.

No more playing nice.

Cocking one arm, I chopped with the heel of my hand. The

front panel cracked, but held. Ignoring the pain, I let fly a second time. The door splintered. Loose fragments fell to the floor.

I inspected my handiwork. The wood was at least an inch thick. Mike Tyson couldn't have split it. Yet I'd smashed it with two blows.

SNUP.

Dizziness swept over me. I dropped to my knees.

My senses dulled, returned to normal.

"Damn!"

Rising, I checked the cabinet's interior. Three items.

The first was an old black-and-white snapshot of Hollis Claybourne. Young Hollis was standing by a stand of longleaf pine, pointing to a pair of eagles swooping low in the sky.

Cole Island! The bastard knew about the eagles!

Below the picture was a manila folder. Inside were legal documents. I flipped through. Records of the sale of Cole Island to Candela. A contract of employment. Evidence, but no smoking gun.

The bottom shelf held a small velvet box. I popped it open.

Inside were two weathered dog tags, one grimy, one gleaming like new.

Francis P. Heaton. Catholic. O Positive.

"Son of a bitch," I whispered.

Any sane person would have destroyed the tags. Not Hollis Claybourne. The egotistical bastard saved them in his trophy case as another souvenir.

Anger blazed anew. Those tags represented Katherine's murder.

Hollis kept them in a box to admire at his leisure.

Monster.

The door creaked.

Footsteps kissed the carpet below.

"What the hell are you doing?"

CHAPTER 64

"Tory?" Chance was still dressed for lacrosse. "Is that you?"

Busted.

My mind blanked.

"What are you doing here?" I babbled.

"What am *I* doing here? I *live* here."

Chance stepped into the room. I tried to block his view of the cabinet, but splintered wood littered the catwalk and the carpet below. He couldn't possibly miss it.

"If you're asking why I'm home early, it's because we lost this morning." A frown replaced his look of confusion. "The others can watch the finals without me. I'm not interested."

"You left Hannah there?" I was still in panic mode. How to play this?

As casual as possible, I strolled back down the catwalk, turned the corner, and moved toward the staircase.

"I dropped Hannah at home ten minutes ago." Chance's eyes tracked me. "Did you try to call? She left her phone in Jason's car."

Oops. Hadn't thought of that one.

Chance crossed to his father's desk, leaned against it. Folded his arms. From his new position, he'd be at the stairs well before I could reach the floor.

I stopped in the center of the catwalk, just above the hearth.

"Why are you up there?" Chance's eyes flicked to the cabinet. "Why did you smash my father's case?"

I should've made an excuse. Lied. Played dumb. Cried.

But my anger was hot to the touch. Hollis Claybourne was a monster, and his son was playing me.

"Just stop it, Chance." My hands gripped the railing. "I know you're full of shit. And now I have proof."

"What's that supposed to mean?" The upturned face darkened. "I tried to *help* you, little girl."

"Help me?" I spat. "By lying? By treating me like a fool?"

"I told you everything I know." The dark eyes said otherwise.

"Jimmy Newman?" I sneered. "Bullshit! Where's your hired goon, Baravetto? Driving someone home?"

Wordlessly, Chance retraced his steps, closed the door, and threw the lock.

I was trapped.

Strolling to a chair, he sat and crossed his legs. His eyes rose again to my perch.

"What is it you think you've found?" The velvet tone was now cold steel.

"I know your father is a murderer."

"How dare you!" Chance shot forward, but quickly regained his cool. "You're lucky my father is in Columbia. God help you if *he* found you here."

"What? He'd kill me too?"

Chance remained silent, but his top foot bounced, dancing the laces on his sneaker.

"I know about Cole Island," I said. "The deal with Candela Pharmaceuticals. Your father murdered a girl named Katherine Heaton to protect his precious land sale."

"You can't prove that. It's complete nonsense." Chance pointed at the smashed cabinet. "And you've committed a felony. More than one."

"Nonsense? Really?" I held up the dog tags.

The foot started winging double-time.

"And that's not all." I was on a roll. "I found Katherine Heaton's journal. I know she discovered bald eagles on Cole Island. That's why your father killed her."

Chance's lips drew into a thin, hard line. For a moment he was silent. Then, "You're right. Congratulations."

I was stunned. Chance was conceding that his father was guilty of murder. And admitting to his own knowledge of the crime.

"You already know the truth," Chance said. "And you're too smart to be tricked again. So why bother? I admit it. The old bastard killed the Heaton girl."

"You knew about it?"

"He called me in here two weeks ago." Chance glanced at the

desk, as if imagining his father behind it. "Told me the whole story. The eagles. The sale. Some meddling girl he'd been forced to eliminate." Chance shook his head. "He was so nonchalant. Matter-of-fact. Heaton's death meant nothing to him. It was incredible."

"But why kill her?" My voice cracked. "She was only sixteen."

"Cole Island was all my father had left." He laughed mirthlessly. "He's a terrible investor. By 1969 the family fortune was gone, and he was up to his ears in debt. Only the Claybourne name was keeping the creditors away."

"That hardly justifies murder."

"My father claims it was an accident." Chance avoided looking at me. "That he didn't mean to kill her."

"And you believe him?"

"Not for one second."

"Then why cover for him?"

"Heaton should *not* have been there!" Chance's fist slammed the arm of his chair. "Cole Island was private property. *Our* property. If she'd reported the eagles, it would've killed the sale. My father couldn't allow that. Too much was at stake."

"He could have tried other things," I said. "Maybe the birds could've been relocated."

Chance shook his head. "The publicity would've forced Candela to back out. There would have been no cash and no position for my father. Our whole future depended on that sale."

I looked down in disgust. "So it was all about money?"

"My father would've been forced to sell Claybourne Manor!"

"So?"

"*So?*" Chance looked up, appalled. "A Claybourne has owned this house since the Civil War. It belongs to us, and no one else. We could never *sell* it. We'd be disgraced!"

For the first time, I was seeing the true Chance. It sickened me.

"Money isn't everything," I said.

Chance laughed bitterly. "Have you even met my father? He'd *never* take a downgrade. He'd rather die than live a middle-class life."

"You're revolting!" I couldn't believe what I was hearing. "You approve of what he did."

"Watch your mouth." Chance jabbed a finger in my direction. "I'm not my father. I'm *nothing* like him."

"That's crap. You're helping Hollis get away with murder."

Chance nodded. "These things happened when my father was twenty-four years old. One day he'll answer for his actions. But done is done. I have no intention of losing my inheritance because of events that took place before I was born."

"Then you're just like him," I said.

"Coming from you, that hurts."

"Go to hell!" My blood boiled. "You've been playing me this whole time. Pretending to worry about me. Calling me the prettiest girl in the room. Please. You never cared about me. You manipulated my feelings to protect yourself."

Chance shrugged. "And it worked."

"You lied to me."

"So I gave you a fake name," he said airily. "You had my driver's fingerprints. What was I supposed to do?"

"But why have him follow us in the first place?"

"We have a mole at the public library. He tipped my father to your research on Heaton. Hollis sent Baravetto to determine exactly what you'd learned."

A mole at the library? That weasel Limestone!

"Of course, Hollis didn't share any of that with his son." Chance's jaw muscles bunched. "God forbid he confide in me *before* confiding in my driver."

"But he *did* tell you," I said. "You're just as guilty as he is."

"Only when he had to. When Baravetto reported back, my father got nervous. Guess he decided I was man enough to dig up a skeleton. Otherwise, he'd have kept me in the dark."

"Poor baby," I mocked. "Sorry about your daddy issues."

Chance glared. Then smirked. "Your stolen laptop story fooled me, you know. I didn't guess what you were up to until I saw the report." He waggled a finger. "Very clever."

"This isn't a joke!" I shouted. "You tried to kill me that night on Loggerhead."

"Kill you? Hardly. I shot way over your head."

"Yeah. Right."

"It's true. My father ordered me to recover the skeleton. Nothing more. You happened to be there, so we had to scare you off." The nervous foot was pumping again. "I couldn't believe you'd already found the bones. Good thing we didn't wait another night. Thanks, by the way." The famous Chance wink. "You saved us hours of digging."

"Screw you," I said. "The only reason I'm standing here is because you're a lousy shot."

"Don't be so dramatic." He smiled. "Did you like the monkey bones? That was my idea. Hollis told me where to find them. He knows people at LIRI."

Spies on Loggerhead?

"Who?"

Chance ignored my question. "The bones were packed in a box by the dock." He laughed. "I wish I could've been there when you showed the police."

"You think this is funny? You murdered Dr. Karsten in cold blood!"

The taunting smile faded. "What?"

"Enough games, Chance! I know you're a murderer. I was there."

"I didn't murder anyone. I told you. I shot over your heads. You're lucky it was *me* out there. My father was furious I let you escape."

"Not Loggerhead. I'm talking about when you attacked us at the bunker."

"What bunker?" Chance frowned. "Wait. Are you're saying someone was killed?"

Now I was confused.

"Thursday night. You and your goons shot professor Karsten on Morris Island."

"I've never set foot on Morris Island."

This wasn't making sense.

"Did you chase Hi and Shelton through the market earlier that night?"

"The market?" Chance rose and moved to the foot of the staircase. "Is this a joke? What are you talking about?"

His tone? His expression? Somehow, I believed he really was clueless about Karsten's death.

Not sure why, but I did.

"Thursday night we were meeting with . . . a friend on Morris Island. An adult." I watched Chance closely. "Men came. They were armed, and dressed exactly as you were on Loggerhead."

"I wasn't there, I swear." Chance looked genuinely shocked. "What happened?"

"We escaped. Our friend stayed behind." My fingers tightened on the railing. "The bastards shot him."

For a long moment, Chance stared into space. A tremor shook his right hand.

"I know nothing about that," he said flatly. "Nothing."

Then Chance looked up, eyes hard with resolve.

"Give me your bag," he demanded.

"What?"

"Your bag." Stepping back so he could see me more clearly. "You found Heaton's notebook. I'm betting you have it now. I want it. And my fingerprint report. And everything you just stole from that cabinet. Game over."

Stupid, stupid, stupid. Why did I bring the notebook with me?

"Hollis murdered Katherine," I said. "And probably ordered the hit on Karsten. People will notice he's missing. The police will investigate. Eventually his body will be found. The truth will come out, no matter what you do."

Chance shook his head. "Not true. Once I destroy the evidence, including the skeleton, the past will stay buried. You just need to let this go."

"You father is trying to kill me and my friends!"

"I'll stop that." Chance's voice expressed a confidence his face lacked. "But I won't sacrifice my family's good name over a four-decade-old murder. And I won't put my father in jail."

It was futile. Chance would never help me.

My eyes sought an escape route. Found none. The staircase was the only way down.

Fight back.

I closed my eyes. Concentrated every fiber of my being on bringing out my powers.

And failed. I couldn't trigger a second flare.

"Tory."

My eyes opened. Chance watched me closely.

"The bag. Now!" He smiled darkly. "Let's not make this unpleasant."

Just survive. Regroup.

I wound down the stairs. Chance held out a hand. I passed him my backpack and the dog tags. What else could I do?

"Good." Chance nodded. "Now get out of my house and keep your mouth shut. This will be our little secret."

I'd been dismissed. Chance wasn't even worried enough to escort me off the premises. He knew he'd won.

I walked to the door.

Looked back.

Chance gave a smirky five-finger wave.

I fled as fast as I could.

CHAPTER 65

The Brennan girl walked right past the Bentley.

Hollis Claybourne nearly swallowed his cigar. He cracked his knuckles. Veins pulsed in his oversized nose.

The little bitch had been inside his house!

His mind raced. Should he chase her down? The girl was only a half block away. He could finish this problem himself.

No. Too dangerous. He couldn't risk grabbing her in broad daylight.

The kid will have to take care of it.

And I can't be here, Hollis thought. I need an alibi.

Hollis pounded his fist against the screen seperating the driver's compartment.

"Change of plans," he said. "Back to the capitol."

"You wanna go back, sir?" the driver asked. "We just got here."

"Now, you imbecile!"

Hollis regretted hiring Baravetto's moron nephew, but he needed people he could trust. His entire career was in jeopardy.

As the Bentley reversed down the driveway, Hollis yanked his cell phone from his suit jacket and punched the speed dial.

Two rings, then, "Yes."

"The Brennan girl," Hollis barked. "She and her friends must be dealt with immediately. I'll be in Columbia."

He heard an intake of breath. Cut off the response.

"And no more mistakes!"

CHAPTER 66

"He's lying," Shelton said. "He has to be."

Ben nodded in agreement.

Hi shifted in his seat, uneasy.

The four of us sat aboard *Sewee* back at the Morris Island dock. No one had any idea what to do next.

An hour before, I'd slunk from Claybourne Manor, humiliated. The walk across town had seemed endless.

The other Virals had been relieved to see me at the marina. Then I told them about my crash and burn. No one spoke during our ride across the harbor.

"I think Chance told the truth," I said softly. "I believe him."

"But he admitted that his father killed Heaton," Shelton said. "Then he admitted stealing Heaton's bones. Chance even admitted shooting at us!" He threw up his hands. "Who else would've killed Dr. K?"

"Chance won't own up to murder," Ben said. "His ego isn't *that* big."

"But why let Tory go?" Hi asked. "If Chance meant to kill us all at the bunker, why not finish Tory off when he had her trapped?"

"Fear of being caught," Shelton said. "He knew Tory would have told us where she was going. And Chance has all the evidence now anyway. Why not let her go?"

"What was I supposed to do, kick his ass?" I said defensively. "He's twice my size!"

But I was embarrassed. Like a dolt, I'd delivered Heaton's notebook to Chance.

"Did you try to flare?" Hi asked. "You leveled Jason at that dance. Chance isn't much bigger."

"I tried, but it didn't work." I shook my head in frustration. "I was flaring right before he showed up. That's how I found Hollis's study and the dog tags. But once I lost it, I couldn't get it back."

"You did the right thing," Ben said. "You had no choice."

"What do we do now?" Hi asked. "Chance can come after us at any time."

"I really think he was being honest," I said. "I don't think he tried to kill us."

"Tory," Hi began. "I know you think the guy is—"

"Just listen!" I sat forward. "Chance admitted to switching the bones. His father told him the location of the grave. But how could he have found our bunker?"

"He trailed us," Shelton offered. "Just like Karsten."

I shook my head. "Ben and I weren't followed from Loggerhead that night. I'm sure of it. And Karsten said he followed you guys from this dock. He swore he didn't see anyone else. It doesn't add up."

Hi scratched his chin. "Then the killers found our bunker some other way."

"But how?" I pressed. "You'd never spot it just by poking around."

"Truth now." Ben looked at each of us. "Did any of you ever tell anyone about the bunker?"

"Nope."

"No way."

"Not a soul."

"Me either," Ben said. "I'm stumped."

"We have to figure out who learned the bunker's location," I said. "And how they did it. We're not safe until we do."

"But we've lost the evidence. And Heaton's skeleton," Shelton said. "We're dead in the water."

"We can't let the Claybournes win," I said.

"No," Ben agreed. "We can't."

"Okay, Tory. You're the commander." Hi snapped a salute. "What now?"

"Chance told me he was going to destroy everything," I said. "The notebook, the dog tags, Heaton's remains."

"So he still has the skeleton," Hi reasoned.

"Exactly."

"I know where this is going," Shelton muttered.

"We need to get it all back," I said. "Find Katherine's bones. Win."

"But where's he got the bones stashed?" Ben asked.

"Claybourne Manor. Where else?"

"She's going to say 'tonight,' isn't she?" Shelton's chin dropped to his chest. "Every time I think I'm done for the night, Tory says we have to invade some fortress."

"Cheer up." I flashed a wicked smile. "This time we do it our way. We go in hot."

"We'll show the Claybournes what happens when you mess with the Virals."

CHAPTER 67

"**D**amn."

I replaced the brick and stepped back from the gate. "The key is gone."

Two in the morning. We were huddled beside Claybourne Manor's outer wall, dressed all in black, cat burglar style. A full moon was lighting the path. Hopefully, the sumacs were concealing us from late nighters strolling the sidewalk.

"Chance isn't stupid," Hi whispered. "He figured out how you got in earlier."

Clearly. We needed another way inside.

"We'll go over the top," I said. "It's the only option."

Shelton glanced up at the iron spikes topping the ten-foot wall. "You're nuts."

"Rope." I held out a hand.

Ben pulled a coil of double-braided nylon cord from his bag.

Sewee's back-up anchor line. I tied the knots and created a two-foot lasso.

"I'll do it." Ben winged the lasso at a spike directly above us. Missed. Two more tosses. Both failures.

"May I?"

Ben handed me the rope.

I whipped the lasso overhead, then straightened my arm and released. The circle rode the air then dropped over a spike. I pulled down hard to tighten the loop.

"Horseback riding camp," I whispered. "Silver medal in target roping."

"Guys, I'll wake up the whole world trying to climb that wall," Hi said. "I doubt I'll make it."

"Not you," I said. "Ben?"

Eager, Ben grabbed the rope with both hands.

"Wait!" I faced the others. "We can't do this without our powers. We need to flare."

"How?" Shelton whispered. "I can't just order one up. They only come when I get really scared."

"Police!" Hi hit the ground.

We all dropped.

"Oh crap!" Shelton whimpered. Then his eyes flashed golden.

Hi rose, brushing dirt from his belly. "You can thank me later."

He squeezed his lids shut. When they opened, two more gold irises burned in the darkness.

"Jerk!" Shelton shoved him. "How can you do that so easily?"

"I just think about how crazy this all is. Bingo. Wolf-time." Hi shrugged. "It doesn't always work."

My turn.

I closed my eyes and reached for my anger. I thought about Katherine's murder. The bunker attack. The experiment on Cooper.

Nothing. No flare.

So I thought about Chance. The winks. The smiles. How he'd held me tight while dancing, touched my hand, and kissed me on the cheek.

Made a fool of me.

Fury spread through my body like wildfire.

Sparks exploded in my brain.

My eyes sharpened. I could hear slugs crawling through mulch in the garden, waves crashing the seawall blocks away. My nose read the air like a roadmap.

I felt amber blaze from my sockets.

"I can't." Ben clenched his fists. "It won't come!"

"Ben?"

When he turned, I slapped him full across the face.

The force of my blow knocked Ben sideways.

He grabbed me with both hands, fingers digging into my arms, eyes blazing with yellow fire.

I held my breath.

"Thanks." Ben spoke through gritted teeth. "Good job."

"No problem. You can let me go now."

He did.

Gripping the rope, Ben scaled the wall, one step at a time. At the top, he grasped an iron spike in each hand, flexed his knees, and pushed off. His feet swung up over his head. His wrists rotated, and for a moment, he balanced in a handstand, biceps straining under the weight of his body. Finally, he flexed, pushed off with his hands, completed the back flip, and dropped from sight.

Beyond the wall we heard his Nikes hit the ground.

"Whoa," Shelton said.

I agreed. Most Olympians couldn't have pulled that off.

Metal clanked, then the gate swung out. I led Hi and Shelton through without a word.

I listened. Nothing but leaves and insects.

Moving quickly, I guided the Virals though the gardens. With the kick-ass moon and my eyes in hyperdrive, the yard was noontime bright.

Surprise. The same door was unlocked. Chance hadn't been careful enough.

The service corridor was as dark and empty as before. At the Alice door, I poked my head through to take a peek. The grand foyer was silent as a tomb.

"Wow," Hi whispered. "Nice digs."

Shelton's eyes were looking everywhere at once.

Ben remained quiet, vigilant.

I led the way. We scurried down the hallway, up two flights of stairs, and into Hollis Claybourne's study.

I started to sniff-search the chamber, but Hi was ahead of me.

"That-a-way." He pointed to Hollis's desk.

Unbelievable.

Everything was there. The fingerprint report. Heaton's journal. The dog tags. Karsten's deposit slip. The evidence lay on the desktop, garbage waiting to be curbed.

Chance had been lazy. And had underestimated me. Badly. He'd pay for his overconfidence.

I stuffed the documents into my bag and pocketed the tags.

"Let's get out of Dodge," Shelton hissed.

"This isn't enough," I said. "We have to find Heaton's bones before Chance destroys them."

"Where?" Hi whispered. "This place is the size of an airport."

"If you had an ancient mansion, where would you hide a skeleton?" I asked.

"The cellar?" Hi guessed.

"Exactly! This house was built before electricity and refrigeration. It must have lots of underground storage areas."

I shouldered my backpack. "We need to find the kitchens. A cellar entrance would be there."

Ben checked the hallway. "All clear."

As I descended the stairs, my eyes pierced the shadows with ease. My ears picked up dozens of ticking clocks. My nose sorted an array of strange scents. None of it was helpful.

The mansion felt empty and we encountered no one. I prayed for that to continue.

On the first floor I detected a storm of food smells.

"Over here." We slipped into the dining room, then down

a short hallway to a tall white door. Through it, we entered an enormous kitchen.

Gray floor and wall tiles reflected moonlight pouring through two bay windows. Modern stainless steel appliances circled a butcher block large enough to dismember an elk.

"Psst!" Shelton pointed to a doorway barely visible in one corner.

I tried the knob.

It turned in my hand.

CHAPTER 68

We scurried down a narrow passage to an iron gate. Through the bars we could see an ancient stone staircase disappearing into darkness. A dank musty smell wafted up from below.

"The cellars must be down there," I said.

The gate rattled and squeaked as it opened. We slipped through, leaving it wide, fearful more noise might sound an alarm.

Testing with our feet, we slowly worked our way down the stairs. Blind. Even flaring, I needed a few light pixels to see.

The staircase seemed impossibly long. By the time I reached bottom, my hand was ice from sliding along the wall. And I was shivering.

Utter blackness. I drank in the odors of damp stone, ancient dust, and rusty iron. Inhaling deeply, I searched for the distinct scent of death. Came up empty.

Ben handed me a flashlight. I thumbed it on. The others did the same.

Four pale shafts arced and bobbed in the darkness.

We stood at the edge of an enormous stone cavern supported by concrete pillars. At dead center were a half dozen high-backed chairs snugged under a round oak table. Flanking sideboards held crystal glassware and bottle-opening implements. Beyond the table, large wooden barrels marched in two rows down the center of the room.

Slowly, I probed the chamber with my light.

Wine racks stood in rows to our left and right, with passages between, like aisles in a library. Thousands of dusty bottles filled the shelves.

I shined my light down an aisle. The beam petered out before reaching a wall. I checked another. Same deal.

"The whole world could get drunk down here," Hi said. "There must be ten thousand bottles, at least."

"Focus," Ben said. "We need to find Heaton's remains, then get the hell gone."

"Spread out," I said. "The bones have to be down here. Ben, you and Hi check the right-hand aisles. Shelton and I will go left."

"My flashlight died." Shelton sounded panicky.

"Use your phone," I said. "It provides enough light if you're flaring."

I stepped left, testing the air like a hound, determined to pick up the scent of bones.

"This is crazy." Shelton was just inches behind me. "I'm sniffing around for a skeleton in Hollis Claybourne's wine cellar. Two weeks ago, my biggest concern was my fantasy baseball team."

Shelton was right. Things had gotten insane. For a moment, I wondered if life would ever be normal again.

No. We'd been changed at some fundamental level. There was no going back.

"Pay attention," I said. "Let's alternate rows. You check this one; I'll check the next. We'll work our way toward the rear of the cellar."

"Fine," Shelton said. "But when we get back, I'm lodging a formal complaint about flashlight distribution."

Row after row, I found nothing.

Was I wrong?

No. And I wasn't leaving Claybourne Manor without Katherine's bones.

"Guys! Over here!"

I hustled toward the sound of Hi's voice.

Hi stood by the table, flashlight pointed at a lone cask beside him. "I walked by it twice before I caught the smell."

My beam picked out a crowbar leaning against a pillar. Ben grabbed it and pried off the top of the cask.

I almost gagged on the sudden smell of death.

Inside the barrel lay a jumble of human bones. Nestled among them was a skull with a small round hole in the forehead.

"Katherine's skeleton!"

I was totally pumped. Hollis Claybourne was going down!

Creak.

The tiny hairs on my neck and arms went upright.

As my head whipped toward the staircase, every bulb in the cellar blazed to life.

I blinked, but the sudden blast of light forced my lids shut.

My flare slipped away.

When opened my eyes, Chance stood at the bottom of the steps. He wore gym shorts and a white tee, and his hair was sleep tousled. It was obvious he'd just awakened.

And armed himself.

"Bastards!" The gun shook in his hand, a Sig Sauer 9mm. Sleek. Deadly. "You just couldn't leave it alone."

My heart stopped. Chance's eyes looked wild.

"Everyone over there." Flicking the Sig toward the table. "Now!"

We did as instructed, hands raised, careful to avoid sudden moves.

"Cell phones. On the floor."

Again we complied. Chance kicked them all against a wall.

I stole a glance at the others. No golden irises. We were sitting ducks.

"I can shoot all of you! No one knows you're here. No one would ever find your bodies."

Chance pointed the gun at me.

"You shouldn't have come back, Tory. I thought you were smart enough to know when you're beaten. I was wrong."

"Chance—"

"Shut up! Just shut up!" His pupils jittered like a tweaker on meth. Sweat dampened his face. "I won't repeat my mistake. I won't prove my father right."

Chance stepped toward me, fingers so tight on the Sig's handle his knuckles bulged white. Despite his death grip, the barrel trembled.

My heart thudded.

What to do? Run? Try to talk him down? Try to take him out?

Chance drew air through his nostrils, steeling for the kill.

This was it.

To my amazement, he lowered the weapon.

"Who am I kidding?" he whispered. "I can't execute four people. I won't. I'm not my father."

No one moved.

I was about to speak when the gate creaked again.

"Chance?" Hannah's voice called down the stairs. "Are you in the wine cellar?"

"Hannah!" I yelled. "Down here!"

Chance raised a tremulous hand. "No! Don't—"

"Hannah, please! We need help!"

Light footsteps hurried toward us.

Chance pivoted, gun hidden behind his back.

"What's going on down here?" Hannah was wearing fuzzy bear slippers and a silk baby doll. Despite the danger, I wondered where her parents thought she was spending the night.

"The boat kids broke into the house." Chance was now sweating bullets. "Some kind of prank."

"Don't listen to him!" I shouted. "His father is a murderer!

We have proof and Chance is trying to destroy it."

"Look!" Hi lifted Katherine's skull from the barrel.

"He's got a gun!" Shelton yelled.

"A gun?" Hannah looked at Chance. "What does he mean? What's behind your back?"

Chance glared at Shelton, but lowered the weapon to his side.

"My God!" Hannah's eyes widened in alarm. "Chance, sweetheart, what are you thinking? Give me that horrible thing right now!"

"But—"

"Right now!"

Hannah held out a manicured hand. For a moment, it looked as though Chance would refuse. Then, sighing, he passed her the weapon.

I drew my first breath in a very long time. It was over. We were safe.

Hannah hefted the pistol, expression unreadable. Then she pulled back the slide, chambering a round. She aimed the barrel straight at my head.

"You really *are* a stupid girl, Tory."

Hannah's flawless smile was pure evil.

"Get two shovels, sweetheart. We'll need to bury the bodies."

CHAPTER 69

My eyes widened. The other Virals froze in disbelief.

Hannah kept the Sig trained on me. I stared down the barrel, imagining the feel of bullets ripping through my flesh.

"Hannah?" Chance sounded confused. "What are you doing? Put the gun down."

"I don't think so." The honeyed drawl was galvanized steel. "They know far too much. I'm going to finish this."

Chance gaped, speechless.

"Close your mouth Chance, you look like a fish." Hannah's eyes were hard. "Did you really think I'd allow you to screw this up?"

"What are you talking about?" Chance said. "Be careful! You don't know how to handle a gun."

"I know more than you think. A *lot* more, actually."

"It was you," I breathed. The pieces were clicking into place. "You led the gunmen to our bunker. You shot Karsten!"

"Don't be ridiculous!" Hannah giggled. "*I* didn't shoot anyone. Baravetto shot the silly scientist. I just watched."

"Baravetto shot someone?" Chance looked as though he'd been punched. "What were you doing with my driver?"

"Chance, Chance." Hannah shook her head. "Sometimes you're like a child. Someone had to clean up your father's mess. And, sweetheart, you just don't have the stomach for this sort of thing."

"How did you find us?" Ben's rage was barely controlled. "How did you locate our bunker?"

Hannah's eyes flicked to me. A tell.

"iFollow," I guessed. "Hannah and I are both in Jason's group. We joined in order to share info for our biology presentation. I never logged out, so the GPS tracked me wherever I took my phone. Even the bunker."

"Nicely done. But, sadly, too late." Hannah gestured with the Sig. "Put your bag on the table. Now."

I took the pack from my shoulder and set it down.

"Back up," she ordered. "All of you."

We retreated several paces. Hannah strode forward, grabbed the pack, then retreated to the foot of the stairs.

"Tracking you *was* hard," Hannah said. "There's no reception out on Morris, so you constantly flickered on-and-off. But we managed." Another smile. "iFollow is how I knew you were here tonight, too."

Chance took a step toward Hannah. She swung the Sig his way, stopping him cold.

"I don't understand." His eyes locked onto the barrel. "How do you know about my father's business?"

"I overheard Hollis telling you about Cole Island and Katherine Heaton." Hannah frowned. "I also heard him tell you what had to be done. Not that you listened." Hannah waggled a finger. "*Someone* has to make sure you don't ruin our future."

"I had things under control!" Chance yelled.

Hannah glanced at me. "Honestly, Chance. Flirting with this poor girl? Did you really think you could *charm* your way out of this mess?"

"You shouldn't have gotten involved in Claybourne business." A vein was bulging on Chance's forehead.

"What? Leave it up to you? You don't have the guts to do what's necessary. To act like your father did, all those years ago." Hannah jabbed the gun at his face. "You're weak. I'm not."

"You can't talk to me like this!" The vein was pumping a gusher. "This is over your head."

"Silly goose. I'm more capable than you'll ever be. Ask your daddy."

Chance went rock still. "What's that supposed to mean?"

The couple locked eyes, neither looking our way. Unnoticed, I scanned the cellar for anything useful. Spotted the crowbar beside the cask of bones.

Ever so carefully, I edged toward it.

"Do you think I could order your father's men without his permission?" Contempt tinged Hannah's voice. "God, you can be dense."

Hannah crossed her arms. "I went to Hollis myself, sweetheart. I told him you weren't able to handle this . . . situation. He agreed."

"How dare you!" Chance exploded. "You had no right!"

"We couldn't let your weakness of character jeopardize the Claybourne fortune. Or my place in the family."

Hannah's eyes slid to us.

"These meddlers have seen and heard things they shouldn't have." She smiled sideways. "But don't worry, Chancey. I'll take care of the hard part."

My mind raced.

Stall!

"Baravetto killed Dr. Karsten," I said. "Why? You could've let him go."

Hannah shrugged. Why not answer? We'd soon be dead.

"We couldn't have a credible adult talking to the police. And Karsten knew too much about other things. Catching him with you at your hidey-hole was very lucky."

Other things?

"The parvovirus experiment," I guessed.

Hannah's eyes became saucers. "Who told you about that? Even Chance doesn't know."

"Check my bag," I said. "I found the deposit slips. Candela Pharmaceuticals was paying Karsten to perform illegal research. We know all about it."

Hannah shrugged again. "True. Hollis was paying Karsten to find a cure for canine parvovirus. Candela's next big score."

She turned to Chance. "Your father truly is a heartless bastard.

If Karsten couldn't produce a cure, Hollis wanted him to make a designer virus. Doesn't that sound elegant? A designer virus."

"What do you mean?" I said.

"Hollis would've settled for a new disease, one that only a Candela product could cure. He wanted a virus that would infect dogs, so that he could sell new drugs to their owners. The man is a business genius."

"That's despicable. Karsten would never have agreed to that."

"Who knows?" Hannah shooed the topic like a bothersome fly. "Karsten failed and paid the price. Just like you will."

I turned to Chance. "Don't let her do this."

"He's not going to help you." Hannah's eyes narrowed. "And keep your distance, Tory. I saw how freakishly strong you were at the dance. You knocked Jason flat."

"Hannah, give me the gun." Chance spoke firmly. "I don't know how my father brainwashed you, but I'll make him pay for it. I'm going to the police."

"Brainwashed?" Hannah shrilled. "Do you think I'm stupid? That meek, pretty Hannah could never have done this by herself?"

Again, she jabbed the pistol in Chance's face. "I'm *not* stupid, Chance. No one *tricked* me into anything. I'm simply taking what is mine."

"And what is that?" Chance's tone was pure ice. "You're nothing now. It's over between us. You'll never set foot in this house again."

Hannah laughed. "It's so cute that you think such decisions are up to you!"

Caught off guard, Chance just stared.

I inched closer to the crowbar.

"Your father and I have an understanding, sweetheart. He trusts *me* to handle his affairs, not you. He thinks I'm more a Claybourne than you are."

"You've lost your mind," Chance said. "You are *not* a Claybourne."

"But I *will* be," Hannah replied. "Your father promised. I will marry into this family and be your wife. Just like we've always dreamed."

Her face hardened.

"It's no longer your decision."

CHAPTER 70

"You're crazy." Chance's voice trembled with rage. "I'll never marry you. Not after this. I don't care what my father said."

"You'll do exactly as you're told!"

Chance recoiled from the shriek.

Hannah was losing control. She could shoot us any second.

I reached the barrel. My fingers brushed the crowbar.

"Don't worry, baby." Hannah's face softened. "We'll get through this, I promise. Once these nosey-faces are gone, we can put this whole ugly business behind us." Hannah beamed her most fetching smile. "I'll be the perfect wife. You'll see."

Hannah's eyes locked onto Chance. For a moment, we no longer existed. Time to act.

Find your power.

I closed my eyes and pictured myself.

Tory Brennan, fourteen. Tall. Skinny. Freckled skin. Red hair. Emerald eyes.

The image crisped.

I added personality traits. Headstrong. Intelligent. Reckless. Loyal.

My mind plugged in memories. Movies and popcorn with Mom. My first awkward meeting with Kit. Reading Aunt Tempe's books on the beach.

Dream Tory solidified in my brain. I recognized her. Knew her.

Shoving that image aside, I searched for the *other* part of my psyche. My baser self, driven by primal urges rising from my genes.

I sought the wolf inside me.

My head swam.

The tunnel called.

At its mouth a figure waited. Coop, leaping and twisting in excitement.

My mind locked onto the wolfdog.

Coop barked once, then turned and ran. I followed, deep into the backwaters of my mind.

Time and space blurred. Strange impressions floated from my gray cells. My tongue lapping the cool water of a woodland stream. My teeth stripping flesh from a warm, still carcass. My throat sending howls into a moonlit sky.

SNAP.

Electricity coursed through my body. The world sharpened. My eyes smoldered with golden fire.

I *flared.*

I screamed inside my head.

Virals! Flare! Now!

The boys flinched at the impact of my message. I sensed their thoughts, faint, like voices floating across a lake.

I broadcast again with all the force of my will.

FLARE NOW!

Ben grabbed his head. Shelton stumbled to one knee. Hi gasped.

All three looked at me.

Eyes glowing.

Don't ask me how, but I'd *forced* them to flare.

Now we were a force. We could fight back.

Hannah's face swiveled our way. The gun followed.

She drew in her breath.

"What's wrong with your eyes?" Her gaze darted among us. "All of you! What are you doing?"

Divert her!

Hi bolted down the nearest row of wine racks. Disappeared.

"Stop!"

Hannah charged forward and fired wildly down the aisle.

Crack! Crack! Crack!

Glass exploded all around Hi. The smell of gunpowder filled the air.

Hi stumbled to the ground and lay still. A red stain mushroomed from beneath his belly.

Chance stood paralyzed.

"Hi!" Shelton screamed.

I grabbed the crowbar. It felt light as a feather. Like the lasso, I whipped it two-handed and, growling, launched it at Hannah.

Hannah screamed and dove sideways. The rod smashed into the rack behind her. Bottles shattered. The scent of wine joined that of sulfur and smoke.

Ben ran forward and shoulder-slammed Chance to the ground. Reaching the stairwell, he smashed one fist into the light switches. The room was plunged into darkness.

Rising to one knee, Hannah fired two slugs toward Ben.

Crack! Crack!

Sparks flew as the bullets ricocheted off stone.

Scatter!

I bolted left toward the rear of the cellar.

Crack! Crack!

Bullets whizzed by as Hannah fired blindly at my back.

I cut down an aisle. Then slammed on the brakes.

Think! Dead end.

Suddenly I heard thrashing and grunting. Shelton? Ben? I reversed course, determined to help whoever was in trouble.

Strangled voices cut through the gloom.

"Give me the gun!" Chance gasped. "I won't let you commit murder!"

"No!" Hannah panted. "Let go!"

Something hit the wall hard. I edged forward, hyper-senses on high alert.

Crack!

Hannah screamed.

Virals, back to the table! Chance needs help!

I crept to the double row of barrels. Lights kicked to life. I froze, prepared to take cover. But only the bulbs overhanging the table were burning. The rest of the cellar remained in shadow.

I heard sobbing.

I peeked over a barrel. A sideboard stood between the table and me. Twenty feet beyond, the staircase was dimly visible in the gloom.

Chance lay sprawled across the first riser, a stain slowly darkening his tee. Hannah crouched over him, crying hysterically.

Still holding the Sig Sauer.

Chance touched his side, then stared at his bloody fingers. His eyes rolled back, then his hand dropped and he lay motionless.

"No!" Hannah wailed.

I was stunned. Chance was shot, maybe dead. And Hannah still had the gun.

Virals! I need a distraction!

A second passed. Then Ben exploded from the aisle to my right and dashed across the open space.

Hannah's head came up. Her face was pale, her hair chaos.

"You did this!" she screamed, aiming the gun with both hands.

Crack! Crack! Crack!

Ben dove between the racks on the far side. Hannah lurched after him.

As she hurried past an aisle, Shelton popped out behind her.

"Over here, bitch!" Shelton winged a bottle at Hannah's head.

Hannah dropped to her knees as the missile flew over her.

Shattered with a crash. Shelton darted across the room with a wail, disappearing into the opposite racks.

Hannah regained her feet, fired twice.

Crack! Crack!

Two misses. Wine ran across the stone floor.

"You stupid little brats!" Hannah screamed in frustration. "I'll kill every one you!" She took two steps in Shelton's direction.

A shadow crossed her face. A big one.

Her eyes darted up.

Too late.

Hi launched from the top of the nearest rack like a pudgy zeppelin.

Hannah scrambled backward, eyes round as Frisbees.

Hi's shoulder clipped Hannah, but his momentum carried him into the wall.

The gun skittered across the floor.

Hi shook his head, woozy.

Hannah recovered first. Scooping up the Sig, she stood and faced Hi, her back to the table. And to me.

There was nowhere for Hi to run.

Hannah raised her weapon.

I vaulted the barrel, landed on the cabinet, then leapt to the table. Crouching, I groped inside the open cask. My fingers wrapped one of Heaton's long bones.

Hannah spun to face me. She was ten feet away.

Time slowed.

Two steps. I launched myself from the table's edge.

Hannah fired twice.

Crack! Crack!

I twisted in midair.

The bullets passed inches from my head.

I hit the ground, rolled, and popped to my feet directly in front of Hannah.

Startled, she raised the gun level with my face.

Squeezed the trigger.

Click.

"Empty."

I moved like lightning, slapping the gun aside with one hand as I swung Heaton's thighbone with the other. The femoral head smashed into Hannah's temple.

Her eyes lost focus.

I swung again, this time gripping the shaft like a baseball bat. The bone connected with a sickening thunk. Hannah crumpled, unconscious.

I dropped my macabre weapon and slumped to my knees. My chest heaved and tears ran down my cheeks. I couldn't believe what I'd just done.

SNUP.

My flare withered and died. I was too exhausted to care.

"Not bad, Tor." Hi leaned against the wall, the fire gone from his eyes. "Those were some primo *Matrix* moves. But a real hero would've dodged *three* bullets."

Shelton and Ben emerged from the racks. Their eyes had also returned to normal.

"Nice work." Ben picked up the femur. "Poetic justice, I'd say."

"Hiram!" Shelton ran to Hi's side. "Aren't you bleeding? I thought she shot you!"

"Red wine. When I saw it running everywhere, I played dead." He winced as Shelton poked his belly. "But I'm not leaping off any more shelves. That was pretty stupid."

"Whatever, Superman!" Shelton slapped Hi's shoulder. "That was money!"

Hi chuckled. "No one outmaneuvers the flying blob!"

I glanced over at Chance. He may have worked against us, but he'd tried to save us in the end. Like Karsten.

Ben put two fingers to Chance's throat. "He's got a pulse."

"I'll call a doctor!" I rushed to the pile of cell phones and dug mine out.

"No signal." I started up the stairs. "Shelton, you and Hi help Chance if you can. Ben, hog-tie Hannah and secure the evidence. I'll call an ambulance."

"And the police." Shelton said.

"And the police," I agreed.

I fired up the steps and along the service passage.

As I crossed into the kitchen, an arm circled my neck and a hand yanked my head back, causing me to choke. A gun barrel kissed my throat, forced my chin up.

"Going somewhere?" The raspy whisper was right at my ear. "Looks like I'll have to do clean-up myself."

Baravetto dragged me toward a corner, out of view of the window.

"Never send a kid to do a man's job."

The gun moved to the side of my head.

SNAP.

My elbow slammed into his ribs.

Air exploded from Baravetto's mouth. His arm relaxed a hair.

I flexed a leg, kicking backward and connecting with his crotch.

Baravetto screamed and collapsed to his knees.

I yanked a rolling pin from the wall beside me.

Smack!

Baravetto went down. I whacked him a second time just to be safe.

SNUP.

My head swam. Stars danced behind my lids.

I stumbled outside, hunting for a cell signal.

Beep!

I dialed 911. The operator asked if my call was an emergency.

"Ambulance," I panted. "Terrorists are attacking Claybourne Manor!"

Then I fainted dead away on the grass.

CHAPTER 71

"Tory!" Hi shook my shoulder. "You okay?"

Blink.

Blink. Blink. Blink.

"Whaaa?" The best I could do.

I lay beneath a mammoth Magnolia, a dozen yards from the kitchen door. Every window in the mansion was aglow. Red and blue lights pulsed from somewhere beyond the garden wall.

"We've been looking for you!" Hi's face was frog-belly white. "Hold on, I'll tell everyone you're okay! I'll bring a doctor."

"Wait." I sat up and tried to clear my thoughts. "First tell me what happened."

"The cops are here." Hi helped me to my feet. "We found Baravetto in the kitchen and got pretty freaked. No one knew where you were."

"I fainted." Everything came crashing back. "Chance! How is he?"

"He's . . . okay." Hi frowned. "I mean, he's alive, if that's what you're asking."

"But?"

"The bullet barely grazed him. He should be fine."

Hi trailed off.

"But?" I prodded again.

"But he won't respond to anyone. He just stares off into space. I think the whole situation messed him up pretty bad."

Not to mention what Hannah said, I thought. *And did.*

"How long have I been out?"

"Maybe thirty minutes," Hi said. "The cops burst in not long after you went upstairs. They thought the building was under attack or something. They kept us cuffed until just minutes ago."

"Did they arrest Hannah? Baravetto?"

Hi nodded. "When the medics revived her, she totally flipped, started cussing everyone out." He smiled. "Especially you."

Shocker.

"She was *completely* out of control," Hi went on. "Basically admitted to everything. That's why they let us go."

Good. Let Hannah talk her way into prison. Fine by me.

"Baravetto was unconscious when we found him," Hi said. "What'd you do to the guy?"

"Kicked him in the balls, then brained him with a rolling pin. Twice."

"Punted and pinned. Couldn't have happened to a nicer guy. FYI, Hannah is claiming Baravetto killed Karsten. She even told the cops where to find his body."

"My God, what was she thinking?"

"Trust me, she *wasn't* thinking. Hannah is hysterical. Yelling, crying, she was offering anything that might save her own ass." Hi whistled. "I think she'll live to regret her loose tongue."

"If the cops find Karsten's body, they'll have enough to convict her and her accomplices."

"They took Baravetto's gun. It's probably the murder weapon."

"Perfect. I wish the two of them a nice cozy cell."

"Hollis may get that honor, too," Hi said. "When Hannah calms down, her defense attorney will undoubtedly cut a deal. You know the police will want the bigger fish."

"Did you turn over the evidence?"

"Everything. The eagle photos, the land sale documents, Heaton's skeleton, the fingerprint report, Katherine's journal. But we couldn't find the dog tags."

I patted my pocket. "Got them right here."

"We told a Detective Borken the whole story."

"What?" I sat bolt upright.

"Don't worry," Hi said. "We didn't mention Karsten's experiment, or what happened to us."

Sudden panic.

"Did you turn over the deposit slip?"

"No, no. We don't want anyone digging into Karsten's secret parvo research."

I relaxed. "Good thinking."

I thought about Hannah's claim, that Hollis hired Karsten to design a new virus to infect dogs. I didn't want to believe it.

Hi read my mind. "Karsten was using Hollis's money to research a cure for canine parvo. He wouldn't have created a new disease. I'm sure of it."

I nodded, hoping Hi was right.

"So everything about our powers—the lab break-in, Coop's virus, the illness, the flares—you kept all that secret?"

Hi smiled. "Of course. No one knows about the Virals, or what we can do."

"We need to keep it that way."

"What about Chance and Hannah?"

"I don't think they'll figure it out," I said. "Things happened way too fast down in that cellar. And if they accuse us of having magic powers, everyone will think they're crazy."

"I hope so," Hi said. "I don't relish the thought of being dissected like a lab rat. If people learn what we're able to do—"

"We won't tell anyone," I said. "Ever. Even our parents."

"Agreed." Hi glanced back at the manor. "You ready to face the music?"

"What music?"

Hi snorted. "I forgot that you've been out cold. Our parents have landed. They're at the front gate."

My groan spoke volumes.

"Tory!" Kit ran up the driveway. "Are you okay!?" I was crushed in an unexpected bear hug.

"Fine," I said. "But I've got some things to explain."

Shelton and Ben stood nearby, talking with their parents. Ben did an eye roll over his father's shoulder. Shelton waved, grinning from ear to ear. Everyone safe and accounted for.

"Why did you break into Claybourne Manor?" Kit asked. "Who is that man in handcuffs? What the hell is going on?"

"I'll tell you everything, Kit, I promise." I took a deep breath. "But you should know that Dr. Karsten was murdered."

"Dr. *Marcus* Karsten? Murdered?" Kit sounded shocked. "Wait, how do you know this?"

"We were telling the truth. We found Katherine Heaton's bones. That man"—I pointed at Baravetto, locked in a squad car—"and Chance Claybourne stole her skeleton from our dig site on Loggerhead."

"Why?"

"Because Hollis Claybourne killed her back in 1969."

Kit stared, dumbfounded.

I pressed forward.

"Karsten followed us to Morris a few nights ago, to confront us about the lab break-in. He still thought we'd done it."

Kit frowned.

"But Karsten saved us," I said quickly. "The man in that squad car tried to kill us, to bury the truth about Katherine forever. Karsten died so that we could escape."

"Who is the young lady they arrested?" Kit asked.

"Chance's girlfriend, Hannah Wythe," I said. "She orchestrated the attack when Karsten was murdered. She tried to kill us tonight, but accidentally shot Chance instead. He's okay, I'm told."

Kit didn't speak for several moments. Finally, "I don't understand."

I groaned. "I'll tell you everything, I promise, but not right now. I've been chased, fired at, and forced to knock two people unconscious. I'm beat."

"Okay." I could see hundreds of questions working in his eyes, but he held back. "The detective says I can take you home, but we have to make a statement at the station later this morning. You kids have caused a serious mess."

Kit was right.

Parked on the street were four ambulances, a dozen police cars, even a fire truck. Several news vans had already arrived on scene.

Quite the scandal for Claybourne Manor.

Walking down the drive, I spotted a familiar figure sitting on an ambulance gurney. Chance, gazing into space.

"Kit, wait one sec."

I walked up beside Chance.

"Hey," I said gently. "It's me, Tory."

Chance didn't move, didn't blink.

"You're a real bastard," I said. "But you tried to save my life. For what it's worth, thanks."

Chance's eyes remained blank, his face slack.

Shaking my head, I rejoined Kit on the driveway.

Crickets floated their chorale best out onto the warm Charleston night. High above, a dove cooed softly.

I yawned.

Time to go home.

EPILOGUE

The sun blazed down from the top of its arc as Ben anchored *Sewee* off Turtle Beach. I popped over the side, anxious to get wet.

A light breeze tussled my hair. The smells of sand and salt blended with those of myrtle and palmetto.

We'd come back to Loggerhead Island.

I'd been grounded for two weeks, and it felt glorious to be out of the house. Confessing to a half dozen B and E's had been enough for Kit to put me on lockdown. And I still hadn't told him everything.

The news coverage had been entertaining. Hollis Claybourne was collared on the State House steps, charged with the murders of Katherine Heaton and Marcus Karsten and a zillion other crimes.

Hannah and Baravetto were each charged with Karsten's

murder, along with four counts of attempted murder. Baravetto's nephew, Claybourne's other henchman, had also been arrested. Rumor had it that Hannah would flip and testify against her partners in crime.

Karsten's body remained missing. According to Hannah, Hollis had dumped him at sea. His car was found in the long-term parking lot at the Charleston airport. One of the three must have driven it there from Morris Island on the night of his death.

Chance was charged with desecration of human remains and obstruction of justice, but avoided anything more serious.

In his case, the district attorney would have to be patient. Chance remained catatonic. No one knew if he'd ever leave the psychiatric hospital to which he'd been committed.

Splashing toward land, I drank in the view. I've said it before: Turtle Beach is the best in the world. I wiggled sand between my toes, trailed my arms through the cooling water, loving the old Palmetto state.

We'd already made one stop that day. Earlier in the week DNA had confirmed that the skeleton was indeed Katherine Heaton. That morning her bones were buried at Holy Cross Cemetery.

It had been a lonely little gathering. An ancient priest. Detective Borken. Sylvia Briggerman, accompanied by a nurse. Abby Quimby. Some parents from Morris Island. And, of course, the Virals.

I'd strung Francis Heaton's dog tags on a new chain, and placed them inside the coffin.

Rest in peace, Katherine.

"Tory!" Hi hollered from the boat. "Help with this mongrel!"

Hi was trying to coax Cooper over the side but failing badly. The fifty-pound puppy wasn't anxious to get wet.

Laughing, I splashed back to *Sewee*. Coop whined, but allowed me to lift him. Even licked my face.

"Come on, boy."

I carried the pup several yards, then planted his paws knee-deep in the surf. He yelped, scampered to the beach, and shook like mad. Water flew from his fur. Then, nose raised, ears flat, he disappeared into the brush.

When we'd all gathered on shore, we looked around. No sign of the wolfdog.

"I guess that's that." Shelton looked disappointed. "The little ingrate didn't even look back."

A cacophony of barks erupted in the bushes. Four animals exploded into view, rolling and jumping in a giant ball. One wolf. One German shepherd. Two wolfdogs. Four tails wagged like excited signal flags.

Suddenly, Whisper's eyes locked on us. Fur bristling, she snarled and stepped in front of her cub.

Ben backed into the waves. "Whoa. That doesn't sound like a welcome."

"So this is how it ends." Hi, king of drama. "Mauled to death by an angry wolf mother. Great plan, Tory."

As we stood frozen, Coop nipped his mother's flank. Whisper glanced down. Coop barked, then slipped by her and padded over to me.

Whisper tensed, but didn't interfere.

I dropped to a knee. Coop placed his forepaws on my shoulders and licked my cheek. I nuzzled his head with my face.

Whisper sat. Cocked her head. Raised her ears.

I sighed in relief. Coop had vouched for his two-legged companions. Mama appeared skeptical, but accepting.

I smiled, happy but sad. "Time to be with your family, little guy."

Coop barked, danced a circle, then fired back to the pack. The canines slipped into the woods and were gone.

We lingered a while, hoping for a return appearance. No such luck. Still, I didn't want to leave.

"He's better off out here," Ben said. "Plenty of space, no one to hassle him. He'll be happy."

I nodded, but couldn't shake the melancholy. I would rarely see Coop in the future. He might forget me.

"Ready to go?" Hi said. "I'm still grounded. I had to beg for a special exemption to make this trip."

"Ready." Not really.

Leaves swished, then Coop burst from the foliage, the rest of the family close on his heels. Without hesitation, he trotted over and sat at my feet.

Bark! Bark!

"Okay, buddy." I rubbed his head. "Your mama's in charge now." I gently pushed him back toward the pack.

The pup darted past me and started wading out towards the boat. I sloshed forward to catch him.

"Cooper!" I circled an arm around his neck and knelt in the water. "What are you doing, boy? Don't you want to go with your family?"

Face lick. Then he slipped my embrace, bounded through the surf, and started paddling toward the boat.

"What's he doing?" Hi asked. "Swimming to England?"

I glanced toward shore.

Coop's family waited by the tree line. As I watched, Whisper stood and barked sharply.

I looked over my shoulder. Coop was still paddling toward *Sewee*.

I made a decision. Kit would just have to live with it.

"Help him into the boat," I said. "Coop's made his choice. He's part of *our* pack now."

Ben and Hi hauled the soaked puppy over the gunwale. He shook, spraying everyone with salt water.

I jumped aboard and pulled Coop's small wet body to me. On shore, Whisper and her family melted into the forest.

"Is that what we are?" Shelton smiled. "A pack?"

"Of course," Hi said. "A pack with superpowers. And a dark secret."

"Tory can order me around *inside* my head," Ben said. "If that doesn't make us close, I don't know what does."

"We *are* a pack." I ruffled Coop's fur. "We're bound by our mangled DNA."

"We're Virals." Hi held out his hand. "Family."

"Virals." Shelton's hand covered Hi's.

"Virals." Ben's hand joined the others.

"Virals." My hand topped the stack.

I grinned, then yelled into the wind.

"And God help anyone who messes with the Virals!"

The others howled in agreement.

So did Coop.

Acknowledgements

First and foremost I would like to thank my son Brendan, without whom *Virals* would not have been possible. Thanks for all your hard work. I would also like to thank my tireless agent Jennifer Rudolph Walsh, and the entire staff at William Morris Endeavor Entertainment, for encouraging me to follow through with this project. I am grateful to Don Weisberg at Penguin and to Susan Sandon at Random House UK for believing in *Virals* from the beginning. Finally, a hearty thanks to Ben Schrank and Jessica Rothenberg at Razorbill for helping me navigate the new challenge of writing young adult fiction. I appreciate you all!